**PURE
SLUSH
BOOKS**

LOSS

LIFESPAN VOL . 9

First published as a collection February 2024
Content copyright © Pure Slush Books and individual authors
Edited by Matt Potter

ISBN: 978-1-922427-36-6

BP#00125

Pure Slush Books
32 Meredith Street
Sefton Park SA 5083
Australia

Email: edpureslush@live.com.au
Website: https://pureslush.com/
Store: https://pureslush.com/store/

Also available as an ePub
ISBN: 978-1-922427-37-3
Also available as a Kindle eBook
ISBN: 978-1-922427-84-7

A note on differences in punctuation and spelling

Pure Slush Books proudly feature writers from across the English-speaking world.
Some speak and write English as their first language, while for others, it's their second
or third or even fourth language. Naturally, across all versions of English, there are
differences in punctuation and spelling, and even in meaning. These differences are
reflected in the work *Pure Slush Books* publishes, and they account for any differences
in punctuation, spelling and meaning found within these pages.

Pure Slush Books is a member of the
Bequem Publishing collective
https://bequempublishing.com/

DEDICATED TO

LITTLE BO PEEP'S SHEEP

AND

VIRGINITY

... poetry and prose by ...

Alex Reece ABBOTT • Carol ADAMS • Edward AHERN
Tobi ALFIER • Dee ALLEN • Kathleen APONICK
Karen ARNOLD • Sandra ARNOLD
Joy Nevin AXELSON • Meryl BAER • Tom BALL
Linda BARRETT • Sally BASMAJIAN • James BATES
Britta BENSON • Henry BLADON • Fran BLAKE
Shelly BLANKMAN • Mark BLICKLEY
Paul BLUESTEIN • David BLUMENFELD
Rose Mary BOEHM • Denise BOSSARTE • John BOST
Lucy BRIGHTON • Howard BROWN • Corey BRYAN
Lynne BURNETT • William BUTLER
John CARNEGIE • Mary Ann CARRASCO
Lucia CASCIOLI • Beth CASH • John E. CAULTON
Guy CHAMBERS • Carl CHAPMAN
Jan CHRONISTER • Robert CLARE • Dave CLARK
Peter CLARKE • Richard CLARKE • Ken COHEN
Sage COHEN • Christine COLLINSON
Suzanne COOKE • Melina CORNELL • Elizabeth COX
Linda M. CRATE • Niall CROWLEY
Anthony CRUTCHER • Brenda CULLEN
Eithne CULLEN • Gareth CULSHAW
Claudette CURRIE • Jeni CURTIS • Steve CUSHMAN
Chris DALY • Charles DARNELL • Sarah DAS GUPTA
David DAVIES • John DAVIS • Jim DAWSON
Tony DAWSON • Gabrielle DE GRAY

… and …

Tanya DELANOR • Doris DEMBOSKY
Bonnie DEMERJIAN • Winston DERDEN
Elaine DILLOF • Mark DONNELLY • John DORROH
Miriam DRORI • John B. ELLIOTT • Steve EVANS
Livio FARALLO • Tom FEGAN • Amalia FISH
Jane H. FITZGERALD • PM FLYNN • Juliet FOSSEY
Natalie FRY • Diane FUNSTON • Laura GARFINKEL
Delphine GAUTHIER-GEORGAKOPOULOS
Flemming GEORGE • Declan GERAGHTY
Nod GHOSH • Gabby GILLIAM • JW GOLL
Jim GORMLEY • Ken GOSSE • John GREY
Pip GRIFFIN • Betty Naegele GUNDRED • Chris HALL
Ronald T. HARDWICK • Richard HARRIES
Doug HAWLEY • Tom HAZUKA • Mark HEATHCOTE
Sarah HENRY • Kathleen HERRMANN
Theresa HICKEY • Ryn HOLMES
Matthew HORSFALL • Paul HOSTOVSKY
Jan HOWCROFT • Ann HOWELLS • Mark HUDSON
Barbara Schilling HURWITZ • GP HYDE
Abha IYENGAR • Joanne JAGODA • Shirlee JELLUM
Christine JOHNSON • Patrick JOHNSON
Terry S. JOHNSON • Connie JOHNSTONE
Fiona M. JONES • Kenneth M. KAPP
Colleen KEATING • Alan KENNEDY
Gurupreet K. KHALSA • Steven Dee KISH

... as well as ...

Pam KRESS-DUNN • Janis LA COUVÉE
Jim LANDWEHR • Jim LaVILLA-HAVELIN • Tim LAW
Diane LEE • Chris LEONARD • Joan LEOTTA
Cynthia LESLIE-BOLE • Louella LESTER
LindaAnn LoSCHIAVO • Tim LOVE • Paul LUIKART
Chuck MADANSKY • Carolina MARCHIORO
Clare MARSH • Carolyn MARTIN
Fabiana Elisa MARTÍNEZ • Joy MAWBY
Katy McKINNEY • Rob McKINNON
Catherine McNAMARA • Mandy Toczek McPEAKE
Jay McPHERSON • Shaine MELROSE
Deborah MELTVEDT • Karla Linn MERRIFIELD
Kate MEYER-CURREY • Neila MEZYNSKI
Lesley MIDDLETON • Karen MIREAU
Amy B. MORENO • Alison MORRETTA
Colleen MOYNE • Remngton MURPHY
Yonnie MURPHY • Johanna NAURAINE • AR NEAL
James B. NICOLA • Ellen NOTBOHM • B. E. NUGENT
Gary PERCESEPE • Darryl PETSKA • Sylvia PETTER
Emma PHILLIPS • Martin PHILLIPS
Margaret PLAGANIS • David L. POGSON
Marianne PORTER • Camila POSADA • Jude POTTS
Gary PREECE • Suzanne PURVIS • Martha RAND
Paul RANSOM • Niles REDDICK

... and also ...

Ian REID • Sally RENO • Danielle RICCARDI
Kay RITCHIE • Jeannie E. ROBERTS • June ROGERS
JA ROSE • Biman ROY • Merryn RUTLEDGE
Ed RUZICKA • Rachel-Anne SAMBELL
Gerard SARNAT • Carla SCHICK
Dorin SCHUMACHER • Carmelita SCIAN
Robert SCOTELLARO • Nolo SEGUNDO
Judith SHAPIRO • Pegi Deitz SHEA • Emily SHEARER
Josh SHERMAN • Michael SHOEMAKER
Joan Seliger SIDNEY • Cheryl SNELL • Amy SORICELLI
Gail SOSINSKY • Adrienne STEVENSON
Robin STRATTON • Marianne SZLYK
Christopher TATTERSALL • Phillip TEMPLES
Suzette THOMPSON • Lydia TRETHEWEY
Lucy TYRRELL • Leo VANDERPOT
Linden VAN WERT • Donald R. VOGEL
Kenneth WAGNER • Zhihua WANG • Tony WARNER
Kresha Richman WARNOCK • Alison WASSELL
B. D. WATSON • Michael WEBB • Brian WESTON
Lynn WHITE • Thomas Reed WILLEMAIN
Jeral WILLIAMS • Todd WILLIAMS • Russell E. WILLIS
Allan J. WILLS • Mike WILSON • Melissa E. WONG
Anne Harding WOODWORTH • Stephen Paul WREN
Mantz YORKE • Gary ZENKER

WELCOME TO
LOSS

Judging by the number of submissions received for *Loss*, a lot of people have lost something.

A partner, a lover, a parent, a child, a job, a cat, a dog, food, their hope, their home, their love, their self-respect, their identity, their dignity …

Loss is, much to my initial surprise, Pure Slush's largest published anthology.

The previous record is held by *Love Lifespan Vol. 4*, coming in at 482 pages and 194 writers, and published in October 2021.

Loss comes in at 566 pages with 237 writers.

There are so many, in fact, that I lost count at times.

And writing this I do feel lost for words.

And it's usually better to let the poems and the stories and the essays speak for themselves, anyway.

Matt Potter, editor and publisher

February 2024
Adelaide, Australia

Poetry

The Heart of the Matter

Peter Clarke

Have you ever held the tiny foot
of a twenty-week premi through
the ope of an incubator?
Gently stroked the sole
the intention of which
is to remind him to breathe.

I am jolted back forty-seven
years, heart thumping, seated
under the eaves of a maternity
hospital, willing my son
to stay with us, to grow,
focus intense through medical beeps.

Another image flashed, leaning against
the wall on a turreted staircase
heaving, buckling under, lost,
a dishevelled wreck of a being,
no longer able to hold in anything,
a puddle of grief folded into a crevice.

Persistent Rain

John Grey

How much the rain wants me to be the rain,
In all its drizzle, all its drape of gray,
Persistently, it drizzles, drips its way
From splattered windowsill to ceiling stain
To be the blood that bubbles through my vein,
To turn my body liquid, feet to clay,
So even when it's gone, the rain can stay
In my damp heart, my weary, flooded brain.

But I will not be rain, I will not pine
For those who've left, who do not call, who've died,
I'll be what I still am, what still is mine
And not the gloom I've felt, the tears I've cried.
I'll be this break of sun, the honeyed shine,
I will not be what's happening outside.

The pink hippo

Stephen Paul Wren

The mission on Saturday mornings
was to reach the pink hippo first.
It was the stand-out poolside prize.
In swim class, we raced other child-parent couples.
We won every race we took part in.
After your passing, I wonder
how much real security or happiness did the hippo provide?
and *how long did these feelings last?*
I do not have the answers but
I do know that you were always searching for something.
The pink hippo was an early example.

Past tense

Anne Harding Woodworth

Last night there were bouquets
and place cards. I recognized the name
next to me, but not the wizened face.

I asked him if he'd dated Sally Curtiss
way back in the '60s.
His eyes squinted toward me.

He married her, he said.
He divorced her, he said.
He lost his children to her, he said.

There's bitterness in the past tense.

Back then, we laughed, not knowing
what would come, what blood would mix
with gentle strokes along what thighs,

what vows would be exchanged,
kisses returned not returned.
In those days, nothing
went beyond the simple present.

To My Mother: On Your One-Year Anniversary

Carolyn Martin

Every week since you died, I've caught
myself gathering news for our Saturday ritual.
You, in your New Jersey nursing home
trying to remember how to answer the phone;
I, roaming our Oregon yard, inviting
you into my life, piece by private piece.
How predictable each call.
I'd only dramatize an opening line before
you'd interrupt with a performance of your own:
how you woke to a man sleeping on your couch,
how convulsions hurled you out of bed,
how you found your way through Italy /
Egypt / Greece but lost the words
for stamp / birthday card / address.
In retrospect, my reports were minor affairs:
a trip to the Oregon coast, a new TV,
the harsh September rains that snapped
our crepe myrtle tree. Yours—like tracking
rowdy clouds each afternoon until they caught
themselves in reddening maple and golden oak—
yours sometimes surprised with poetry.

Of Necessity

Darrell Petska

How couldn't you love Sis:
her smiles and laughter, her frowns.

Free-ranging farm kids smelling
like hay, we wore bib overalls

except on Sundays
when Sis wore a dress.

We were "those whippersnappers,"
and sometimes "the Bobbsey Twins."

Sis learned to play piano and sew.
She never learned to swim—

I know she'd have married,
had kids, lived close by.

There'd be no need for this poem.
We'd simply call or text.

She'd ask could you come Sunday.
I'd reply what time.

Obituary of a dead poet

Mark Heathcote

One day, he'll have a name tag around his big toe
like he belonged someplace and didn't have far to go.
The slate will be wiped clean; all will be reimbursed.
His Caucasian toe is free of lesions and blisters that burst.
All that will be left shall be pages and pages of verse
and a body that can't afford a burial or the price of a hearse.
And few other than a priest will mourn or even attend;
as he can count his friends on one hand, let's not pretend.
The obituaries – let the 'record show,'
that custom tears did somehow flow,
and angels banked both sides of his coffin, row on row,
and God was in attendance as his guide when he died.
That God removed the name tag.
That God, in His heavenly ascendance, was by his side.
And God was in attendance, and some say even He cried.
The day they tagged his big toe
like he belonged someplace and didn't have far to go.

It's Been Too Long

Patrick Johnson

I know you only in the turns of calendar pages,
each year, the same month.
You are small, now tall, now taller,
playing with rattles, now dolls, now no longer playing.

I know you only against the backdrop of snow,
when time slows to ice on pine needles,
and we allow ourselves to celebrate,
to remember.

You say you miss me
having quickly learned kind adult lies.
For you it is merely routine pleasantry,
like crying at the weddings of strangers.

But for me,
there is a pain in my spine
that remembers our piggy-back rides,
a cold ache to feel that weight again.

Sorrow of the Sea

Shaine Melrose

Long brown weed piles hide her possessions in a valley of flattened sand. Knit purl, knit purl, along Merricks beach, crustaceans spun into plastic bags, coarsely woven seagrass, woolly rows waiting for waves to cast off to the sea.

Shaggy dog
patiently stands guard,
night fall.

A mourning tide has washed her gently ashore. Rolling foam rises with salty buoyancy through splayed toes, fingers, reaching an absent husband, too long in the afterlife. *Is there an afterlife?* This ocean will always be here, has touched the flesh of millions who have perished. Gives life to billions who live still.

She took her life
into the arms of an amniotic sea
at dawn.

Downsizing

Chuck Madansky

I'm 5'4" and at 72, not getting any taller.
Which is to say I grew up through all
the straits of being short, though
in the Peruvian rainforest and
Balinese villages I lived more
freely among men my own
size and temper than in
Baltimore or Boston.

Which is also to say that now the project of
trying to be taller is over, I can begin to
downsize in earnest—jettison a lifetime of clutter, rooms filled with
trophies—a few firsts, mostly
honorable mentions—for
being a somebody.

Now, as my thighs grow thin, my muscle
mass melts, my footprint fades, my
presence can open, thicken and
stretch. and time can reduce
and release me until
I've downsized
into nothing,
and back
into
all.

For the Man
Behind Your Iris

Corey Bryan

Forgive me, please.
but I took a peak
into the empty space
      behind your tongue.

I saw the image, carefully
held by your bated breath.
The weight of it
      cracks your molars.

I see it now, the grief
passed through your parents
poverty neé pain neé a cupful
      of bleach in his lower intestines

I can see it flecked in your eyes
Lord, forgive me for looking
Darling, forgive me all the sins,
      all the times I never said I missed you.

glad you're gone

Linda M. Crate

not everyone you lose is a loss,
although sometimes it feels as
if they might be;

i don't mind being headache free
and having the freedom to be me

with friends who love and appreciate who
i am instead of one who has known me
since childhood and doesn't know a thing
about me—

you only knew need and you had no shame,
always the victim even when you weren't;

you always wanted everything for free

instead of supporting me like my
true friends do—

i just don't understand how you could
simultaneously make it seem as if i didn't
matter to you, and then turn around and
demand things as if i owed them to you;

but you were a real piece of work,
and i am glad you're gone.

Keeping in Touch

James B. Nicola

It's not that we fall out of touch (although
we do, even with family and friends
we love) but out of time. Before we know
it ...
Each day, new beginnings and new ends.

Yesterday I heard my cousin Chris
died of an overdose two years ago.
His dad, my cousin William, told me this
gently when I asked how Chris was. "Oh,"

I said, or tried to say.
Bill said he still
attends a help group, something like AA,
for parents. He will sit there quietly
not taking a turn with *My name is Bill*,
and so on, which he had done every day
last year, but just to be, for those like me.

Lost then Found, Jennifer

Allan J. Wills

My sister found her DNA.
Who were those ancestral souls?
Lives, losses mourned by generations unknown.
Colombians, Aztec, and Inca
fused with Devon and Cornwall folks.
Celtic thrown in too, somehow.
Self as chemical codex.
Yet no mere genome,
fleeting courier between past and future
bearing the factory plan.
Oh! More!
A gentle,
imagining mill of emotions.
Wise writer of luminous text:
Children and grandchildren,
amalgams of her and other scripts.
A revelation of those long lost to time,
and the message in and of herself.

Oy Vey Iz Mir Watching Rachel Maddow in Pajamas

Gerard Sarnat

Rain or shine, COVID or no,
distanced in their backyard
or inside it doesn't matter,
end of week dusk must
mean dress for Shabbes
with kosher daughter's
family; but now after
a month of Friday's
which too has come
to its end
            at least for
interlude while post
the New Year's scare
they get parent bearings
that allow both toddlers
to play with other kids …
whereas vulnerable elders
stay more cautious course
not letting down our guard
waiting to get vaccinations

so tonite instead oy atheist will boil to-die-for pork shumai.

Shade

Ian Reid

Now midsummer's longest shiniest day
brings news that suddenly deepens the line of shade
angled across a corner of this window.
Another friend is lost to all

but one-way memory, joining a crowd
of silent apparitions. Once they were more than that,
these parents, partners, workmates, childhood cronies,
who have left the bright living room early.

Thinking of them now is like turning the pages
of a battered old photo album,
pages that are heavy and stiff
and thick and black.

Consolation Prize

Karen Mireau

When the other baby, the first one
(the one that took them by surprise
and didn't even know they wanted)
suddenly fell from her that afternoon
in a briny, shapeless mass, they married anyway
had already named the infant girl
because it was the '50s, and that—

that was the thing to do, then, and maybe
even now they'd have done the same

There was no burial—
what happened to the body is anyone's guess
but the next one came along so quickly
they pinned no hopes on it, a second girl,
always there to remind them
of the one they'd lost, the one that set their lives
in motion, although it was never spoken of

they seemed happy to have a child, yet astounded
she'd survived, and kept a careful distance

There were three more after that—all boys
so easy then to suspend their grief, so easy
to ignore the one that served as placeholder
for the other, never-to-be-forgotten one
or the memory of her body's awful original failing
the mourning that would never be extinguished
because of her, their first born

the consolation prize
her gaze forever unmercifully upon them

I Was Never Good at Sharing

Gabby Gilliam

I cannot write a eulogy
for you—snippets of life
on paper—reminders of memories
we'll never get to make.

I could spend days
                    a lifetime
telling stories about you
but none of them transfer
well to a page.

                    I could pull
the beating heart
            from my chest
                        offer it up.

See how it curls in on itself
trying to hide its new scar?

                    See how the mourners nod?

They recognize
that battered thing
     so brave to offer it up
          such a marvel.

But I want to cling
to my suffering
wrap it tightly
hold it close.

Why should the world get
to share these precious memories?

Who says I owe them any of my lifeblood?

Everything is Lost

John Bost

Lost keys, lost fobs
Lost ways, lost jobs
Lost wallets, lost means
People living in lost dreams
Ain't no use sighing
Ain't no use trying
Everything is lost

Lost socks, lost places
Lost walks, lost faces
Lost days, lost years
Paths are strewn with lost tears
Lost letters that may have been tossed
Everything is lost

Seems like every time you head off across the floor
Something else is out the door

Lost meetings, lost glances
Lost voices, lost chances
Lost connections, lost calls
Lost leaves on lost falls
Look out again, trees covered in frost
Everything is lost

Every time you go and walk on by
Things disappear up to the sky

Lost tickets and lost notes
Lost luggage, lost totes
Lost legroom, lost naps
People crying over lost maps
Roads are followed, streets are crossed
Everything is lost

Since We Traveled to the Shore

Sarah Henry

I google your recent snapshot.
It feels like getting a sunburn.
You look young for an older
man but your hair has turned
gray as a car we drove home
from our last beach vacation.
I'm unprepared to study you
because no one is ever really
ready to witness an accident.
Pressing on, I observe an old
man who also appears in the
photo and imagine he's your
close brother. The fellow has
bifocals and smiles so openly
his big wrinkles are showing.
It's possible he's enjoying an
excellent long life. I note you
are planning to leave or have
now arrived. A gray cashmere

coat and black tie are tip-offs.
Next I watch an old Teutonic
woman. She might be a super
snob you married. I am extra-
jealous of her. Two little girls
stand in front of my bad rival.
I suspect they function as the
granddaughters you certainly
would have been longing for.

The females are all smiling at
the camera. You must be very
distracted. I have seen enough
and don't want to come across
more painful souvenirs online.
I prefer to recall our swims in
the summers at a favorite spot.
I have walked a plank of poor
luck for over fifty years. You
didn't really go for me much,
friends said, just to be honest.

Where Did It All Go?

Jan Chronister

I remember black Irish good looks,
pale blue eyes,
my first time at a jazz club,
the trip to his parents' home in a rich suburb
north of Chicago.

The man I find on Facebook is bald,
fat with a big red nose,
sitting in what appears to be
a hospital bed in a messy house,
crumbs on his dark t-shirt.

Memories of love
dilute like wine in water.
I console myself with the fact
that his loss is greater than mine.

The Chill

Ken Gosse

On Valentine's Day, cold, darkened skies
won't chill two hearts which wildly race,
nor can winter's freezing guise
deplete the heat of love's embrace.

Flames of true love bond each heart
where two will lay, where dreams entwine,
and whether near or far apart
they'll find both heaven and hell align

but bitter cold lies deep—the cost
to those who suffer desperate ache
from hearts seared when all hope was lost
where true love left it in its wake.

When A Young Male Goes to A Residential Treatment Facility

Danielle Riccardi

It's best to wear black.

I removed 5 water bottles,
a dozen empty wrappers, took
all of the dirty clothes out,

found again the wood floor. Put
his Invisalign teeth into a box.
I didn't make the bed. Well,

it's partially made as if he's still here.
Put his chrome book and charger
on the dresser. Tucked the loose money

into his wallet, then into his underwear
drawer. To be saved for later. I hung
his dress pants and Hawaiian shirt, too.

Closed his closet doors.

I passed his neat room at the top
of the steps – on the way to mine,
look in, knowing

that the cleaning crew made the bed,
and there is no—body to leave an imprint
on the slate-colored sheets.

For now, I imagine
it is best to wear black
to contain the bleeding:

A circular counting of days from,
days until, of meals without, wondering
in what mindset the young male might return.

The first loss

Melissa E. Wong

Losing that dog was my
First big loss in the world.
She was not my pet
She was my sister
She was there for me
And now a steel urn
holds her dear ashes
It still sits in our house in
The spot she loved so much

There is a new puppy now
He is a similar breed
Not a replacement
Just a new member of the family
Just a new soul to love

That pup found all her old toys
He knows her
By smell if by nothing else
I don't know if this puppy
Can understand my words
But I tell him about his
Big sister dog and say:
"She would have liked you"

The Lost Ship Amistad

Tony Dawson

I'm afraid to tell you that your ship has sailed.
You used to be first mate on it but that's no longer true.
The ship that was your raison d'être is now *Mary Celeste*,
a mystery ship devoid of crew, and that's including you.
While there are ships that end their days in the breakers yard
and others, storm-tossed by the waves, at the bottom of the sea,
some of them will fade away exactly like your friendship has,
a ghostly memory to be recalled in some old sailor's yarn.

All gone wrong

Brian Weston

This isn't right
When did this happen?
I shouldn't be here
The sound of the ocean wave
Breaking against the shore
Should be my alarm call.
The gentle cool breeze
Giving some respite
From the tropical heat
As the curtains dance.
The aroma of fresh coffee on the balcony
Entices me from my king-sized bed.
All gone wrong

This. This isn't right
The music of the dustbin men
Wheeling, banging, clattering and shouting
Drowns out the annoying early morning birdsong.
The putrid stench of the bin lorry
Suffocates the tiny, cluttered bedroom.
Her snore makes me jump.

The dog gives a little grunt.
One of them farts.
I don't know who.
She rolls over
Pulling the duvet with her
Cocooned.
The dog pulls the last square of duvet
I am left bare
Resigned to my fate
This. This isn't right
When did this happen?
I miss you.
I really, really shouldn't be here.

The Day I Heard the News

Richard Clarke

Early summer and the shadows were lengthening.
It was still warm though the evening was near.
The spacious footpaths were deserted.
The passing traffic was silent.
I was sitting in a car near a towering church
in Johnston Street, Annandale, the widest street in Sydney,
with a schoolfriend, soon to be my best man.
        When the radio told us that John Lennon was dead,
it seemed like ours was the only car on the road.
Lennon was 40 and I was sorry
the music had died when it was only just
starting over.

Late spring, across the lawn lay the Harbour.
sparkling in the afternoon sunshine.
I was sitting in a crowded staff room,
thick with conversation as the daylight waned.
        When a phone call told me that my best friend was dead,
it seemed like I was the only one in the room.
I'd barely seen him since he turned 40
and looking back down that narrowing road
to the warm evenings we had shared in youth
and then the long summers of silence since
I was sorry our friendship wasn't
starting over.

The end of a marriage

Mandy Toczek McPeake

You weren't taken by death, you walked away from life.
No white light, no silver dust, no rising spectre,
yet still we saw you leave.
A slower breath broke the rhythm, a long pause drew our attention.
We held our breath, Mum, and I, until, beyond expectation,
another inhale, then no more.
You didn't move again but minutes passed with an infinite,
a finite settling of bone and muscle.
If we'd had another, a higher sense,
we might have seen a shimmer
Surround that shape, consolidate into an image of you
Rising, striding to the door,
not looking back.
You left life as you lived it: resilient, determined
and with choices made.
We left that place rich in knowing we'd been there
to perceive your infinitesimal farewell.

Long Lost Family

Richard Harries

A long time ago
1970 in fact
I became an uncle
Again

Zoe
A bundle of joy
But her Mum could not cope
And had no home
Struggled with life

So Zoe
Seen
Loved
Filmed
Held and cuddled
Was adopted

My sister married
Emigrated
And sadly died
So no trace of her in Harrogate

No one with our surname still there
So if Zoe looks for her Mum
There is no clue
We registered with a tracing site
But maybe she hasn't looked
Or not seen us

We don't know her new name
It's 50 years now
But I still think of my niece
Wistfully

I Talk with Dad

Dave Clark

I talk with Dad
    but he doesn't talk back
        He's no longer around
            Buried in sodden Adelaide ground
    We talk more
        than we ever did before
            A solid sounding board
                He's a better listener now

I talk with Dad in soft tones
    as I thought I was losing the plot
        'til I read that many folk
            still natter to their loved ones
    once they're physically gone
        We don't stop and start again
            We go forward with them
                The heart's got room

I banter with Dad by the herbs
  and a potted competition's on the go
    to grow the juiciest tomato
      He's up forty to zero and though I pester him
  he won't give up his sprouting secrets
    on that solanum fruit
      I want to grow at least one so I can
        throw at least one at him in jest

I ask questions of Dad
  about sending me to boarding school
    in another country at age seven
      That kid was so scared, so lost
  That kid's still scared and lost
    and we'll never fully conceive the cost
      of that decision on our connection
        These are borders we're still crossing over

I call out to Dad
  One day I was down
    and out I walked for a K and a whistling
      kite hovered above the whole way
  Was it chance? Was it Dad?
    Was it tracking the muesli bar I had?
    It's hard to say
      though I regained some peace

I chat with Dad about the footy
      He never saw his beloved St Kilda lift the Cup
         I tell him they're looking alright this year
            but not alright enough
     I hanker for when the Saints go marching in
        and I give Dad the play-by-play
          of how his team won the day
              and that devotion to the underdog pays off

I talk with Dad
     without knowing if we'll meet again
        I have my faith and I have my doubts
          I have my guesses, I have my hopes
     I've scanned the Scriptures, trawled the tropes
        and the one thing I know for sure
          is that 'til the day I die
            I'll keep talking with Dad

On Leaving Us Both

Gareth Culshaw

We sit as if waiting for the last train
to leave the station. Our hearts
tandem to mother's eye blinks.
The room closes in as the light
pulls away. And the stars try
to hide the size of the universe
above the roof. Silence creeps
leaving us both to look at the woman
we've known become someone
else. The turning of this earth
reveals mother's skin lost to time.
I've nothing left to say like a wind
that's reached the top of the hill.
Murmuring its way to the clouds.

Father waits, head down, shovelling
memories of my mother.
In hope to unearth the source
of the woman we love.
Now unclamped to float away,
float away as if released from us both.

The Incessant Loss of a Wild Flower

Declan Geraghty

I remember the soundtrack
I was listening to
the number of the song but not the title
I think about that song sometimes
the one I listened to
the night
just before you passed
when things were still bad
but a little better
than they are now
I go back to that song
every now and then
locating it by number
there's a comforting melancholy to it
even though you probably
never heard it
I'm connected to it now
whether I like it or not.

the hole
in the ground
is nowhere near six feet
it's barely four and a half
as they lower you down
I inhale deep
from the cigarette
I had
from years back
the one I promised meself
I'd never smoke.

Masks

PM Flynn

Tonight
go where tomorrow will be:

to moonlight and all things bending
darkness into light that swallows
the pained shapes of withering leaves,
masks falling to the forest floor; a forest
of standing water reflecting the moon;
a road of silent faces; once with trees.

While driving
what appears instead:

trash debris scattered for grazing deer
on crew cut right of ways; a road
guarding ditches lined with weeds;
faces like barren houses with eyes open
and doors shut; more loss spoken
in stumbled sighs, eyes barely open
that flow downstream in deep rivers
with stars falling in.

Closed Bookstores

Diane Funston

Once, in a city of cold,
buildings beckoned,
places of coffee and book-talk
comfort away from the storm,
pages away from problems.

Once, in a city of warmth,
writers gathered together,
for a repast of pastry and prose
leather chairs,
hours into late night.

Once, on island of paradise,
poets wove verses,
kindred spirits
crackled humid evenings,
through passing trade winds.

Although doors close,
structures change hands,
books will live
Way of the craft, forward—
one page at a time.

Sacked

Michael Shoemaker

Like a formidable train barreling out of a tunnel
in a billowing blur directly at you,
you hear the somehow controlled and practiced dispatch
"Take everything with you.
Your services are no longer needed."
Not even one word for each of the
twenty years of service-sterile-efficient-economical.

A security guard escorts you out while
you carry heavy frozen productivity in a cardboard box.
What do they think a 54-year-old man is going to do,
stab someone with scissors that were always too blunt
to open a bag of Cheetos?
Your body slumps, as you push fingers
through your hair and tears drop
　　　　－ too early for any final whistle
　　　　and too late for the sinking knife of reality.

What will you tell your wife?
Sitting in the driver's seat of panic, desperation
and a vocational disappearing act, you mutter
"I'll think of something, must think of something."

Nano and Pawpaw

Russell E. Willis

A pair, these two,
But a pair of what?
Wasn't always clear,
Yet never in doubt.
Never separate,
As in Nano and …
Or, Pawpaw and …

She, one of the last New Dealers,
This Rosie-the-Riveter on B-26s,
This Rosie-turned-foreman,
Turned career government servant.
This new type of working-mom,
And working grandmother,
Sitting on the floor making placards
For our favorite candidates
During summer-time conventions,
Teaching me, even at that early age,
To take my politics seriously
And myself with a grain of salt,
And vice-versa.

She, growing ever smaller as
I grew up around her,
Ever in her orbit
Cajoling me to be whatever self
It was my destiny to be, a
Project she never grew tired of
Even as she grew tired.

He, ever-whistling.
Smelling of cigarettes and sweat.
Smiling the Cheshire's particular grin.
Eyes gleaming, a gleam
That sometimes harbored mischief,
But always promised love.
Filthy hands that were busy doing something
In that magic place – his workshop;
Filled with greasy, dangerous things
That made grandchildren conjure adventure
And their mothers live in dread.
Sawdust and oil.
Drawers half-open, beckoning small hands.
Pegboards on every square inch of every wall.
Dangling tools, each in their place, but still somehow haphazard
(as in "potentially, but not probably, a hazard").
Just like Pawpaw.

He finally wore down to next to nothing,
"Damn cigarettes!" he'd mutter as he
Chatted up his brother, Joe,
Sitting there at the foot of the bed,
Or so we gathered.

Her great big heart
In that small, frail, but determined body,
Finally failed, so many years later,
But granted just the time, just one more day
To say goodbye to those close by.
Then, that night, on her own terms,
As it almost always had been,
She slipped away.
We heard the news in Iowa
While wrapping Christmas presents
Sitting on the floor, hers among the rest,
With her now among the resting.
But take even that with a
Grain of salt, as well; for, after all,

This is Pawpaw and Nano,
Or was it Nano and Pawpaw?
We're talking about.

Laid Off

John Davis

The first week without work
Donald bought bourbon
admired gold light in the glass.
He admired his spit.
He admired fists of ice
under the car he didn't drive.
He got to know
the gray crust in his eyes
and the soft crust on his lips.
He befriended the slow weight
of silence and the fast blaze
of headlights through his window.
The cold oiled everything
even the sawdust barges
that smoothed the channel
going out to sea, deck hands
mufflered, cheeks red as sunrise.
Not much of a moon.
He learned to shiver.
He learned to bitch.

He learned the buzz
of overhead lights
was the same buzz that fuzzed
in his ears after years
of ripping rails at the table saw.
No beard of sweat.
No crook in his neck.
But he talked to the ache
in his arms—old friend.
He heard the bell
for morning break.
This was just a break.
A week, maybe a month.
He would feed rails into the saw again.
Someone would.
He would be the one.
Of course he would.

Her Closet as She Left It

LindaAnn LoSchiavo

Deprived by his wife's absence, grieving guts
My father. The cremation over now,
Her ashes urned and glowing with repose,
Inspection of her closet is the next
Unmaking, contents intimate, perfumed.

Attired in nightgowns longer than a year,
My mother needed nothing stored inside:
Complacent church clothes, pastel linen sheaths,
Insomniacal sling-back heels, upright,
Attentive, waiting for the toll of tread,
Accessories forgotten, unloved, cold.

Sharp hangers await uninvited guests,
Prepared to fight. Should caretakers encroach,
Conspirators rise: bouclé knits scratching,
Steel eye-hooks, belts resisting, stuffy air
Redolent of her scent almost forcing
The trespasser to leave belongings there,
Mourned privately by what caressed her skin,
The nude audacity of death dismissed
As long as things remain, her door pulled shut.

To a Friend
a Continent Away

Nolo Segundo

You turn up often in my mind, though it be
in subliminal fashion, iridescent flashes
of your quiet image flit into consciousness
like flies in spring, when they are quick.

I think of you in your silent parade, you
marching in your eastern–black robes,
your body and face towards the sunset
but your mind and soul see the sunrise....

During our brief piece of the vastness
we learned thoughts, taught codes and
traded essences, so now you can never
be away from me, for my imagination
and memory and will, shall, like some
formidable trinity holy, penetrate
mountains and forests and oceans
to sense your presence
in the movement of my arm
lifting a cup of tea ...

Time Lapsed

Donald R. Vogel

30 YEARS AGO

Writing is who I am.

20 YEARS LATER

Wife and kid out. Third in charge again. Shit, 'honey-do' or write?

ONE HOUR LATER

Still blank screen. Jazz channel will set the mood.

FIVE MINUTES LATER

Ooh, Game of Thrones marathon.

10 HOURS LATER

Who left the goddamn computer on again?

NEXT DAY

Check one off 'honey-do' list. Too tired to write. Get Starbucks.

THIRTY MINUTES LATER

Damn, hot barista! Gotta come here more often.

2 HOURS LATER

Finished 'honey-do' list. Gonna get some tonight. Remember
hot barista.

NEW YEAR'S EVE

Resolution: write more. Start January 1.

10 HOURS LATER

Feel like shit.

ONE DAY LATER

Joined writer's group. Share something each week.

ONE WEEK LATER

Fucking wannabes.

30 YEARS LATER

Who am I? Never heard of him.

Ode to Fallen Leaves

John Dorroh

1.
All this talk of dying leaves my thirsty
for life – the old brown dog that fell from the back
of a truck when the young male driver swung hard to avoid
what turned out to be some kid's doll, its gingham dress
torn from over use, its bulging eyes indicative of
the turmoil in her body. He didn't stop. I saw it all
from the backyard deck; hurried to help the poor hound
in what was the last few minutes of its life.

2.
He tells me with no uncertainty that the deck
is dying, its support posts rotted from weather
& age. I'm not ready to hear this but it's been said
more than once, just as he predicted that our two
dogs would be dead within a year. He has an old soul
like his grandmother. I hate her for being right.

3.
The leaves are dying now, that time of year
with their weakened petioles, exhausted from holding
them up for almost eight long months. In turn

there will be a parade of color, one last hoorah
before they blow into the wind, waiting to be
mulched, composted into nutrients for the next
line of living things. It's all so tiring.

4.
My Uncle Jim moisturized until he was 99.
And then one morning he said *What the hell*
& stopped. Just like that. In his last 10 years
I watched him cling onto shopping carts
which had nothing in their massive scaffolding
except Neapolitan ice cream, a two-liter Coca-Cola,
& a carton of eggs. He sprang from his recliner
like a cricket when someone knocked on his door;
kept two bowls on his kitchen counter. And then everyone
he knew was dead. *Why me, Lord?*

5.
When you told me that you might need open-heart
surgery, I believed you only a little. Because you've
been right most of the other times. I'm praying
that the law of averages works in your favor this time.
You need to be wrong. I sit on the deck & feel the temperature drop.
There's a front moving in from the southwest, & I want to see the
last of the leaves fall to the ground before I need
to put on a coat.

reminder

Colleen Keating

air is riven with grief   a low
slow pall of whispers   shrouds
our small communal world

heads shake in disbelief
gasping sounds like that of fish
stranded at low tide

yet in this laden torpor
cicadas still ring their song
timid blue-hearted pansies nod

and in a corner of her garden
a young hibiscus bursts
into flower   its yellow suns

quivering with search for meaning
as today at the funeral
many search for words of comfort

dragonflies on the mirrored–
surface of our loss   and from
a screen memories draw us in

her toasting with wine laughter play
arms lovingly encircled
hugs of celebrations

to a backdrop of a tended garden
multi-coloured petunias rambling
golden roses that give and give

this is life   it is beautiful
it reminds us of the fable
where a fish asks 'where is the sea?'

and the wise fish answers 'you're in it!'
back at home the sweet scent
of camellias wafts from her garden

Rainbow

Mantz Yorke

When the seagulls follow the trawler, it's because they think sardines
will be thrown into the sea.
Eric Cantona, sometime Manchester United footballer.

The rainbow's brilliance
arcs across the thundery grey.
A scarlet trawler, caught
by the sun, is coming in,

pursued by a bright white
fluster as seagulls seek fish
guttings, or possibly sardines.
I anticipate a striking shot

when boat and rainbow meet:
I raise my camera in readiness,
the image almost burnt out
by sunlight on the screen.

I take the picture. Eagerly,
I review the shot in shade
to find the camera still set
for monochrome. Sod it! Shit!

Ten Years Ago

Guy Chambers

train stranded
station ten years ago

cracked windows
curtains half closed

unpunch tickets
lay on the shelf

an old English hat
dangling on the hat rack

foot prints eroded
on the rugged wooded
dusty platform

a jagged bench
is where yesteryear
stories been told

suitcases astray
baggage cart
deprived

windblown papers
scattering the corners

    signal light
    on the long tall stand
    staring down the track

green burnt out
but still waiting
for the thundering
rumbling echoes
of the tracks

    cable gram
    asleep on the down lines

letterman's bike
frayed flat tires
decaying in the ditch

    sunset over the boarded up houses
    rigid wooden sidewalks
    sagging in the tall grass

streets weathered
and moss grown
a gray horse grazing
in a patchy empty field

old school yard
voiceless
playground eroded
swings too rusted
to wave into the wind

the church left behind
holding the green gunnysacks

wooden crosses
rest on the hillside
abandon
flowers bone dry

west rooted away

evening settled
the in road
in the pocket
hereto
here unto

Dining Out

Remngton Murphy

He goes to the same
24/7 greasy spoon
Beneath the same waning three quarter moon
And orders the per usual
Two grilled chicken medallions,

Corn on the cob, Pennsylvania Dutch style
Lima beans smothered in vinegar,
And a salad, ranch dressing on the side.
He's gotten used to eating by himself
Even if he feels deranged

Like a horror film loner,
Uneasy in his own skin.
The restaurant has a counter.
All the same, he'll still insist
On sitting at a table

As if his wife were still alive.
He wonders if the waitresses
Gather in the kitchen or the employee washroom
And have themselves a high old time
Laughing and telling a few stories

About the strange sixty-year-old.
He wonders if he's reached the stage of notoriety
Where they've given him a pet name,
Like Hop-a-long, Five Dollar Tip,
Or Mr. Toad.

Puking

Mark Hudson

I failed out of college,
because I got sick, and my
girlfriend broke up with
me. So I quit drinking,
but I still smoked cigarettes.

The cigarettes were no
good either. I smoked two and a
half packs a day, and sometimes
I would vomit.

I got a job at a movie theatre.
A girl would come in named Carey.
A lot of people thought we were
dating each other, but we kissed once
in a movie theatre for twenty minutes,
and that was it. But we became really
good friends.

She called me the guy who
"Pukes on command." I don't
know if she thought that was funny,
but I thought that was kind of gross!

I also had a friend named Steve,
who was a Desert Storm vet. One
day I had a big chicken dinner
at my parents' house. I got in
the car with Steve, headed to his house.
I lit up a cigarette, and puked up
my chicken dinner onto my shirt.

Steve just laughed, and when
we got to his house he put the shirt
in the washing machine, and
temporarily gave me a shirt
to wear. At the end of the night
my shirt was clean. Steve dug out
a rock n roll magazine with the band
the Sex Pistols, and Sid Vicious
claiming one of his hobbies was,
"Puking for Pleasure."

I eventually went to a
Stop Smoking Clinic, and quit
smoking. So I don't really
puke anymore.

I hadn't heard from my
friend Carey in a while, so
I called her parents. Her
mom answered. She said
that Carey had died young
of a Cerebral Aneurysm.

So another friend who
died young in my life. I'm
fifty-two, and I'm a survivor.
But I know what loss is, and
the older you get, you know it
more and more.

My Books

Rose Mary Boehm

It did not start with one book. Of course.
I brought some from home
the moment I left to forge my own way.
The German edition of 'War and Peace',
and a German Dickens collection,
three heavy, bound volumes of 'Die Dame'
with an illustration of a fascinating device
that helped Edwardian ladies fart at the dinner table
without making a sound.

Beautiful leather-bound
volumes of the collected fairy tales
by the Brothers Grimm,
by Hans Christian Anderson
with drawings
of strange animals
and art–nouveau writing
like extra-terrestrial bindweed slithering over
the cover and the back.

The page edges of 'Der Zauberberg' by Thomas Mann
were dipped in gold leaf, the print
like little insect legs.

And, oh, the chapter headings
for the collected sagas from around the world:
etchings and drawings of dwarves, elves,
and assorted unholy beings or entwined lovers;
and always, always that bindweed
winding its way through
the first letters of every new chapter.

The books multiplied, perhaps
during the nights when I wasn't looking.
But my new ones became thinner and flimsier.
There were no saints and angels.
I do understand the lack of decoration on books
by Jean Genet and Albert Camus.
But even 'Madame Bovary' and 'The Three Musketeers'
were now just paper and cardboard, the font—
like almost every book—Times New Roman.

I have learned to appreciate my Kindle,
especially in my new home country where books
in my preferred language are not easy to find,
even though I mourn the loss of the satisfying
feel of paper under my eager fingers.

But sometimes I indulge in a secret communion
with some old friends. Books that have survived
travels, moving vans, container ships
on rough seas, and lazy hands that didn't
want to carry another box with useless stuff.
Together we sit in the big, black armchair
and remember.

Remains

Cynthia Leslie-Bole

how odd to receive your remains
in a black plastic box
with a typed yellow label
listing the formal name you no longer used

they were delivered by a stranger
who said "sorry for your loss"
then had me sign a form

how odd to place your remains
on my desk in a shrine
with a photo of you in your prime
and your true name written on bamboo

I worked with what had been you
beside me for weeks
cherishing our proximity

how odd for that to suddenly feel wrong
and hear you say
"time to turn toward your own life
and separate the living from the dead"

I dismantled the altar as you instructed
hugging your blocky remains
as I carried them to the shed

how odd not to know
what to do
with the black box
of you

Coming Apart

Ryn Holmes

I am completely undone,
brought to my knees
by the unexpected sight of your slippers
placed side by side in the trash bin.
Useless and abandoned,
their toes touch in a final kiss
as sad metaphor of our married life.

Every step taken apart
has the strangest effect:
it severs the present,
causes preoccupation with the past.
Returning to an intimacy
once squandered is hopeless.
Longing for you pulls at my skin.

Trolling empty streets for remnants
of an uncoupled life is futile,
that story over.
Associations melancholic and uncomfortable
are pitiless resurrections.
In sorry attempts at keeping you close
I surround myself with your discarded things.

I cannot breathe.
Two minus one just doesn't add up.
Others wrenched from a union
have parted ways before us,
managed solitary lives in empty places,
spaces filled with echoes of grace and fury.
Changing the sheets, I catch a trace of your scent.

What a love we lived.
Such heated play of words
shall never be repeated.
You have gone on ahead now,
hung it up and walked away
from our here to your forever there.
I could not care more.

blue

Amy B. Moreno

This is the first poem I have written about you
it has changed; and so have I
I remember the damp weight of hot chips wrapped in
newspaper on my lap, coming home just us two;
why does that memory visit so often?
And your hands – dry and warm, they cooled

they have changed; and so have I
I sit up late and put the pieces together
then stack them on my shoulders
And your hands – dry and warm, they cooled
under the skin; inky arteries sing of things I forget

I sit up late and put the pieces together
then stack them on my shoulders
I thought I heard you in the sunflowers,
but you preferred the blues of cornflowers
under the skin; inky arteries sing of things I forget
You left some other parts behind – your wide laugh,
your brown eyes; your favourite flowers

I thought I heard you in the sunflowers,
but you preferred the blues of cornflowers
You left your nose here; on my face
You left some other parts behind – your wide laugh,
your brown eyes; your favourite flowers
And my voice, somehow, sounds like yours on the phone;
people thought I was you, so I had to tell them over and over

You left your nose here; on my face
I remember the damp weight of hot chips wrapped in
newspaper on my lap, coming home just us two;
why does that memory visit so often?
And my voice, somehow, sounds like yours on the phone;
people thought I was you, so I had to tell them over and over
This is the first poem I have written about you

The Visitation

Amalia Fish

You came into my room:
a spirit light as air.
You brought your love and kindness to me,
lying by my side.

Your body lay
so many miles away,
still and cold but not yet spent.
The nurses attended to your body's needs:

the earthly shell,
not knowing that your spirit left
and came to see me as I slept.
'My mind has not been right for quite a while,' you joked,

'but I'm so proud of you
and all you've done.
You are my darling daughter
and my number one.'

I felt your hand lift up to stroke my face.
How can you be here
when you're not yet dead?

but here you were beside me

and loving words
were all you said.
How can I feel alone
when you are so close,

watching over me
and knowing me for who I am?
Your spirit's young again,
light without the world's constraints.

I think you came to say,
'Don't grieve. There'll be freedom in my death.'
How can I doubt this transformation
playing out before my eyes?

When the suffering
of your final days
has turned
to dancing light?

Loss … and Gains

Pegi Deitz Shea

(Based on the life of Jeanne Baret,
the first woman to circumnavigate the world.)

Docteur visits my tavern between expeditions.
I sit across from him, and order us
a fine Burgundy, kite stuffed with pomegranate,
roasted pork with pineapple.

I listen to his descriptions of specimens
from Madagascar and Réunion.
I promise to visit him, but I won't,
don't want to, don't need to
be lectured, be humbled, be asked to fetch
this book, that scalpel, that magnifying glass
while, here, I gladly pay others to serve me.

But after three years—an urgent letter,
and I do go to Philibert. Oh…
no salve can save him now—
gray veins barely pulsing beneath
paper temples, breaths faint
and far between, limbs lined
with blood-crusted bandages.

He presses a pouch into my hands,
wheezes, "Wages…
for walking the clouds."

Inside—diamonds!
The red, blue and black ones from Brazil.
I lift my gaze to his eyes but his eyes
and mind—impossibly, finally
still.

"Merci."

2.
I didn't think I'd miss him, but
the worms irrigating my soil,
the seeds sprouting in pots,
the birds wheeling in sea breeze,
the leaves dripping soft raindrops,
the monkeys squealing in glee
have me beckoning *Look, Philibert!*

I thank him for the time
and space to ask questions,
for his patient replies to them, or
for his demands, often maddening,
that I find my own answers.

I thank him for his confidence
that I could.

QWERTY

Karla Linn Merrifield

Quite satisfying,
typing with my eyes
closed—words flying blind
into foggy bereavement.
The keyboard nosedives toward *Death*.

★

I'm ordering the cremation online. *"Excellent service and thoughtful care! The best in the field ... I wouldn't trust anyone else. ... he always called my mom "mom" instead of saying "the body". ... no pressure about which urn I wanted.* Sounds fine by me. I complete the form, but, then—long pause—I do not, emphatically do not, click *Submit.* I'll call this Andy and Scott exit-burner duet tomorrow. After all: *Tomorrow is another day,* so saith Scarlett O'Hara in the annals of Hollywood, so saith my mother when teaching me, at age seven, to type on her heavy black Smith-Corona. *Enough typos for today, missy.*

The so-called arrangements can be made Wednesday ... or Thursday ... or Friday ... . He's got time yet until he slips away (s-l-i-p, s-l-i-p-p-i-n-g, s-l-i-p-s-l-i-d-i-n-g a-w-a-y), and return home as cremains in an antique Chinese ginger jar.

★

Not mind but body
fingers stirring syllables
ad infinitum

Nazar to Protect Against Losing You

Jay McPherson

I can't call you mother anymore.
Nights of bittering beer
have washed you away.
I can't say 'I love you,'
not to the woman who would sooner
abandon her sons than her drink.
But alone in my room
tucked beneath sheets you made,
I am a child again,
freshly showered, kissed.
A snow monkey asleep in Jigokudani,
Hell's Valley,
even though it wasn't yet. I remember
before addiction dammed you,
before your love was
a threat.
You spat snapshots of my childhood
as if you expected me
to stay frozen,
then anticipated praise
when you bought me a men's shirt.

You engulfed my experiences,
twisted my gender
into an open forum,
then insisted you had no say
in what I am.
You drowned my first chance to
transition, said you'd just
cut me off,
then wept when I asked Dad
to help me in secret.
But despite torrents of torment,
I reach out my hand
from that
undertow
to show you
I'm still here,
waiting for the flow to ebb.

Women with Dead Husbands Have Questions

Connie Johnstone

Some answers are provided them, at first. Obviously.
They know, now, how their marriages will end.
And when.

Love can live forever or die, but marriages? They end,
one way or another.

At home, later, when they look in the mirror, they say,
Oh, I am not a married woman, often still wearing
their wedding ring and, quite possibly, his, on a thumb.

> *Who am I, then?* But that's later.

Arguments with Death make no sense, but women with dead
husbands change position, drop their pleading arms, lower
their weeping eyes, direct their questions to the corpse.

> *How could you do this? Die,* they mean.
> *Be dead,* they mean. There's no quick comeback,
> no defensiveness, not even a shaky alibi.

It's disorienting, no one to argue against.

Or lean against. Faced with the silence of one-way arguments,
looking upon the bulk and muscularity of the unmoving
male body, the next question these women might ask,

> *Who? Who am I going to lean against?* Leaning.
> Its meaning built on a foundation of flirting.
> Leaning into. Tipsy in bars.

Then leaning down, to say *Yes,* when he knelt, to propose.
Leaning back against him, in a nursery peering down at
babies they've made. Leaning toward. Leaning on.
For support. Flashes of all that leaning. Gone.

> *Look at those shoulders. Those hands. Those fingers.*
> *I paid extra for all that gold to go around your meaty*
> *finger. Where do I put it now, the ring?*

Touching the body mass, cradling the size-Large head,
stroking the long leg bones of a dead male,
can make women with dead husbands say,

> *How can all of you, your entirety, be dead.*

The greatest fear of aging is not death

Jeral Williams

I. The Fear

Alzheimer's disease is death before death, and I'm terrified of it.
— Joey Comeau

Dreaded loss of living,
perceptions slowly transform to fog,
retrieval ebbs as a rainbow fading,
and familiar words decay into blinding white.
Scrambled connections ooze
into the abyss of the living dead.
Null echoes cross the sound of silence
and touch what is felt no more,
even music ceases.
Behind a gaze of blank panes
lie tasteless tunnels of no thought, no emotion,
and declining reflexes
accompanying mute echoes
through a vacuum.
No sunrise, no sunset, only night.
Evil leech sucking life
digesting into permanent unconsciousness.

An invisible sponge
absorbing axons, dendrites, engrams
evaporating into silence.
Blood and breath,
only blood and breath,
until death.

II. A Difficult Road to Trek Together

*Although your loved one may not remember you or might do
things that frustrate you, this is the time when he or she needs
you the most.*
— Angie Nunez Merryman

Her first evaporated memory—
an old friend unremembered,
signaled a rainbow fading.

Over time birthday cakes lost flavor.

Cues failed to stimulate what was lost,
as fear in her eyes sought comfort
his heart reflected concern.

Each anniversary, roses lost more color.

Side by side
they traveled the same road
in different lanes.

Residents ate Thanksgiving dinner; memory care had no aroma.

Her lane paved with quicksand
absorbing thoughts, emotions, senses.
In fading eyes, even dread stopped growing.

Children opened presents, but her Christmas heard no laughter.

As limbs withdrew
her carapace slowly hardened
to benign emptiness.

The church was full, but her Easter had no sunrise.

His lane paved with hot stones,
thawing memories frozen in tears,
morphing into affection, enriching dread,

Weddings and births passed in silence; she could not cry.

Enveloped in bittersweet pain,
every day he came
and kissed the vacant shell.

He buried her in purple.

III. The Caretaker's Report

Dementia care—it's not rocket science, it's heart science.
— Gail Weatherill

As we walked
I watched dead grow in the living,
one memory at a time.
Where footstep trod
quicksand covered dissolving time
In the end
I held the unfeeling stone
that was love
and kissed the carapace
of torpid death.

I just can't do for me what you do

B. D. Watson

Don't come looking for me as soon as you get home
Don't immediately hand me some chilled Manzanilla
Don't remember to ask me how the chat with my friend went
Don't smile and let your eyes wander all over my face while I talk
Don't lift my straggly fringe gently back from my glasses
Don't pull me into you and massage my shoulders
Don't be so nice to Mother
Don't always walk the dog when it's raining
Don't read to me so that I drift off to sleep
Because
If I lose you I don't know what I'll do.

Catharsis

Betty Naegele Gundred

A dark day matches my mood,
my façade of calm about to crumble.
The pressure builds as I sink deeper
in a sea of bad news.

The fissure open as tears scatter
in a full circle spray,
tears of loss, of frustration,
I am so sorry to disappoint you,

as long-awaited plans dissolve in the saline bath,
tears of fear, anger expelled, leaving the ruins of an aging body–
though I remember supple, silken, strong,
adjectives that no longer define me,

a constricted thought,
my throat swells to close,
as my tears rain like Thor's heavens railed today,
until my reservoir of pity runs dry.

I pull myself up, walk to the window,
and search for a rainbow through bleary eyes.
I know there is a sun waiting—
beyond the storm.

hey dad

Jim Dawson

i came to say hi
i love you,
clean your stone
and be with you.
i remember your
arm holding me
securely against
your thin legs,
the smile behind
those horn-rimmed glasses,
how calm funny gentle
you ran the family,
how your shirts smelled
of old spice,
how you deferred to your mom
disappearing to let me
cook with her,
and letting me steer
on the dump road
and dig through the trash
for junk like the adding machine
that never worked.

you taught me to save pennies
in the white lighthouse
and enjoy ice cream walks
and riding waves.
you taught me
i could trust.

Instructions to a Big Man sitting next to a Big, Big Man at the Theatre

Kenneth Wagner

The battle for the arm rest is already lost,
and a quarter of your seatback has been donated
to his spreading shoulder even before
you get to your seat.

So as you make your way across the row –
after you've stepped on toes and bumped into knees –
try not to audibly exhale when you see the big,
big man sitting in the seat next to yours.
Take a breath and try to find your inner mouse –
remembering the extra piece of pizza and slice
of chocolate layer cake doesn't matter to you now,
you have – for the moment – the benefit
of looking thinner – or at least not as large
as you always feel.

At the seat finally, there is no way
to avoid contact. There will be a small amount
of jockeying for position – you will lose.
Get used to the fact that your shoulders
will be rolled forward and your arms
will be squeezed into your lap for the first act.

After you've made it through intermission,
as soon as the house lights dim, there will come
a strange sensation – a relaxed second
of quiet security. And as the second act rolls
along you'll begin to lean into the warmth
of the big, big man – and a regressive happiness
will sweep across you – sporadic, calming memories
of what it was like to be held by your mother.

That comfort comes only as a quick flash,
seconds before the curtain falls. The house
lights will come up, and you'll finally rise and walk out
into the cold night air – your freedom from
the big, big man will be bittersweet, and you will be
a little bit sad, and a little bit lonely
like you've just left home for the first time.

Southern Ice

Jane H. Fitzgerald

It's northern December
We have escaped to
Florida, land of warmth
Our old cat, Sasha
took a dim view
She became lethargic
refusing to eat

Sasha is our rock
She rules our family
including the dogs

Her shuttered glances
speak volumes
Liking or criticizing
our actions
She curls up
on our laps if happy
or rubs her head
against our legs
When displeased,
she haughtily
leaves the room
tail raised high

While we soaked
up the sun
Sasha kept sinking
We rushed to the vet
His frown said it all
Leave her here
I'll operate
see what's there
A few days later
our betraying phone
rang, Caller ID, Vet
Our hearts chilled
Suddenly, sun and sand
had turned to darkness
Our grief turned us back north

Widow's Fund

Melina Cornell

Here's the link to a Go Fund Me to help reset my life,
funds will be allocated to cover the cost of a basic start over
mattress, whose foam hasn't sunk and imprinted
with the years of our love making,
one without coffee stains from clumsy afternoons;
where there weren't enough towels to soak up our
messes, all which have dried now
and don't matter anymore.

Another few hundred will be used to rip out
that old beige carpet,
where you'd prevent my slumping remains from falling
between the fibers after so many exhausting work nights,
where you gripped my body under the lights of
our 4ft Christmas tree as we wrapped ourselves
in holiday paper.

A couple more dollars will be used for a new couch,
where the impressions of your muscle and bone no longer dwell,
where I still sit each night, hoping the shadow of your
body can hug mine that somehow still lives and breathes
without you.

Donate your cash to help replace all of my
furniture, so I may find a new spot to place my
heart, a tchotchke now collecting dust on a
shelf, standing still in the memory of you.

Please fund my passage through time,
help me save up whatever it will cost to
be ten, twenty, another lifetime away
from the aching actuality that you are
no longer here.

And with the remaining pennies,
toss them into the Connecticut River,
pay the current to take me back to
Brattleboro, where we stood on a bridge
between mountains promising each other a
forever that came too soon.

Donate today.

In the Hours
Since I Lost You

Gurupreet K. Khalsa

In shadowed hours, since I lost you,
ten times each night I lie awake
and ache for bright resolve of day
where troubles fade for love's true sake.

In whipping storm, for I lost you,
beneath my quilt, I curl, and bawl;
beyond my windows, slashing winds
thrust branches, stones into the wall.

Some time long past, chanteur or bard
sang of true care, our world aligned;
safe in your arms, I fain would be
where ardor dwells, a peaceful mind.

I ring bright bells ten thousand ways:
fond stories of our futures tell;
I'll find you again, trust sighs of ease –
our hearts, in time, will all be well.

Half Diminished

Paul Bluestein

The passing years smeared my vision, stoppered my ears
and seasoned my food with bland.
Arthritis lamed my knees and took my hands
that once spidered jazz arpeggios and wove a web
of major 7th and half-diminished chords.
The changes were so gradual that, nearly without noticing,
I learned to live with the losses and infirmities.
But that was nothing like losing you to the malignant thief of time,
a hurricane that blew my heart out of my chest and flung it
onto piles of rubble that once had been my life.
Our forty years together was ransacked
by a cruel and careless robber,
that stole my peace of mind but left behind this grief.

Growing Pain

Anthony Crutcher

A seed sprouts in our lives
growing in our nurturing care,
ever stretching taller,
ever growing stronger.
Maturing
until it outgrows our space.

A lump of clay placed in our hands
temporarily.
We twist it, mold it, and smooth it,
but we cannot complete it.
It slips from our hands all too soon
for life to refine and fire.

This process like a flowing river,
natural.
We can observe and influence.
but no matter;
it will follow its own course,
Ending in a destined place,
at a destined time.
Our children grow up.

We futilely try to push it back,
but the moment comes.
The dreaded moment arrives.
The one no parent can stop.
The moment of goodbye and hello.
The last exhalation of childhood,
The first inhalation of adulthood.
Our child dies,
and in their place an adult is born.

Mom's Obituary, First Draft

Katy McKinney

Because of the newspaper's word limit, I had to leave out
how she never ordered dessert but would take instead
one bite of the pie on my father's plate, until, after 52 years,

he finally exploded, accusing her of always taking the point,
and – too loud for the restaurant – *The point's the best part!*
I had to leave out how she loved to watch her great-grandson

flip her cane upside down and vacuum the carpet with its handle.
I chose to leave out how I hated her nagging, though now
in my 60s, I realize it's possible as a child I was lazy.

I left out how she loved to grow orchids. Her mother's slit wrists.
The matching dresses she sewed for her daughters.
Our fights over curfew. I stuck with the basics: birth, death,

survivors – a few good anecdotes. But where will they go,
the left-out stories? What will happen to the motorcycle ride
she took on her 90th birthday, the first of her life?

And what will happen to her ordinary days, the years of them,
the times she sat, content, library book on her lap?
I hope they'll rise – all of them – like sparks from a bonfire:

some hot and fast from the fire's center, while others
take the slow path, ascend in lazy meander above the snow,
past darkened trees to linger and glimmer like stars.

Vulpine

Emily Shearer

Find something remarkable, they said, to write your poem about.
Let it show how one thing mirror-images another.

The bugle's resounding echo tapers to a pregnant hush,
the radio reports horizontal theories.

A hurricane is to grief what grief is to a carefully planned outing,
then, everything left behind—the picnic, the music box, the map.

It doesn't matter, or as the French say, *peu importe.*
Little matters. Tell that to the woman alone in the graveyard.

Little matters? Foxes weigh less than a box of ashes.
The first inkling of a breeze out at sea

can change the course of a poem
or a life. Her there, studying pawprints,

evidence of who has passed this way
the day after the hurricane.

Hell Has

(for the Chevalier O'Keefe)

Matthew Horsfall

Leave me be, because
There can never be
an us.
Fatal, scandalous,
ludicrous, a consummation
of hideous fantasy.

An improbable intersection:
your irresistible force,
and my long-lost youth.
A three-way collision course
between fantasy, truth and you;
you are oblivious.

You remind me of death.
You could destroy the world.
What on earth made me think
that you ever wanted me?
Your radiant fury, (hell has)
your haggard beauty.
(She has) a triple face,
(hell is) a terrible place
reserved for ....

Cat Orange

Zhihua Wang

1

You were almost three
when we adopted you,
pampered by a loving lady
at the beginning of your life,
now trapped in three pairs
of green hands.

2

You literally sniff everything
and I feel nothing.
Only when you smell the flowers,
I feel different.

3

I'm immersed in learning
my second language,
you challenge me by talking
with the only-word
in your vocabulary.

4

In the morning, when
my daughter is still asleep,
I hear you croon
at her window.

Your soft, turning,
and tactful voice is different
from the demanding meows
to us parents.

She treats you with songs
and notes from her keyboard,
so you speak to her
in a different tone—

it's your understanding
of music; they are
your songs.

5

With me, you scream
in order to play outside.
You sing
while trotting back.

You dash into my room
before I close the door.
You crouch outside,
beg for your bedtime snack.

Sometimes, I see you in me,
sometimes, I see me in you.

6

Not sure of our own tomorrow,
I put your cutest pictures
in a group chat,
hoping someone is willing
to rehome you.

After two months,
the guy who queried me
confirms that he wants you,
I know our real separation

is in the corner,
my tears run
unbridled.

7

In what way
will you know
or should we do
to let you know

that we are seeing you
off today—

      like marrying off a kid
      and never seeing him come back.

Your new home master
will drive hours to pick you up—

there are many cues in the air,
many talks among us, and many
are addressed to you—

but you will never know
until the moment comes—

      until we put you in your travel carrier
         zip it up, and mount you
            onto a new car,

until you think back
about today
later.

8

We have you
    in our pictures
            and videos,
you have us
    in your memory.

Lost Sock

Paul Hostovsky

There is a dark side
to the dress socks
in the top drawer. They sort
according to some dark principle
of chaos and the estrangement
of identical twins—the precipitous
divorces of the happily married
are no less confounding
than these fine upstanding socks
you could once trust with your ankles
and your pedigree,
your onward and upward mobility,
suddenly turning against you
and each other
and themselves.
The motley characters
one sees gathered around park benches,
passing the joint or the bottle,
are this kind of lost—
the transient attachments,
the fleeting allegiances
dissolving as soon as the spirits stop flowing,
each going his own way.

Everything is Different— every Hour.

Amy Soricelli

Her husband's death was not the front page.
It wasn't the pie in the oven or
the perfumed letter.
Her husband's death slipped off her lips
and then dragged itself through their
old neighborhood;
the one with the coffee shop
that smelled like roses.

She sat in front of the mirror after
he died, waiting for her reflection
to show her open mouth.
Her cat curled around her legs,
purring and rusty from the rain.

When her husband died she showed
us pictures of couples in love.
She held them up to the screen
with a flat hand.

Sometimes after the sun set,
she ate ramen noodles and
pointed with her fingers.
She gave us a poem on the third day,
but scrubbed the words first so
they wouldn't sting.

Who could blame her for the creases in
the bed, the songs on the radio in
a steady loop,
the car sirens in the middle of the night?
She considered changing her hair.
or whispering secrets in the dark.

When her husband died there were so
many ways to make her cry.
First, there was that bowl of soup she
settled down to eat with us.
We watched with her as the noodles
danced in her bowl.
Then, there's the unfinished soap that was
blue at first, but slowly became
gray and light.
We all cried as it slowly melted down the drain.

A Day in the Life

Jim Gormley

It's October 17, 2006
He's nine years old
He isn't going to school today
His mom is dying

She is sleeping
Next to the window
In her new hospital bed
For the first time

The doorbell rings
It's Elise, his mom's sister
His mom is dying

The doorbell rings, it's Trish
His dad meets her, crying
His mom is dying

The doorbell rings, it's Gayle
The doorbell rings, it's Arthur
His mom is dying

The doorbell rings, it's Paul
The doorbell rings, it's Teresa
The doorbell rings, it's the Hospice Nurse
His mom's dying

The phone rings, it's Peter
The phone rings, it's Babette
The phone rings
Her parents are calling to say goodbye
His mom is dying

They are playing music for her, tapes made by Paul & Jot
Just for his mom
Someone wonders can she hear it
Gayle says hearing is the last thing to go
his mom is dying

He is lying on his bed
with his cat, Carlos
His mom's breathing is loud
Elise thinks his mom is suffering,
His father calls the nurse
No, it's all right, this is how it works
More morphine on the tongue
The doorbell rings
It's a package for him!

Halloween toys from Oriental Trading Company
He is very excited,
Lays out the skeletons
In their coffins in his room
Goes into his mom's room
Asks if anyone wants to play
It's 4 o'clock,
His mom is dying

Everyone is in the room, around the bed
His mom sits up and looks right at him and his dad,
She lies back down

It's 5:30
The wheezing stops
No more breath
No more Mom

Some people suggest we take him for a walk
NO
He wants to stay in the room with his mom
We take turns lying next to her, hugging her, talking to her

The doorbell rings
The nurse comes to tell us
What
We already know

8 PM, the doorbell rings
The men have come to get his mom
He waits at the bottom of the stairs with his dad
The men bring his mom down,
wrapped in the soft, warm brown blanket
He puts two of his favorite stones on the blanket
"I am sorry for your loss" says the big man
As we close the gate

9 o'clock
Everyone is gone
He says to his dad
"Now it's just boys living here, you, and me, and Carlos"

On a Raw Morning in Wiltshire

Elizabeth Cox

Tyres squelch through cattle-churned slurry,
rubber sucking the ground like hungry leeches,
as I drive along meandering muddy lanes.
Bare trees loom through dank grey fog
slithering around black branches
like tendrils of Old Man's Beard,
strangling life from limbs yet to show signs of spring,
piercing cold visible in morning light.

This is familiar to me.
These lanes were once my home.
The bone-chilling fingers of icy mist
stroke me like a ghostly lover.

I pass dwellings I once loved,
now someone else's joy.
Feel nostalgic for the times
when I lived and loved
within their sheltering walls,
surrounded by warmth
and kinship.

This is no longer my place.
The loss of belonging,
bruises me.
And I am shorn of comfort.

The Young Girl and the Old Woman

David Blumenfeld

Young girl:
Old woman here, I cry to you of what I dreamed today.
A wrinkle came upon my face and would not go away.

I rubbed and creamed and washed it off to hide my sad disgrace.
But when I rubbed the wrinkle out, two more came in its place.

My waist is slim, my skin is smooth, I'm young and lithe and lovely.
But Time will make its silent mark and soon I shall be ugly.

I prithee help me hastily that I may find a way
to sidestep steady Time's advance and never, never grey.

Old Woman:
Oh, foolish lass, there is no way to run or hide from Time.
It hounds us like the rhythm of a never-ending rhyme.

It follows us in every path and never slows its pace.
No matter how you wash or rub, its mark will not erase.

But fear it not, oh maiden fair, forget its mournful knell.
You only see its painful toll, but it brings gifts as well.

Your mind is dull, your spirit dim, you're young and lacking vision.
Time will bring experience and with it shall come wisdom.

Young girl:
What voice is this that echoes here with lies and self-deceit?
Your words are hollow as your eyes and pallid as your cheeks.

What made me think that one who's worn could ever know the way
to stop the ancient traveler and bid fair youth to stay?

I should have guessed before I spoke that you could be no aid.
Your withered body Time has claimed and caused your mind to fade.

What wisdom is there anywhere or vision, truth or sight,
can e'er replace these golden curls or eyes that sparkle bright?

The One

Linda Barrett

When I first met you at the Bible Study,
I thought you were the One
That God-given mate I searched for
In every Bible-believing church single's group
You told me you were a believer
You promised me you wouldn't pressure me for sex
Like the other guys I went out with
Who weren't followers of Jesus Christ.
My psychologist wanted me to find you.
She had hopes that I would have a good sex life.
That's all she obsessed on for $40.00 an hour
You were the One
Even when you threatened to break up with me
Because we weren't having sex,
You were the One
When you gaslit me into spending
New Year's Eve at your parent's house.

You were the One
Even after you fought with total strangers
In department stores and restaurants
Even when I was away from you,
Realizing you manipulated me
Just to keep your parents happy.
I went to my church's rector
Who said This One pushed me and pushed me
Into marriage
And you didn't love me after all.
The Holy Spirit made me realize
If he loved me, he would wait.
After that New Year's Day morning
When you, The One, took my physical innocence,
The Holy Spirit gave me
The marching orders to dump you
Because you weren't the One.
Sometimes, singleness is a God-given gift
And sometimes loss is Good.

Lost Days

Rob McKinnon

Sitting and looking without focus
through her room's window
she saw through the pristine lawned garden
to the years of her past
where she now lived.

She remembered the day at Primary School
with her friend in the playground
when the good-looking boy smiled at her
and said hello.

She remembered the day years later
when she married the boy who had become a man,
the dress that she wore, the guests at the Church,
the joy of the Reception.

She remembered the birth of their two children,
the first days at School,
the birthday parties, the happy holidays,
the family being together.

She remembered her husband becoming sick,
the hospital stays, the awful treatments,
but at least he got better – did he get better?
Where was he now?

She remembered many things
but the morning and yesterday
were lost.

The bulb catalogue

Juliet Fossey

I need to know your favourites,
or at least the ones you prefer.
Each page is a colour-chart of sweets,
like the liquorice torpedoes
we gobbled as kids.

The bulbs arrive in brown paper,
silvery skinned, the size of garlic cloves.
I bury them in handfuls to warm
my mind, with orange and red,
when the spring comes.

Trying to negotiate this parting with you,
between now and then, is fraught.
You won't have my terms, refusing
to pick a colour for your birthday.
I must accept that,

what I'll remember with the flowering
of these tulips, is your stubbornness.

Casket

Kate Meyer-Currey

wicker lets souls breathe
bones dance ash fly light
on the wind beyond this
momentary resting place
where we gathered within
grief's blank stone walls
sun filtered through
impersonal glass bricks
paperweight heavy as
mournful roses left for
last goodbyes or notes
of farewell dropped like
torn petals by someone
waiting until it was nearly
over to stand at your side
and lay a hasty hand on
the bars of your woven
cage and hope you might
hear the muttered words
of loss through its chinks
before you slipped away
a spark on the grey hills
swallowed by low sun as
the afternoon faded and
we became ghosts of that
shadowed day.

The Poke Bowl Lunch with Matthew 10:14

Jeannie E. Roberts

Heartbreak is a loss. Divorce is a piece of paper.
—Taylor Jenkins Reid

We ordered the same poke bowls
bought the identical pair of jeans.
I told her how shame had settled
solidified in my body.
After four marriages
and three divorces
she remained my friend
knew me—
my heart
wish for one marriage
one family
one life
built on love
trust and truth.
It never feels good
to be judged

treated like debris
told you'll go to hell.
I guess that's the point.
She reminded me of the Gospel of Matthew.
If we're not received nor welcome
it's best to shake the dust off our feet   leave.

We were the same but different.
She with one marriage
me with four.
Like the seasons
there's no shame nor judgment in repetition.
Moving forward
I'll whisk away the dust
stand in my own garden
where the dust will fall
meet the ground   mix with the earth
where it'll flourish
grow into edible ingredients
like those served in poke bowls.
At our next lunch
I'll be clean
like spring.

Times passed

Lynn White

As the day ends
I tick it off
on my calendar.
Finished!
Done!
Gone!
Lost!

But some will remain intact
to be pictured
sometimes
even heard
almost re-lived
as my memories.

If only
I could choose
the ones to remember,
open a window and look through,
revisit those days
and throw away the rest.

Watch them leave
forgotten,
lost,
gone
really gone!

But I can't.
They're self-selecting,
those memories of
passed days
or ebbing and flowing
outside my control.

ER, Vancouver General Hospital

Lynne Burnett

Last night, watching the reality TV show, marvelling
at the array of patient issues—stabbings, overdoses,
malaria that can kill, cyclist hit, pedestrian hit, a
flailing foul-mouthed drunk—each with a short
update later in the show and then—the last one—
a guy in his early sixties like us, who, diagnosed
with a form of lymphoma and told it had a 70%
cure rate, suddenly had a heart attack and looked
dead but was brought in because a faint pulse was
detected—then none—CPR—now a pulse again
but then fading, finally his wife called in and the
family doctor, all the staff around this white-headed
buddha-bellied man with the grey-tufted chest
hair cresting like smoke signals from a dying fire
and the doc in charge saying they could do no more,

his body wasn't responding, then taking the tube
out of his mouth to make him more comfortable and
telling his wife to hold his hand and everyone standing
silently, the woman weeping, thanking the staff for
all they had tried, the man mostly naked lying there,
my husband and I on the couch with a box of Kleenex
knowing exactly what the other was thinking
and him not a handholder but he let me hold his
until the show was finally over.

Losing It

Pip Griffin

Yet another nightmare
astride me in early morning dark.
I am lost in my own street
made unrecognisable by developers.

This much is real:
a light-blocking monster looms –
impending renovation to my Siamese twin dwelling
the party wall to feel the saw
of brutal separation.

I will be besieged by armies of trucks
thump of wrecking balls   whine of power tools
piles of debris, bricks, metal, timber
to be negotiated on the narrow footpath.

I've read change can be upsetting
for the elderly
that stress attacks brain synapses
already losing their way.
On the other hand I've read change
challenges the brain to form new pathways.

Let's hope it's not too late.

That Morning

Biman Roy

Spring was almost over.
An invisible viral hand had slammed shut the door.
Summer was somewhere idling outside
and winter was playing hooky on the other side of the mind.

Inside
            the glass jar
                        filled with absences,
you waited
for the doorbell to ring.

Then a man with a hat and raincoat ambled in,
greeted us in a foreign language, and sat quietly in the corner,

as if waiting for someone or no one,

until you came down the stairs, wearing
                        a gown, borrowed from the night
and smiled.
Then the man stood up,
bowed gently as a bough to the wind,
            held your hand, and walked out through the door
                        as silent as death.

Absence

Kay Ritchie

It wasn't that I didn't ask but that I asked too late
about his childhood & his early days &

now this spectre of the man he was,
a ghostly presence cloistered in his nursing home.

We discuss doctors, diet, medication,
television programmes.

Our talk so small
as all his memories have left the room &

left just empty chairs.
He grasps for them.

They haunt his days & nights
but like the autumn,

once the curlew-song has flown,
they've gone.

Loss Pup

Neila Mezynski

His sweetness remains; you didn't go far; only as far as my outstretched arms. Your hand fit so well in my pocket; you spread your wings without thinking it through, flying too close to the terrible heat, singeing beautiful you. Too many nights hatching your plan. Those terrible words I couldn't ask, afraid to ask, make them real. Too bad I left my wings in the shop along with my crystal ball to head you off at the pass; magic wasn't in the works that day. It's so permanent my pup.

Vertical, or: Horizontal

Britta Benson

When that last leaf falls,
when autumn becomes all,
we hold on to sinuous fibres, bend
tangle, gnarl our anxious souls
into awkward, bloodless knots
clumps of quiet devastation

Green leaves in its own sweet time
disoriented, early, late, excited, a collection
already played with by determined winds.
Brothers, sisters, on canvases far from their core,
each breath creates wings, all things possible:
Composite families, frameless pictures of loss

When that last leaf falls,
when autumn becomes all,
we bind hope with old spider thread,
collect conkers, seeds, fill pockets
in our need to preserve futures, pasts,
gone, long before we were ready

Can I fit another memory into my veins?
Drying, dying, clustered recollections spill
like snowflakes in anticipation of darkness,
prodigal dust filled with nostalgia. We're preppers,
caressing our secret stash of goosebumps, until
structures disintegrate. Celebration of change

When that last leaf falls,
when autumn becomes all,
we gasp, watch warm breath disperse,
then resist this most courteous invitation
to traverse the air, forget destinations,
let go of fear and regret, just because

Arriving to a garland of fairy lights
wrapped loosely around a rowan tree's heart,
we applaud nature's reckless self-sacrifice.
Forever scared, we touch graves, waiting for signs:
Last berries, shiny red baubles of remembrance.
I am cold. I am tired. And I know, I am home

What the Map Doesn't Show

Ann Howells

Unfamiliar names on my map. On road signs.
In three days I must return home,
but I want to see it again –
that farm central to Grandma's stories.
I recall a single lane, steep hill,
sharp curve, tunnel
under overhanging branches, but all I see
are tidy houses, golf course lawns.
Where is the quaintness? The country?
Big white house, stone floor kitchen
down a step? The wraparound porch?
Lilac bushes?

I remember slanted cellar doors –
basket after bushel basket
of empty bottles: condiments, tinctures,
tonics – nothing useful tossed away.
The house burned, I know,
but I need woods,

Uncle Owen's tidy cottage just beyond,
at the tree line, surely that remains,
and the adjoining field
where he ploughed up the lavalier
passed down to me.

I fade like an old Daguerreotype,
into the past – light coal oil lamps,
ride to church in horse and buggy,
play the parlor's pump organ.
GPS can't help me, I'm trapped
in the nineteenth century.
But perhaps it's best –
how disheartening to find Seven-Eleven
where the chicken coop used to stand,
Starbucks where childhood stories reside.

Pacific Pulse

Bonnie Demerjian

Last living salmon in the stream.
Last among your kin, now finally at home, your
salty journey done. Late summer's beam
of slanted light shines on the bones

and ragged bodies, starvation torn,
once lustrous skin surpassing weaver's art.
Life's meaning spent, your eggs soon born
while river's might speeds your departure.

Here on the bridge I watch your toil
still fondly hoping for a happy end.
I know the plot no human will can foil,
together in this helix, unbending.

Unfailing is your purpose and your way
to teach hard lessons on this autumn day.

The Yard

Edward Ahern

I let the wild back in.
Discreetly, so the neighbors
would only slowly notice.
At first, thistles and ferns
sprouting on the edges
of lawns gone weedy.
Then briars and ivy
filling in and choking
bland shrubs and bushes.
As the neglected manicure
tangled and splayed
creatures came and stayed.
Skunks under the front porch,
chipmunks and mice scurrying
past the edges of the house,
a possum in the swamp oak,
moles and grubs in the lawn,
somewhere unfindable a raccoon.
The true nature of the yard
hidden under cursory
mowings and prunings
like a bad haircut.
Not a revolt, just subversion

what we learned from death

William Butler

when our aunt passed away
and
we were so very young
alive, playing chase in the backyard
her pale, frail face framed by her dark hair
became iconic tragedy
moving us only briefly, superficially
then
our mother's father in his sterile hospital room
my father frothing at his straining mouth
our cousin of breast cancer in her twenties
grandmother suddenly/uncle of alcohol/another uncle
another aunt/mother/others
we reckoned we should be done in the accounting
but
death's lesson is never long remembered
even in its inevitability
even as we age;
it seems never pretty
and not always welcomed

Dear Jules,

Ed Ruzicka

Dear Jules,

We could be basking in time at a café
   witness to the untamable lust of the French
   as they floor then brake Lemans, Citroens
   Peugeots in their out–sized, ludicrous traffic circles.
You could be seeing for yourself
   how the Eiffel Tower is a great needle
   pointed at stars & satellites. Or in
   the stacks with me at Shakespeare & Co.
Like F. Scott Fitz. was a decade before
   the world fell apart. Instead, you are
   in Stenton KY. hearing lawn sprinklers
   sizzle and watching your husband
Drop yet another Marlborough
Into yet another craft-beer bottle.

My Brilliant Tattoo

Todd Williams

Grief has a season, the doctors say,
but I wear mine as a tattoo,
   brilliant and burning when new,
   swollen in the razor-sharp sting
   of its Technicolor freshness.
Even in lifting the gauze to share
its hazy shape with friends
and family, I am alien to myself
   in a form forever altered by
   the permanence of colored ink
   and lingering absence
I feel the curve of its line redefine
paths where the hair was shaved away,
no strip of well-placed tape
or dark garment able to disguise
the image reversed in my mirror.

Through the years, this stain will
        quiet my tongue
        quell my smile
        and slow my gait
through days made more difficult
without your soft, still voice,
fading but always with me
until I am nothing more
than memory and fine dust.

I Should Have Been a Better Friend

A Dream Poem

Mike Wilson

You're different –
still self-contained, manly,
but wrecked, like your mother.
Yet tidy as feminine hygiene.

You wear ear studs
but they look like thumb tacks.
I can't tell if it's fashion or medicine.
If I ask, you'll see it as intrusive
so I don't, but you want me to.

You are telling me something.
I hear words.
What you don't say is louder.
What you don't say is a cloud.
No one lives there but you.

You've always been this way,
a gruff saint concealing sacred sorrow.
But something brings you to me, now,
defenseless in a dream.
Something's changed in you,
and changed in me.

The Living Monument

Doris Dembosky

I couldn't take my eyes off her –
a living, breathing antiquity
of priceless porcelain.

Her skin (ancient, opaque parchment
over oriental bird bones),
her backbone (made of Bethlehem steel
tempered with resolve),
and her propriety
belonged to another age.

She was an anachronism
removed from race riots,
unsoiled by the inner city,
distanced from the disenfranchised.

Her carriage and her clothing
marked her as a woman of means
who had cultivated standards.
She was a monument
to the refinements of the ruling class.

But as my train left the station,
I saw the monument crack.
This detached, cloistered woman
widened her stance and stoically stood
as her body betrayed her
and urine fell
between her silk-clad legs.

Love: Where do you go?

Theresa Hickey

The inscription on his stone read,
"In the end, it is love that lasts"

But on the ordinary days
when nobody paid attention,
was it on his lips, in his mind,
on his heart, in his steps?

If so, perhaps this wife, these children,
all gathered around to say goodbyes,
may have had a glimpse
of it, known it to be true,
claimed it as their own:

In the end, love *will not* die

In the end, it weaves its way
like a river, past the eulogies
in the oratory, past the days of loss
and grief, resilient in hearts
where it's been planted

Heat lightening in the wake
of a storm, love illuminates
the night, purifying
visions, purging sorrows
with a fire that brands the flesh

No ... love does not die
but chisels us towards a new beginning,
breakthroughs of the mind and heart.
Like a young bride and her husband
on the threshold of new life;
like an infant at the breast,
a passion fills our veins again
because love endures

Last Seen

Elaine Dillof

In March still vital
I wrote a poem.
In April May and June
I wrote nothing.
I hovered
in dimness, bandaged
as if wounded, an invalid,
a mummy, an assemblage
of clogged responses,
a glob stuck in my own throat.
Worse, a bare outline,
a stick drawing,
an erased presence.
July, I occupied chairs,
walked across rooms,
scrubbed, windexed.
picked crumbs off the floor,
I watched CNN
Turner Classics in the afternoon.
In August, I zapped a hornet.
looked a finch in the eye.

In the Fall
I wrote a line of poetry
It buzzed in my head.
but like a fumigated fly
fell dead. December,
like a switch on the wall,
I clicked on and off.

The Taint of Her

Tobi Alfier

It was a day so clear
you could see the ends
of the earth, yet
it left her in a rut
of melancholy.

She couldn't shake
a bitter taste
like the last swallow
of cold-dregs coffee.

A mash of echoes
filled her head,
a ghostly chill
filled her bones,
and an old ballad
filled her saddened heart—

she's so far down
she doesn't know
if she'll ever get up.

She keeps to herself
as she walks into
the shallow surf
in a column
of ivory light.

Being Nailed to a Cross is Not the Only thing that is Excruciating

Carla Schick

excruciating (adj.)
1. Latin *excruciare*: in other words, to crucify / literally /
as in death penalties / metaphorically / as in cross-questioning
while your hands are in cuffs / intensely painful or causing
intense suffering: as in being nailed to a cross / consider
yourself a martyr /

do you know what it means?

2. *I don't think you mean / nails in your back /*
not excruciating pain / not a loss
that lodges in my spine down my leg / my father's
back / his laughter when he visited me
in dreams not yet dead / just out of reach.

3. Tortured as when we sat beside my father's hospice bed
counting each rasping breath / masked with sweet melodies /
Tony Bennett's singing / romance / wandering around the garden
near his window / brilliant yellow pink   orange marigolds and roses
preparations for mourning.

4. Not the look of the dead / bleeding tiny punctures / brain bleeds
my father doesn't have time / I ask him why
he returns / to sit with me / he asks me to teach
him to throw a baseball again / for a moment
the pain subsides and I follow him over a hill
where fog absorbs his face.

5. Excruciating as in: to wipe out / as in we can never
rest / pierced at the edge of fingertips / dissolved
touch / a brain that slipped beneath
his words / lips moving / no sound / a tumor
spread out like a spider's web / entangling his lips.

6) *Excruciare* / as in each crooked step / sending
shooting pains / body on the rack / up through my legs
to hips / out to a hollowed sky / I walk
to retrieve the bodies I've left behind.

Hindsight

Brenda Cullen

I miss seeing the white around her nose
just visible in the night behind the screen door
the greeting in her pearlescent cataract eyes
cradling her to bury my face in her warm black fur
and breathing her smell mingled with grass and freshly dug soil.

I was frustrated at times with the constant slow sharp click
of her nails on floorboards trailing me.
I mistook company for dependency
blind to my own
now violets flower opposite the front door.

All the Time

JW Goll

the time we broke into my neighbors's house, stole *Lolita*,
      read it all night, and ended up disappointed
the time we beat up a boy peeping at an undressed bride
      in my father's church, feeling righteous afterward
the time our UFO made of dry cleaner bags, balsa wood,
      and candles lit our school on fire
the time I beat you at tennis, you smashed your racket
      and got kicked off the team
the time we took LSD, swam across an algae-filled quarry
      at 2am and woke up green
the time my dad asked if you were a Christian and you said
      you weren't sure but certainly hoped not
the time you bought a 1200cc Harley Indian and
      hid it in my backyard
the time we drove to California, met a girl on Stimson beach
      and slept with her together
the time our good friend came out and I warned you
      against sleeping with him out of kindness
the time you lied to me about sleeping with our good friend
the time you introduced me to Phillip K. Dick and I said
      now I know why you are paranoid

the time you refused to wear shoes in Las Vegas
  and we got kicked out of three casinos
the time I introduced you to Heinrich Boll and you said
  now I know why you think the world will end badly
the time your father got drunk, told his old FBI war stories,
  then got angry when we thought they were funny
the time you worked nights as a stripper and
  I did my community service work on the highway
the time you married, moved to LA, got robbed by your wife
  and divorced, all in two months
the time the French Moroccan woman sold us bad dope
  in Tangier and you went to the hospital
the time the French Moroccan woman narced on us
  and we got to Ceuta just in time
the time we argued, you moved to Mexico City, me to Vienna,
  and we didn't speak for three years
the time I went to graduate school in photography
  and you learned how to fly
the time I wrote a poem, you gave it to a woman in Barcelona
  and you made out in the street
the time we got robbed in Girona and squatted with addicts
  until the passports & money arrived
the time you came to South Dakota, met my girlfriend,
  and told me I was luckier than deserved to be
the time my girlfriend left me and you talked me out of
  acting like a fool
the time you bought a Piper Cub, crashed it,
  and walked away, unscathed and laughing

the time you had a son and said no more traveling
>I've got work to do

the time I tried to change your mind

the time the mother of your child held a gun
>and dared me to step into your yard

the time you said your second son was disabled
>and you finally knew your life's purpose

the time our friend died of AIDS, we drank, and you said
>you'd fuck him again if he would just come back

the time your son joined the Marines and you cried

the time you died in a motorcycle accident
>on the mangy outskirts of Tampa

the time I spoke to your adult son and he didn't want to know
>anything about you before him

the time I realized I no longer had a best friend

the time I realized I didn't want another one

all the time that has passed since then

Ex / Ash

Pam Kress-Dunn

A cross marks your box
embossed like moss
on the wide side,
a blot on the spot
your body never thought it would come to.

A cask of masks
all soft save for one
leftover bone, knocking
on the side of your urn,
a hard marble. That's what's left
of the trouble
you bungled
the slow slide
of your expired life.

Seized and trussed
your flailing limbs
can't reach me, restrained
in their mean container,
the crock they locked
you in. I swear
I hear you sneering.

Unloosed, shook out,
I could see through you:
you must be dust,
save for that one
spared rock. Is it your hand
twisted into a fist,
your ankle, that kick
you tricked me with?

All your anger
sifts to ash
past forgiveness
passed over
like the flame, fueled
by the blue gas,
in your spent end place,
your final gasp.

Loss as the Beginning
of The Shunning

Jim LaVilla-Havelin

… so this is one of the places where the shunning begins,
though sometimes the shunning overstates the case
and it is merely a turning away

> a turning away that
> constitutes a loss

A bad trade, a fan favorite let go – monetary differences
                        the realities, the cost of "free" agency
A bonehead play, another losing season
Out of the hunt in by the fourth of July

The threat to move the franchise if the city doesn't
        pony up with the big bucks to build a new
        stadium

Ticket prices doubling

Equivocating front office in the face of a player/wife-beater

Taking a stand, not taking a stand

Cheating to win

Loss
      of face
           of faith
                of patience

The voice of the franchise on radio and television
      dies after so many years and I can't listen
           to the game in any other timbre

Loss
      of spark
           of sparkle
                of prospects from the minors

So not really a shunning
just a loosening of the ties
a distance

Some questions no one answers.

The Glutton Club

Eithne Cullen

Charles Darwin, I've been told,
eagerly ate many of his specimens
iguanas, armadillos,
a huge rodent and some insects, too.

At Cambridge, he'd presided over
the Glutton Club: seeking out
"strange flesh" – birds and beasts
which were before "unknown to human palate."

Returning from its expeditions,
the Beagle was filled with precious
specimens and creatures.
The tedious journey was a chance
to savour new pleasures.

The galley bustled, finding ways
to cook and serve wondrous new delights.
The rhea, he'd spent many hours
trying to catch, caught in his throat.

One of the tortoises was such a hit,
so flavoursome, so tender,
they served it many times, baked,
fried, boiled, marinated.

When Darwin went to check
the inventory of species he'd collected
one was missing, lost to science
lost to the world, tasty, but extinct.

The sailors took the shells home,
used them for table tops and bowls,
dreamed of the taste, the smell
of tortoises now lost forever.

The aftertaste of loss.

Soft Machine / Hard Bargain

Winston Derden

Nearly five-foot-seven tall,
he liked to "smoke and drink and ball."

Until an inebriated spill
traversing a third-story trellis

left Robert paraplegic-sprawled
in the courtyard below.

Saved him from death
by drink, he later said.

No more drumming
with dead legs,

a drummed piano instead,
and songs sung in a piping voice

at the edge of tonality
on such topics as insomnia,

bacon protesting in a pot of soup,
and the United States of Amnesia,

recorded for Virgin, Rough Trade, other
minor labels, and occasionally rereleased.

Now Wyatting means queueing the jukebox
with a string of his songs

to annoy fellow patrons pop-schlock
poisoning the airwaves of a local pub.

June 5, 1968

Charles Darnell

I lost it
somewhere
between now and
the last time I
held it.

I wore it
on my lapel
every rally
but after,
I kept it
in a plastic flip,
a momento
from my youth
and from his.

Stamped metal,
with a sharp pin
tucked
into the curved
edge,

it would prick,
draw blood,
if not careful.

Red, white, and blue,
initials
in block-black center

RFK

I still have the flip.
lost the button.
Gone now
like a dream,

like him.

Ghost Love

Gary Percesepe

I

It took years to locate you. Your flesh not a dreamt of destination but our point of departure, most often in a hotel room in Tribeca. Your coiled body flared like an apparition, calling me to come, and please leave. Your face made up with desire, both shelter and storm. To sleep here on Duane Street, together.

For what in our single beds would we have ever known of poetry?

II

What I did not know when I was young was that nothing can take the past away. You taught me the meaning of unpredictability. In each moment what you were about to do was unknown and this delighted us both.

III

I felt the need to disappear; you were someone easily disappeared, unformed and chaotic, a body flared in light then lost in shadow. I wanted to lose myself, you wished to remain lost.

IV

Separated, unhappy, we were expert at taking. We knew how to look distance in the mouth, to judge pain by its teeth. Two hearts to carry it all, harvests, coffins, water, roads, flowers, trees, earth mounded up around your open grave. Our freight, your ticket. The price was high. We made the language quiver.

V

The opposite of love is not hate but separation. Love and envy glued us together. Love aims to close all distance, but death gets the job done. I don't know where you came from. I've no idea where you've gone.

Passing

Linden Van Wert

Her grey-blue eyes are now dark, almost that deep brown
which waits in the cloudy shadow of burgundy
as does the parent's face in gesture
flicker through the transparent child.

The nurse knew
bringing her a saucer of floating jasmine blossoms
a scent come indoors from our backdoor climber
to her bedside.

Mark this
this foreshadowing, a beginning of that quiet
for which I have not sufficiently prepared
to do right by us both.

It seems I have already begun the walk ahead
never before witnessing the death of a loved one—
she who offered so much—
kin, teacher, listener, writer, inspiration.

Unknowing, unimaginative that a preparation was possible
I've been offering less than she was to me.
New understanding reveals itself as I fall into that deep brown
once grey.

Losing It

Merryn Rutledge

After my first lover left, I lost the keys to the car
I agreed to share until he could find a job.
He had gambled away my money on the sly.
Endings are complicated.
Years later, a necklace my husband gave me
disappeared after his horrid death,
while I was locked in No Exit hell
with several who sought to steal everything.
Fear slid in, rattling
under lawsuits, illness, even mail
like this, from a medical lab—
We regret a records security breach
by unknown actors has occurred.
When COVID struck, poisoning the whole world,
someone slithered into my computer.
Sucked out the brain that held my writing life.
Pneumonia nearly took me.
But here's the thing.
I just found my necklace,
nestled in a pouch I so secretly stowed
I lost the memory.

Power

Rachel-Anne Sambell

When I sit down at the computer, and complete the transaction,
The rush I feel is power to me.
A head of lightness to mask the inevitable
vulnerability underneath.
I remember –
I remember when he first held me down, and, you know.
Pinned my arms in place.
Entered my most secret space.
Negating my right to a choice in the matter altogether.
About that time, I made a purchase
with some of my hard earned, brought it home,
And lo, got the scorching of a lifetime.
I think it might have been a backpack.
It felt so good, though.
To buy.
To control my money.
To control –
Me.

First to Go

Adrienne Stevenson

oil slick on ditchwater calls up ham & pickle sandwich mix
an early memory, one of many evoked by sense of smell

tiny molecules invade the nares, those cavities
where odour and savour mingle, taste an adjunct to smell

or is it otherwise, since latterly, as perception of aroma
declines, flavour remains, perhaps less overtly, contrast

noticed most when attempting degustation of wine
fine distinctions lost—the nose no longer knows

how much worthier the loss of evil reeks
vomitus, excrement, stagnant sewers, toxic fumes

if senses must decline with age, perhaps it's best
to dull smells—hone vision, hearing, touch

Dying in process

Suzanne Cooke

As the evening fell

You died quietly alone

I got a phone call

I visited you that day. The doctor spoke with me about
discontinuing life support. I signed some papers. But you had
died before I got home and I got the dread "we regret ..."
phone call. I was suddenly alone in the world.

I won't bury you

Put you aside forever

I bought a small box.

I so wanted to be able to prepare your body for your last
journey. There was no boat but at least there could be fire. It
was 4 days before I could make arrangements with a mortuary.

The young lady at the crematorium told me, "He's not been embalmed; you really don't want to see or remember a 4-day old corpse". I signed some papers. A few weeks later, she brought me your ashes.

You haunt me sometimes

Talking from your wooden box

sometimes I talk back

We had always promised to haunt one another. You do get through now and again. I've even heard you call my name. I have concluded that it must be very hard to pierce the veil between us. I talk to your box. I scream at your box. I cry and my tears wet your box.

I found a tattoo place that will mix your ashes with their ink. I signed some papers.

The Wreck of the Alba

Lydia Trethewey

After Alfred Wallis

(1)
the boiler, charcoal black
slimy with half a century of brine
just visible where the waves break

I want to swim to it,
let the white surf engulf
and set fire to my soft
warm-blooded
nerve-endings, immerse myself
here.

I dip a toe in the bay,
and the frozen latitudes of the Celtic sea
surge inhospitable and violent,
prove me a mere visitor.

stranger,
I run, numb-footed, for safety

(2)

this rag-and-bone man
melancholic
treats generosity as a
black-hearted bitch.

suspicion
in the steep tilt
of a ship angling against
bad weather

the Alba, laden with Welsh coal
turns back from a storm
pounded by
brushstrokes
and mistakes the shore lights
for Godrevy lighthouse   runs aground.

a rush of blue oil
paint
breaches the hull

silvery gloom
of his last days

the fatality of a receding present
in undulating white

Dear Ravi,

Sage Cohen

It is a year since you
gave your brother

the good seat
though it wasn't his turn

as you always gave him
the best you had to give.

You left your brother
untouched in his seat

when the car hit
the guardrail.

You left us unknowing
how to be left.

I promised you I would live
but I lied as the living do

when we want to be better
than we are. You made me

want to be better, Ravi.
I stood today

among the high branches.
Spring relentlessly

ushering the world forward.
I looked for you

where the birds twist
our best scraps into nests.

Petals blown open
to leaf.

Five Levels of Loss

Shirlee Jellum

for JoAnn

I: Innocence

groping fingers
probing tongue
robbing trust
one thrust at a time

how does one so young
cope with such gut-punching gall

how does one so young
make sense of the senseless

how does one so young
justify the genesis of sex

how you cried
on the beach
drunk with shame
while I held you
helpless

II: Death

how do you handle
the horror
the sudden jump
from life to death?
the suffocating silence
after the splash
the news flash
the sinking
into obscurity?

how do you cross the bridge
from violation to volition?
accept the unthinkable?

was there ever a moment
of vindication
a nod to god's
answer to prayers?
what faith grew
from this act of fate?

III: Addiction

nights drinking
three beers to my one
sometimes four or five
morning coffee
doctored with
peppermint schnapps

wild rides
by the grace of god
we survived
your driving
me blithely unconcerned
when I should have
taken your keys

what cup needed filling
time after time
with mind-numbing
mood-altering poison
that severed sanity
and rocked relationships?

does why even matter
when the past is dead
each day a test
and tomorrow unknown?

IV: Betrayal

the pain
intermittent at first
a dull ache
an annoyance
easily forgotten

then stabbing
shocking intensity
crippling fingers
buckling knees
hips throbbing with heat

everything hurt
nothing helped
life became a series of
sacrifices
compromises
excuses

my apologies
for leaving you behind
while I blind to your needs
flew toward the fire
breathless anticipation
fueling mine

V: Estrangement

to lose a child
not by death
but by choice
staggers my mother mind
the heart-wrenching agony
of alienation
the gut-pounding permanence
of separation
has shattered my faith
in forgiveness

how can one adored
be so hateful
whose words
flung so heinously
hold love hostage?

you try
so hard
to accept
the inevitable
while I wait
to embrace
what's left

Drop

Natalie Fry

After Christmas you suddenly couldn't raise
your eyes up to your granddaughter in my arms.
Neck drop, they called it. At first, Mum sent you
to acupuncture, then there were exercises to do.
Next spring, still smart in a suit, dapper
at eighty-five, the fuss was mainly about
the cake for your golden wedding.
I was breastfeeding the baby and trying
to keep the toddlers quiet and I needed
you, even though I thought I could be strong.

But you were already departing, the dad I knew.
The doctors said you would never be
as well as you were that diagnosis day.

A shadow of you stands by the sink of my house,
just there, rhythmically dipping and scrubbing
dishes. Outside the bedroom on the landing,
creaking the floorboards, getting ready for bed.
Home. That comfort, that feel of your movement.
Not your awkward bids to grip the gearstick
with gardening gloves, or the scratchy way you signed
with your stiffened fingers, or your legs locked tight
on the hospital bed so not even a team of nurses
could turn you over that final week.

Baby of the Family

Marianne Szlyk

Drifting past the stained-glass windows,
he hears his grandmother's
cheerful question: remember when
wc lived near here?

He cannot. He was not
born then. Instead
he remembers this morning
at the bus stop
watching Mom
duck her head and run
down into the subway.
Late to work again,
she didn't wave goodbye.

Still he says he remembers
standing beneath a green canopy
and winning a teddy bear,
the one his oldest brother won.

His grandmother nods and smiles,
brushing back her iron-gray hair
not quite long enough for
a ponytail.

She calls him her memory
and says she can't ask
anyone else,
not his brothers or
his mother who is
at work somewhere, not her
husband who has been dead
for three years. Once again
she asks her grandson
his name.

Once more, he repeats
his oldest brother's name,
the name she has always
called him by.

Promises Kept

Beth Cash

I promised that I would take care of you
I would never let you get hit by a car
that I would love you and consider
you a member of my family
and not return you to the shelter
if you made me mad.

You promised your loyalty
you would follow me when I changed rooms
understand if I stepped on you
that it was an accident
watch me intently with your brown eyes.

The beginning was hard for you –
you had never lived in a house
you spent your first days
with my hand
on your head
while you shook
until you felt safe.

We walked country roads
down the back hill to the quarry
looked at wildflowers
chased deer
hiked through
mountains of snow
you leaped over
while I trudged through.

You tussled with a coyote.
I heard two sets of teeth hitting
but, he returned to the newborn and mate
he guarded,
you and I to the house.
We met a mountain lion
as we were getting the mail.
I stared in awe
and you didn't notice.

You grew older,
your back legs weakened
a tumor grew at your neck
you walked along the pond
lost your balance
fell into the pond
unable to pull yourself up.

You followed me to my art room
until I blocked the stairs
because unable to see
you took one step
and hit the wall at the bottom
you were loyal.

I kept my promise
I cared for you
loved you
you didn't get hit
by a car
but you grew older
unable to stand
I cared for you
and was with you
as you took your last breath.

Wearing Thin

John Carnegie

I do watch the sun rise
if I'm still up
or am forced into service
at an early and indecent hour
I always give it a sincere salute
even on the bad days
and I try to stay
you know
positive
but there are
things we just bear
and keep on
bearing
and my patience
which was once a
densely woven carpet
of silk and hope
is baring its threads
and I no
longer always
know where
to kneel

I'm haunting myself (with memories of my lover)

Denise Bossarte

It's been a month
since my lover gave up
on me.
We had a misunderstanding
and exchanged words
and hurts.
I was triggered.
But when I tried to explain
my trauma response,
he labeled it as "drama."
He told me he didn't have
patience for drama.
He didn't revel in it,
didn't seek it,
and to the
extent possible,
he tried to steer
clear of it.

He told me that
being with me
was not good for
his mental health.

It's been a month,
and I'm still conjuring
memories of him.
Memories of laughing
together, making love.
Memories of the hurts,
frustrations, and
disappointments.
The shattered pieces
of my heart are
searching for the part
that he stole
when he left;
longing to be whole again.

It's been a month,
and each day I
think of him when
I look at the picture
that was to be
his birthday present.

I hung it up in
the spare bedroom
and each morning
I see it when
I work out.
Ironically, he was
supposed to hang
it in his office to
give a boost to
his mental health.
But here it is,
challenging mine.

It's been a month,
but hopefully,
in a few months
I'll be able to say
"It's been X months
and I don't think of
him at all."
I'll be able to
see that picture
on the wall and
not remember him.

I'll just remember
that gorgeous summer
day in the park
when I lost myself
to the sunlight dabbling
the water, and the so,
so green reflections
of the trees on
the surface.
The time I was
fully present,
and wholly me.

Aftermath's Beginning

Terry S. Johnson

i.

We wash the body, learn
to dress dead weight, wrestle
to pull on his favorite shirt.
Frame his face with fresh
flowers. Call his sister
in Mumbai, share
a Hindu blessing.

After dark, the nurse signs
the death certificate. She
leaves as his daughters flee.
The chaos of dying done.

I stroke his cooling
lips, his arms, his hands.
Katydids, crickets accompany
this hush of loss.

Late evening, the hearse
arrives. Two old duffers, both
gasping for breath, struggle
with the stretcher, a sweaty
slapstick in summer heat.
They cover him with a hospice
quilt. A red, white and blue
extravaganza. As a naturalized
citizen, he would have chuckled
at such patriotic display.

ii.

Next morning, D-Day plus
one. Deceased Day. Dismal
Day. Day of turbulent weather.
Inundation of death's dreary
bureaucracy, duties filled
with despair. Phone calls, forms,
followed by the frenzy of sorting,
cleaning, packing up. The list
grows like cells dividing.

A storm swirls a tornado
in my heart. Tasks delay
the crush of grief. D-Day
plus two, plus three.
My new eternity.

Patchwork Quilt

Colleen Moyne

A life filled with loved ones can feel
like a pretty patchwork quilt
that wraps itself around us
and keeps us warm and content.

A loved one's leaving, though,
can tear a jagged hole
in that once perfect fabric
and usher in the cold.

But, given time, we may find
another pretty patch,
maybe not a perfect match
but one that mends the hole

and brings
a new kind of warmth

My quilt has many patches
each one pretty and unique
and each one fits
where once were jagged holes.

And though at times
the patches may change,
the beauty and warmth
remain the same.

murder

Livio Farallo

pre-dawn
of the bird
splashing in the bath,
now several.
now more,
raw as laughter.
if i could crawl
with shovel
silent as a cat,
they would be mine:
snapped feathers mingled
with
water crashing
over the sides,
a stew reddening
in the quick dark. their
small bodies floundering
like wind
in the dead of almost night.
and then the froth
lessening with a few of
their last chirps,
their final paralytic breaths.

fine silence then, drifting over the yard.
shovel glistening in the dripping grass.
my crimson smile laying with hands behind its head.
and not once
did i mention cold blood.

Titanic

Laura Garfinkel

At her hometown high school,
my mother was the pretty one.
Smart.

When I was in high school,
I'd bike home each afternoon
find her sitting on the deck
dark glasses, sun on her face
angry, tearstained, wrecked
storm hidden behind shields.

Like a clarion call:
All aboard, I would embark
despite horn-blown warning

as though I could change
fate, steer to avoid
the iceberg. Unaware
of the impending disaster,
the inevitable end

that would leave
some dead, and survivors
who would remember
her sinking only and not
her maiden voyage.

Lexicon

Gabrielle de Gray

The first time I encountered death
I was still learning to read at the long glossy table
in the dining room. I was four.
Flash cards with Spot and Dick and Jane.

I would knock on my neighbor's door
to see if she wanted to play with me.
We would walk slowly along the streets
behind the houses in our neighborhood.

I liked to reach up to hold onto her arm,
to touch the soft skin behind her elbow.
She smelled like warm sunshine and baby powder.

One young girl, her life a long stretch of time
unspooled before her. The other, older, elder,
closer to the fate Atropos who cuts the thread of life.

One day I knocked on her door. Some woman
I did not know answered. I asked when my friend could come out
to go on our walks, our gentle talks of nothing in particular.

It was explained coldly that she was not coming back.
I would not cry in front of this indifferent woman at the
half opened door. I could not name this strangeness in my chest.

I had not yet learned the word, *grief.*
I still miss the old woman whose name I do not remember.

on her birthday she writes her sister's eulogy

Jeni Curtis

whoever tells the family
myths holds power   a weapon
the sword of truth   the shield
of justification   or the bow
where   between the bending strut
and string   lies air   space
wide enough to let   the stripes and slants
of variation   slip in
refashioned   rehoned

yet it is difficult   the years
passed   memory rebounds on
memory   the child   the bride
the mother   the deserting
wife   and you were not there   you
wore your own glasses   looked askance

what to admit   what to
include   old truths glossed
with new sheen   polish these
varnish those   and you know
there is a vanished story   the one
she would have told
before   she   was silenced

Sister

Clare Marsh

You'd asked for a William Morris calendar
on my Christmas visit to the hospice—
the prints to remind you of home
and his influence on your artwork.

You ask me to hang it on the wardrobe
in view of the bed you'll never leave
where you lie beneath twining Acanthus covers.
You still surround yourself with the beautiful
following Morris's decree, in this room
where everything else must be useful—
hoist, drip-stand, oxygen. Staff check you
four times an hour. I give you teaspoons of water
as we giggle at remembered childhood games.

You ask me to mark future appointments
and birthdays, through to next December
despite your second terminal diagnosis.
We can't articulate our mutual thought
that one of these luscious textile prints
perhaps Pimpernel or The Strawberry Thief
will preside over your final day.
Now the innocuous blank oblongs
wait until only I know the date
when I strip this room and remove this calendar.

After Eden

Carolina Marchioro

Our genesis went like this:
In the beginning you were drinking
apple cider out of a red polystyrene cup
when I slithered into your life trailing
temptations like a well-practiced
party trick. I'd said:
Hey baby, did you know the first sin
was a woman eating? I can swallow
you whole if you let me.
I'll be forbidden and you be the fruit.
Eden's a classic and we were too;
The scratchy record player of ennui,
entropy, ephemerality, or whatever
pretentious new word we'd learned
that week in Philosophy 101 in lieu
of admitting we were just afraid
of dying and maybe a little afraid
of life too. And I was just vintage
like that, baby. Rock and roll,
a rebel, a counter-culture queen.
Anyways, wasn't it so much more fun
to sin with me than to kneel down
in the dirt breaking some man's ribs,
mud to the elbows, righteousness to the chin?

In the between we'd toasted to Eve,
toasted to you, toasted to me,
and I imagined how delicious you'd taste
once I bit through your seams. I salivated
over your sugar-dusted, soul-encrusted,
candy-apple dreams. Savored the saccharine
saturation of our summer trips, acid trips,
tripping over words we were learning
how to feel. And maybe I didn't protect
you from myself but I protected you
from everything else and didn't that
count for something? Was that so bad?
Wasn't it love, or something so close
that you could have eaten it too?
We could have been neverending, you know,
you inside me, me inside you.
The snake devouring herself
into that age-old dance of eternity.

By the end Eve would have rolled in her grave
but you were never biblical in the first place.
You made your own Gods and they looked
like a husband, seasoned to taste,
two kids here and a third on the way.
Or maybe they just looked like you.
Either way, I could have eaten them too.
Hosted your sepia-colored, cookie-cuttered,
claustrophobic suburbia somewhere
between my liver and my spleen.
Gods are nothing without a sexy
underworld; gotta give the penitent
something to fantasize about at night
to block out the sounds of rent being due
and children failing school and his snoring.
I get it, I do.
I have an appetite the size of creation
and if a woman's hunger is large enough
it can choke down all of the rest of your world.

Forgot

Steven Dee Kish

Buzz ... Buzz ... Buzz ...
My cell phone vibrates ... an incoming call from ...
Ugg, I see your name on my phone.
Damn, I was just starting to forget you.
I erase your messages. So, I can keep forgetting you.
Every day, my eyes see something that reminds me of you.
I close my eyes so tight ... So, I can forget.
You gave me a bun in the oven, and we put on
Our running shoes to the altar.
You became my husband ... You were not ready
For the responsibility.
I wish I could have read the tea leaves and made better choices.
I could have saved everyone from heartache.
Every time I look at our daughter's cherubic face ... I see you.
Our family became unimportant; the only thing
That mattered was your narcissistic ego.
The calendar flips, and our daughter
Evolves into a rebellious teen.
Where is the father figure?
Check the bars ... Go to a strip club ...
Drive the red-light district.
I can't forgive you for the way you treated us.
We became expendable, and you shifted the blame on us.

Stay away! Hell, yes, I am bitter!

Every bit of extra cash

Goes to therapy for your daughter and me.

Buzz ... Buzz ... Buzz ... Stop calling me, get lost!

Every buzz of the phone rips my heart again.

Hate overtakes me, and I vow to never talk to you again.

Can anyone hear me? Save us from suffering!

My only hope lies with the Grim Reaper.

You must pay with a pound of flesh,

A third of your heart, and your sanity.

We want the Reaper to take your soul ... if you had one.

We despise that we are related to you.

How many times have you lied right to our faces?

You pretended to care when, in reality,

You were plotting your subsequent indiscretion.

You showed us how to lie and pretend to care ...

So, we followed your lead.

Just to get away from you, we miss things on purpose.

Our excuse ... We forgot. The truth is

We remember all your failures.

We can remember to give you presents:

A box filled with isolation. A neatly wrapped loaded gun.

A bottle of poison as a stocking stuffer.

Each gift is topped with ribbons shaped like nooses.

You are your own worst enemy;

You will be the cause of your downfall.

Maybe you will give us our gift ...

Cease to exist. Leave us alone!

When you're dead, we will pretend to be sad.
But there will be a joyous private party.
Pass us a tissue, for these are tears of joy.
We will wear black. But our souls
Are as white as the heaven you are not in.
The next day will provide relief …
There will be no more phone buzzing.
You are gone … and I already forgot you.

to a lost lover

Janis La Couvée

what strange compulsion
propelled me to find you
almost fifty years since those
tumultuous nights
eating raclette in Zermatt
meeting for clandestine rendez-vous
in upscale Paris hotel rooms
days when communication meant
letters and not instant messages
there you are, smiling
painting a fence
proud of your new puppy
a wife I do not know
small grandchild
snow in your small Australian town
how strange to see
your life laid out before me
what would my life tell you?

The Thief

Kathleen Aponick

for Tony

It was the year of the break-in, remember?
We'd come home to open doors, rooms
he invaded, rifling through drawers, closets,
desks, a small lockbox with bonds,
jewelry, old bank records.

We called the police, filed a report
that went nowhere. Sorry, they said.
So we move on. After all, why pine
over material goods? At least
we had life's necessities. At least
we escaped with our lives.

Decades passed: births, deaths, work,
warm embraces, disputes, moments
of darkness and light casting shadows,
snow covering the house, pines
howling in wind, heat and rain
pressing on the roof.

Then a call from the South,
a sheriff asking if your college ring
was missing. Part of a stolen cache,
he reported. It had your name, the college,
its beaver inset, symbol of
the school's industry. And your own
diligence in those years—

tests you crammed for, nights in the lab,
out drinking with friends, on your finger
the ring you'd one day set in a metal box
you thought secure, ring carried
in his pocket traveling south with
resentments, misdirection, unmet desires.

Who knows what became of him?
Had he paid a price? We'll never know.
Yet who am I to judge? Haven't I
taken what wasn't mine, forgotten
to return books, clothes? Don't I
still "borrow," as they say, a phrase or two,
ideas from those I admire?

Thinking of him now, I try to imagine
the child he was, the teen, his surround,
his circumstance, how vast
the canyon between your life and his,
the journey taken before he paused
to assess the ring's value that day,
that hot summer day.

Gasoline and Propane

Margaret Plaganis

for my brother Harry

It's a good thing we talked a long time on the phone.
You were surprised when I called you, camped
somewhere in Colorado, asked questions about
your old Dodge Four by Four pick-up truck,
you'd rigged to run on gasoline and propane.
I said it was mustard. You said it was yellow.

You laughed, *"How did you remember that shit?*
That was back in 1979."

I told you I kept notes, photos of you and the truck
on our road trip from Oregon to Massachusetts.
I confessed, I was afraid it wasn't safe,
afraid we'd break down or blow up.

"What the hell," you chuckled. *"We made it didn't we?*
The system worked fine at home, so I figured I might
as well test drive it cross-country. Only I wasn't sure,
didn't know if it had enough power to cross the mountains.
But it did, didn't it? Made it over the Tetons on gasoline
and propane! Even that damn old drive shaft held up!"

I remember we played Supertramp's *Paris Live,* relentlessly,
Dreamer, Take the Long Way Home, all of Carlos Santana's
Abraxis, over and over, and your Greek blue worry beads
and brass bells dangled and swayed off the rear-view mirror,
clicked time back and forth like a highway metronome.

It's a good thing I kept notes, good we took time on
that phone call, good you explained how you secured
two twenty-five gallon propane tanks in the pick-up's
back bed, how you installed a toggle switch to control
your gasoline or propane fuel feed to the engine.

Good you promised to call me soon as you got home.
You sounded like yourself, but you choked,
"I had a stroke – somewhere in Nevada."
You paused a long time before you spoke.
"Words – don't come – out – they stop –
in – my – mouth – they – just – stop –
I'm – afraid – to drive – my rig – don't –
know – how – I'm – afraid – don't know –
where – I am – I – can't drive – my truck."

Once Upon a Time

Kathleen Herrmann

By the time I arrive, you are long gone
Laid out on hardwood floor
Bare feet protrude from too short red sheet
Our goodbye must be face to face
I draw back sheet little by little
Receding hairline retains strands of brown
Brow creased, eyes closed, thank god,
Nose angular in profile, lips set like plaster

This last time we share a bedroom reminds me of the first time
"Linus and Lucy" propped on keyboard,
Film noir posters on adjacent wall
Pants and shirt tossed aside, glasses atop disheveled papers
I stand in the quiet of your deafening absence

Once upon a time, we made a playful pact
Whoever goes first will signal the other,
Who must remain vigilant
"What's that gentle rapping, rapping at
My chamber door?" I feigned
"'Tis some visitor, my dear, only this
And nothing more," you lisped with sly grin
We joked about Houdini's widow, contemplated Einstein

Concluded maybe Carl Sagan was right,
Or better yet Gary Larson
Yeah, drop me a line from the Far Side

Out your window, gray finch scales pine tree with tiny hops
Fly away home
Daughter and son-in-law cocoon downstairs
Their sorrowful eyes have seen enough
Warm hands stroke backs, fragile glances flicker
Fresh tears spill with urgent longing, but you are long gone

Restless night brought lucid dream
Running errand at the store, I line up
At checkout and there you are
Shoulders rounded, penetrating stare
I clutch my bags, freeze right there
Eyes downcast, you turn away
As you did that broken, hopeless day
Two became one then two again
Nothing more to do or say

Sad truth plays on in me as I wake from goodbye reverie
Cello solo languid and low, melancholy notes rise from bow
It has no ending, fermatas, or rests, this tune of dissonant legacy
What was and what would never be once upon a time

Finding Your Soul

Shelly Blankman

The mind is always prone to believe what it wishes to be true.
Heliodorus

I lost you long before you died, paid the price
for the wreckage of your life – the shattered
pieces of your childhood and a marriage that
went all to hell. I was bullied at school and you
were bullied at home. You didn't believe in hugs.

Your mantra was there is no such thing as love.
The first time and only time you told me you loved
me was after Alzheimer's had impaled your brain
like a shrike. You died within months. But years
later, you came back to me in a dream, sitting

across from me at the kitchen table in the house
where I'd grown up. Just you and me. You were
smiling warmly and holding both of my hands
lovingly. You spoke softly for a long time. I don't
recall the words, but I remember your eyes,

baby blue. No name calling, no laughing at me, just a gentle, reassuring tone that I'd never heard from you in life. And then you were gone. I'd seen your soul. The mother I'd always hoped would be there. For you and for me.

Your wreckage was gone and your soul had emerged.

Confession

Deborah Meltvedt

The robe was all I wanted
the one we joked made you
look like Hepburn wooing Tracy
in those late night movies you loved so much.

It was meant only for adornment
the pinstripe one you left behind
too impractical, too lightweight
for sterile beds on cold hospital floors.

Months later when we packed things up
and gave away the suit and silverware
and divided up your life –
I took that robe.

Most days it hangs in beauty.
too impractical. too lightweight.
but on those nights when I need something
silky and tender and timeless
I cinch you tight around my waist.

Letting Go

Lucy Tyrrell

How do we adjust
to the mental slights
brought on by others—
deletion of friendships,
lost opportunities,
being left out of decisions, invitations,
experiencing relationship ruptures
that touch us deeply?

Letting go would seem like a loss,
but the kind that is kindest to us—
we can abandon rancor, grudges,
we can move on, smooth the hard edges,
start again, cross the bridges,
forge new friendships,
emboss goodness on our hearts,
make peace with our best selves,
be bold, watch the river flow on,
let abundant life unfold, go on.

Stars and Bones

Steve Evans

I stand overlooking the town
with my arms outstretched.
I am a cross with stars in one hand
and small bones in the other.
This is not a metaphor.
It is, however, a kind of ritual,
an offering to your absence
and to your memory.

I recall that final night,
how I lay with you —
the quiet of your breathing,
rain on the window,
leaves brushing the glass,
and then no breathing
except my own,
which came
from another planet.

I walk down from the hill
along the path we used to take
and see our house in the distance,
the square of the kitchen light
I have left on
as if you are in there
waiting on my return,
gazing out at the darkness
for my approach.

I'm no good at this —
the summoning and unsaid prayer.
The house will be empty.
I will place your art–class stars
and painted bones
back on the shelf
by one of your paintings.
Rain is forecast for past midnight.
I will be listening for it.

Prose

.

Escape Artist

Robin Stratton

We greet the owner of the Houdini House in Budapest with the typical American greeting, "How are you?" and after a moment of thought, he says with unexpected gloom, "My heart is the same since I opened this place ten years ago."

We're not sure how to respond.

Houdini, obviously, was from Budapest. But did we know that Tony Curtis, who played him in the movie, was also from Budapest? No, we did not know that.

We do know about the pact Houdini made with his wife, Bess: if it's true that there's life after death, whoever dies first must "come back" and deliver this secret message from beyond via a medium during a séance: *Rosabelle, believe.* We know that Bess tried for years and years but Houdini never came back. "Of course not," mutters my husband the atheist.

We move slowly past the Houdini paraphernalia: handcuffs, chains, newspaper clippings. My husband marvels at how easily people were duped into paying someone to contact the dead. I think about my brother, gone four years. I think about how I sometimes ask him to give me a sign, any kind of sign.

Turn, turn, turn

Sylvia Petter

1. Your parents gather their small family and emigrate to the Antipodes because Australia doesn't sound too different to Austria. But it was and still is.

2. At the age of reason, you reason, you leave on a ship to see your birthland. You study, work and fall in love. That love takes you where it will: north, south, east and west.

3. You marry for $25 in Vegas, now speaking German, and in Geneva a daughter is born. Bon Courage! You say as she leaves for Australia. Not so different, she says. But it is.

4. She marries in Sydney and the decision is made to join her when your Austrian partner of 51 years passes away.

5. Home is where the heart is people tell you, but what if it's broken?

6. All that remains is to pick up the pieces and carry on, no longer here but there.

Comedian

Paul Luikart

Two Februarys ago, my friend Marty cashed in all his chips and hit the road for LA. Like in that Billy Joel song, only real. He has two kids and was married to Diane—not even necessarily unhappily, either. They're still in Tennessee, Diane and their kids. I saw them yesterday in line at Aldi.

"How are you?" I asked Diane, and then asked about the kids.

She asked about him. "Is he still out there telling jokes?"

He has a new gig as a waiter at this place that serves fricassee of mourning dove, but he hits the open mics when he doesn't have to work. I know this because we still stay in touch.

"Do you speak French now?" I asked.

"Oui. But, ee-poo-vin-table," he said, "I think that means 'bad.'"

"How's the big dream treating you?" What'd be the point of bringing up Diane and his kids? Or his regrets, if he had any? Or anything at all? What the hell would be the point?

"Listen. I sat my ass on the beach the very first night I got here. I watched the sun dip all the way down into the Pacific. Not 'into.' More like through. All the way through. And I swear to God, I could hear it. All that screaming neon orange way up in the sky."

I didn't say anything for a while, this big pause.

Finally, I heard his voice on the other end like he was shouting at me ten feet away from his phone. "Bud, hey. Did I lose you? Bud? Are you still there?"

Illusion

Fiona M. Jones

I am walking down a crowded street when I glimpse her again: short, upright figure; grey hair dyed blonde; that olive-green coat; or a certain turn of the head.

I stand my ground or continue unslackening in pace. I am startled, but I am no longer afraid. Before she died I learned to stand my ground or hold my course against harsher jolts than this. And in a moment or two the illusion will resolve into just another stranger with a momentary echo of appearance or mannerism.

This one quickens her pace or turns her face, and the haunting impression fades. In time my tendency to see her will fade away too.

People sent me flowers when she died. With Deepest Sympathy and Heartfelt Condolences. "Praying for you in your grief," one dear lady wrote, and went on with something about the undying influence on my life.

Did I cry on the day of the funeral? Yes, I did. Not crocodile tears, but real grief for my loss. The loss of my childhood; the blighting of life's opportunities; the doors that stand closed to those who have learned the wrong lessons in life.

Filling Extra Space

Louella Lester

When his wife can no longer handle anything but the main floor, the basement works its way up. Pipe wrenches, jars of bolts and screws, and various lengths of plastic pipe crowd the steps. The upstairs' bedrooms make their way down. Lamps needing rewiring, puzzles missing pieces, and his grandson's old Lego sets trip over themselves on the stairs. The barn-shaped garage bulges outwards. Warped paintings, rusted bicycles, and wobbly chairs shove one another into the yard.

When his wife moves into the care home, their bedroom climbs the walls. Creased shirts, over-washed towels, and threadbare sheets explode into the air. Kitchen cupboards spill over. Plastic bowls, chipped cups, and dusty spice bottles spread along counters. The dining table overflows its top. Newspapers, grocery receipts, and sheets of paper filled with uneven rows of daily blood sugar levels drip onto the chairs below.

He drives into town each day, returns home to pick wild blueberries, dig in the garden, or putter with something in the garage. His mind sinks and shifts, he refuses a plumber, buys bottled water for drinking, fills pails in the rain barrel and uses them to flush the toilet when he's unable to repair the water pump.

His daughter does what he'll let her. Sweeps, changes bedding, plays cribbage, balances the chequebook, stops him digging a well in the basement ... until his choices dwindle to one. Finally, she convinces him to sell up and move into a building two blocks away from his wife.

He's never lived in an apartment in town and he mutters about dirt, stains, and the stupidity of a light beige carpet, things that have never concerned him before, so he buys rugs to protect it. Some are meant for front doorsteps or the beds of trucks. At first they're scattered, like his mind, but he waits for sales and buys more. Soon they're overlapping and the carpet is almost obscured. His daughter fears he'll trip one night on his way to the toilet. Still, unable to relax, he searches out and covers even the tiniest spot of beige.

Without a Trace

JA Rose

Nothing

   Zilch

   Dot

The day is sunny, but clouds loom from somewhere long ago. We park the campervan outside the fence. There are no parking bays marked, just pink dust. Off beyond, near the dam and creek bed, majestic river red gums grow, their feet rooted in sand and buried water. Car doors slam and we cross to read the plaque that gives a potted introduction to the Beltana Cemetery.

I'm looking for the grave of my paternal great, great-grandmother, Johanna Bralla. She's buried in this cemetery. Her last baby, the eleventh, is there, dead the day after her birth in January 1881. A month later, in February, Johanna is also dead.

On the plaque is the story of a family buried there in December 1881. Mrs Johnson and her four children were burnt to death in their tent at seven in the morning. The inquest was held later that day. William, the husband, a teamster, was away when it happened, but arrived in time for the inquest. The deaths were deemed accidental. No one was to blame. The husband was distressed.

Why were they living in a tent? Didn't they have even a slab shack to live in?

Did Johanna live in a tent too, with her nine surviving children, or were they lucky enough to have a cottage and a proper kitchen outbuilding? I look at the plaque again. There's a plan of the town with nineteen buildings identified, among them the train station, the school, the butcher's house, the Presbyterian manse, a mission house, and the telegraph station. The Royal Victoria Hotel and Doig's and Martin's houses. Two are named simply: 'stone cottages.' Was one of these where Johanna and her husband Clement lived?

On the day of her death, the house must have been crowded. Clement was about to lose his thirty-five-year-old wife. Mary, the oldest daughter, heavily pregnant at eighteen, wed the father with Johanna present and preparing for her own imminent death; the other children farewelled their mother, sorrowing and anxious. Ruphina, seventeen, was to take over as 'mother,' assisted by Louisa (5) in caring for the boys Amos (16), Edward (15), Alfred (13), William (10), Edgar (8) and Arthur (2).

None of Clement and Johanna's sons would go on to marry, have children and continue the Bralla name. Of the boys, only Amos reached old age, dying at 66 years. Mary, Ruphina and Louisa all married and had children. Ruphina, my paternal great-grandmother, was as fertile as Johanna, delivering twelve children, before her death at 48.

There's an atmosphere of sadness and ruin at the cemetery and the town itself, back down the track.

We wander around for a bit, searching for Johanna's grave. There are few stone or marble headstones. We find the Johnson's. It looks so formal, proclaiming the tragic demise of Anne and the young children: William, Anne, Bertha and Agnes. A teamster like William probably couldn't afford the headstone, so a Mr Pearce erected it as a mark of respect. Who was he? Did he know Anne and William senior well? Was he acquainted with their hopes and dreams, their ambitions for their family?

Iron fences drunk with age surround the odd grave or two. There's a headstone broken and fallen on its face, half buried in the sand, too heavy for me to lift and discover who is buried there. The saltbush and other native shrubs are reclaiming this hallowed ground. Here and there we see pieces of slate scattered on the ground or sticking up, as if shoved into the hard earth by a desperate hand. Any scratched or painted writing is long gone from the surface of these memorials to the modest, brave souls whose bodies lie below.

There is no visible trace here that Johanna Bralla or baby Amelia ever lived or died.

Cry of the Soul

Marianne Porter

Once heard the cry of a man who got the phone call voice on the other end broken barely able to utter their baby boy had died the infant you met once in your office when your boss and his wife became new parents all smiles showed him to everyone to coo and make faces his father held the baby facing out for all to see their matching blue eyes the man whose office had a glass wall who answered the phone mid-morning and you heard the phone crash to the floor rose from your chair when a primal scream burst through the ceiling a deep keening an unbelievable wail emitted from his throat so loud the word *NO* penetrated every cell in the room racked your spine shook the office floor silenced ringing phones the busy newsroom the press itself. Everything stopped. The man picked up his chair propelled it through the glass wall every particle of life surged out of him smashed to pieces. He peeled out of the broken room raced down the hall skipped the elevator flew two steps at a time to the parking garage drove home to hold his baby boy for the last time the three-month-old he bottle fed that morning rubbed his fly-away blonde hair kissed his satin cheeks said see you tonight to his wife and son the paramedics attended to the baby who laid in his crib for a usual mid-morning nap now you're shattered with the possibility that babies die. Suddenly. You stand frozen beside your desk barely able to breathe.

Painted Lady

Christine Collinson

As Eva dandles her daughter on her knee, the little girl watches a butterfly flit between blooms. Her plump finger points, a giggle erupts. Eva catches her hand and kisses the tiny palm. Lottie gazes at her mother with eyes like rain-soaked earth. His eyes, over again.

"Eva, join us for boules! Nanny will take over." Harriet glides across, cheeks carnation-pink, gliding on newlywed joy. Harriet's endearing spirit is pure; the one sibling who always saved her last toffee for Eva.

"I'll stay with Lottie for now, but later perhaps." Eva's smile, a gesture failing to dwell within. Embedded, her role in a daily charade. Wearing chic dresses which sag over bony hips, adorning an unkempt knot with jewelled hairpins, daubing sallow cheeks and thin lips with poppy-red rouge.

Harriet's husband survived the desert, despite her endless nightmares. They married in late April beneath a cornflower sky. Eva wore pale silk which made her skin look translucent, but everyone said she looked pretty. Pity makes people kinder. Shrouded in her silk cocoon, Eva persevered. 'Are you sure you want to do this?' Harriet had asked. 'Yes. I absolutely need to do normal things.' The smile alight again, like a traitorous signal across enemy lines.

Henry was lost to Eva at Tobruk. He knew of Lottie, for which she felt blessed. When he returned to the front for the last time, their daughter was merely ten months old. This, Eva's eternal anguish.

The Painted Lady has flown. As Eva watches Lottie plucking grass, her soul yearns to be beside her daughter. For only when Eva smiles at her, does it fly straight from her heart to her face.

In distant summers, Eva's wings may yet unfold to the sunlight again.

Trophy

GP Hyde

It's up the stairs. I'll go on up first as I'll have to unlock the room. Good of you to come all this way from Down Under, visiting all of us long-lost family! Few of Bob's family took much interest while he was alive so you're doing better than they did. He had this room to himself. He called it his Trophy Room. Always kept it locked. Not that there was much of value in it but he thought of it as a special place where he could go of an evening.

There we are. You go first so you can take a good look. It's not a bad sized room. I'll open the window as it's got a bit stuffy in here. You could get a child's bed in here but that never happened for us.

This was his Trophy Cabinet. This is the shield for the Grimsby and Cleethorpes Bowls Tournament. That cup is the All-Lincolnshire Darts competition. This one's for golf and those are for snooker and darts. Yes, all of these cups are silver. Well, silver plated. They could do with a polish. He used to polish them every week on a Sunday evening.

As you can see, all around on the walls are the certificates. There're ones for swimming, cycling proficiency and chess club. Here are all the secondary school qualifications. That's a university degree and this one here is very splendid, isn't it? A master's degree from Cambridge University!

Your Uncle Bob left school when he was sixteen. His dad found him a job running errands and making the tea at GGD, that's Grimsby Graphic Design. One day, when they had a big rush job on, he helped out with making up one of the publications and they spotted he had a bit of talent. Soon they took him off the odd-jobbing and put him on the layout work. He quickly became good at setting out the titles and banner headlines in the magazines and brochures. We used to do plenty of those.

Back then, the graphic artists used Letraset on the artwork before it went to be photographed and made into plates for printing. I guess you won't know what Letraset is but it was sticky letters on a clear backing sheet. You took the sheet, positioned the letter over the paper and made the transfer by rubbing the sheet from the back. You would build the headline up from individual letters. In the stockroom there would be hundreds of different sheets, each with a different font and a different size of letter. Tedious and time-consuming but Bob really enjoyed it.

That was how we met. I worked in the Accounts department. Part of my job was to check the stockroom to make sure that we had enough materials and order in whatever we needed. But Bob would know what we needed. He knew his way round that stockroom so instead of me going and checking, I'd go straight to Bob and he would have a note of everything that needed ordering in. 'We need two more sheets of Baskerville in 36 and 24 point, please, Gillian,' he'd say and I'd go back to my desk and order them in.

He was at GGD all his working life. Only ever worked at the one firm. Of course, it changed tremendously. As a firm, it liked to keep up with the times. When computers started to come in, GGD were right on it. Bob was thrilled when the first Apple Macs started to appear. I wasn't so thrilled when I saw the cost of them but the boss told us that this was the way of the future.

'No more messing about with Letraset,' he said. 'Everything will be done on the screen.'

Bob saw the way the business was going and knew if he didn't get re-trained, he might be out of a job. The art college in Eleanor Street began doing an evening class in computer graphics and he would take himself off there every Tuesday evening.

See this certificate here? The one with the golden frame? He was ever so proud of it. This was his Level Three in Desktop Publishing.

All these certificates are ones he designed himself. He began doing them as projects for his evening class but then he continued designing and printing off all the qualifications he never achieved.

He loved seeing his name on them. He told me that he did them as a pastime, as an amusement.

Those trophies – he used to buy them from charity shops. In America, they call them thrift stores, I believe. What do you call them in Australia? Op shops? Ah, that's interesting. Of course, opportunity shops. Well, Bob used to go to all the charity shops and to car-boot sales, junk shops. Trophy hunting he'd call it. He taught himself engraving so he could put his name on to the cups and shields.

Here's the last piece of artwork he ever did. The design for his tombstone. Nice, isn't it.

I'm clearing this room next week. Selling up. Downsizing, they call it. I'll have to ditch all these certificates. I'll keep that

Level Three Certificate. Send the trophies back to the charity shops where they came from. Unless you might like to take one back with you to remember your Uncle Bob.

Memory Seeds

Barbara Schilling Hurwitz

I feel an anxious flutter in my chest as I try to recall the voice, the blue eyes and auburn curls bouncing as she approaches. But my head refuses to place her. Who is this lovely woman touching my hand like she knows me? I mirror her smile. I want to ask who she is, but I don't want to break this magic spell.

She lets go of my hand and slips off her pale pink rain jacket. She likes pink. My memory tries to open, but just as there's hope the door closes before another clue is released.

"I stopped at the farm and picked up your favorite Winesap apples, Dad."

Dad? She's my daughter. I look away trying to hide my welling eyes. Winesap apples?

She passes me one, and I study it. "My favorite?"

She nods. "Yeah, Dad. I love them too." She pulls one from the bag for herself. I watch her teeth pierce through the crisp, ruby-red skin before I follow her example. Savoring the tart juicy flavor, I feel my head bob as the memory is revived.

"Yes, I used to eat one of these every night, core, seeds and all … while reading … What kind of books did I read?"

"Detective stories, Dad. You were always devouring the latest David Baldacci or Mickey Spillane mystery along with your apple."

I munch, savoring the memory, and stare out the window watching the heavy raindrops spilling down the glass, splashing onto the sill. I turn back to this woman sitting beside me, smiling. "Evelyn? You look more beautiful every day." But as I reach for her hand, her smile fades.

"What?" I jump at her using an angrier tone than I intended.

"Dad," she speaks in a whisper, "I'm Jody, your daughter."

"Where's my Evie?"

"She's gone, Dad." I hear her voice crack.

There's a gentle knock on my door just before it opens, and a woman in a green uniform calls out my name. "Mr. West, there's a music performance about to begin in the social hall. Why don't you and your daughter come join us?"

I shake my head while waving her away, but something reminds me, I used to like music. In fact, there's a picture on my wall of an orchestra. I'm in the middle of the back row playing the clarinet.

"Where's my clarinet? Did someone steal it?" I hear someone bark before realizing it's me. I apologize to my beautiful Evie who passes me the aged instrument case, and I smile back my thanks. Rubbing my hands over the cracked leather, I absorb the oozing history I can't put into words then I open the case and fit the polished pieces together. I wet the reed with the sweet saliva still clinging to my tongue, and soon the solo clarinet passage from Gershwin's "Rhapsody in Blue" is singing from the other end of my clarinet.

I feel the joy, the peace in my soul as our eyes connect, and I set that instrument on my lap.

"Not bad for an old guy." I wink, still hearing the music in my head.

"You've still got it, Dad."

Dad, I nod. "Yeah, I've still got it. We better get going. The show can't start without me."

A Revolutionary

Tom Ball

I, Ophelia, said to Harry, "To survive in this modern World, you have to be courageous. It's not for sissies!" He said, "If you want to be a mover and a shaker, then you need to be brave. But if you just go along with the culture, life is easy." I told him, "But most people are dissatisfied and want change." He remarked, "Maybe, but few people try hard for change. They sit on the fence, most of them …" I said, "But we need better rulers than the so-called "wise personae." All they do is take; they take money to enrich themselves. And they take and use lovers to get their thrills and reserve the best drugs for themselves, as if they don't want the people to be happy."

He opined, "I guess, they don't want to spoil the people. And keep them hungry for improvement." I said, "But they are not improving in any meaningful way. That's my whole point." He said, "Every day someone is promoted to be one of the wise!" I said, "It's just a drop in the bucket out of a total Worlds' population of 11 billion humans. I don't know why the people don't rebel against this nowhere civilization?" He said, "Maybe they lack courage, just as you say. Or perhaps they feel that they have too much to lose, and are simply conservative, or both!" I said, "I am going to form a group of democracy advocates and at least try!" He said, "But you are careless and don't realize I am a spy for the wise personae. All I have to do is blow my whistle and you will be arrested." I said, "But surely you believe that my heart and thoughts are pure?" He said, "You are just another shit disturber for which we have no need." And he blew his whistle, but nothing happened.

He explained that, "I too, was looking for change and I just wanted to test you." And he said, "Welcome to the underground. But I hope in the future that you do not act in such a careless fashion. This is serious business, here." And he introduced me to a contact in the organization I could correspond with. And my goal henceforth was to "Recruit others who are interested in revolution." And he told me, "I can't reveal to you how many of this are there. Nor can I tell you, when we will take action. So be prepared."

As it turned out the group of revolutionaries was in the thousands and pervaded all walks of life. I didn't find out until they launched a general strike against the tyrannical rule of the wise personae. And many people jumped on the bandwagon when they saw what was happening and finally the wise personae stepped down.

And we formed a new government as stewards of the Empire and held an election. Many of us revolutionaries won Mayoralties and I was elected as one of the 12 ruling councilors for the Empire.

Our agenda was vast. We wanted to renew science which had been dormant for many years and develop eternal youth drugs. And also, drugs which stimulated the imagination. And strongly bolster the few colonies that existed in Space. But we continued the previous administration's ban on AI, which we thought was anathema, just like they did. And we planned to reinvent the arts and make a lot of movies and bring back old movies out of storage.

And as for business, we set up an almost free market in the place of a largely centrally controlled communistic regime. This made many people greedy, but we thought that avarice was good for the people. To never be satisfied. More of everything.

And we made love into a big deal. Previously true love had been forbidden. And I couldn't figure out why?

Anyway, we made sure everyone got an advanced education, which had not been the case previously. Before only the top 1,000 who were leaders were well-educated.

And soon our Worlds were prospering like never before, and almost everyone was content. Of course, any civilization would have its detractors and ours were mostly people who wanted progress even faster. We told these people to be patient and gave them powers in Space to enhance progress.

And throughout all these developments, I wondered how civilization had fallen so low under the previous regime … And so, I became the official historian of the previous wise personae rulers. And I discovered there had initially been a powerful Emperor who was assassinated and those who seized power were the wise personae who figured progress had gone too far and wanted to be able to better control the people, so it became a regressive regime.

And so, we lived happily ever after!

Sixty Minutes

Gary Zenker

I'm dreaming. But even in the dream, I realize it's a dream. I'm standing in an amalgam of my childhood home and my current house. Things I recognize are mixed with things I don't. And it's all in color. I read somewhere that people don't dream in color. They may be muted but it's definitely color.

My dad is sitting on the green sofa that my mom bought in the early 1970s. It's the fifth dream of him this month. My last dream was that he had moved away, not telling anyone where he went. I somehow knew he started a new life in another state working as a staff accountant. It's hard to understand since he had owned his own accounting firm. Despite begging and pleading for him to return contact, he wouldn't. I spent that entire dream trying to understand his new life and why he left. It was perpetual heartache.

But today, here he is: sitting on the sofa and smiling. Despite it being a combination of the homes I've lived in, I recognize it as his home. He stays seated as I speak to him.

"I'm so glad you're here."

"Actually, *you* are here," he corrects me and laughs like he just told one of his old, often repeated jokes. It makes me smile. Then, I remember. He's dead. Dad died four months earlier in a traffic accident. There were no chances for last goodbyes; he was gone before I could reach him. It simultaneously seems like yesterday and a lifetime ago. His appearance here confuses me but makes me happy. I don't say anything about my confusion or his death, afraid that he may suddenly disappear if I acknowledge it.

He pats the sofa cushion next to him. "Sit down on the couch and let's talk."

So I sit. It turns out that I do most of the talking. My heart is filled with happiness. I tell him how much I love him and miss him. "Seth and I have been looking at old family photo albums, even the ones from before he was born. He's a good kid but it takes a lot of energy to keep up with him." I pause. "I think *you* taught me how to be a good father."

His smile grows bigger at my comment. "Thank you."

"I like this. It makes me feel good. Will you come visit me again tomorrow night?"

He is quiet and the non-response gives me the answer I dread. "We only get an hour. It's a gift to us and the people we love. But just one hour."

It seems amazingly generous and cruel at the same time. It's not nearly enough time. I want more. "That means you'll be going away again?" He just nods but with a funny smile on his face. I don't know what it means. "Why don't Steve and Penny ever dream of you? When I ask them, they tell me that they don't."

"Because you need me the most. I gave my sixty minutes to you." I know that he's right. They didn't … don't love him any less. But for some reason, their grief seems less intense. Mine feels crushing and unbearable. I feel selfish and start to cry. I can feel the wetness of the tears roll down my cheeks and taste them in the corners of my mouth. My heart grows incredibly heavy and my throat tightens so that I can't speak. He answers my unvoiced question.

"There are rules with the sixty minutes. I can't control the dream. I can appear but *your* mind guides it. Sometimes I can push it a little in this direction or that …" It makes sense, in a way, but does that mean this was his conversation with me or mine with him? I probably would never know.

"You may dream of me after but that will be all you and not really me." I want to ask him more questions, about why some people are ghosts, whether reincarnation is real, and whether our destinies are open or set. We never get to those answers but he answers the question I couldn't bear to ask. "This is my last time. And I have to go."

He stands and I follow. He holds out his arms and I sink into a close, protected hug. I can feel the warmth of his arms on my body and he strokes my hair like I do to my son Seth, when I hug him. I'm teary but comforted.

He smiles again. "The secret is creating memories for each other, over and over." Scenes flash through my head at lightning speed: I'm four with the two of us in Halloween costumes; six with him holding the back of my new two-wheeler without training wheels for the first time; nine in a deli eating breakfast on vacation; fourteen with him by the roadside changing a flat tire; twenty-two with him in the audience of my college graduation; thirty and visiting the first house I bought. Memories with my dad are rich and plentiful. "Memories outlast everything else."

He is almost through the doorway but turns to add one last thing … "Don't waste your time focused on what you can't do. Figure out what you *can* do. And have faith. I may not be in your dreams but I AM watching over you. Every day." Then he walks out and I wake up. My pillow is wet and my eyes sting.

I lay there a bit, then get up and shower. I think about the day and make a list of what to do ... my first in three months. I have a little more faith in what I can make happen today. I have to. Because I know he's watching.

Men don't cry at funerals

David L. Pogson

'Don't let them see you crying. That's when they know that they've won.'

My father's words throughout my childhood. He'd expected me to apply them on all occasions – after a fight in the school playground, a bust-up during a soccer game, a caning from the headmaster. They came to mind as the Vicar asked us to spend a few moments reflecting on the deceased. I envied girls. Fathers didn't say those words to them. They cry openly whenever they feel like it and no-one thinks any the less of them.

My friend's wife had died suddenly, just before the restrictions. He'd gone into the kitchen to make a brew. Thought she'd nodded off in front of the telly ... until he offered her the mug. No symptoms, no warning. That's the problem with Covid; it affects different people in different ways.

A sudden unexplained death. The post mortem suggested an undiagnosed, underlying heart condition triggered by the virus. My friend had to self-isolate for fourteen days on his own. By then the lockdown was in place and new funeral rules imposed. Ten mourners only when the Crematorium should have been packed.

I'd wanted to go to support him but her close friends outranked me. Then came a late call-up when one cried off because she felt at risk.

I drove alone along empty roads to be stopped at the locked Crematorium gates. Security checked me in, the last to arrive before the hearse, to pick any spot in a deserted car park. We ten queued outside the doorway in the sunshine and filed in, two silent metres apart, to sit on the ten spaced-out chairs in the cavernous hall. No flowers, just an on-line donation to the RNLI. No cards, no hymn books, no printed order of service, nothing to touch. No human contact. Hopefully no contamination. Only masks, personal hand sanitisers and recorded music.

Luciano Pavarotti singing 'Nessun Dorma' from *Turandot*, her favourite song from her favourite opera. None shall sleep … maybe a foretaste of how it would be for my friend until his grief passed? A heart-rending aria designed to make grown men cry … if we let it. But that would show the virus that we were beaten. I'd glanced across at him. He was holding it together.

Half an hour later we filed out. No hugging, no hand-shakes, no comforting arm around his shoulders. Just strained conversation as we stood in a makeshift circle facing each other, maintaining our safe distance, to say what a nice service it had been. As nice as it could have been in the circumstances.

No tea and buns afterwards. Just the drive home again along those same empty roads. Home to talk it over with my wife. My friend bound for the isolation of an empty house and an empty bed with a grief-filled heart. A loss made harder by the circumstances. Men don't cry at funerals but they weep when they're alone.

DS

Doug Hawley

As an eighty-year-old, all of my previous generation are gone, as well as a former best friend.

Of my two previous important relationships, the first ended because of my foolishness and her ego, the second because of her past trauma and my immaturity. Of the not so important:

Neither of us was that excited.

She became a full time Lesbian (says what about me?).

She was more interested than I was.

It took a long time, but the last one and I have made it through fifty-three years.

I had intended to write about a recent friend who I had spent a lot of time with. After several years of hanging out, I got entangled in a feud I was not part of, and he cut me off.

DS dying months ago changed all that.

When we moved back to Portland Oregon twenty-five years ago, DS and RS helped us settle in many ways. We had just started with the Lake Oswego hiking group. They had started with the group a little earlier, and showed us the ropes about what to wear, and what the landscape was like. At the time, even though they were eleven to fifteen years older than we were, we had a hard time keeping up.

On trips, we frequently rode in their van. We spent several overnights at their cabin on the Siletz River which starts in the

Coast Range and runs to the Pacific. We'd fish in the river, but I struck out completely. I'll never be a fly fisher. We were slightly more successful at mushroom hunting in the local hills. We backpacked with them a few times. The slim and light DS would take a much heavier load than we did, even though we were younger and stronger. He insisted.

DS loved telling jokes; his only problem was that he was so amused that he would laugh during the punch line, which we couldn't hear.

DS and RS slowed down over the last ten years or so, so they were neither hiking nor backpacking much or at all. Contact became infrequent. After they moved into Sunset City (my name for retirement homes, my wife likes it better than God's waiting room), they mostly kept to themselves. We would see them at times for coffee or drinks.

DS had lived long and knew a lot about a lot of things. He told us that since he retired as a doctor he could give us advice, but couldn't charge us. We used that a lot.

DS had a history of heart trouble, but we were shocked to hear that he had collapsed and quickly died. DS and RS have been a huge part of our lives for twenty-five years. Wife RS is now in assisted living.

The Memorial

Mary Ann Carrasco

I knew it was coming but was still surprised upon receiving it. The black envelope, addressed in gold ink, held a trifold invitation, that when opened, read "Come join Philip's family and friends in honoring his memory." The red rose at the end was meant to add some color, as if the memory of Philip did not add enough color.

I met Philip's lover, Ken, first. It was 1988. My late husband and I were referred to Ken for a home refinancing. Our friendship grew and invitations to social occasions began to arrive. Philip was an event planner for a prestigious hotel and had a flair for hosting lavish parties.

Their annual holiday party was our first experience of Philip's talent. A Christmas tree decorated each room. The buffet held such delights as caviar, smoked salmon, fresh crab, and champagne. The guests also exhibited flair, dressed in bright colors, accessorized with boas and flashy jewelry, parading throughout the home as though sashaying down a runway.

Philip's customary perfectionism in hosting showed in his lack of patience and temperament.

"Why aren't the salads on the table? I told you to put them here, next to the ice sculpture," Philip could be heard saying to Ken in exasperation as, hips swaying, he flailed back and forth between the dining room and kitchen.

Ken would glance at a guest, roll his eyes, and hurry off to cater to Philip's order.

As each guest for the Cinco de Mayo party arrived, a sombrero was placed on their head, while forced to sit on a burro by the front door as their picture was snapped with a Polaroid. For the party game a two-by-four was placed across the pool. Many guests were goaded into walking across it while wearing four-inch spiked heels.

Philip was diagnosed with AIDS in the early 1990s, a death sentence at the time. Months later Philip became very sick.

Forever the event planner, Philip began orchestrating his funeral from his sick bed.

"I want to be cremated and I want an elegantly lavish memorial service. My parents will want their own service but promise that my remains will never go home," he pleaded with Ken. "I love my family, but I just don't want to go there again. Promise me."

"Of course," Ken assured him.

Philip planned the service to the last detail; including the speakers, songs, and the champagne to serve. He arranged for the catered party in the grand hotel where he had worked, conveniently located across from the park where the service was to be held.

Months later Ken called.

"Philip has passed away," Ken said, choking back tears. "Everything is arranged but his family wants their own service, and I promised Philip that I wouldn't send his remains back home. I am at a total loss as to how to get out of this."

As if by divine intervention, I responded, "Well, what if you filled the box for their service with kitty litter?"

Ken chuckled. "Well, I'll deal with it somehow. The service here is in a few weeks, and you will receive an invitation."

My husband and I arrived for the service. Men in tuxedos poured champagne before escorting us to our seats. In front of the podium stood a beautiful ice sculpture of an angel with hands extended.

As guests arrived, a chorus sang. Two limousines pulled up. Ken emerged, dressed in a black tuxedo and top hat. Ken somberly walked to his seat in the front row. Philip's family emerged next. His mother and father and five sisters, each dressed in a floor-length black dress and long white gloves. One sister carried the wooden box holding Philip's ashes. She placed the box into the hands of the angel ice sculpture and sat down.

After the eulogy, one of Philip's sisters rose to speak. She lost her balance before gripping the sides of the podium with her gloved hands. She began to speak while trying to hold back tears. She spoke of her younger brother very lovingly.

While listening, I noticed a puddle on the ground and traced the source back to the ice sculpture. As if in slow motion, the wooden box encasing Philips' remains slid from the grip of the angel's melting hands and crashed to the ground. The lid flew open, and ashes spewed out.

In that awful moment, Philip's sister – the one who had just spoken – stepped down from the podium, fell to her knees and began scooping up the ashes and dumping them back into the box. All that could be heard was the scraping of those gloved hands across the earth as she continued scooping until there was only a gray film left.

Philip's father put the lid back on and placed the box on the podium. He turned to Ken and said, "It seems Philip has put on some weight since he was last home."

Ken nervously shifted himself in his chair.

Philip's sister continued, "My brother's memory will now always be part of this park," eliciting chuckles. As we stood to attend the reception, I noticed Ken take the box that held Philip's remains.

The hotel banquet room was decorated with Philip's signature flair. A video continuously played photographs of Philip. We stood off to the side of the room sipping champagne, watching the video. Philip's sister who had spoken at the service approached, gloveless and stumbling. She gulped champagne before turning to me and said, "Did you know that when Philip's service was held at home, the box was filled with kitty litter?"

I took a gulp of champagne swallowing my amusement and widened my eyes in surprise. "Really?" I replied before turning back to the video, feeling very content that Philip's wishes were carried out, happy that my divine inspiration assisted with his final planned event.

Gone

Robert Clare

As I walked into the bathroom, I bent automatically to pick up the bathmat. Always heavy with water, it was left there outside the shower. I had long ago given up trying to get anyone else in the house to take responsibility for hanging it over the shower door to dry. It just became one of my daily routines – invisible to everyone else and automatic to me. Shower mat. Toothpaste lid. Dripping tap. Wipe the toilet seat. Switch the light off. Morning and night for nearly thirty years.

Today the bathmat was where it should be, hanging over the shower door.

Everything else was as it should be.

It was exactly as it had been when I switched the light off last night.

I pulled the bathmat from the door and folded it on the floor in front of the shower.

I stepped onto the dry soft pile.

I switched on the shower and as the steam warmed my skin, I knew there were no longer secret ways to show I cared.

Sandra Breaks Out

Sally Basmajian

Everyone over the age of fifty had one. Her husband, her friends. Everyone except Sandra.

Sandra didn't care much about her husband's bucket list, but she hadn't given up on their marriage—yet.

So she feigned interest and asked, "What's on yours, dear?"

"I want to see the Taj Mahal." Bob steepled his fingers in a mystical way.

Sandra thought, *"Pompous asshole,"* but replied, "How lovely."

She couldn't repress a snicker. He'd never lever himself out of his reclining chair to get himself a snack, let alone venture abroad.

She was saved by a pocket buzz. Her best friend Amy was calling to suggest meeting for coffee later. Sandra agreed, then asked, "Do *you* have a bucket list?"

Amy's alto grew husky. "I've always wanted to climb to Base Camp at Mount Everest."

Sandra dug her fingernails into her palm to keep herself from chortling. Amy hadn't worked out in ages and one of her knees was wonky. She had as much chance of getting to Base Camp as she did twerking with Justin Bieber.

Bob interrupted their chat. "I'm starving. When's dinner?" He didn't even look up from the television.

"Soon, dear." Sandra hung up and began to bang pots around with more vigour than necessary.

While the cozy aroma of roasting chicken filled their small kitchen, she pondered the question marks that floated within her soul. She didn't crave an exotic trip. She simply yearned—a keen, clean ache of wanting something more.

But what was it she craved? Freedom? From this humdrum existence?

As the chicken crackled and browned, she realised one thing for sure. She wanted to lose that deadweight Bob.

And now, when he called, "Hey, hon, get me another beer," with the certainty of prompt service, Sandra snapped.

At first, it was the quietest rebellion imaginable.

"Ff-f-f-f." This was most unsatisfactory, as snaps go. "Ff-f-f-f," she tried again.

She paused, wiped a bead of sweat from her forehead, and made another attempt.

"Hey, where's my beer?" Bob hollered.

"Fuck it," Sandra whispered. This time, no hesitation. She savoured a sensation of power, laced with glee. "Fuck it!" she said again, this time out loud.

"What?" Bob yelled from his comfy couch. "And where's my drink?"

"Try the Taj-fucking-Mahal." With a lilt in her voice and a song in her heart, Sandra abandoned her chicken mid-roast, shrugged on her old jacket and her practical, woolly hat, grabbed her purse, and slammed the front door behind her.

Sandra charged downtown in the invigorating evening air, feet slapping the pavement. What did she want to do? Not in a few months or years, but this very minute. What dreams could she fulfill?

A bucket list sounded way too final, and Sandra had a lot more living to do. But, maybe, just maybe, it could be a fuck-it list.

A shiver of naughty excitement rippled down her spine.

As she passed the first row of stores, she paused to look in a window filled with bright hats. Absently, she touched the sad relic perched atop her own head.

At that moment, her friend Amy yoo-hooed outside the grocer's and crossed the street to join her. She toted a bag overflowing with veggies, but a chocolate smear above her mouth betrayed her. When she saw Sandra admiring the hats, Amy pursed her Snickered lips.

"We're too old for those styles. We'd make such figures of ourselves."

Sandra looked at Amy and pulled a tissue out of her pocket. As she dabbed away her friend's chocolate smear, she whispered something under her breath.

"What's that?" Amy asked.

"Ff-f-f-f it."

"Speak up. You know I have a hearing issue."

"Sandra placed her hands on her hips. She raised her chin. "Fuck it!"

"WHAT did you say?"

"I said, fuck it! I'm buying a hat. A fluffy, pink one. And not shell pink, either. I'm going full-on Barbie."

Amy tried to shrink back against the outer wall of the store, but Sandra tugged her inside. She popped a vivid chartreuse hat on Amy's head.

"You're gorgeous!"

Amy, trembling like a mouse who has just seen its reflection in a tabby's eyes, squared her shoulders. She looked in the mirror.

"Yeah, not bad," she said. "It's not meant for someone my age, but—"

"Fuck it!" Sandra interrupted. "I'm buying it for you, and this pink one for me"

"What will Bob think?"

"Fuck Bob," Sandra said. "I'm tired of his shit."

"Oh, dear, really? You two have always seemed so happy."

Sandra patted Amy's arm, like a mom comforting a child who has learned of his parents' impending divorce.

"*Bob's* been happy. I would be, too, if I had someone waiting on *me* hand and foot. Wouldn't you?"

Amy nodded. She stood up straighter and tweaked her chartreuse hat into a rakish tilt.

Sandra slapped some bills on the counter. "Our new lives begin right here and right now."

"If you say so." Amy's voice was soft but hopeful.

"We'll lose our old baggage. Do new, exciting things."

Arm in arm and with their jaunty hats aloft, they sashayed out the door. Amy no longer favoured her bad knee.

"But what are you going to do about Bob? And don't use that awful word!"

"That's the zillion-dollar question. I'll call you when I've decided."

As Sandra entered her home, the smell of incinerated poultry was almost as infuriating as the ratcheting sound of Bob's snores.

"All I need is courage," she said to herself. "And to remember that for every loss there will be a greater gain."

She passed the kitchen, ignoring the dirty dishes and pots. She tiptoed by slumbering Bob in his padded chair. Upstairs, she opened the closet and yanked out her suitcase. It was time to improve the balance sheet of her life.

The first thing she threw into her suitcase was her new pink hat.

Gerald and Phillip

Leo Vanderpot

It's just as well that cousin Maurice has the black and white photo of Gerald and Phillip, left at Maurice's house by accident, the picture taken in the dining room at 15 Washington Square. It's a snapshot of my two brothers, taken on a Thursday, perhaps, in that time just after the end of World War II. They are both wearing cotton jackets, as if they have just come home from work. Both look tired, their faces drawn. They show no eagerness to please the camera or the person who points the camera at them, as Phillip was in my memory inclined to do. They may have been solving a problem at our house on Washington Square: a roof-leak or a clogged drain. Phillip would have been living with us – Ma, me, Bette and Bobbie. Gerald lived across the Square. So many questions. Why a weekday? Why a picture? It must have been Bette's camera. I do not like the mood of this picture. I don't want to see my brothers tired and somehow defeated by the day, not able or willing to give hope and pride to me so I can say to those who will look at them in the future, "These are my brothers. They were at our house that day and Bette took their picture." My memory is so much better than this picture. And it must not be true that the camera does not lie.

Anita goes shopping

Tony Warner

Saturday afternoon. The market is crowded. Anita is shopping. She stops at a stall, sneaks a strawberry from one of the punnets, pulls a face at its under-ripe sharpness, pops a couple of tomatoes into her bag.

Cucumbers are cheap today, in mid-season. Elderly women jostle as they squeeze and assess individual items, judging tomatoes to be too fat, peppers too scrawny, aubergines past their best. Anita is not choosy, taking two of the nearest tomatoes. Peppers are a problem, being large, bulky and blazingly conspicuous. Celery hearts, trimmed down from their original flourish of growth and now squeezed into plastic wrappers, are less difficult.

She totters on, ignoring both the butcher's and the fish stall, grabs a handful of abandoned cold chips from their cardboard container as she passes on her way to the cheese counter. As usual, they have a 'special of the day' for customers to try. Anita picks up a wooden fork, spears a cube of orange and green cheese. Holds it on the end of her tongue; swallows. Pulls a face. Tries a second cube, passes it voluptuously round her mouth. The third disappears more rapidly. 'Too salty,' she declares with a sigh. Heads off towards cold meats.

This is her favourite destination. If she had time, she would stare for hours at the pastramis, prosciuttos, black puddings, venison patés and hands of honeyed hams. But she has no time; she must be quick. While the store holder has her back turned to slice a Westmoreland ham, she filches four slices of pastrami, slips the greasy meat into her coat pocket. Winks at the astonished customer standing next to her, and continues on her progress.

The police cadet and his mentor have been watching Anita for the last half an hour.

'Did you see that?' gasps the cadet. 'Brazen as you like, out in the open. Funny business on the quiet with tomatoes and cucumbers is one thing, but a whole handful of meat in front of everyone! Aren't you going to do something?'

'Yes, I suppose I ought. Come on.'

The older man rolls slightly on his stiffened legs, aiming towards the meat stall. 'Missing anything?' he asks of the owner.

'Bit down on the pastrami. Saw Anita earlier, so I can guess where it's gone.'

'This should take care of it,' says the policeman, tendering a bank note.

The stall holder shakes her head. 'Don't worry. I'll leave out something cheaper next time, one of those patés which have a short shelf life.'

The police pass on. Anita is scanning the backs of the food stalls where the rubbish is left, just in case a tasty morsel has been relegated there by mistake.

'We'll check on her tonight,' mutters the policeman, taking the cadet by the arm. 'The doorway of M and S, her favourite shop. Used to see her in there all the time. Ex-mayoress, you know. Best we ever had. Fell on hard times. Helped Mum when Dad was going through a bad patch. Never did no-one no harm. Poor old dear.'

The Petals of Yellow Roses

Carmelita Scian

You never gave death a thought when you met him, did you?
The illusion of eternity cuddled you both in your spring world.
Good looks and young dreams opened the golden gates to
paradise, you lucky wanderers. Death hovered over the old, the
ill, the hopeless, those sorrowful pilgrims wading through the
desert regions of lovelessness. You were embarked upon a
yellow road of silky promise, dazzlement, the titillating discovery
of soft fingertips, wiping out the ponderous and exacting world
around you in a flash.

Love didn't arrive in a golden chariot. You were married to
someone else for six years, someone you couldn't even look at
for all your disdain, a forced proxy marriage arranged by your
mother when you were only fifteen. You hated Mauel's
bargain-store jokes, his bowed legs, the dribble running down
his chin when he laughed. Your mother knew better. She hasn't
spoken to you in four decades since the day you left. Ronnie,
too, wasn't free, engaged to someone with adoration in her eyes.
Cupid's arrows didn't care. What could you do? Yet spikes and
thistles appeared along your long journey together through the
years, passions colliding like tectonic plates. Ronnie was a
possessive lover, "Love me only, Milita, me ... Me ..." He
couldn't share your affections. The yellow brick road
disappeared, then, like a fading star in a tempestuous firmament,

not a handful of words spoken for days, sometimes weeks. But love remained, watchful, non-judgemental. After the storm, the world was recreated anew with each embrace, each promise.

You recall his first touch. You'd taken the Bathurst street-car to work, and there he was! A rainy day and his new green Dodge wouldn't start. You'd been working together for a month. The street-car lurched forward; he grabbed your hand. It was at that moment that you understood the meaning of completeness and the dread of loss. Months later, were words spoken? What do you remember? Hungry tongues and grasping fingers. The haaaa! of his spasm.

Now you're alone.

You wait …

What is it you're waiting for?

Unlike Penelope, you don't have a death shroud to weave and unravel for twenty years while waiting for your hero's return. You know Ronnie won't be showing up disguised as an old man.

He'd staggered down the front steps on the way to the hospital, life already seeping away, drop by drop, like water dripping out of a rotting vessel. *Il mio dio dagli occhi azzurri,* my blue-eyed god.

The cemetery is empty of visitors on your first visit but it's not peaceful. The dead do not rest in peace. A silent disquiet fills the air. Skeletal fingers reach out behind tombstones in protest, clawing their way back to the living.

There's no grass on Ronnie's grave. Not yet. It takes time for the earth to adjust to its new resident. Settle. Dust to dust. Alpha, Omega. The in-between doing and feeling, loving and hating we call life, finished, obliterated with that first shovelful of dirt.

Wait ... That's too poetic. Words bathed in spurious sentiment grasping for a kernel of beauty in death's stab. The yellow bulldozer had stood like a powerful brute next to the grave, waiting to pounce.

A square of dirt, that's all he's become.

The ground is wet from the rain the night before, the leaves of the old willow arching above the grave drip with opalescent dew drops in the sunlight. For whom are they crying? For him, so soon departed? For you?

You spread the petals of yellow roses you hold in your hand across the soggy earth—he'd given you twenty-two yellow roses on your twenty-second birthday. The petals float down like fragments of memory, sorrow, doom, loss.

Life became too much for him at times. Like Hephaestus, he forged ahead at the smithy of life, creating beautiful art, crafting stained glass, writing haikus, filling your needs, but his deformity, unlike the god's, wasn't visible. His friends all doing well; he did too, but could never see what he'd achieved. It was never enough; he was never as good as others.

Now he lies under this muddy earth.

Oh, the weight of it all!

★

It's the banality of death that keeps you awake while others sleep. You'd always imagined the hooded black figure announcing itself at your door, regal and solemn, like a king or queen proclaiming their intentions to their subjects. But death arrived in a three-minute telephone call—a vagabond in ragged clothes. Official. Clinical. Unadorned. A duty, according to the day's list. The clock is always ticking, isn't it? The cosmic engine moves only forward. Did you fill Ronnie's thoughts before his last breath merged with the miasma of all other last breaths uttering their sorrowful goodbyes? You'll never know.

What do you know?

You know that all that remained was the busy sound of a hung up receiver. The kitchen, where you stood, the city where you live—where you both lived—the infinite space beyond the everything, became a vacuum. Hollowed out. The June morning sun shone in shame through the kitchen window. What did it care?

Death brings on the breathless heartbeat. The universe, up to that final moment, a cornucopia of hope and good intentions, collapses within you. All is shattered. The dreaded scythe leaves no room for alterations, corrections, apologies. The old man carrying the dead souls across the turgid river for a coin will not bring Ronnie back. Charon's boat morphed into a black Uber.

In your garden, the August evening is sultry, but a cooling breeze brings relief to the scalding day. The cicadas fill the air with their mating song, the earth, itself, pregnant with desire. The flowering oleander, bougainvillea and hibiscus in clay pots around your patio, remind you of places you visited in those halcyon minutes of your lives—Pompeii, Nassau, Mexico. Warm lips and silky fingertips. The eternal hunger.

Ronnie is everywhere and nowhere; nowhere and everywhere.

Captain on the Bridge

Niall Crowley

Standing by the upstairs window, binoculars at the ready, I am the captain on the ship's bridge. The room is stripped of its former purpose, except for table and chair. The logbook is laid out, ever at the ready. On one side of the bridge, my watch scans over the bay and beyond, to capture the dramas of the ocean. On the other, it looks out across the stippled remnants of barley, and on up the road for whatever that might have to offer.

This ship, however, can no longer withstand the toll of internal abandon and external distress. Mortality beckons. Walls of ageing white, stained with threads of grey mould, surround. Faded green carpet tiles are rendered rigid with time. That logbook, previously a record of incidents of note, is now no more than a receptacle for doleful musings.

All and any efforts of preservation on my part have been in vain. Hope has been devoured in the growing intemperance of the sea, and any aspiration of salvation disappeared down that road some years ago. The sea that had always fascinated, now rises in search of revenge. The road, previously of merely functional interest, now provokes ever-disappointed scrutiny of any movement cresting its hill.

I can make out the detail of the corpse below even without the binoculars. It's laid out on the rocks along the dark mass of what we've always called Table Rock, as if prepared for sacrifice. The head is twisted out of place to open a gaping hole, otherwise there is peace in its repose. Even at a distance, the yellow daub is apparent on the chest.

The tide was high last night. A full moon lent a shivering glow to the sea as it swelled to cover Table Rock. The water flushed out beyond in impetuous discharge, to feed hungrily on the underpinnings of the cliff face. These tides reach higher every year, demanding their toll on our bulwarks, a source of growing consternation. I track the phenomenon with resignation, and was out early morning to survey the damage when I found the body.

People are gathering now, word has spread. Gruesome demands an audience and is rarely disappointed. They circle the corpse, in ritual formation. Death elicits silent awe, both a mourning for what has been lost, and a premonition of what is to come for the onlooker. They stand to attention, mobile phones raised in response to the imperative to record catastrophe, however intrusive. The sea surrounds, but has withdrawn to respectful distance.

Tales of the sea had fired my imagination from early days. I grew up to trace its secrets, with papers written and projects undertaken. Its distress supplanted celebration of its dramas, as my work honed in on toxic warming from contamination, and unmanageable burdens from waste. With the melting of faraway ice caps, I came to fear as much as revere the sea, inexorably rising to draw us into its destructive fold. Now I am resigned to mourning, sorrow and trepidation my companions on the bridge.

Two people kneel by the body, dressed in white hazmat suits, hooded and masked. I watch, through the binoculars now, as one cuts deeply into the chest, lips of flesh pulled back from the incision to release bulging innards. The knife wielder picks at these with apparent distaste, or perhaps forensic care. The other writes notes on a clipboard, which they confer over from time to time.

The basking shark, still a novelty in these parts, merits such scientific attention, though this is not the first to die in this manner. The yellow daub marks its fatal encounter with the hull of a fishing boat. Basking sharks never had a place in these waters, only finding their way with more favoured habitats poisoned.

I 'WhatsApped' him when I returned home after discovering the corpse. I do so when there is some drama or anything that might make an impression. Not regularly, but insistently. Photographs of the cadaver winged their way across the world or maybe closer. I no longer know. Two grey ticks against the message indicated they had arrived, and, later, two blue ticks that they had been read. There is no response. My watch from the bridge is further accompanied by distance and longing.

The bridge is where I pick at old sores, the hostility of the seas through one window, the deserted stretch of the road through the other. The immediate pain gives some distraction from the constant itch of grief solidified as melancholy. I wanted to leave him a better world, I worked fruitlessly for that future. In the end he left me. I might as well have looked to the present, working more diligently for us to appreciate together the time allowed.

The parental bond had fractured abruptly. It could have been rejection, my failure to deliver in a moment of crisis nullifying a history of being there for him. Maybe it was an inevitable shedding of shackles, the claims attendant on interdependence become too restrictive. It could have been insight, a mature dawning that parental knowledge and understanding was lacking any substance. Maybe it was just the unavoidable clash of lives at different stages, become too taxing as they evolved along different lines.

The scientists pack their tools and samples, the onlookers pocket their phones, and the undertakers arrive. The basking shark is sprayed sanitary, wrapped for transit, and loaded into a battered horse box serving as hearse. The carcass will be stripped to whatever can be preserved, a further monument to our disinterest in a future. The village park will play host, the remains become another desperate call to the exigent tourist. I will remain alone on the bridge, as custom demands of the captain.

Portal

John E. Caulton

Maria sat at the front of the top deck; and as she peered through the window, she could see the small, circular light gradually becoming bigger and brighter. When, at last, the bus drove out of the tunnel and entered the interchange, the world had become more luminous. The sun shone and the town buildings appeared newer and shinier.

Maria waited patiently under the market clock for twenty minutes, safe in the knowledge her daughter would be her usual, late self. When Anne finally arrived, she gave her mother a quick hug and a curt apology, before making it understood she was famished.

As usual, Maria paid for breakfast. She ate a muffin and drank unsweetened black tea while Anne had a creamy doughnut and two sugary espressos. As Anne vaped and stared vacantly through the café window, Maria gave news from home which she thought might be of interest: Dad, the dog, her old school friend Billie, pregnant now. Then Ann spoke for a long time, seemingly without catching breath, about herself: her job, her flat, her new boyfriend, her skin problems, her money problems and her old boyfriend problem.

Back on the street, bright sunlight bounced off the shop windows. To protect her eyes, Maria wore her shades, which made Anne laugh and Maria in turn. Laughing with her child made Maria feel great. Really, really great, even if it was at her own expense.

As they wandered around the market, it felt to Maria like the old times. Herself and Anne and nobody else. Mother and daughter on their big day out; just the two of them; blood on blood.

And, as in past times, Maria purchased items from the stalls which she insisted Anne have. Not children's necessities now, of course, but the things women need; lady's things. Soon, Maria was carrying a full shopping bag because Anne had her hands full: a vape in one hand and her phone in the other.

When Maria, being adventurous and thinking of mixing things up, suggested they visit the art gallery for a change, Anne poo-pooed the idea, moaning she desperately needed some new gear for the evening. So instead, they wandered to the department store on the main street.

It was fun, though. Maria giggled as Anne tried on several skimpy tops and increasingly revealing skirts. Anne's heart finally fell for a glittery-golden one-piece and, because it was somewhat out of her budget, Maria bought it. However, proud of her own financial independence, Anne purchased a piece of junk jewellery to complete her new look.

Back at Anne's flat, Maria boiled the kettle and opened the chocolate digestives she'd bought at the pound shop. They sat together on the sofa and watched a TV shopping channel until Anne said she needed a little nap, to freshen her up for the night on the tiles. So, Maria brought a pillow from the bedroom, placed it under Anne's head and covered her over with a throw. While Anne snoozed, Maria took the chance to tidy the flat and water the house plants.

As she was tending to the parched Yucca on the small balcony, Maria noticed dark clouds filled the sky.

After cleaning the bathroom and ironing the washing, Maria sat down on the spare chair and watched TV with the volume off. Eventually, Anne stirred and Maria re-joined her on the sofa. Resting Anne's head on her lap, she gently stroked her hair. The room had become dark but Maria felt an inner-illumination. If only, she thought, it could always be like this.

Feeling cosy in the dim light, Maria began to tell Anne the funny story of how her own mother had once cut her hair to disastrous effect. At one point in the tale Maria could feel Anne gently convulsing in her arms but, when she looked down, saw Anne was chuckling at a friend's text.

Before it was time to leave, Maria attempted to arrange another mother-daughter date but Anne was non-committal, citing work and social obligations. In the end, it was agreed that Anne would text Maria when she got the chance, hopefully with a mid-week date in which to shoe-horn her mother.

When Anne began running the shower and preparing her toiletries, Maria realised she would be walking alone to the interchange. Putting on her coat, she felt the urge to tell Anne how much she loved and missed her. But Anne's phone began to ring, so that ruined any chance of that. Before the door was closed behind her, Maria had to be content with a hurried kiss and a quick 'I love you' and 'I love you, too.'

Outside, she walked the wet pavements. Light rain fell on her bowed head. As the bus left the interchange big drops plashed against the windows and the town was only visible through streaky-blurred glass.

Cold and damp, Maria sat apart from the other passengers, downstairs towards the rear of the half-filled bus. From her higher position, she stared indifferently at the backs of people's heads, until she spotted a small boy leaning against his mother. She imagined they were gently holding hands. Maria's eyes fixated on mother and child until, in the dark of the tunnel, the spell broke and thinking of Anne again, she instinctively turned her head to look out of the rear window. She stared for over a minute, as the tiny light shrank to a dot and then, as she blinked her eyes, closed.

Losing It

David Davies

It had happened many times since, but the first time he wondered if he and his dog were psychically connected.

His wife had bought him the puppy on his retirement thinking it would get him out of the house. Then she made it a parting gift by promptly dying. He was devastated. No warning. A heart attack. The dog was now a good age for a Lab at thirteen, but still needing walks.

It was his habit each morning to pop into the local supermarket, get a few bits, then do the walk on his way home, but on that particular day something had upset him. Something that undermined his confidence and kicked off a chain of events that left him confused.

As he walked out of the supermarket, a young man with disturbing tattoos was angrily pacing in front of his car, and worrying the dog. It seemed he had straddled two parking spaces. The young man's face was as red as the blood on the crude dagger decorating his neck, his language as blue as the spiderwebs covering his arms.

He tried a few remarks as a counterattack, but if he was honest, he found it a bit frightening. He couldn't count on a respect for the elderly on physical violence. That was another era. It was a generation and fashion thing he knew, but tattoos still worried him, and this man was losing it. He thought it best to leave.

As usual, he drove up the lane to the footpath where he always walked the dog. He was re-running the whole incident in his head, editing the parts where courage failed him, and inserting the withering remarks that always come with hindsight. Relishing his last cutting word, the dog sitting next to him turned to look, then after a second or two resumed the straight-ahead non-partisan demeanour of a DVLA driving tester.

Had the dog picked up his imaginary rant? The words may have seemed sharp enough to be a command. He did a quick test by silently repeating them. The dog remained unresponsive. It was official. He had been talking to himself.

Driving home, a car flew past at speed laying on the horn. He turned sideways to see a snarling face mouthing obscenities and saliva through the prison bars of two upright fingers and more crude tattoos. A different young man but the same attitude.

He had no idea what he had done wrong, then looked in the rear view mirror to see a tailback of at least a dozen cars. He checked his speedometer. He was cruising a 15 mph.

Back home in his cul de sac, he carefully navigated the garden path that ran beside a shaggy unmown lawn up to his front door. Concrete cancer was proving a challenge and tufts of plantain were taking full advantage of the puddles and newfound light. Nature was waging a war to regain territory.

There was a parcel delivery wedged into the postbox, but he had no recollection of ordering anything. He unlocked the door and watched as the draught rolled a tsunami of dust and fluff up the bare floorboards of the hallway.

He laid it on the table and used a bread knife to cut the tape. He recoiled as the open box revealed what looked like an animal pelt. Cautiously, he removed some tissue paper. It had a silver sheen like an arctic fox. He lifted it out and a card fell to the table. He held it at arm's length to be able to read it. *Thankyou for buying the Celebtops ANDY WARHOL hairpiece (ref. 12570).* **Warning.** *Dry clean only, and store in the packaging provided to reduce static.*

He shook his head. He returned it to the box and placed the box on top of all the other parcels lining the walls of what used to be the dining room, to be dealt with later. He looked around the room. It resembled a cardboard cave targeted by street artists Prime and Amazon. So much to be 'dealt with later'.

Opening the French doors, he stepped out to feel a passing moment of sun on his face. He was a prisoner marooned on the cracked tiles of a patio. The garden was now ravaged by a marching army of nettles and bindweed scented only by the sickly sweetness of mayflower on the overgrown hawthorn hedge. The neighbours, always standoffish, were now not even a distant memory.

He shuffled between dog excrement and broken pieces of terracotta pots and their dried-out contents. Standing on tiptoe, he could see the heads of Arums at the end of the garden. He smiled remembering the old yearly joke to his wife. *'Those haughty French nuns are in our garden again ... looking for snails no doubt!'*

The smile dissolved from his face with the realisation that he had lost it again. Her name. Was it Lily? The dog was at his feet waiting for the next command. Maybe it would come to him later.

Mother's Milk

Mark Blickley

My lips tremble as if I am about to cry. Please let your mother's milk steel me against the animal I become when my brain confuses intellectual arousal with physical pleasure.

Why do I nurse wounds that flow from the expectations of others? Sometimes it feels like I'm the suckling of a Tin Woman who warns me she has no heart, yet dopamine builds with each puckered kiss swallowed in humiliation or spit back in defiance.

You lactate a complex flow of contradictions that dribbles down my chin with the shame of a stain. I want to forget the day I found, at nine years old, that first red stain on my Wonder Woman panties. Terrified, I run upstairs to tell Nana. My gentle grandmother slaps me across my face.

I cry: "Why did you hit me?" Nana says, "Ask your mother when she comes home from work."

The moment I hear your key click in the keyhole I run to the door. When I speak, you slap my face, too. You, who never laid a hand on me. Why? You shrug: "I don't know. It's what mothers do. That's what Nana did to me."

Why doesn't your mother's milk offer me the nourishment and immunity from judging myself as being nothing more than my menstrual flow? From fertility to maternity to menopause, must I believe that I am simply what I bleed?

Your milk sours in my mouth whenever you try to convince me your slap was done with love to awaken me from my childhood slumber. I was nine years old.

If I'm ever blessed to one day suckle my own daughter, I will offer up a kiss, not a slap, when she comes to me with her first red stain. I will celebrate her menstrual flow as sacred, not shameful, as it honors her passage from childhood and will continue to do so right up to her old age.

And should someone ever claim her blood is a curse, I will ask why is it painful to be reminded of your youth each month?

Uncle Fred

Ronald T. Hardwick

I went to my Uncle Fred's funeral. To the best of my recollection, for this was some years ago, it was a vile November day, freezing cold with sleety rain sweeping down straight from the Urals. I think I was ill with influenza, but I made myself go, for my dad's sake.

There were about a dozen of us gathered in the chapel of rest in the cemetery when they brought in the coffin. The air smelt stale and musty and the paint was peeling from the damp walls. Being in that chapel was like being in one of those refrigerated rooms where butchers hang carcasses of beef and pigs from hooks on the ceiling.

My dad had made sure it was an expensive coffin – dark oak and gleaming brass handles. Uncle Fred had left more than enough cash, in suitcases, bin-bags and stuffed inside his mattress, to cover the cost of his funeral.

The vicar arrived, out of breath. He was a small, wasted man with a fringe of silver hair round a bald pink pate. He wore a permanently anxious expression, as if he might discover that very afternoon that God didn't exist. The vicar had never met my Uncle Fred, and he offered up an almost apologetic valedictory, reading from a postcard my dad had given him, giving his feeble address in a monotone entirely in keeping with the dismal surroundings.

I stood at the graveside for a while, contemplating how short and generally useless life is, when my mother called for me to come away. In the car, driving to my Uncle John's for the obligatory cheery meal after the funeral, I pondered what Fred would have thought of it all. Not an awful lot, if I knew my uncle. My mind went back five years, when I came across him again, after an absence of almost forty more.

'I've found him!' said my dad, 'I've found him, after all these years.'

He could scarcely conceal his excitement. For a man in his seventies, you wouldn't have thought he had that much to be excited about.

'Who have you found, Dad?' I asked. 'Lord Lucan? Amelia Earhart?

'Only your Uncle Fred,' he said, delighted with himself. He was well used to ignoring my sarcastic remarks.

Uncle Fred. That ghost, that wraith, that man who disappeared one day in nineteen sixty-five from my grandparents' house, never to be seen again, until now. That war hero, who took a shell fragment in the cranium at Amiens in nineteen forty-four which destroyed his life thereafter, and which turned him into a moody and miserable misanthrope. That man who changed his name by deed-poll from Fred Mountford to Fred Newlands while he was still living with Grandma and Grandad at home, because he had fond memories of that eponymous city in South Africa, where he had worked as a storekeeper for fifteen years after the war. His greatest wish was to go back there. He grew to despise the surname with which he had been born, much to the chagrin of the rest of the family.

Even in my teenage years, when I was preoccupied with girls, acne and sport, once a week on a Sunday, I used to go round and visit my grandma, a lovely, plump, jolly lady, and grandad, a cheery, lazy soul with rheumy eyes and a chin coated with stubble. Fred would invariably be lying on the couch in the front room, staring into space. He never, ever spoke to me. He was undoubtedly a member of the male line of the family – all six brothers were short, slim, and had the same handsome chiselled features and piggy eyes. Fred was darker, swarthier, a testament to his time in South Africa. I used to think to myself that he looked very like a tawnier version of Rod Laver, the Australian tennis player.

What a bad-mannered wretch, I thought, when I saw him lying down, with no socks on his feet, staring out of the window into the back yard. I didn't realize then his inner turmoil due to that piece of metal in his head, so near his brain that they dared not operate for fear of killing him.

John, Fred and my dad used to meet up every week in the pensioners' café for cut-price bacon and eggs. I asked Dad if he'd seen what was inside Fred's bin-bags.

'Rubbish, mostly,' he said. 'Clothes and the like. But there are several bags of cheap religious things – what do you call them – figures of Christ in plaster of Paris, that sort of thing?'

'Icons?' I suggested.

'Yes, icons. There are also a couple of old pasteboard suitcases which must contain papers and other bits and pieces. I haven't seen what's inside them.'

★

I got a phone call a few days later. It was my dad. He sounded very upset.

'I just wanted you to know that I went up to see your Uncle Fred this morning. I couldn't open the door. I had to get the caretaker to open it up. I knew there was something wrong, the minute I stepped into the place.'

'What was the matter?' I asked, mechanically, for I had already guessed the answer.

'Fred was dead. He was still sitting on his bar stool in the kitchen, the way he always did. His eyes were open, and his head was tilted back. He was staring up at the ceiling.'

'I'm sorry,' I said. I couldn't think of anything else to say.

Later, amongst all the detritus, we found an exercise book full of poetry, written by Fred at some period in his life. It was mainly flowery Victorian doggerel, and of absolutely no merit whatsoever to a modern reader, except one verse which arrested my attention:

> *Alas! Alas! Old age of late*
> *Had on my strength began to tell*
> *And this accounts for my defeat*
> *The night of this November's gale.*

The Rising Cost of Loss

Jim Landwehr

We were a family of seven children raised by tragedy and loss. At the age of five my older sister, Linda, fell sick with what would later be diagnosed as a Wilms tumor, a rare kidney cancer that mainly affects children. Her sickness and death were swift, and she passed away when I was just four months old. While my older siblings have memories of her, my two younger brothers and I, have none.

My father did not know how to process the grief that comes with losing a child. The stresses of providing for a family of six and the loss of his beautiful daughter led to a drinking problem over the next five years. Despite my mother's attempts to remind him that his family needed him and that his drinking was affecting their marriage and his role as a father, he continued down the road of depression and drinking. In 1967, they separated, and he took an apartment in a rough part of St. Paul. My mother moved our family into low-income housing projects in another part of the city.

On a warm night in June of '67 my father was beaten to death in a bar fight by a gang of youths in a racially charged incident. He was knocked to the ground where he was punched and kicked in the head and died of a skull fracture. He was pronounced DOA at the hospital, leaving my mother a widow with six children.

By the grace of God, our mother pushed on and raised us on her own over the coming years. She worked full time and eventually managed to buy a house and sent us all through the Catholic school system. It is a textbook example of how two people, linked through matrimony, dealt with loss in completely different ways. I can't condemn my father for what happened as I know the demons of depression and despair can take over a person's life. I cannot imagine losing a child of my own, so I've spent my life trying to extend him some grace for the actions that led to that fateful night.

Nevertheless, I can't help but wonder how different our family's lives would have been with him in it. At the same time, I've heard from people whose memories of their father are filled with abuse, ridicule, and narcissism, and think that maybe sometimes loss is a better story than the pain of an abusive parent. Questions like these still pass through my mind at sixty-two years old.

It is the December of 2010, and I am speeding westward in my Santa Fe SUV with Arcade Fire's *Suburbs* album on the CD player. It is a great album that laments the banality of life in the suburbs. It is also a CD I will soon grow to hate because of the circumstances behind this trip. I'm on my way to visit my brother Rob at the Mayo Clinic. A month earlier, he was diagnosed with a chondrosarcoma tumor on his spine. They removed the tumor, reconstructed his spine with rods and screws, but the cancer spread to his lungs.

It is known that this type of cancer does not respond well to chemotherapy but with no better options, he has been admitted for his first chemo treatment and I am anxious to see him. Part of me is going to show my support and encouragement, but there's a bigger part that just wants to see him, to spend time with him. Time is short. Time is all we have left together. Time is precious.

As I drive and listen to the music, tears well up in my eyes. The road blurs like I'm looking through stippled glass. Without warning, my chest heaves as my body quakes in a torrent of tears. What is happening to me? I never used to cry like this. This emotional gut punch is entirely new to me. I cannot help but think it is the upwelling grief of loss that I never had the chance to reconcile after my sister and father's deaths so long ago.

After I arrive and settle in, we talk for an hour about the intricacies of his treatment and the unfortunate side effects of the chemotherapy. To add to his difficulties, the pressure of the tumors on Rob's spinal column has paralyzed him from the waist down. As much as I dream and pray for a miracle that he might someday walk again, all signs indicate differently. We talk for a bit about his "lasts." The last time he went golfing. The last time he played softball. His last swim. The whole discussion is sobering and stark. At the same time, I was glad I had come.

The first five rows of the Methodist church are filled with immediate family and a few close friends. The minister closes out the service with a blessing. As he readies to leave the sanctuary, the enormous pipe organ revs up Widor's "Toccata" from *Symphony V.* The piece begins with a carnival carousel melodic lightness. The notes twinkle and flutter around us like starlight and fill the space with auditory brilliance.

In my grief, I am comforted by the impact the music has on my soul. As our family exchanges hugs, the colorful notes celebrate the life of my brother. Right now, it tells his story better than words can. The sadness of the moment is overtaken by the brilliant uplifting notes coming from this marvelous instrument and this wonderful composition. The music rises from the floor of the sanctuary up to the ceiling, and I immediately visualize Rob's spirit rising with it. Through my tears I can almost see his spirit dancing on the notes above us near the ceiling of the church, his journey into the company of my dad and sister, to the loss of the rest of us.

The Man Who Left Too Soon

Martin Phillips

David stands among the loose huddle of mourners. Crouched under umbrellas outside the church, the wind buffets their brollies and the rain slants at them as they wait for the vicar. They're here to mark a loss. To bury Alastair's ashes.

The ashes are surprisingly heavy. David's arm aches through holding them in his left hand while clutching the umbrella in his right. He could put his old friend down; he's safely jacketed against the elements in an undistinguished green plastic urn. But it doesn't seem right to park him in the puddles. Holding the urn in the dry is a final act of dignity. A last connection with important personal cargo.

Some weeks earlier, in crisp autumn sun, David had collected the urn from the crematorium. A strange business, it involved showing ID at an office on one side of the site, collecting a ticket, and then walking the length of the graveyard to a red brick Chapel of Rest. On the door was a notice inviting you to "ring and enter". After some minutes, an elderly man wearing a grey work coat had emerged through a very large, ornately panelled door. In a hushed voice, (to avoid disturbing those at rest?) he asked for the ticket. David handed it over, uneasily conscious that it was beginning to feel like a trip to Argos. Minutes passed, then the keeper of the urns returned with a brown cardboard box. As David took it from him, the curator of ashes leaned purposefully forward and whispered,

"Could you just check the name, please sir."

David looked at the brown box. It had no label or writing on it. He turned it up to look on the bottom. In a more urgent, though still reverentially hushed tone, the curator said,

"Inside!"

David lifted the flaps on the box. A neatly typed label was stuck to the lid of the plastic urn: Alastair Nigel Thomas. David nodded.

Carrying Alastair in a backpack, he caught the bus back to Putney and the overground to Waterloo for a last walk along the river. In an old Young's pub, he'd self-consciously set the urn on the bench beside him while drinking a pint. They'd shared many pints in many pubs over many years. Alastair would often hurry them off after one pint to get another pint in somewhere else. David would always acquiesce, even though he often felt they were leaving too soon. He looked at the urn and realised Alastair had done it again. Left too soon. Fifty-six was no age to head off. But then Alastair always was a leader. One step ahead of the pack.

Eventually the vicar arrives. David and the others shuffle into the small nave of the church. The vicar struggles into his surplice and muddles his way through the service. Would they like to read aloud the words of a hymn? Mumbling words not designed to be sung, David imagined catching Alastair's eye at this moment, watching his friend raise a quizzical eyebrow at the bizarre muttering.

Soon they are out into the rain again. The wind snaps at the umbrellas, worries the vicar's surplice and displaces his comb-over. They trail after him through the wet grass, past the bones of others long gone, towards the stone wall and the neat hole in the ground with the mound of wet earth beside it.

The vicar sets off on another monologue while David drifts into his own private memories. His thoughts don't dwell on how mortal we are. They are packed full of life. Bright flashes of moments past. Fragments of shared laughter.

He thinks of the night in his local pub when Alastair had predicted his own early death. Aged 53 he'd just had a heart by-pass operation ("make mine a triple" he claimed to have said to the surgeon). "I'm not expecting to see 60. I've been on these (he waved his cigarette) since I was 10. I've had a bloody good run."

Then the vicar brings David sharply back to the here and now. He's about to bury Anthony. David briefly wonders whether to say "Could you just check the name, please sir" but quickly decides against it. After all, it's him who took the label off. It didn't seem quite reverential enough to have the shiny green plastic urn interred with what looked like a raffle ticket Sellotaped to its lid.

For a moment the world might end not with a bang or a whimper but with an identity crisis. At the last moment, as David steps forward to place the urn in the hole, God must have whispered to His man. There's a stuttering correction and an embarrassed smile. It is Alastair they're burying after all.

The earth closes over the urn.

★

Back at the pub they reminisce. And then David chinks his glass to give an informal eulogy.

"One thing I'm sure we'd all agree," David begins, "is that Alastair, that great raconteur, would have dined out on certain aspects of his own burial. If there is an afterlife, he'll be seeking out some like minds – John Lennon, perhaps, or Jean-Paul Sartre – and while shunting them from one celestial bar to another, he'll regale them with an embellished version of the day he was nearly despatched from earth with somebody else's name."

All that then remains is for his assembled friends to raise one final glass in memory of Alastair:

"To the man who left too soon."

Saturn in the First

Martha Rand

Sometimes, I look at charts and I can see Fate playing out.

Charts, you know, astrology charts, star charts, birth charts, horoscopes. Certainly, you've seen them. They're so popular now. Sometimes, I look at them and they look like pizzas. Pizzas that are cut into 12 pieces. The planets are distributed over the pizza, like ummm, like sausage slices. Perhaps a better way to describe it is that it's metaphorically a clock. It's a circle. Geometrically, that's 360 degrees. And if you divide it into 12 houses each house has 30 degrees. We could talk house systems now, because different house systems show the houses sometimes having more, sometimes less, sometimes an entire sign will be encapsulated in a house. A sign has 30 degrees. I'm getting too technical for you now, I can see you glazing over and this isn't really the point of my story. So, imagine it's a pizza cut into 12 slices. Or a clock. Either way. The chart starts at the 9 o'clock position, that's the ascendant. Sometimes that's called the rising sign. I'm sure you've heard of that. It is sooo popular now.

The child had stopped talking.

She was in kindergarten or maybe it was pre-k. Saturn was in her first house. The first house goes from the 9 o'clock position to the 8 o'clock position. There was an entire stellium in her 12th house. That's the 9 o'clock position to the 10 o'clock position. The first house begins with the ascendant, 9 o'clock and goes counterclockwise. The sun was in her 12th house among this stellium.

Oh, a stellium? Of course, I should define my terms for you. It's when there are more than 3 planets in a house or a sign, if you use whole sign houses. But, I promised not to get too technical. You just have to know that when the planets travel through the chart, as you progress it or look at transits, the planets are going counterclockwise. What that means is that all those planets in the 12th house will eventually, as you look at the progressions, get to the same degree as the planet Saturn in the birth chart. They're all going to hit that planet.

Saturn is the planet of Fate.

There's probably nothing you or I can do about it. The planets have their own timing. This child, with Saturn in the first house, she never got to be a child, really. Saturn grows people old. The first house is what a person is born into, and this child was born into adulthood, really. Something in her childhood environment was not letting her be a child. Consequently, she went mute.

She was four or five that year. Her grandmother died. She was overheard to tell the four-year-old across the street who came by to say how sorry she was that her grandmother had died. I have no idea where this child got this idea. Perhaps some sort of religious training. I don't know. Are people still doing religion? Anyway, the child was overheard to say, "Don't feel bad for me, Anita." That was the name of the little girl across the street. This little girl, Zoe, continued, "Now I have an angel in heaven looking out for me."

Yes, that was what she was reported to have said. The mother brought this child's chart to me.

Did the child give permission?

I have no idea! Are you about to go ethical on me? I know that's an issue, but the mother was my client and she brought her daughter's chart. The girl was in kindergarten. After all! I didn't see it as an ethical dilemma, that I was looking at someone's chart without their express permission. It was the client's child.

And all those planets in the 12th house. That's always too much for a young person. All this introspection. No wonder she went mute. 6 people died in the course of that year. The year the child went from pre-k to kindergarten. The planets from the 12th house passed over that Saturn in the 1st house.

First, she lost her grandmother. She passed. Yes, I mean she died. And then the grandfather was very ill. His death bookended the other four. After the grandmother, there was the father's cousin's wife. The family didn't go to that funeral. It was a little distant and between the grandmother dying and the grandfather having a heart attack, where he didn't die, but there was a long recovery. Then there was an uncle in Chicago. The family did go to that. It was the grandmother's brother. That was sudden, it was a car accident. Then the child's godmother, who was affectionately known as Grandma Bethie. Hers was a long slow ride through the big C. That was traumatic for the child. The family went to the funeral parlor and the little girl refused to get out of the car. She wasn't stupid. She knew what was going on. She knew it was another death, another loss. So first one parent stayed with her in the car. Then the other. That way each could pay their respects. The child said, "That's too much death. I don't want to go in." Such maturity to know her limit. Like I said, she was never meant to have a childhood. Yes, that's what Saturn in the first house often does.

Then the grandfather died in the hospital. Congestive heart failure. He was in his 90s, being that he was considerably older than his wife, the first to die. It was at his funeral that she stopped talking. But, I don't know the child personally so, I'm just getting this from looking at the chart and with all those planets in the 12th house, she could have stopped talking to us here. Gone mute. But with all those planets in the 12th house, I bet, I'd bet anything, that during that year, she kept talking to the angels.

K Pasa

Tom Hazuka

My blind date wants to meet at K Pasa, a dorky name for a restaurant if I've ever heard one, especially since I don't think the food there is even Mexican. I'm not sure what it is, Polish maybe, or Jamaican.

She probably plans on breaking up with me. Ignorant people claim that can't happen on a first date, but I know better because it has happened to me, and more than once—twice, to be exact, which I pride myself on being. Precision counts in this world. Otherwise, we might as well live in a zoo. I know what you're thinking—ha, ha, this world *is* a zoo—and all I can say is ha, ha, you might be right, but I don't live my life that way.

One good thing about K Pasa, at least I can walk to it and not waste money on an Uber. It's only a mile and there's sidewalk half the way. I'll get there early and if my shirt is sticking to my back, I'll duck into Pinky's Liquors across the parking lot and dry off in their arctic AC. I'll peruse the champagne section and watch the window. With any luck I'll see her drive in. Odds are she has some terminally cute car like a yellow VW bug. She'll check her makeup in the rearview, because they always do, right? Then I'll know she's meeting someone, and odds are it's me. When she walks in alone—smoothing the skirt on her flanks? tossing back her casually perfect hair?—I'll leave Pinky's empty-handed, with a casual mention that they don't carry the vintage I'd sought.

Should I shave? The Internet says a two-day beard makes women's hormones kick in, they can't help it, but mine is three days going on four so there might be diminishing returns. Love is a complex thing to navigate, and I don't care what the chat room experts say, most of the voyage is in uncharted waters. I break out the Barbasol.

OK, smooth as a baby's butt for Sugar Lips. If I have a beer now that will be one less I'll be tempted to purchase at K Pasa's undoubtedly inflated prices. I wonder if she's the type to order the most expensive thing on the menu, insist on going Dutch, or somewhere in-between. There's $91.47 in my debit account, so I'm good unless she spends like a Kardashian. If that happens the least she can do is chip in.

Why did she pick K Pasa? She mentioned something about reading a review, but you know how women ramble on, if you paid attention to everything they say you'd be as crazy as they are. Maybe her uncle or somebody owns the place and she's trying to keep the sinking ship in business, though in that case we might at least get a free dessert or appetizer.

I'll take this can of PBR for the walk. I'd hate to lose the deposit, but maybe I'll find a bush to stash it behind and pick it up on my way back. That is, if she doesn't hand me the keys to her car to drive us to her place for unbridled carnality till dawn.

Hey, it could happen. From a law-of-averages perspective, the universe might decide that I'm due for such an eventuality.

Put the Binaca bottle in your pants pocket, even if it does make a suggestive bulge. Masking beer breath is worth the awkwardness. If she says, "Is that a Binaca bottle in your pocket or are you just happy to see me?" you'll probably need both of the prophylactics in your wallet tonight. Think of a witty comeback to that line during the walk to K Pasa.

Well, that beer disappeared in a hurry. This one for the road tastes even better. Damn, barely to the sidewalk and I need to go back and whiz again. Is it going to be one of those nights? Trip after embarrassing trip to the K Pasa pissoir? She'll probably grin and make some snide remark about Flomax.

Shell out perfectly good simoleons just to listen to her get on my case? Screw that.

I've got three more PBRs, a pack of hotdogs and my favorite self for company. I exit my bathroom and turn on the tube. Say what you like about me, but I'm no fool.

The bitch was probably going to break up with me anyway.

Frozen Eden on the map of lost places within the Arctic Circle

Tanya Delanor

> Celia remembered how her grandmother always began her stories with "It was the farthest north they had ever been …", never with "Once upon a time …"

The total of all of her tales wrapped their way around the Arctic Circle, mapping aeons of legend. In Celia's mind, she pictured skipping from berg to berg, skating over wafer ice, and sailing in a ghostly ship on a never-ending voyage of ice and mystery, accompanied by the little girl ghost her grandmother promised was looking over her.

Celia struggled to remember the lyrics of a song about loss. She hadn't meant to spend the evening in the pub. But the weather changed for the worse, and after leaving evensong at the Arctic cathedral, there was nowhere else to run. Her hotel was on the other side of town. Too far to risk without a soaking.

And then she remembered.

Some think it's brave for a woman to travel the world alone. If you're careful, Celia noted, you can remain invisible. Look confident, she learnt, after studying the European businessmen who always seemed on a mission. Nobody can touch you then.

Even the man at Heathrow, who mislaid his case on a connection from Oslo to the Philippines, would eventually find his way home. As in all the best songs, one wonders what lies overseas; one sails, if one is brave enough, and if one survives, then one returns home to … Never mind all that, decided Celia.

The musician started playing another song. While Celia had never grasped more than a handful of Scandinavian words, she soon recognised the tune, and of course the catchy chorus to 'Har du Fyr'. At first she guessed the title meant 'Heart of Fire'. She was wrong. It translated literally as 'Do you have fire' but there was no question mark. A puzzle. Celia liked puzzles. She had all the time in the world for puzzles. Google produced 'Have you a light?' This made more sense, for that would explain how the singer initiated a conversation in song. How the singer grabbed the attention, by asking somebody who was already smoking to light his cigarette also.

Celia's husband had been a heavy smoker. But that really was another story and not relevant to 'Har du Fyr', although the person who came up with the song might possibly have lit up a fag or two along life's way.

Celia Googled a full translation of the lyrics. It reminded her of her research in a former life when she worked as an intern for a lecturer who specialised in Ancient Nordic culture. She came across the meeting point of three different cultures, the Vikings, Sạmi and Fenns, and decided to write her own version of the song which encapsulated the merging of time, peoples and ideas:

> Do you have a light, old friend?
> And I'll tell you a tale of
> A far-away land, as far as it's
> Possible to sail,

In a ship with a fragile cargo on
A voyage across the sea.

They say that when God made
The Earth, he said, Let there be
Light with the sun, the moon and stars,
But those left behind were forever
Doomed to fly in the wind,
The fog and dark night.

Do you have a light, old friend?
A house by the sea that survives?
Do you have lanterns to guide you
To your path? A lamp that glows and
Brings you home again?
Or do you wander, as I …

Again Celia remembered …
The tale of the drowned priest,
And how the lake was named for him.
The walk she had taken despite being drunk.
Her cries and screams for help.
But nobody heard her in the howls of the storm.
She hadn't dressed sufficiently.
There is no such thing as bad weather, they said,
Only bad clothing.
Celia had never been bad. Not really.
Before she slipped into a frozen coma, she recalled …
A man telling a joke badly …

For a time, Celia dated a PhD student writing a thesis on fungi, and evenings in the bar with him were gripping. When after three vodkas and orange, he said the word 'underland', he regaled everybody with tales of how fungi see our world as their underland; radioactivity never fazed their activities, whether it be from Hiroshima's blast zone or the sarcophagus at Chernobyl. 'Indeed,' said Dr. Phil, 'they positively thrive where humans dare not tread.' When somebody asked, 'What about climate change?' the good doctor assured them that our future was fungi.

Another all-night session informed them of the legacy of the Anthropocene. The following night Celia dreamed it all through: she was standing at the iron doorway of the burial chambers at Onkalo, reading the sacred text: *We shall tell you of what lies underground. This is a warning to future generations. This waste was created after the manufacture of nuclear weapons, aka atom bombs. We believe we have an obligation to protect future generations from the hazards we have created. This message is a warning about danger. We urge you to keep the room intact and buried.*

Along with good historians, and poor futurologists, when Celia walked up to the podium to collect her degree, she was on a packet of Consulates a day. She and Phil broke up, then. It was a fading away rather than a row. 'Look after the little one,' he said, and walked off down the road towards the station. Just before he rounded the corner, he did one of those little sideways kicks, both feet in the air at once. Then he was gone. Like water, he had no roots; he was just passing through.

He lied to me. He took you away with him. Celia's little ghost girl protector.

Yet after all those years, she found her way back to Celia. Cheeky little thing. All the time she was there hiding within that frozen lake *waiting.*

Echoes of Loss

Joan Leotta

In the autumn of my life, now I feel much closer to the season that echoes my age—when leaves skitter across our cement drive, some colored, some dead brown before they fall and propelled by chilly breezes, pile at the base of our neighbor's pine tree. Then I must endure his annual phone call, instructing me to come and rake the leaves that he, having planted an evergreen, has avoided. At first I was indignant at his loss of civility—after all, it was not my fault the wind considered his lawn as fine a resting place for leaves as mine. I never tell him that leaves at the base of his tree would compost and enrich its soil. Instead, each fall, I silently rake the detritus into a small pile, take it to the curb.

If only this small loss of civility were the only indignity my autumnal years must endure. No, it is the larger losses that fill my heart. My own sight quivers on the verge of darkness until the right surgeon manages to overcome my hereditary condition and restore clarity to my lenses. My other neighbors, one by one, began to send out notices of the loss of a pet or this illness or that, and then last year, the heavier notices came, by email, by telephone, in person—the loss of their spouse. Five widows joined us last year as we attempted to remain thankful in this time of loss. Their solo status left my husband Joe, as the only male at the table. Yet, we are not strangers to sorrow, to the loss of someone who should be sitting at the table, laughing, joking with us all.

Twenty years ago, our beloved son, Joey, at age nineteen, stepped off a curb while crossing the street on his college campus and instead of reaching the other side to continue with his errands, he crossed into paradise. This loss echoes through our lives, especially loudly at the holiday—our Joey enjoyed them so very much. Yes, there are those who have written that their children are not lost, unlike a misplaced pen or notebook. Yes, we know where he is as the others do, according to their faiths or lack thereof (in which case, the comfort place is the cemetery).

This loss echoes in all I do, every day. From the time I wake up and miss him passing by my chair while I finish a second cup of coffee—the way he would touch my shoulder and whisper, "Love you, Mom" as he passed by. Sometimes, at the grocery store, I find myself reaching for cinnamon bagels or cranberry juice as if Joey were coming to visit.

My own loss of agility, my own health struggles, losing even my mother, father, older relatives, these echo in a minor key, through my autumn. They are so much a part of the season, that the sorrow they engender seems a part of the wind that blows those leaves of memory across the lawn.

It's much harder to accept the out of season loss of Joey, at the time of his life when he was on the cusp of leaving the spring of childhood to enter the early summer of life as a young adult. Joey's loss does not merely echo; it resounds like a cymbal in my psyche even now.

When he left, I felt the world shudder. Clocks and hour-glasses shattered. Time's shards pierced my heart.

It is easy to accept the losses of my old age, the normal flow of my life now in deep autumn. Soon, I will be in winter. Soon, I myself will become a loss.

He spoke to her in dreams

Ken Cohen

He spoke to her in dreams. She'd stir in her sleep when she heard his voice punctuated by the ticking of the grandfather clock.

"Soon," he'd whisper. "Quite soon."

"What will be soon?" she'd mumble, her eyes tight shut, her mind drifting.

She'd sense his presence. Not just in the room. Not just next to her. Not just whispering in her ear. But stroking her hair. Touching her cheek. Smoothing her brow. It was strangely comforting. Oddly reassuring.

"Don't be afraid," he'd whisper.

"Afraid!" she'd reply, tartly, her body tensing, her muscles tightening. "When was I ever afraid?"

"Don't be afraid," the voice would repeat, every word caressing her soul.

She'd lie in the darkness, unearthing deeply buried memories of decades past.

It had been a blistering afternoon. They'd driven to town chattering happily as they searched for somewhere to park.

"Wait here," he'd said, switching off the engine. "Just need some cash. I'll only be a minute." He'd crossed the road and headed for the bank. She'd sat in the car watching the bustling shoppers, humming a tune she'd heard earlier on the wireless.

She'd tapped her fingers on the bag on her lap, wishing he'd hurry.

He'd been gone ten minutes when a car pulled up outside the bank; a Vauxhall, she'd thought. Or a Ford? Black, she'd told them later. But then, she'd conceded, when pressed, it could have been dark blue. She hadn't really been watching but she'd thought three men jumped out. Yes, maybe there had been four? They were dressed in dark blue jeans and black hoodies. Or black jeans and dark blue hoodies. But they were all wearing balaclavas which she'd thought odd on such a sweltering day.

Why should she think anything of it? She was waiting for him. Minding her own business. Distracted by someone along the street she'd thought she'd recognised.

When she'd looked again, the men had disappeared. Maybe they'd gone into the Post Office. Yes, it could have been the bank. But it could equally have been the launderette on the other side. She'd not been watching.

"It all happened so fast," she'd told them between sobs.

She'd opened the glove compartment in search of the bag of pear drops he'd usually kept for her. She always loved a pear drop. None to be found. She'd fiddled with the fraying straps of her handbag as she looked for him again across the street.

Then there was the sound of a car backfiring. Yes, she was sure it was a car. No, she couldn't tell where.

Why would she think they were gunshots? She'd peered through the front windscreen but ... nothing! She'd turned, craning her head so she could see through the back window but still; nothing. Then she saw them again, scrambling into the Vauxhall. Or the Ford. Yes. It might have been dark blue after all.

She'd opened the car door and climbed out. It was a miracle she hadn't been hit as she ran across the road. A split second and she would have joined him. Maybe, in the weeks and months that followed, she wished she had? But the car swerved, and she reached the other side.

Blue flashing lights.

Sirens.

Police tape stretched taut across the pavement.

"You can't go in there," the officer said, his arms tight around her so she could scarcely breathe.

She struggled against his hold.

The officer's grip grew stronger. "You can't go in there," he repeated. Then, with a little less ferocity, "Honestly, it's better you don't."

Better for whom, she'd wondered?

Later they'd told her he wouldn't have suffered.

What did they know? They couldn't have asked him. "Did you suffer? Did you feel anything when the bullet tore through you, splintered your ribs, ripped through your spleen then bore into the wood panelling behind? Was it instant? Ah! You felt nothing! Well, that's alright, then!"

So many years later, she remained unconvinced. But she always remembered their kind words and empty gestures. "I'm sorry for your loss," they'd said. As if she'd mislaid her keys, or left her cardigan behind at the shops.

When he spoke to her in dreams, she always asked. But though his words were soothing, he never answered. He was always just as she remembered. Just as young. Just as neat. Just as well-groomed. A hint of a smile, perhaps. Calm.

"Please tell me you didn't suffer."

He'd smile in the dark, and she'd immediately feel better.

She missed him so much, yet no matter how lonely she felt, she knew she was never really alone.

And she knew in her heart she'd be with him again.

A lovely little City

Kenneth M. Kapp

The real estate agent bubbled with enthusiasm. She had passed her license examination two months prior. "I've the perfect house for you. I know you'll love our *lovely little city*." She glanced down at her clipboard. On top lay some background information on the Kellys, Anne and James, recent graduates from Boston University, moving west for teaching positions with their state college. "But I wanted to make a slight detour on the way so you can see my favorite peak while there's still snow on the upper levels."

Faith pulled into a trailhead a few miles from the base of the mountain and continued, "Plate teutonics [sic], just like the knights of old. They push up more on one side – we got the steep side – than the other. So the road to the pass at the top here has lots of switchbacks. You can see them going up the side right there. And now there's that new slash going up and stopping – it's called a runaway truck cut-out. In case the brakes fail on the way down, trucks can go up the ramp until they can stop. All the people in town call the road to the scenic pull-off at the top 'The No Brake Rise.' You'll be able to see it from either of the homes I'll be showing you. And since everyone here loves to hike in nature, that's why I took you here first. Now let's see that first home I told you about on the phone."

★

The Kellys decided to rent an apartment near the University, but two years later, when both of their contracts were renewed and Anne became pregnant, they contacted Faith and asked about one of the homes she had shown them initially. It was still on the market. James said he had the whole summer to whip it into shape.

Kate, the oldest Kelly child, was 16 and going to be a senior. Her hair, a bright pink her junior year, was now a cerulean blue. Her parents encouraged her to fight the good war for equality for all. "Equality is a foundation stone of civilization." Hair color is a minor skirmish on the way.

Most high schools have a rite of passage when students enter their senior year. Here, senior boys would pair up in August and have until Labor Day to make the run up to the scenic pull-off at the top, switch drivers, and make it back down in under five minutes – the qualifying time. Anything over and you were called a wuss and had to wear a green bowtie to school for a week. The winning pair were guaranteed dates with the co-captains of the cheerleading team.

Parents who grew up in the *lovely little city* knew of this ritual but were unable to put a stop to it in spite of several fatalities on the race to the bottom.

This year Kate and her friend Shelly decided it was time for the girls to break through this gender barrier. A couple of beers gave them added courage and they bragged to one of the timers at the bottom of the road, "We win, we get to go out with the captain of the football team and the basketball team. And tell those Yahoos they'll have to brush their teeth first!"

Shelly drove up. Kate was behind the wheel on the way down. As the car rolled over, Kate kept count: E – QUAL – IT – Y, E – QUAL – IT – Y, E – QUAL – IT – Y, until the car landed and burst into flames.

The Kellys stuck it out. University jobs for couples were hard to find and they had tenure. Their other child, Ted, was seven years younger than Kate. He missed his sister, but his parents kept him busy with seasonal sports. He didn't need cautioning about the senior rite of passage. There was now a memorial plaque at the bottom of the hill – Catherine Kelly was the fourth name from the top.

Seventeen years after Kate's fatal race, Ted who worked in Tampa, flew back to help his parents move. They drove up to the scenic pull-off at the top of No Brake Rise one last time. Looking over the *lovely little city* Ted said, "You're going to really like your condo on Middle Key. Beautiful white sand instead of the snow and about an hour's drive up to Tampa where I work. There's not a mountain in sight."

The language of grief

Sandra Arnold

Language often fails when we try to describe a bereaved person. Phrases commonly used, such as 'breaking down' and 'losing control', are those used in describing dysfunctional machinery. Grief is spoken of in the same terms as an illness from which people 'recover' and 'return to normal'. To describe the bereaved status of a wife, husband or child, the words *widow*, *widower* and *orphan* are used. Unlike some cultures, such as Israeli, there are no words in the English language to describe a bereaved parent, yet parenthood is an existential fact, not merely a sociological description.

Evelyn Waugh in his satirical novel, *The Loved One* (1948), and Jessica Mitford, in her explicit exposé on the American funeral industry, *The American Way of Death* (1963), describe the way traditionally direct terminology referring to the dead and their disposal was supplanted by funeral directors with invented, indirect vocabulary. Such words as funeral director for undertaker, caskets for coffins, floral tributes for flowers, loved one for corpse, slumber room for laying-out room, cremains for ashes and memorial park for cemetery or graveyard, became the norm in the USA. In the decades since Mitford's book was published, many of these terms have been adopted by other Western countries.

The vocabulary used in Western societies to talk about dying is often euphemistic and clichéd. Such euphemism is exemplified in the Death Notices columns of local newspapers. Instead of the unambiguous 'died' we see 'passed away', 'peacefully at home', 'suddenly in hospital ...', 'slipped quietly away', 'goodbye ...', 'gone to Heaven,' 'laid to rest'.

Avoidance of direct language is also found in condolence cards which show ethereal scenes and messages such as 'time will heal', 'we are sorry for your loss', and 'your loved one is in a better place'. Many of these cards reflect Western society's traditional stance on the correct way to grieve, which is to move through stages, let go and move on, while cards acknowledging the first-year anniversary or beyond do not exist. Platitudes and expressions of divine will such as 'It's God's will' and 'God loved your child so much he took her back' are extremely unhelpful.

The difficulty the non-bereaved sometimes have in empathising with the bereaved is encapsulated in an article in the *London Review of Books* (2007) about the missing English girl Madeleine McCann, who was allegedly abducted at the age of four while on holiday in Portugal with her parents, Gerry and Kate McCann. The writer of the article, 2007 Man Booker prize winner Anne Enright, says, 'I was angry at their failure to accept that their daughter was probably dead. I wanted them to grieve, which is to say, go away'. This extraordinary statement is made worse by Enright's lack of understanding about how grief may be expressed as she berates the demeanour of the McCanns during television interviews. 'I find Gerry McCann's need to influence the investigation more provoking than her flat sadness'.

Callous though Enright's statements appear, studies of bereaved parents (Dean et al., 2005; Grinyer, 2003; Riches &

Dawson, 2000) have shown that those who have not undergone the emotional trauma of losing their child can never fully empathise with those who have. This was exemplified for me when friends and colleagues stayed away after my daughter, Rebecca, died from cancer at the age of twenty-three. Some told me later it was because they didn't know what to say. One colleague who did come to visit said, as he was leaving, "Well, you're lucky you have two other children."

Collectibles

Niles Reddick

Magnolia Park is located in the older part of Burbank and is also where many of the hipper antique stores, independent coffee shops, and fantastic bookstores can be found. Manning had been in the collectible business since he and his wife moved to Burbank in the 1950s. Marie had started as a secretary at Warner Brothers, but before she retired after thirty years, her title had become administrative assistant. Her job duties hadn't changed, but she had never complained and had loved her career at Warner Brothers. She'd told Manning, "It's the symbol that survives, like the WB one on the water tower."

Manning had responded, "You're always right." He'd brushed her cheek with his fingers, and when she died of a massive stroke, he brushed her cheek and said, "I'll miss you, Marie."

It had been Marie's idea for him to open the shop, and he named it after her: Marie's Collectibles. Through the years, he'd scooped up some nice antique pieces in Burbank, pieces he located at early morning garage sales. If the garage sale was at an actor's house, that was an automatic mark-up. He'd collected and sold a wooden ironing board from Doris Day, a broach from Jane Wyman (President Reagan's first wife), a signed copy of *To Kill a Mockingbird* to Robert Redford, and some weights from Denzel Washington.

In addition, Marie brought home anything discarded at WB, and if there was a story associated with it, that was pure profit, profit to put their daughter through UCLA, pay cash for her first car, cover her wedding expenses, and help them with a down payment on her first house, a bungalow near the Frank Lloyd Wright homes and Griffith Observatory that overlooked Los Angeles.

Collectibles Marie rescued from the dumpster were an ashtray Bette Davis used in her dressing room that Manning had sold for twenty dollars; a hairbrush used by Joan Crawford that brought fifty dollars; a broken watch left behind by Douglas Fairbanks fetched two hundred dollars; and a broken cap gun used by John Wayne that brought nearly five hundred dollars.

If Marie and Manning became aware of a major change in society, like the development of cellular phones, they scooped up items like rotary phones or phone books. They even found several Burbank phone books with Johnny Carson's photo on the cover, and those items brought high dollar. When there was a lull in business, Manning expanded. He added an online store on eBay, which increased his sales to worldwide audiences who might never visit the Burbank store. Success followed, and he and Marie had talked of retirement, moving into the Santa Monica mountains.

When Manning arrived at Marie's Collectibles a few weeks after Marie had died, there was a rare rain coming down, and he stood under the checkered awning, opened the door lock, heard the bell jingle, and smelled Marie's perfume. It wasn't overwhelming, but just a brief whiff, and he heard her words, "It's the symbol that survives." It was as though Marie whispered it in his ear.

Manning knew it was truth. The actor doesn't survive. While the film or television show technically survives, it isn't constantly shown. The times don't survive. The one thing that survives is the symbol, like the WB symbol on the iconic water tower. Recently, in a video tour, Ellen DeGeneres welcomed visitors from the small balcony that circled the tower, but Manning's friend Ralph who was a retired teacher and had taken a job as a tour guide told him: "They filmed her in the studio and projected the image of her onto that balcony. It would be way too dangerous to hoist her up there." It made sense to Manning.

Warner Brothers had sets that were used over and over like the New York Street set complete with an overhead subway track. From *Yankee Doodle Dandy* in 1942 to *Wonder Woman* in 1975 to *Friends* in 1994, the New York Street set had survived. The Jungle Lagoon was another example of a set that first appeared in the 1956 feature film *Santiago*, later in the 1993 Spielberg film *Jurassic Park*, and again in the 2018 film *Aquaman*. The Midwestern town square with a gazebo was used in feature films from the 1960s such as *The Music Man* and *Bonnie and Clyde* to television series like *The Dukes of Hazard*, *The Gilmore Girls*, and *Pretty Little Liars*. Viewers were not aware that these sets appeared in multiple films or television series that spanned decades or that they might be rented to other studios who were scouting for sets.

Marie's whisper prompted Manning to pick up the phone and call his friend Ralph.

"Funny thing you should call," Ralph said. "I was just thinking about you. They've tossed these signs from the New York, Lagoon, and Midwestern sets in the dumpster that haven't been used for years. Making some new ones. You want me to get them for you?"

"Absolutely," Manning said. "Signs bring a great price." Manning knew he would get top dollar for them. He added, "Glad you are on the inside of the studio fence. Since Marie's gone, I need someone to get me some treasures, so I can supplement my Medicare."

"Supplementing Medicare is the main reason I came back to work. That and to see if I can get discovered and be an extra in a film."

"They've already made *Cocoon* and *The Golden Girls*. It would have to be a new film or show with Seniors."

Ralph laughed. "Yeah, you're probably right. I'll drop the signs off later this afternoon."

"I appreciate it and I'll split the profit with you."

"Sounds great."

Manning hung up the phone and knew Marie had steered him in the right direction. Their love and marriage bond seemed to survive death. He'd see to it these new collectibles, too, would survive long after he and his friend Ralph were gone.

The Gift of Losing

Tom Fegan

Several years ago, as I crossed the Dallas County line in my new model red Dodge pickup with big wheels and roll bar with lights, I promised to find myself again.

Years prior to this I had departed for San Antonio, Texas to seek the success I felt I deserved. The bigshot of sorts I dreamed of being. A layoff at Dallas-based Texas Steel had occurred. My manager and friend Joe Lomax was retiring. Bill Wilcox, his assistant, took over and my position was eliminated. Recession stormed nationally across the country. With unemployment benefits, I ventured to South Texas. My furnishings I placed into storage until I was settled. A furnished apartment would be suitable for my plans. All I needed was provided. I had prayed for help in that matter and received the answer. Joe Lomax wished me well and told me to keep in touch.

A set of apartments that advertised for a night or a lifetime became my temporary home. I visited a nearby state unemployment office and transferred my account. I rented a post office box and opened a bank account. My Toyota Camry was in good running condition and so I began the job hunt. Weeks passed and discouragement began to overshadow me until I walked into a one-story office building to apply for a logistics position. Job references from Texas Steel secured the position for me immediately. The company was Monclova

International Steel. I was hired by their international office. The parent company's plant and home office were in Coahuila, Mexico. Their storage facility was in Eagle Pass, Texas across from the Mexican border town Piedras Negras.

With exuberance, I began the following day. I was responsible for the outbound truckloads out of Eagle Pass to clients in the U.S. and Canada, as well as auditing freight bills, tracing railcars along with conferring over regulation matters for commercial transportation. I implemented changes and raised the level of standards for the company in a short period of time. I studied Spanish for a semester at a junior college.

Former cohorts had teased me about working for Monclova Steel International and their noted history of zero logistics practice. Within two years the jokes ended. I was proud to be employed by a Third World nation business that was beating to death major U.S. steel companies because it was cheaper to import our products than buy theirs domestically.

During this period, I had got rid of my former furnishings and stylized a singles pad with modern furniture perfect for hosting ladies. I bought stylish clothes and found a hair stylist, too. My Toyota I traded in for a new model Dodge Ram Pickup that was fiery red with roll bars and lights that adorned the top. Oversized tires as well. I thought it gave me a flashy appearance. It was worthless and impractical. The apartment complex I was housed in was loaded with many like me as well. Weekends were for partying, except for my weekend reserve meetings.

I joined a group of singles called San Antonio Professional Singles. A college degree was necessary to belong. Thusly my romance interludes increased as did my drinking. Hangovers were more common than before as were failed relationships that could have led to a worthwhile union. A dream I always had; to settle with one woman and raise a family. Booze blockaded this. I would set out at night for one drink and leave after "last call." In a conversation with Joe Lomax, he asked if I was still attending church. "Hangover mass," I joked.

The Episcopal Church I was a member of had a five o'clock mass on Sunday. Perfect after a Saturday night of partying. Soon drinking-based activities were all that I imbibed in.

A quota system placed on foreign steel importers by President Ronald Reagan phased out my position. After a few more nights on the town, I filed for unemployment and phoned Joe Lomax.

He was direct with me as he always had been as a manager. "Your reports on partying were amusing but even I noticed a change in you. You used to give a damn about yourself and others. I saw this coming. Yes, it was a lay-off but I know that your drinking expedited the decision. I have dealt with problem drinkers before. Some got help and others left, and their lives cratered. What plans do you have for yourself?"

I could not answer, only ask for help. "You are welcome at my home. Rent will be paid but you must seek help. Your life is not over." I thanked him and agreed to the terms. I had lost myself and had adopted an unsuitable lifestyle. Ego overran common sense. With women I sought only what I could get from them rather than a worthwhile life with one. Once I ended the conversation with Joe, I hit my knees in prayer. I took his deal.

Joe Lomax had a room prepared for me and restated the deal he was offering along with a phone number of a charity-based counseling practice. I phoned immediately and was soon in session. I stayed on unemployment a few weeks longer.

Through counseling I learned I was alcoholic and joined a support group to aid in my staying sober. I needed a job. My time in reserves had ended with an Honorable Discharge and I secured a position with a private security company.

I remember as a child stating I wanted to help people when I grew up. In this profession I found my calling. I have dealt with medical emergencies, domestic disputes, protected others from harm and prevented criminal incidents by using my head and prayer. I have been promoted to supervision and live in a small one room apartment. My vehicle is a practicable Honda Civic. The gift of losing opened a locked door where I found myself again.

Pale Green Walls

Mark Donnelly

I moved in yesterday to this old wooden house, a two-story white job. I'm in the top floor apartment and out my window I can see woods. Most of the leaves have fallen, but there are still some bursts of color here and there on the trees. Nice oranges and reds. I like the contrast when they mix with the brown ones on the ground. I took a little walk this morning. Plenty of leaves on the trail and I kicked my feet in them, shuffling along like a kid again. I always enjoyed this time of year – playing in the leaves, hearing that crunchy, crinkly sound when you walked through them, jumped in them, threw them up in the air. Freedom.

I'm gonna have trouble with the walls in this apartment. Maybe because they're such a contrast to the leaves. These pale green walls. Not inspiring. Institutional. I bet the landlord got the paint cheap. I didn't pay attention to the color when I scouted this place. The price was right, and I needed to move in fast. Now I'm faced with them. Overcome by them. But it's not just the walls. My first Sunday night here and I've got that sad feeling I used to get back in school. Homework due tomorrow and I'd rather watch TV. All these years later and I still dread Monday mornings. Add to that the tension over a new job.

Kathy leaving … that shook me … bad. Deadness to the heart. After the divorce I just couldn't stay in our apartment on

Long Island anymore. Couldn't or wouldn't stay in the area even.

It's different Upstate. Less traffic for sure. Wonder how it'll be working for a weekly here. Not the same action as a daily back on Long Island. What the hell. I'm not a kid anymore.

When I interviewed at the weekly, I didn't even think about the walls in the newsroom. Probably white, with books piled all over and photos pasted up. Maybe not lots of books – we're all geeked out with the Internet now. I really didn't pay much attention in the interview. Kind of drifted through. But the walls are not green like these. That much I'd remember.

Too busy yesterday to notice these walls in the light, humping stuff up with Tom's help. We just dumped it here, then grabbed some beers and a bite at a local bar. Last night I was so exhausted I just plopped on the bed. Tom headed home to the Island. Said he had to get back to see his girl, it being Saturday night and all. I was out cold till this morning. Then the walls hit me.

This cheap furniture sure follows me around. Junk from before I was married that I stored. Wonder what new stuff Kathy bought besides what she took with her from our apartment. Our wedding furniture ... Wonder what she's having for dinner ... She always was a good cook. Not like me with the hamburger and peas in my one frying pan and pot. No curtains on these windows ... no shades even ... tacking up bath towels and my extra set of sheets till I buy some.

What a bum ... have to find a store during the week. Probably at that mall off the highway. I hate the measuring part about curtains and shades. Women always know how to do that stuff. For certain Kathy sure didn't move into a new place like a nomad. She has class.

I feel sort of like I'm in a lighthouse here. No water nearby, it's not that – but being on the second floor with no other houses close by. That wind rattling through the windows – here at the end of the block – more like the end of the road …

Great, Riley. Way to psyche yourself out. Better change the attitude so I don't fuck up my first week. From *Newsday* to the *Libertyville Leader.*

Just keep telling myself that a newspaper is a newspaper is a newspaper. I've got the writing, listening and observation skills, the intuition, and the instinct. So why can't you apply listening and intuition to your personal life? Why couldn't you?

Now, veteran writer, you can report about abandoned hope and the wretchedness of living in this beautiful country escape you've chosen …

Have to keep my head on straight and not go drifting off about Kathy like I've been doing all these months. She's gone for good. And I'm here on the edge of this strange town. That gray sky late this afternoon really brought me down … And I thought I could handle it. Lone wolf. Always trying to make it on my own … that's what Kathy said … that I couldn't share what was going on. If she only knew how I felt … like I was spinning inside a washing machine most of my life. Then I became the lighthouse that couldn't give off a signal. Couldn't bring her into anything. Couldn't give her safe harbor. Couldn't let her be mine. Distant.

An old, battered lighthouse. Maybe it's the chipping white paint outside. Maybe it was climbing those narrow, rickety, creaky stairs. I CLIMB THE LIGHTHOUSE TOWER TO FREEDOM! Sure. Plenty of freedom … A crumbling lighthouse with no light … because you couldn't open up to your own wife.

You're at it again … Mr. Self-destruction. All problems handled internally … Was it me who drifted out to sea or her? You! You shut down because you couldn't open up, show your pain. Fear crippled you, man. How many times did you pull away before she finally got sick of reaching out? Stop. Getting nowhere, this inside-the-head talk. Sleep, wake up fresh tomorrow. I'll go out early before work and walk in those leaves, feel the crunch again. Maybe pitch a piece on the beauty of fall for children to the managing editor.

The Psychic

John B. Elliott

The four of us were at a bayside restaurant, not paying attention
to the boats passing by or the pelicans floating on the bay. We
were finished with lunch and Barry, as usual, was the most
talkative, which at the time we didn't mind since we were
relaxed after the meal and our minds were only half listening to
him.

Evelyn, his wife, gazed at him with the indulgence of one
who had often argued with him but now had a resigned
acceptance of his foibles. She had decided that his personality,
which never accepted he might be wrong, was beyond
changing, and the effort of trying to do so not worth her energy.
Today, there was more amusement than usual in her smile, and
she listened indifferently as she tapped a fork against her water
glass like a metronome.

We'll have a female president in our lifetime, Barry was
saying, in fact, both a female president and female vice president
at the same time. I'm certain of that. But before that happens,
there will be a bad recession.

Anyone could predict that about a recession! I said.

Yes, but not the president bit, and I can predict something
about everyone in this room if you'll give me the time.

Evelyn looked at my wife, Alejandra, and the two of them silently stood up and left for the restroom, an event so common no words were necessary.

Barry continued without missing a beat: See that couple over there? She's young, very attractive in a natural way, very little make-up, and he's middle aged, probably an MD or an IT executive. He's managing the 18-month-old, doing all the work, elated to have the child. The thing is, she'll stay married to him until their child is eleven or twelve, then divorce him, take him to the cleaners and, newly rich, find some executive her own age.

How would you know that?

He smiled broadly. I'm psychic, Marco, just accept it. And that woman over there, the obese one, she's already on insulin and she'll soon have a heart attack. She won't live more than three years after that.

Maybe, but I know a lot of older heavyweights who are living beyond expectation.

Not her, he retorted. Now look at that young kid at the next table, he's twelve I imagine. He'll get hurt at summer camp this year, a bad cut or a broken leg or need to be rescued from drowning, and that mother of his will freak out and not let him go to camp the next year.

If you're psychic, why don't you know which way he'll be hurt?

I do! Exactly as I said, all of them. He'll fall from a boat and his femur will cut through his flesh. The injury won't let him swim, so he'll have to be rescued.

Any good news in this crowd?

Not much, but that guy there, the one with a light beard and wearing a baseball cap, he'll get a dog this year and meet a gal while he's walking it at the park. You might say that's good news … at least while it lasts, he added with a grin. I told you, I'm psychic. Look at that couple next to him—divorced by the end of the year.

I wasn't about to ask him about myself or Alejandra. We have a good relationship and I didn't want to hear that something bad was going to happen. So far, most of his predictions were sorrowful.

That thin lady, he said smugly, has cancer but doesn't know it.

I shook my head in hopelessness, then saw my wife returning. I was happy because I wanted to make my escape. Evelyn wasn't with her, and Alejandra stopped several tables away and started a conversation. She's good like that, sociable, having an easy manner I envied.

Barry continued: look at the people sitting alone. Every one of them is reading their cell phone. If we had been here a month ago some of them would have been with someone, and I could have predicted for you which ones would have had that relationship killed by now. Then you would have seen the proof that I'm psychic.

He smiled, then added: Where have our wives gone off to—did they elope?

He laughed at his witticism, and frankly, I was getting anxious for Alejandra to return. We were going to summit Montecito Peak that afternoon, and I certainly didn't want to learn Barry's prediction about our outing. I said: Wouldn't you have known if Evelyn and Alejandra were running off together?

A joke, man. Of course I would have known! But tell me, don't you think the two of them would be good in bed together? I'd like to see that.

I held my tongue. Sharing anything like that fantasy with Barry is the last thing I wanted. Thankfully, Alejandra returned to the table. Barry looked at her with a quizzical look. She shrugged.

After realizing Alejandra had nothing to say, he asked: Where's my wife? Where's Evie?

Don't you know? she replied.

Know what?

Alejandra was again silent.

What's going on?

Alejandra sighed. I thought you would have known. She's left you.

You're joking, aren't you? You two are playing a practical joke on me! He smiled with the joy of one in on the game.

She told me to tell you she took out half of the savings yesterday and an additional amount to see her through until the divorce. She put a deposit on an apartment and will need to get groceries, pay utilities and so on. And she took the car. She said we should give you a ride home.

Barry's round face flushed red with humiliation. He took two rapid breaths. Perplexed and trying to speak, his lips moved, but no matter how hard he tried, he couldn't push his words out.

The Hint of an
Almost Invisible Smile

Alan Kennedy

Winter's ebbing gasp snuffed the life out of the day Pierre lost the only two people he ever loved. That morning, half a century ago, a black haze billowed from nearby charcoal kilns when the last surviving Villeneuve buried Daisy and their unbaptised daughter. Inky snowflakes powdered down over the rock-hard mud. Three spades broke before his scalding tears melted the frost enough to fill the grave.

Pierre left his shattered heart and shredded soul in the village where the Villeneuves had lived for generations. Like a sunflower searching for warmth, he drifted from village to village, from job to job, from bad to worse.

Thirty months in a cardboard box factory, a year as a debt collector preceded three winter seasons as an artists' model in a Parisian attic. His senses clouded by substantial quantities of illegal liquor and opium, Pierre consumed endless, mindless hours; silent, still, naked.

Quarts of numbing absinthe left him incapable of imagining further than the following day until, moonlighting as a jazz club bouncer, he married the owner, Fleur, became the stepfather to her fifteen-year-old twins and woke up.

Six months after the ceremony, a fondness for cosmetic surgery, fresh masculine meat, ever smoother-faced youths blossomed in Fleur. Not once, but at least five times a month. Sometimes she invited Pierre to join in her midnight games, but, except for a young sax player with the same cadence and features as his Daisy, he always declined her kind offer.

Incapable of feeling anything as strong as desire, hate or jealousy, Pierre cared little for her infidelities. Fleur could do whatever she wanted with her body as long as she signed the club deeds over to him.

Her boys, Yves and Jacques, waged a virulent campaign against him. They cut off two of his fingers, dripped acid on his only photo of Daisy, laughed about his impotence.

The twins, as it happened, wouldn't survive long enough to contest the will. War found Yves and Jacques collaborating with the occupying army, and hanging from the apple tree in the yard once peace came.

Their mother never discovered who had turned them in, and, after a costly but botched operation to restore her tear-furrowed face, Fleur wilted away petal by petal.

With the meagre sum he hustled for the sale of the club, Pierre rented a room in a medieval village on the Atlantic coast, bought a typewriter, reams of paper and scrawled out steamy features for one of the many sensationalist magazines that sprouted after the war.

He lived that way for twenty years, selling his scribblings and sordid anecdotes under a name that wasn't his.

In his darkest, yet unfinished novel, he wrote that only two heartbeats are relevant. The first and the last. The others are merely there to mark time. The duration of life is mirrored in a sigh. The depth of the inspiration and how slow the out-breath is all that matters.

It was a stormy morning many years ago, when Pierre Villeneuve buried his two loves. That same raging Arctic blast greets him on his return. Hunched over their tomb, he clears away the weeds, polishes the tarnished nameplate, prays.

Uncoiling years tighten his chest. He wants to share his fast-approaching last breath with them. A weak, poppy-red sun peeping out between the clouds illuminates a heavily pregnant Daisy's youthful features on the pewter plaque.

As Pierre stretches out on the marble to slake his decades-old thirst with her image, the hint of an almost invisible smile ripples his face.

Exercises for a Tender Heart

Catherine McNamara

Do not move with a sudden lateral motion, for you may lose your precious balance and, once again, fall. Go forward, towards all obstacles, tackling these with your full frontal horns, for in this way the heart will be dissuaded from participation, preferring more interior acts. Ignore the prevailing weather with its telling seams, find sections where these seams have been unpicked, and slip through with your slender body. Or this can be vacated, left somewhere safe.

Ignore signs, guidance, prattle, for trees rise as green nibs from the soil, usually caught between crevices where they pilfer nutrients.

Sully your clothing and make sure this sullying reaches your skin. An earthen sullying or the prickles at ground level in a meadow, or the sea sluicing, given you can fly.

Stretch. Further. You are made of beams. And when the beating is a bomb, and the cascades shooting through your atriums are blue with hurt, stay there, be with your ticking, your fruitless archery. Wait for cadences, changes of key. The F sharp minor chord through the mesh of your lungs, a buzz through the ribs.

Curve. Don't forget there is a soul in there, the great anticipator, the *I-told-you-so* made of short cusps, the revelling past lives that you drag on and on, recidivous, the milling audience in your gut. Hold your breasts in your hands, their loving lenience. The heart is close, it is moments to the left, performing sticky gymnastics that would dry out in the sun.

My Father

Fran Blake

My father sits most days. A blanket covers his body up to his chin. He remains incredibly handsome, especially considering his advanced age, but his body reveals all the difficulties he now has.

My father and mother were very much in love. They were a couple nearly reaching the status of urban myth, so known for their interest in one another. Their song was "In My Reverie" and every day I hear my father singing it now though he laughs at himself because it was my mother who had the splendid voice.

My father remembers one hundred years but not always clearly. Time is out of order. Yesterday, he held my hand to warm it. "Why are your fingers so cold, baby?" he asked with concern. He wrapped my left hand in the edge of his blanket— he is always cold now and rarely sits without his throw upon him—"now let me warm the other," he said.

When we were little, my father would gather us around him and ask us to sing for him. I suppose his recall of songs is his way of maintaining contact with a past long gone. My mother died with her face raised to the sunlight whispering their love song, "Make my dream a reality; come to me in my reverie."

Sometimes now I sit with my father holding his hand or I let him lean his head against my shoulder. Sometimes if I hum a tune, he smiles and throws me a kiss but other times his blue eyes get teary and my stomach tightens. I feel so much sadness for him.

There are many ways of losing everything and old age is one of them. For a while, we accrue experiences and knowledge and friendships and then our minds cloud over; our friends die and our knowledge is forgotten. I tell my father to please try to remember who I am. That loss would be so hard to bear.

Dad sings, "*Last night we met and I dream of you yet.*"

"I don't know that song, Dad? Sing it again."

"I can't carry a tune," he says sadly. "I'm a lousy singer."

"*Last night we met and I dream of you yet with the wind and the rain in your hair.* That was the one playing when I met your mother."

"Yes, you sang it very well. C'mon, Dad." With my fingers, I comb the hair from his wet eyes.

"Our love is a dream but in my reverie," he sings.

"But what about the wind and rain?" I ask.

"Nothing matters," he says. "Rien, rien. You know what that means? Nothing."

Post Script

Joy Mawby

'You want me to teach you English?' I was incredulous. He was Polish, 96 years old and had lived in England for fifty years without learning more than a smattering of the language. As this went through my mind, Konstanty Wladyslaw Nieczuja Dzierzek was nodding enthusiastically.

And so our lessons started.

Each day, he peered at a different photograph in his ancient album and haltingly, tried to explain it, often aided by his daughter. I wrote down the story which lay behind the picture and together we read what I had written.

I saw photos of his family's stately home, Palac W Michalowcach, of him fishing, shooting, on a fungus foray. I learned that he had attended a Russian public school alongside the Tsar's son. One photo showed him as a highly decorated colonel in the Polish army.

One day, he held his album up in front of me and said, 'Before war this. After war – nothing.' And he shrugged.

I'm not sure Konstanty's English improved much but he loved to talk about his youth and his days as an officer and gentleman.

He didn't talk to me about his life in wartime. After his death, however, I was given access to Konstanty's translated diary. I discovered that his father had been a pioneering railway designer and that Konstanty had worked with him until he joined the army.

He recorded his capture by the Russians, of never seeing his mother again, of transportation to a Siberian labour camp, of torture but then being freed when the Soviets joined the Allies.

He had shown me his Monte Casino medal, during one of our lessons, although there is nothing written about that battle in his diary.

He wrote that at the end of the war, he found that many of his compatriots were stranded in Soviet-held territory, homeless, hungry and hated by the Russian people. He used his knowledge of the Russian language and psyche and of the railway system in his mission to help thousands of them leave Soviet-controlled territory and reach safety. He was often hungry himself and just scraped by. Meanwhile, his reputation grew and later he was awarded a medal for this resettlement work.

Konstanty came to England after a spell working for Polish intelligence, in Italy. He became commandant, of a camp in Cheshire and continued his task of re-settling his countrymen and women.

Finally, he and his uncle managed to scramble together enough money to buy a damp old house in Manchester, into which Konstanty moved with his wife and daughter. They took in lodgers to help make ends meet. The only employment he could obtain was in the local Dunlop factory, hard, unpleasant, and unhealthy work.

At weekends, he was a volunteer for Polish charities. He helped to run 'Pogon', a paramilitary group, in the belief that a new Polish army would return one day to reclaim their homeland. However, world leaders decided that Poland should be one of the prizes awarded to the Soviets for their part in winning the war against the Nazis and Konstanty knew, then, that he could never return home. A couple of his friends who did, had simply disappeared.

Now he threw himself into other Polish causes. He raised money to build and maintain a Polish club, church, priest's house. He supported the Saturday club for Polish children and helped to set up Polish scout and guide groups

Although he took pride in all these activities, he never recovered from the bitter disappointment of not being able to return to Poland. Even after the fall of the Berlin Wall he could not return because it wasn't *his* Poland any more.

He remained, for ever, a stranger in a foreign land.

As the years passed, the people who had known Konstanty as an officer and gentleman died and his status in the Polish community died with them. His mother and brothers had been lost during the war and of course, he had lost his true home and his homeland. Konstanty died in 1997.

★

Konstanty's death certificate recorded his occupation as 'manual worker'. When I read those words, I thought of the ingenuity and the courage he had displayed while fighting for his people in so many ways. The piece of paper, in front of me, seemed to sum up Konstanty's final loss.

Clichés

Tim Love

When Bert Bacharach died, his songs were playing everywhere – on radio, TV, even in shops. He'd praised Hal David's lyrics – they touched so many people's lives because they talked about what mattered. Though each of us thinks our love is unique, the clichés ring true. We make our own magic moments from them.

A few months later Berlusconi died. I must have been one of the few people who wept on hearing the news. My late wife was Italian. We watched the Italian news each evening while we ate, and he was usually on it. When we met new people, his name often came up.

Grief reaches out from kitchen table to the country lanes where we used to walk, the sunsets and stars. Its unique details spread until they merge with the unique grief of others, into the supermarkets where the music plays, where I see an old couple suddenly hugging in tears by a 2-for-1 toothpaste promotion and I so much want to go up to them, even though I'm not old, to tell them that whatever happens, it's been a good life.

Jaquith

Chris Daly

My creative writing instructor wasn't "William", he was Bill or another name I can no longer remember which he sometimes went by for a reason I may have never known. Bill was a speed freak, naturally I think, and in the jam-up of ideas things could get in the way and his own writing had a tendency to go off the rails, or so he often said. If teachers, like coaches, break down into two types, he was a player's coach, with the associated strengths and weaknesses.

What's a good writing teacher? Like most he was ok, he was not crazy. I remember him more as a person I knew and talked to. "How many?" the question (not from me) might be when he came in the room, and he might answer, "four and counting." In another, the personal insomnia might have been too much info, but Bill was peeled open, maybe more than he needed to be for his own good, and was more than good-natured about it, and practiced a sort of advanced form of self-deprecation. He liked to cite a funny bit about a kid learning to stutter when made to hold the nail dad was whacking.

He was one of the boys at Cal State Long Beach with the poets Locklin and Stetler and before that he was one of the boys at Cornell with Pynchon and Farina, both of whom he claimed stole words right from his mouth to put in their books. I believe him. He could imitate Nabokov drifting off into a frenzied daydream in mid-lecture. Bill lived his classes, he was a method-teacher.

One story. There was a certain gentleman student of limited mobility who used to situate himself on a bench in the main hallway in front of the library and emit a constant stream of what sounded like over-vocabularized automatic writing. Since coherent dialogue was not possible, most people faded him into the woodwork, which made his rap take on that much more of an edge. Some of us young intellectuals liked to meet the challenge now and then of playing the anarchy game, drawing out his theatrical, embittered persona, but the guy was good, the best I've seen, you could not get a remotely straight sentence structure out of him, you could throw a big rock in the stream but the water just coursed around it.

One day Bill somehow corralled himself into giving the one whose name was not readily forthcoming a ride, dealing with the chair and the whole bit, and for his trouble the anarchist, sensing a good nature, put him through all kinds of shit via the medium of mumbo-jumbo, my teacher was still stuttering (we were both laughing) the next day as he recounted stopping just short of dumping the guy we referred to as The Oracle in a heap on a random corner.

You remind me, he said one time, of Alyosha in Karamozov. Which one is that? I asked. The innocent one, he said. I said, likewise, I'm sure.

If it took a rare asshole not to like Bill, he was not necessarily ready to back down when that individual came along. One night in a bar in a part of town he didn't need to be in he got in a fracas which ended up outside and a week later at a small memorial I heard something about his head and a concrete curb. I got lucky that night with one of his later students. About this I might have heard some shit.

May have been the same year I stopped in at the new campus tavern and there at a big table, not exactly the life of the party but no wallflower, was the anarchist gone social. After a manner I congratulated him, though it felt somehow like a commiseration.

Remembering Ira

Meryl Baer

Ira and I were never close. Our moms were friends. Ira and I attended different elementary schools, but the same junior high and high school. We saw each other occasionally, passing in the halls, and infrequently hung out together. We did not have a lot in common. Our friends did not overlap. I did not participate in a lot of school activities, and Ira took part in less.

Ira was a geek, although that term was not used back then, the middle of the 20th century. He was short, thin, gangly, and sported thick, black-rimmed glasses. He usually wore a white shirt and slacks. Most everyone else switched to more casual attire. He was one of the smartest kids I knew and seemed a bit off; in a private world I could not enter.

We did not stay in touch after high school. I did not see Ira again until twenty years later when we met at our high school reunion.

It was the late 1980s.

Dr. Ira worked at a hospital in a major city out West. I was not surprised when he told me he was gay. Looking back, I knew. But we didn't talk about the subject of sexual identity openly, or furtively, back in the dark ages when no one came out during their teen years in a public high school. Girls were girls, boys were boys, and anyone internally questioning their identity did not candidly discuss their feelings with peers – or anyone, for that matter – afraid what people would say or do, worried they would be bullied, shunned, or worse.

Ira was not the only closeted gay in my world. One of my girlfriends had a crush throughout high school on a football player. Nothing happened. At the same reunion where Ira and I reconnected, she saw her high school crush once again. He confided to her that he knew she liked him, but didn't say or do anything because he was gay. He worked in finance, a conservative field, and, although the 1980s were supposedly different – more tolerant, more open-minded than years earlier – the ex-football hunk had not yet openly declared his sexuality.

Ira was unlucky enough to be born a few years before he could honestly express himself.

Ira and I caught up on each other's lives at the reunion. At one point he announced, "I'm sick. And I'm going to die. Don't tell your mom. My mom doesn't know yet."

Ira's mother knew he was gay, but had no idea he was sick. AIDS devastated the gay community, but Ira still looked healthy and continued to work full-time. As soon as Ira and his friends realized the severity of the scourge striking their population they began to take precautions.

But it was too late for Ira.

Less than two years after our reunion, Ira died. I mourn the loss of a bright, educated, caring person. I wish we could have been closer, but in the dark ages of the 1960s I was naïve about sexual identity issues, he was struggling with inner torments, and neither of us could bridge the gap.

Capsized

Cheryl Snell

We stacked up the decades like laundry, losing track of details just passed through; only looking ahead. Now, our house floats by on the river of forgetting, brass knocker rapping against the door. *Who's there?* we ask, even as sorrow enters. It has taken years for our belongings to slip into the water, cliché first. Youth, beauty. Health, happiness. Age, wisdom. We wait patiently for some to surface again. Here they come, out of context, altered – a glimpse from blue eyes now filmed over, a set of knuckles like keys left in the sugar bowl, the same question echoing in a soundproof room. You, a flicker of light upon a spine, lean out the windowsill, taking inventory. There's Father's silenced heart, the lungs your sister drowned in, her scarred synapses a series of dominoes collapsing. There is nothing to be learned from all this, no lesson, just as there is no reason why you should turn inside out over a pair of gloves left in our wake, earmarked for oblivion. Yet you pick them up and shake them like the hand of an old friend whose face you had almost forgotten, but whose features you would recognize, if you ever saw them again.

Sam

Lucia Cascioli

Sam.

I uttered, giggled, tsked, whispered, and cooed his name so many times, I could wrap it around the world twice.

He's been the man in my life for 15 years. Always pawing me. Flopping on my couch. Eating my food without complaints, and up to no good now and again. He's the one who nudges me awake before my alarm clock screams. Panting for attention.

Sam is my dog.

What were you thinking?

If ever there was a need for a furry, four-legged friend over the last 730 days, twelve hours and nineteen minutes, it's been during this time. If ever there was a need for unconditional love, it's been during my entire lifetime.

I never really knew what love was until I looked into Sam's deep brown eyes. He's golden. A retriever to be precise, but his colour seeps through to his core.

There's something about a dog who smiles and wags his tail every time he sees me. Sam speaks with his eyes and they never disappoint. We may not speak the same language, but we understand each other perfectly.

As a bonus, he's kept me fit over the years, chasing squirrels and rabbits, the scent of a fox lingering on Saturday morning dew, or a mourning dove waddling across the driveway teasing him until a last second takeoff. He'll bring me one, someday, and dump it on the welcome mat before grinning and kicking his hind legs to make his point.

I say this knowing it won't be true. Sam is going to leave me soon. He has the C word. I can't even say it. It's spread. He's on meds for the pain, yet he still smiles while my heart breaks.

His love has healed me, but I can't heal him.

If there is a heaven where our souls can meet again, Sam will be there to vouch for me.

Here boy.

Knife-a-geddon

Alex Reece Abbott

"Helllllll-p me!" Von jiggles, she wriggles, she steps back and wriggles and jiggles some more.

"Canya wait till half-time?" Greg bellows from the lounge.

Compete with the All Blacks in a test match? Nah, Von knows the score. She looks around her new streamlined galley kitchen they saved up for years to buy. She mutters to the shining slow cooker. She glares at the stubborn bastard knife drawer that's stuck again. Won't open. Won't close.

"Wassaproblem?" Greg keeps his eye on the oversized station clock, a prop propped against the kitchen doorframe. Von points an accusing finger at the drawer, now gaping two centimetres. "Ahhhhhhh," he exhales, in that Grasshopper tone that really gets her goat. He gives the drawer a gentle ruckish shove. "Nahhhhh. She's jammed. Suppose you've tried — "

"— The spatula, the egg slice — *and* the tongs. No joy. I think one of those damn santoku blades is wedged."

"Ahhhhhhhhhhh." Greg swirls the dangling waistband cord of his rugby shorts like he's warming up for a *poi* dance.

Von flicks his sensible, furry, tree-trunk thighs with the damp tea towel. "My brand-new drawer!"

"Your *very* old father." He scratches his salt-and-pepper cactus jaw. "Amazing really. The Old Man's in care with his dementia, and yet - without fail - he still remembers to send you a set of kitchen knives every feckin' Christmas — "

" — And e-v-e-r-y bloody birthday. Jamie Olivers. Fujiyama Mamas. Messerschmitt 501s. The Gourmet Selection by Jean-Claude Poncez. QVC channel has a lot to answer for. If he buys one more set of staysharp knives ..."

"Have another word with the manager at his care home." He runs his hands over the jutting drawer, trying to gain some purchase to shunt it open. "And you could maybe get one of those — "

" — Don't even go there." Her inner Marie Kondo screams *Clutter!* A knife block on her new counter does not spark *her* joy. It reminds her of a very long Neighbourhood Watch meeting about knives on display being a weapon-invitation for slabby, stabby burglars.

"There's people out there ..."

Von shakes her head.

"People who'd really appreciate a nice new knife set. Or five."

She grimaces. "I can't."

"Ohhhh ... you don't want to lose them cos they're from your father? Re-gifting is very environmentally friendly." Greg gets coaxy. "All these knives ... they're only going to waste sitting in your brand-spanking-new kitchen ... babe, y'could keep one or two sets and give away the rest. No need to tell The Old Man. And even if you do ... he's never gonna bloody remember."

Von rolls her eyes. "You can't give away a powerful object like a knife as a present because then you lose power — *and* giving a knife severs the link between the giver and the receiver." She sighs. "Bad luck."

"Superstition." Greg puffs out his cheeks. "Though, to be honest, I wouldn't mind cutting ties with your Old Man — I've never been pick of his crop."

"Very funny. He said *you* are an acquired taste."

He jerks his thumb in the direction of The Game. "Duty calls."

After the match, Greg rattles the drawer again.

Von winces. Full-time score: Fourteen all. "Gently."

He sucks his teeth, signalling that a great insight is about to be imparted. "Sorry luv ... might have to take the bugger apart." He sighs and jangles the loose change in his pocket.

She grins. "Eureka! Got any cents?"

"Bit rude, babe. I'm Mensa material ... they just don't know it yet."

She growls. "Dosh. Wonga. Moolah. Spondoolicks. I'll give The Old Man ten cents for every set of knives, then we're buying them. See! That'll stop the bad luck that's jamming the drawer."

Greg taps the drawer. "Ummmm ... I think ... even allowing for a dollop of ... ahem, bad luck ... that your conflict between your current quantity of knives and the capacity of your drawer is contributing to your ... jammage situation." He wrinkles his nose. "Babe, we've got a fundamental storage problem here. Do we *really* need nine knife sets ... or do we need a bigger drawer — "

" — And munt my whole design?" Von slaps the marble counter. "No! We'll give him a few coins for the knives, then they're not gifts."

"Yeahhhh ... do we really want to encourage him by giving him bloody money? We're already living in Knife-a-geddon." He tilts his head. "You could always open a cooking school."

"Ha-fucking-ha. No knife, no dinner."

He grins. "Hon, trust me, a knife shortage is not your issue here. I'm getting a ruler to unjam your unlucky knife collection from your *very* unlucky drawer. Don't sweat it."

Von's shoulders drop. "Oh, thanks — "

" — Pick one set, then I'll put the rest of his knives on eBay and hoping that the police don't arrest me as some knife-fetishising-mass-murdering-mofo-terrorist-nutter."

She blows a kiss. "Ohhhhhh, thanks babe. I'm going to email his care home and ask that bloody manager to stop The Old Man from ordering stuff. And then, *I'm* gonna do something *really* nice for you ..."

Greg grins. "Yeaaaah ... ?"

"Ohhhhhh yeah." Von smirks and pulls out her *Edmonds Cookery Book*.

Hidden Treasure

Jan Howcroft

Mum died a month ago and my sister and I have come to clear the house. I'm on the carpet wrapping ornaments, Heather's upstairs; she's finished clothes and wants to sort the jewellery.

There's not much: Mum's watch and her engagement ring; a locket from the seventies with our photographs inside; a string of pearls; some sandstone beads I brought her from Nepal.

The room's almost empty now, apart from furniture. Heather lifts a blue glass bowl from the dressing table and underneath the pink and white check runner there's £60 in ten-pound notes. She gives me half; it's the second stash of money we've found.

This afternoon we're going to the crematorium to scatter Mum's ashes. My father was the director of the crematorium before he retired; it's where our parents used to live.

'The flowers look nice,' I say, as we drive in through the gates. 'Dad would have liked that.'

The house is now the office. I knew but I'd forgotten. Suddenly it seems a very different task. To allow a bit more time, we park as far away as possible

'That used to be the junk room,' I remind her, pointing at the net curtains as we cross the tarmac. 'I see they've repaired the crack.'

'I don't remember that.'

Round the front by the hedge, where there used to be a gate, there's now a line of monuments on display. They've extended on the front of the house and built a ramp and porch which lead into the main office.

The new reception is what was once our parents' sitting room and while the secretary picks up the phone, I try to match the space to photos I remember from their Ruby Wedding, but it doesn't seem to fit.

A door opens.

'Would you like to come this way?' the director asks and we follow her into the hall, past the stairs and into a small rectangular room with a desk and computer.

Something caves in underneath my rib cage and I'm back: that first Christmas when the sanders were on strike. Home from Goldsmith's College. 'Song for Guy', 'D'you Think I'm Sexy?' playing over and over on the portable tape player; sitting in here trying to write an essay on mixed ability teaching, although I've yet to step foot in a classroom. The wallpaper's two shades of green on a cream background, in a textured woven pattern.

Another day. Aunty Bessie and Uncle Eli sitting at the table, facing the lawn, my back against the window because we've pulled the table out and it's a tight squeeze. Mum's bringing in a cake stand with slices of angel cake and home-made buns. I'm listening to my dad regale some story I've heard at least five times before. Mum's smiling. Eli's face is red with laughter and he's mopping his eyes with a handkerchief.

'We can't be in here,' Heather says and we head back into reception and out onto the ramp. I'm staring at a massive oak, the one my kitten ran up and had to be rescued from with a ladder and a mop.

'I'm sorry,' I say to the woman. 'That used to be our parents' dining room. My father was director here in the eighties.

'Oh, of course,' she says, 'I'm sorry I wouldn't have ...'

'You didn't know ... can we do this in reception?'

Inside I look around for chairs but there's only one, so we stand over the reception desk and discuss memorials like we're ordering online furniture. Then it's time.

Our mother's ashes are brought from a back room. The room where she stored her dress materials in egg boxes; where my dad typed documents on an old Imperial; where seedlings sat on window sills poking through compost.

Heather walks back to the car. She doesn't do ashes. I walk with the deputy. It was the same man when I came with Mum eight years ago, to do the same for Dad.

'Your father gave me my first job,' he says. 'He was a lovely man.'

We walk to the tree with the urn.

'Today Daphne is reunited with her dear Herbert ...' he reads. I have a manic urge to laugh so I focus on the plastic-covered paper till he's through and wonder if they ever bother to read it when they're filling in the names. Then he pauses for me to remember them.

It's evening. They're beyond the hedge behind us, in their garden. Mum's weeding in a sun dress; Dad's tying up the beans.

Suddenly a high-pitched squealing from the cabbages – a baby rabbit with its foot caught in the netting. It's tunnelled up inside the vegetable patch and has been destroying brassicas for weeks. Dad picks it up, threatening to wring its neck and while he struggles to remove the netting from its paw, it screams.

'Poor little thing,' says Mum.

'Go on then,' he says, releasing it. 'And don't come back, or I'll have your guts for garters.'

There's a dead blackbird on the grass and I'm about to pick it up when the man starts emptying the urn and the ashes fall in zig zags on the grass but I'm prepared: this time I do not weep. He walks away and leaves me then. I wonder where my mother is. Wherever it is, it's not here.

Back in the office, the receptionist asks me for twenty-seven pounds. I look in my purse and all I can see is Mum's money from this morning. Suddenly it's the most important thing in the world not to use it, like it might save her in some way. I rifle through my purse looking for something, anything, else. Time passes, too much time. I'm fumbling and I don't know what to do. Two of the twenties are mine but by now, the receptionist will think they're counterfeit. Anyhow, she has no change, so there's no choice but to hand over Mum's hidden treasure. I doubt that's what she was saving it for.

A jammed-up heart can't keep its beat, so how can time heal it?

Jude Potts

Her heart didn't break.

It just jammed up with sick slicks of regret, sharp shards of pain, coils wound too tight without you to release them. Cogs turn uselessly without making contact. It ticks an erratic beat, sometimes so slow she barely feels, barely feels, then-its-too-fast, too-fast, nopauseforbreath-or-thought-just-plough-on-through-it-full-of-caffiene-anxiety-and-last-night's-wine.

She doesn't want to 'put herself out there'. She doesn't want to 'meet someone nice'. She doesn't want to just see whether she'd get on with her neighbour's son, her workmate's neighbour, her best friend's boyfriend's brother.

She

doesn't want

to bother,

because her heart's jammed up with you and your lazy smile and your soft voice and your eyes that pinned her to the floor and made it impossible to breathe unless it was to breathe

you

in.

She doesn't want to join-a-site, set-an-age-range-and-the-number-of-miles-away-someone-should-live. She doesn't want to scroll through men who visit Machu Pichu to stand and have their photo taken; who want to meet up, hook up, get hung up on her pale blue eyes that never meet theirs because

they

are

not

yours and they cannot hold her heavy gaze.

Her heart's a barely ticking thing because you were the space between beats, the hope, the dreams, the heat that kept her heart beating in time.

And hasn't she tried to unjam it?

She's walked endless beaches, joined night classes, learned Italian, thrown pots, joined a joyless choir, bought a damned dog.

Hasn't she tried to slam-it-back-to-life-with-nights-out-and-too-much-drinking-and-casualfucking?

But-men-who-weren't-you-have-mouths-that-taste-wrong, -move-to-rhythms-that-feel-wrong, -stroke-too-soft, grind-too-hard;

are

not

you.

Fleeting pleasures let her lose herself in friction but twist her heart into complicated coils of betrayal, guilt and regret.

They tell her time heals all wounds and she wonders how much time. One year? Two? Ten?

Her heart's rapid-rattle rips through her like bullets and she knows there is no healing. It can't keep time, her not-broken heart that just keeps on beating long after she wishes

it

would

just

stop.

So she curls around the dog in a well-worn spot and they howl until her voice is hoarse and she tastes the sharp tang of blood. Her swollen eyes close, she breathes gently in time with the snoring dog. Inside something slowly uncoils and her heart holds time for a few beats.

Ketchup Sandwich

Flemming George

Sam squeezes the last of the ketchup onto a slice of bread and slapping another bread slice on top, makes a sandwich. He drops the empty bottle into the bin and using the order of service from this morning as a makeshift plate, places the sandwich on the kitchen table.

He slips off his black suit jacket, loosens his tie and sits down.

He turns the pages of a newspaper and skims through the news. He stops on a headline:

"Shortage of table sauces leaves shelves bare in supermarkets following row with brand giants over inflation."

"Damn. I haven't left any ketchup for the kids," Sam says, turning his attention back to the sandwich.

The shadow cast, where the two slices of bread meet, resembles a grimacing, downturned mouth.

"Please don't look at me like that," he says to the sandwich.

Sam hears footsteps and turns around as Maria walks into the kitchen. She rests her hand on Sam's shoulder.

"Are you okay?" Maria asks. "How was the funeral?"

"It went as well as it could do but I feel bad. I didn't know my aunt very well," Sam answers. He glances up at Maria and continues, "Now she has gone and I can't make up for that."

Maria sits down on the chair next to Sam and takes one of his hands in hers.

"Don't feel bad," she reassures him. "You could've woken me. I would have come down and made you some food."

"I know. I didn't want to disturb you."

Maria looks at the food on the table.

"What have you made for yourself?" she asks.

"A ketchup sandwich," Sam answers.

"It seems sad."

"Yes," he says through a sigh.

"Did you finish the ketchup?"

Sam closes the newspaper and nods his head.

"Ok. I will pick some more up tomorrow," she says.

Sam looks out of the kitchen window. He can see snow falling in the orange of the streetlights.

"It's started snowing," he says to Maria. "Let's go out and have a look."

Sam picks up the sandwich. Heading out of the kitchen, he opens the front door and steps out onto the driveway.

Maria sees the order of service on the table covered in crumbs and shakes her head. She pulls on Sam's jacket and joins him outside.

Sam turns to Maria.

"I can't deal with how mournful this sandwich looks. It's making me feel guilty," Sam says and then he hurls it across the drive into the street.

"Condimental," Maria calls out.

Whatever Works

James Bates

We were walking along a favorite woodland path when I turned to Mom and asked, "Say, I was wondering. What's your favorite memory?"

Even though she was slightly hunched over and walked with a cane, she was still a spry lady. She also had a wicked sense of humor.

"At my age, too many to mention," she grinned. Then she winked and added, "But, I'll tell you this, Jack. Walking in the woods with you is among my all-time favorites."

Mom always had a way of making me feel good. Wanted. Something that meant a lot to me since I was one of those guys who was quieter and more withdrawn than most. Expressive and outgoing I was not. Not like my other brother Marc for instance, a successful insurance salesman with friends galore.

I lived by myself in a single bedroom apartment with my cat Ralph near where I worked stocking produce at a local grocery store. A job I liked. I must have, since I'd been hired in high school and now, fifty-three years later, I was still there.

I liked routine. Walking like this with Mom had been a Sunday tradition for us ever since I'd left home and moved into my apartment. We used the time to catch up. It was where Mom told me she was leaving Dad because, as she put it, "I'm sick of his fooling around and womanizing." It was where she told me she had earned a BA degree in early childhood education and was going to begin working with at risk preschoolers. It was where she told me she was moving into the Lakeside Senior Living complex. And it was where she told me she had an inoperable brain tumor.

I was on my way back to the car when my phone buzzed. I grimaced. I had a feeling who it was. I looked at the screen. I was right.

I picked up. "Hi, Marc. How's it going?"

My older brother had strong opinions. One of them was he didn't agree with me "communicating" as he called it with our dead mother. Especially out in public on my woodland walks with her. Too bad. It worked for me.

"Just fine, little brother," he said. I waited for a biting retort but none was forthcoming. Instead, Marc asked simply, "Are you still coming for lunch?"

I metaphorically wiped my brow, glad the two of us would not be arguing, especially on this day, this tenth anniversary of our mother's passing. "Yeah," I said. "For sure. Wouldn't miss it for the world."

I liked seeing my brother. Plus, Marc was a great cook. His nod to the anniversary of our mother's death was to prepare her favorite meal, chicken and rice casserole. He'd fix a simple salad to go with it, and he and I would share a glass of her favorite wine. "Still on for 1 pm?" I asked.

"Absolutely. Like always."

"Sweet. See you then."

A pause on the other end of the line. Then, "Out communing with Mom?" he asked. Then, without missing a beat, he chuckled.

"Yeah, I was."

"Thought so." Another pause, then, "Well, whatever works."

Interesting, I thought to myself. My older brother must be mellowing. Not wanting to break the ice of this delicate détente. I said, simply. "Exactly."

He chuckled again, then said, "Okay. See you at one."

"Sounds good," I said, glad to have dodged a potential brotherly bullet. My stomach suddenly growled. I hadn't realized how hungry I was. "See you then."

★

With the chicken casserole baking in the oven, Marc set the table with cream-colored Spode plates accented by an ivy border, his mom's favorite. He put down a setting for him and one for Jack: a knife and spoon, a dinner fork and a salad fork, linen napkins with wooden napkin rings, just like his mother always liked.

He thought of his mom as he finished setting the table. The divorce so many years ago had been hard on everyone. He'd sided with his father, his brother with their mother. It was just the way things went. Their father had remarried only a week after the divorce was final and within a year, he'd died of a massive heart attack. Their mother stayed happily single for the rest of her life. He smiled. She'd been a teacher, a wonderful grandmother to his kids, and when it came right down to it, a really good person.

He wiped an unexpected tear from his eyes. Honestly, he really did miss her.

A sudden urge came over him. He took out another plate and made up a place setting for their mom, right down to the linen napkin and wine glass. When he was done, he poured a glass for her and one for himself. Then he raised it in a toast.

"Here's to you, Mom. Thanks for everything."

He took a sip and was turning away when he thought he heard something. What was that?

He turned to the table. *Oh, my lord.*

"Mom?"

"Hi, son."

"What are you doing here?"

She smiled. She always did have a nice smile. Open and honest.

"I just wanted to thank you."

"For what?"

She cast her hand over the table. "For including me," she said.

Wow! This is crazy.

It was, too. But, nevertheless, it was great to see her. He smiled. "I'm glad you could make it."

She grinned. "I wouldn't miss it for the world."

So, this was what Jack was talking about. *Communing with Mom.* It felt good. He made a snap decision. "In that case, how about Sunday, I'll join you and Jack on your woodland walk?"

"Your brother would love that." Then she smiled. "So would I."

"All right, then," he said, and sat down next to her. They had a lot to talk about. "It's a date."

The Mumbling Parrot and the Queen

Sally Reno

I

When Beau, with Lori, knocked on his neighbor's door to ask permission to pick a gardenia, she invited them in for iced tea. Because they were neighbors who hadn't yet met, in Key West terms, this was a festive occasion. Mrs. Bell brought a plate of molasses cookies and a pitcher of iced sweet tea out to her back patio.

"I have a friend," said Lori, "who has three good lime trees in her yard."

"ah," said Mrs. Bell.

"And a good well."

"ah"

"So she made gallons and gallons of limeade for her family. Over time."

Mrs. Bell nodded.

"But she was using mangrove honey to sweeten it."

Mrs. Bell winced.

"She's from Vermont."

"oh …"

"Her husband's from Baltimore."

Mrs. Bell looked at Beau.

Beau had heard the story about Lori's friend who accidentally stripped the enamel from her family's teeth. He was looking at a very large and empty birdcage with its door standing open set against a frangipani thicket at one end of the garden.

"There were two of them," said Mrs. Bell. "Parrots. My husband bought them as a mated pair from a dealer in Boca. We called the big one George and the little one Charlotte."

Beau walked over to the cage. He looked back at Mrs. Bell and smiled. The frangipani smelled like striped ribbon candy.

"We learned that Charlotte was actually Jon-Jon which didn't really matter as we had never expected eggs," said Mrs. Bell. "George was … a social problem."

"Because of the swearing?" asked Lori

"No. Well, partly. You expect that with a parrot. At first, it's funny, then it's annoying, eventually you don't notice. George is very vocal and all you can make out of what he's saying are the curses. So we never got past being annoyed."

"*Is*? Not *was*?" Beau asked.

"Oh yes. George is still around. That's why I leave the cage door open. Maybe you've seen him …?"

"So what was the problem if not the cussing?" asked Lori.

"George was very abusive to poor little Jon-Jon. Screamed at him, bit him, kicked him, muscled him away from the food. Jon-Jon complained bitterly but never fought back. He took to plucking out his own feathers. It became rather worrisome. Then, one day George figured out the latch and flew away."

"Problem solved!" Said Lori.

"Not at all," said Mrs. Bell. "Jon-Jon finished the job of snatching himself bald and died of a broken heart."

"That's just weird," said Lori.

"Yes, it is." She agreed. "Now George just flies around the neighborhood, muttering curses."

"Wait," said Beau, "I *have* seen him. He flies around in the early morning. You never see him in the heat of the day or the evening. I always called him The Mumbling Parrot."

"Yes, that's Georgie. That's our boy."

II

Walking into the coffee shop, they saw the newspapers next to the cashier stand. All the headlines said the Queen had died. They did not buy a paper. When the hostess had seated them, given them menus and brought them ice water, Lyle said,

"Once he was gone, she couldn't last."

"I'm going to go all in and have a stack of blueberry pancakes," said Kate. "They seemed to have a good marriage."

"They did seem to but I don't think that's the point. I think it's the longevity, not the quality, of the marriage that accounts for that. Couples who just bicker for 50 years usually don't outlast each other by much either," he said.

"Maybe they despair when they realize that after 50 years of a bad marriage, it's too late for a good one," said Kate.

Lyle laughed, "Could be."

"Are people *fatally* averse to change?" asked Kate.

"I don't know what it is exactly …" he said.

"Quantum entanglement?" she suggested.

"Oh yes, I think so. Quantum entanglement at the least. And cognitive entanglement and existential entanglement. You hold each other's memories and expectations. He'll say, 'Who was that woman, with the hair?' and she'll name some woman 20 years gone and it will somehow be just the person he meant.

And the divisions of labor that were never discussed or decided but become habitual, like one will be the one who always refills the ice-trays until the other one no longer remembers where ice comes from. Grief is ... confusing. And any sort of loss is a kind of threat."

"You and Elinore, 40 years?" she asked.

"Yes, 40."

"Happy?"

"Mostly, I think," he said, "we had a rough start, my fault entirely, but that didn't last too long. I was happy. I think she was happy. I think she liked me. She treated me well. I certainly loved her. Then, at the end ..." He shook his head.

"Are you trying to tell me you aren't planning to live much longer?" she asked.

"No. Not at all. Just making an observation."

"Because if you are, I gotta warn you I'm a poor choice for a traveling companion if you're planning to drop dead en route. What the hell would I do with you?"

He smiled, "If I get an urge to drop dead, I'll try to do it someplace like this. You can prop me up behind a newspaper and you can just walk away. Be sure to leave a nice tip."

"Maybe I'll get a paper ..." she said.

"I'm not going to croak right now!" he protested.

"I didn't mean it that way," she said.

The waitress took their orders, collected their menus, refilled their coffee.

Kate said, "It's just, *funny* ... the Brits don't seem to like Charles."

"They liked Diana." Lyle said. "I'm not sure why. I've never been attracted to coy women myself."

"Me either," said Kate. "About the queen, think how many people were born, lived and died, entirely within her reign, thinking she would be dead soon and they would not. Millions probably."

He nodded. She peeled the lid off a plastic cup of half-and-half, poured it in her coffee.

"Do you ever go out where there are other people all around, mostly or all strangers, and look around and think, 'Soon we'll all be dead.'?"

"No," he said, "I don't." He steepled his fingers and touched his index fingers to his lips.

She looked at him, then looked away, watching for her impending pancakes.

Else

Paul Ransom

Everything is replaced. Day by night. Youth by age. Presence by absence. Even memory, by its merciful twin. Forgetting.

Lest we remember.

As I linger over them for the umpteenth time, the reality is stark. If not for this trove of remnants, there would barely be anything left of you. For it is the photographs that anchor my dissolving recollection. So too this handwriting, swirls on a time-softened slip of paper. You, supplanted by phone numbers and pictures; and by this temple I have imagined. The one made of aches. And myths.

I gather up these bits and pieces. Their weight is insubstantial. Here now, the enormity of it all, lightly contained. Living … replaced by kindling.

There is a clenching in my throat. Like thirst. Like strangulation. A build–up of tension, followed by breath. By letting go.

A cord snaps. I am floating. Giddy. It feels like awe. The indescribable beauty of distance. Its liberating erasure. Formerly sharp details, textured foregrounds, smoothed to broad horizon. Such ordinary transcendence. As though the divine were commonplace. A simple function.

… Next, next, next.

Once, when we carried the burden of mystery on our young and sturdy backs, we measured our unknowing in the metrics of striving and deciding. Novitiates, afraid to be wrong. To be found foolish. Wanting in any way.

Now, in the ocean, we are droplets. In the desert, grains. From afar, I cannot distinguish you from me; and in this way I navigate the brutality of years. Collapsing distance to a semblance of touch. With such tricks I escape the quantifiable tyrannies. Dates. Certificates. Mirrors.

Is this my foolish fantasy? Or rather, a subjective rendering of reality? As with waves, which can be experienced as sound, and sound, which may be heard as music, the further away you are, the nearer I am.

I carry my souvenirs outside. The air is gentle. Like you once were. It kisses me in your stead. Tenderness replaced by twilight.

For years I called your name out loud. Now I rarely think it. We move in lovely silence tonight. Only the birds are singing as I walk to the circle of stones.

You used to light candles to stare at flames. "I wish I could dance like fire," you said. There was often a sadness in your voice. It was how I first recognised you. The echo.

Yet, it is your absence that resonates now. The shape of hollow space. You the empty room, me the walls. Painted by flickering light. The radiant pas de deux of fires outside, shining through the windows of leaving and remaining.

You are not lost, merely somewhere else.

I fix myself in relation to you. As far as you are from me, so I am from you. Hence this fire, which I am fumbling to light. Shaking hands. Hesitation. Last bandage.

When it is done, I will no longer love you with wounds.

These mementoes at my side … one by one they are receding to the distance of ash. Like birds uncaged. Briefly, a flurry of wings. Then, a speck in the sky. And shortly thereafter, the immensity of night.

Here on Earth, the usual sounds. Insects. Leaves ruffling. The tempo of breath. Above, the astronomical quiet. Your interstellar remove.

Looking up, out, I sense it. There is a subtle realignment in my body. The knowledge is physical. This is the difference between losing and realising that nothing is mine, nor ever was. The agony of permanence replaced by the relief of change. Grasping by releasing.

When you first left, it was rupture, something torn from my flesh. Disorientation. Numb progression.

Then, slowly, beauty. The scent of blooms, the salty cooling sea. Another.

Later, gratitude. For your advent, and ultimately, your passing. What is gone cannot be lost.

Now, tonight, the miraculous banality of light years. Impossible, inevitable expanses. You are truly beyond me now; and therefore, beside me. Your warm proximity has become this ghostly configuration. A perfume, barely discernible. Is this what they call diaphany?

One long, centring breath. In. Hold. Out. Exile recalibrated as return. Death as life.

Flames dance, as you once did, before stilling to a smudgy glow and, thence, to cinders. Tomorrow morning, charcoal and dust. Over time, atoms re-purposed. Forms reformed.

I drift back to the house. In the bright electric light, I briefly startle. I too have been reconfigured. And will be over-written again. So simple. Such ruthless grace. Now that I have yielded the weight of old treasure, the space is made for new jewels. The mystic clichés seem true tonight.

A low-level tension across my shoulders subsides. The routine dulling of senses sharpens to clarity. My grief was selfish. A story I told myself. Replaced by this one.

Soon, stripped of triggers, I will forget the guns, and the myriad detail of curated despair will be lost.

In their place? Something else.

Words that Fail and Words that Flow

Miriam Drori

Words that fail and words that flow,
Words that shadow and words that glow.
The most important thing to know?
Words won't change the status quo.

At the time of writing this essay, my husband of forty-five years has been dead for three months. Yes, *dead*, because he collapsed, hit his head and *died* early one morning while I was sleeping. For me, those are the most suitable words to use because they describe reality without recourse to euphemisms. I want to be sure in my mind that this really happened, and the word *died* does this for me much better than *passed away* or *departed* or *left us*. I don't have a problem with anyone who prefers to use those other words. I'm only giving my personal opinion. I seem to be doing that a lot recently. During all the years of my marriage, I was never so clear about which opinions were mine.

"He's better off," appears in the list of what not to say to a grieving person. Yet it's something that I've said myself. I hope no one regards it as callous. Does it become acceptable if I'm the one who's grieving? "He was afraid of what was to come," I've said. "Dying suddenly without losing any of his faculties was, considering the diagnosis, the best thing that could have happened to him." I don't really believe he's now in another place, but I do believe it was for the best.

"Life goes on" is another no-no. I've said this, too, while repeating my current motto: "I will always cherish the memories, but I'm not going to be stuck in the past. That phase of my life has ended; a new one will begin as soon as I can get out of this limbo stage."

When my mother died, twelve years ago, there were plenty of annoying phrases from well-meaning people. "I know what you're going through," was one. *No, you don't*, I thought. *I lost my mother five years ago when dementia turned her into someone else.* What I was going through when she died were thoughts of being a nasty person because I couldn't experience the grief I was supposed to feel, and that phrase made it worse.

"You're so brave," people have said, although I don't think that's true. I'm simply doing the things that feel right for me. Three months on, I'm slightly bothered when someone tilts their head and says, "How are you?" Am I supposed to say something sad? "I'm all right," I reply, and I am because I have accepted what happened and am trying to move on. "You're so brave."

Anyone who knows me knows I'm not the best conversationalist. Even so, I'm not sure why certain words drown in deep water while others are always bobbing about on the surface. When I'm asked whether it was unexpected, I reply with ease, "Yes and no. He was diagnosed with incurable cancer a year before, so we knew he didn't have long to live but we didn't expect it to be so sudden." Yet when they ask what sort of cancer, I stumble over the answer. It's not the name itself, as I've memorised all six syllables of the word *mesothelioma* and always get it right as long as I take it slowly. No, it's the explanation that has to follow that little-known name, especially the phrase: *exposure to asbestos*. Why does the word *exposure* continue to evade the hook of my fishing rod?

"Have you managed to return to your routine?" I've been asked. My answer is that I don't want to return to anything. I want to make changes in my life. I want to feel I'm entering that new phase. When I told a friend I was thinking of moving house, I was pleased she mentioned that she'd once advised another friend to wait before moving from her rambling house and not do anything rash, but realised her mistake when she visited the friend in her new, compact abode.

Advice is always welcome. I listen to it all, but I know it's up to me to make the decisions that suit me best. When I say that to family and friends, my words seem strange and selfish to me. How can I decide anything that's solely for myself? Probably the last time I did that was when I said "Yes" to the love of my life, forty-six years ago.

I recall words my husband said, especially during the thirteen months of living with the diagnosis. "I'm thankful this happened to me now and not when the children were small." "I'm grateful for all the things I've managed to do in my life." Now, as I look around a room adorned with his beautiful works of art and remember our amazing trips to near and remote parts of the world, those words make me smile rather than cry.

Those things people say about loss? As far as I'm concerned, it's not necessary for anyone to worry about getting them exactly right. I'm not about to sever contact with anyone over a word or a sentence. That's just as well, because I've said several unfortunate things over the years and wouldn't have any friends left if they were all so sensitive.

Ghost Shark

Phillip Temples

Ray's gone. I still can't believe it. He'd have been twenty-eight years old next week. In fact, I was riding with him just two days ago. Ray was a good friend. He was a true "shark."

They're holding the funeral for Ray at the UU Parish Church next Tuesday. Just family and close friends. That truck did a number on him. Closed casket. I'm told it would have taken too much effort to reconstruct what was left of Ray's face.

Ray would have wanted to be dressed in his blue and white biking shirt with the spandex jersey shorts. Instead, they will dress his remains in a suit and tie—something Ray would never have worn while he was alive.

Ray didn't take shit from anyone or anything. He held his own on some of the busiest urban streets in Boston alongside the four-wheelers. Once I saw Ray get cut off by a distracted driver only to catch up with the car a few blocks later. Ray pulled in front of the car and slammed on his brakes then he simply glared back at the driver. When the driver honked at Ray, Ray turned and slammed his fists hard on the car. He bruised both his hands. The blow left a noticeable dent in the car hood. The driver wisely decided to leave.

Ray frequently lost his temper with motorists. And he could be downright rude to the "non-shark" civilian bikers. I recall one time when he hassled a middle-aged man and his young son on inexpensive, three-speed bikes, deriding them for going too slow. Yes, Ray could be an asshole sometimes. But he could be equally generous of his time and energy when it came to promoting bicycle projects and initiatives. What can I say? He was a complicated guy.

I've ridden to the scene of the accident at a busy intersection on Massachusetts Avenue between Harvard and Porter Squares, where Ray's friends have erected an elaborate shrine on the sidewalk to honor him. His jersey is prominently displayed. Candles surround a photo of Ray posed with his trophy after winning second place in the Beverly Grand Prix in 2019. There are other knick-knacks there, like: a tire pressure gauge; a set of Allen wrenches; and a pair of half-finger bike gloves.

The quintessential item Ray would have wanted there the most: his Savadeck 22-speed carbon fiber road bike with its hydraulic disc brake and thru axle system. Sadly, the Savadeck was destroyed.

Instead, there is a plain, nondescript street bicycle that's chained to the light post. Everything about the bike—its frame, chain, seat and tires have been spray-painted white. It's a ghost bike—the kind of thing that gives cyclists like me the creeps.

All Ray had to do was yield to the tractor trailer.

Proposition Play

Dee Allen

It's neither a story with ghosts made for campfire gatherings nor the classic children's fairytale variety, but it's my favourite story to tell:

LOS ANGELES 1945

Leaving the studio lot of Twentieth Century-Fox was the best move she'd made at that moment. Results from her screen test were a bust. What young aspiring actress Bettie Page saw was a heavily made-up, whorish-looking character acting in her place, under her name. Hollywood didn't need another Joan Crawford.

One of the biggest, flashiest cars moving on the Fox lot pulled up alongside Bettie and stopped. The big ugly driver in a double-breasted Brooks Brothers suit stepped out, long enough to shower her with compliments and a proposition. Bettie remembered him from the screen test. His was among the many faces who saw her crash and burn while the big cameras rolled for her and fledgling actor John Russell.

The driver told Bettie he was a very important man at Twentieth Century-Fox. His lips spoke of a request to join him for dinner, but his intentions were clear as a brand-new wine glass. He wanted to make her a star—in his own production. Consisting of two characters. Set in a *boudoir*. Her, posing horizontally. Him, the leading man. The only man. No cameras shall roll.

Bettie's answer to the proposal was a cold, hard <u>no</u>. Convincing didn't sway her. With pride wounded, the ugly studio exec got in the last word before driving away, hurled with the weight of a threat: *YOU'LL BE SORRY!*

Bettie Page never made it onto the silver screen in the manner of her girl, box office success and acid-tongued ice queen Bette Davis. She became a star anyway. By-passing the casting couch way to acclaim and acceptance. A glamorous star in the minds of her billions of fans across decades, myself within the enormous number—

Cigarettes

Steve Cushman

You come to me with nothing more than a smile, your hands cold from an early morning smoke on the porch. When I'd said you could smoke inside, you shook me off, said you'd been taught early by your father, then first boyfriend, to smoke outside. Your hands were cold on my neck, my ears, beneath my hair. Our bed warmed you quickly; your body hot against mine. You'd be leaving for college that afternoon, but I stayed inside of you for as long as I could. I wondered how deep I could go, how far you'd let me. *It's all flesh, nerve endings, and blood vessels* my tenth-grade biology teacher had told us, trying, I think, to ruin sex for a bunch of teenagers. But he didn't and it's not. You can't stop the warm flame of a body on fire.

After, as before, you stood at the window, looking outside, wanting a smoke. *Here,* I said, holding the lit cigarette up toward you. You turned, lips parted, as if frightened. I inhaled and exhaled and you walked back to the bed, your hand out in front of you. I watched you smoke that cigarette slowly, gracefully, sweet queen of my world. Fell asleep with my lips against your naked shoulder. When I woke, you and your two plastic storage crates were nowhere to be seen. The only thing remaining was an inch or two of a cigarette dangling from the edge of my white coffee saucer. There were lipstick marks on the butt, so I lifted the cigarette to my mouth, tried to taste a little of you. But it was no use; you were already gone.

Subterranean

Robert Scotellaro

He'd lost his job at the plant and was in the basement where his good-for-nothing teenage son lived. The father found the tightly rolled marijuana joints in a drawer and lit one. It had been many years since he'd smoked and he sat in the bean bag chair, a bit dazed, stared up at the ground-level window and peered at a fat robin flapping about in a puddle of day-old rain. He had finally made it here, he thought: *subterranean*, and put on his son's virtual reality headset: the one that said, *Aladdin and the Forty Thieves (Cave of Riches)* and walked slowly through a cave ceiling-high with gold coins, diamonds, ruby-encrusted goblets, and it was all his/there for the taking. He removed the headset, sat back down, saw that the robin had flown off, which, inexplicitly, made him a little sad. He took the small bit that was left of the joint and smoked it, was going back in.

Dolls

Emma Phillips

The other kids held their noses when Patty passed, called her *Stinky Pants*, left an empty chair by her in the dinner hall, sulked and demanded their parents write a note of protest when teachers sat them next to Patty in class. It wasn't the fact she had accidents, that had happened to some of them too, it was the way she denied it, sat with a wet patch that spread like a lake across her skirt, so that when Miss Holly or Miss Morgan made Patty do the walk of shame to the spare clothes drawer, she left a puddle in her space on the carpet. They said when she was home, she still wore nappies.

Patty lived in her head most days. When her classmates found a dead baby bird on the football field, Patty was the only one who would pick it up. She scooped it into her upturned palms, as if she were afraid it might break, and held it out to them like an offering. Nobody smiled. Later, Patty wrapped its corpse in a bandage stolen from a medical kit and held it close to her chest, like she could somehow breathe life back through its open beak.

She learned to keep watch at the foot of buildings for fallen fledglings, filling her pockets with twigs, wool, and pieces of thread that she'd weave together to line a nest. Sometimes her fingers shot out to pluck feathers from the ground or hedgerows. When Social Services finally called, Patty was sat on the floor in a room that reeked of death. All around her were tiny boxes. They said she cared for those birds like the dolls no one had ever bought her. They said she couldn't bring herself to bury them.

A Man for All Seasons

Sarah Das Gupta

I watched my father's coffin disappear through the crematorium curtains. I almost expected the lid to be pushed open and that familiar figure to sit up in his old mac tied with bright orange binder twine. I looked at the crowd of mourners. Ex-pupils, the local football team, the town's Cactus Society, old men in dark suits with collections of war medals, the dog racing fraternity, at the back of the hall. Then the family: aunts, uncles, distant cousins who just showed up at weddings and funerals. Only my mother knew the delicate details of affairs, second marriages, scandals, all the skeletons in the family cupboard.

The wake, in the sitting room, was much more relaxed. Alcohol certainly oils the wheels. The funeral urn stood on a side table as if my father were keeping an eye on his favourite tipple, the bottle of navy rum. Snatches of conversations drifted across the room. Horses, football matches, the war, farming, music, gardening, dog racing, markets, poultry, Burmese cats – he would have talked about all these and more, with quiet authority. I looked through the windows out into the garden. It was hard not to imagine that figure in the old mac digging potatoes or watering broad beans. I glanced at a fading wedding photo of a handsome, young naval lieutenant and a pretty girl in her wartime dress which was to be passed on to at least six other young brides. Few could have guessed then what lay ahead.

As with a whole generation, the Second World War altered and influenced my father's life. He had just finished training as a teacher when the War broke out. He told me once that on his first week as an officer, the recruits were sent into Plymouth which had been heavily bombed in July 1940. As well as rescuing the injured, the young men had delivered a baby among the rubble. Even as he told me thirty years later, I could see the deep impression it had left.

He served as an officer in command of a gun crew on the cruiser, HMS Orion. It was only on very rare occasions that my father spoke of the war. In fact, I only discovered last week when researching, that the Orion shared the distinction of winning the highest number of naval battle honours in the Second World War. She was also the first ship to fire a shot during the D–day landings. We found his medals after he died, hidden away in the back of a drawer.

One of the most tragic episodes for my father was the death of his best friend, Tommy. He was aboard HMS Curacoa, escorting the liner Queen Mary with 10,000 American troops, to Greenock. The two ships collided off the North Irish coast. The 82,000 tons of the liner cut through the 4,000 tons of the cruiser, like a knife through butter. The two halves of the Curacoa sank in minutes with the loss of over 300 men, including my godfather. We never talked about this. Tommy's sister sent me handkerchiefs on my birthdays. I thought them too sacred to ever use.

After the war, my father resumed his teaching career. He was extremely good at explaining complex ideas in a clear, practical way. A boy in his class suffered from epilepsy, and as a result he was very withdrawn. Then, George started helping my father with our menagerie of animals. I was amazed to hear the two chatting away while mending a fence or feeding a hawk with a broken wing.

Animals played a major part in his life. He was able to communicate with creatures from hedgehogs to nervous horses. Just his presence would calm them. He would often take the syringe from the vet and inject dogs or horses himself. They would just stand quietly, ignoring the needle. My father always refused to admit defeat with animals. A newly hatched gosling with bandy legs was given matchstick splints. A piglet, the runt of the litter, recovered in the slow oven of our Aga cooker. Unfortunately, he forgot to mention this to my mother. To say she was surprised to find a live pig when she went to bake an apple pie, would be to slightly underestimate her startled screams!

He would buy hens from battery farms and 'rehabilitate' these featherless chickens. Within months, they strutted round the yard, new plumage gleaming, and rewarded us with delicious, brown eggs.

The Gregory Peck Affair was typical of my father's dedication. Gregory was a white gander who had outlived the flock and followed us everywhere.

When we were painting some poles red, he dipped his head in the paint. The result was goose from a Stephen King horror story. My father decided he needed romance in his old age. Two grey females were bought. One started sitting on a nest of eggs. Gregory kept guard, developed a cold and died in the cause of love!

I shall always be grateful for my father's love and knowledge of the countryside, especially of wild flowers. My sisters and I had collections of pressed flowers, carefully researched and labelled. We understood and valued the passing seasons: the grass growing in Spring, the hawthorn, emerald green by April; Summer evenings in the hayfields, loading the sweet-smelling bales. Autumn followed, with the chill of the first frosts in the air.

Winter, snow deep in the fields and no Christmas 'lunch' until late evening when we had struggled through drifts to feed the horses.

Every Saturday afternoon my father refereed the local football team, Farleigh Rovers. Years after his death, an old man I met out walking, hailed me with, "Hey! You're Bob's daughter. He was the best referee the Rovers ever had."

As with so many experiences in life, hindsight is a wonderful thing. Only now, looking back over eighty years, do I appreciate how privileged I was having a father who truly was 'a man for all seasons.'

Rounded Edges

Joanne Jagoda

Grief can be soft. It can have rounded edges. It can call to you at any time during the day or night with a whisper or a shout. It can also be a gnawing ache, a scar that doesn't heal. It can sidle up to you when you are not expecting it, when you are at the market or on the treadmill at the gym.

Grief can be a quiet companion that travels with you day by day, co-existing in your consciousness with a tender reserve until you feel a ping, bringing sweet memories or the stabbing jab of painful remembrances.

I lost my older brother a few years ago, but I really lost him a hundred lifetimes ago. He suffered from schizophrenia which struck him when he was a senior in high school, the typical time for onset of this difficult illness. I was four years younger and from the time he exhibited troubling symptoms at age seventeen, our tight-knit family was afflicted along with him. My childhood essentially ended.

He was the golden boy; blonde curly hair and deep blue eyes, a cherubic face, the first child of our hard-working immigrant parents. All their hopes and dreams were pinned on him. One of my treasured photos shows the two of us on the front steps of our family home. He is wearing a sharp sport jacket with a bow tie and a collared shirt. His pomaded hair is carefully combed. I'm in a party dress, my stick-straight hair curled. I don't know where we were going but I'm sure my parents were bursting with pride at their American-born children. Who knew then how the life of this smiling, hopeful boy with a life of possibilities dangling in front of him would turn out.

My brother was a handsome teenager, a good student, a weightlifter, and involved in track, where he threw the shot put. He had a few friends who stuck with him through high school, though he was not particularly smooth with girls. It was his senior year when he started exhibiting troubling behavior, becoming very distressed, especially worried about getting in to college because the Vietnam War was looming and he needed the college deferment. The doctor diagnosed him as having a "nervous breakdown." Though he was accepted into college, he was not able to stay in as he could not deal with the pressure of school. This was the start of a lifetime of difficulties and though he was smart and talented, he could never be the success he wanted to be above everything.

When the first symptoms of his illness struck – troubling thoughts, delusions, and confusion – my parents were bewildered and frightened. What was happening to their healthy, beloved son? We learned that whatever he had wrong could not be cured by a quick-fix penicillin shot. We were the baby boomer kids and most everything in our day could be handled by a shot of that miracle drug. The little blue pills prescribed by a psychiatrist were not helping him, and my parents did not know where to turn. Once my mother was so upset, I was the one taking the phone from her to speak to the psychiatrist. We learned to live with the elephant in the living room, trying to keep his situation private – like him having to drop out of college, bailing him out of trouble when he bought a car with no money, and his sometimes scary behavior, like yelling and creating arguments. My sister and I intervened at social events when his ranting got out of hand. We always tried to protect him.

He became a very talented scenic photographer, able to capture the rare beauty of clouds and crashing waves and took many classic photos of San Francisco sites, but his disordered thinking messed up his attempts to create a viable business even though he won prestigious awards for his work. His delusions made him believe at different times he was an advisor to Presidents, the problem solver of world crises, a religious scholar. He was always waiting for a big check to compensate him for his "advice." He spent countless hours calling elected officials and sending reams of letters. He imagined affairs with the most beautiful, famous women. However, one of his constant sources of pleasure and comfort was music and he owned a large, eclectic collection of CDs and DVDs and possessed extensive knowledge of recording artists and their best concerts and albums. There were happy occasions when he entertained his nieces and nephews with his music collection.

We waited for the proverbial shoe to fall and sometimes it did. We prayed the police wouldn't be called before we could intervene and smooth things over. In good moments he was funny, had an incredible recollection of family stories and could be sweet and charming. In bad moments he was difficult, unreasonable, and selfish. We never blamed him for the illness that he didn't ask for or bring on himself. His illness also precluded him from taking care of his health. Eventually this caught up with him.

So many nights in fitful dreams I begged him to improve his life or take better care of himself. I keenly felt the loss of him never having a serious relationship or family of his own. I grieved for the talent and potential which could have given him the fame and recognition he craved but never achieved. I grieved for my parents who watched their beloved son suffer. I missed the normal brother and sister relationship we never could have.

His last years were increasingly difficult with him needing to be in a convalescent hospital. It was a wonderful facility and he adjusted to living there as best he could. The staff was kind to him and put up with his often difficult behavior though he also could be a flirt with the nurses and many had a special relationship with him. Sadly he ended up with a hip fracture and complications. When death came softly on a Saturday morning, my sister and I were at his bedside. It was a quiet exit and in the end a blessing. He is at peace. We are at peace too. I will continue to grieve for him in my own quiet way.

Out of Sight

Christopher Tattersall

Tracy twitched as if dreaming of playing tennis, or maybe punching a clown, it was hard to tell but lying beside her, Paul froze so not to disturb her any further. Her breathing soon settled back into a slow and rhythmic pattern.

Tracy was beautiful and funny, one of those rare partners Paul hadn't worried about showing off to his parents. She ticked all the right boxes. She was perfect in every measurable way, but there had always been something missing.

With darkness only lasting around five hours, four of which had already passed, Paul lay alone in the world of consciousness. He removed the covers from his side of the bed to find some unobtainable breeze, and continued reminiscing of Jennifer, a past, and his first love.

This time of year was always hard as the memories of Jen never seemed to fade. Summer had always been his favourite season with her. He should never have let her go. His desires for his past love weighed heavily on him.

He closed his eyes. He edged slightly away from Tracy so not in direct contact with her. The symbolism of the increased distance between them added to his guilt.

Jen had curves in all the right places, she was always immaculate, smelt great and although some considered her a little too loud, the majority of men, and a fair few women were drawn to her like bugs to a headlight.

Just being in her presence was life affirming.

Now entering middle age, Paul was embarrassed to even think of how he acted back in his younger days. He was intolerant, selfish, not like he would be with her now if they could meet again. When Jen would find life hard, he would be far from understanding of what he termed her 'break downs'. Then there was the most shameful of admissions – he recalled his annoyance at always having to wear protection. It was crazy not to be safe, but back then, with the immortality of youth on his side, all his thoughts and actions were controlled by rampant hormones. He had been stupid in making such a fuss, and even more stupid for letting her go.

As Tracy slept the sleep of a princess, Paul slid out of bed. Creeping across the hallway in the blue semi-darkness he eased open the door of the study and sneaked to the bookshelf. The photo albums were resigned to on top of the bookshelves, almost unreachable and not even worthy of a real shelf to call their own. Out of sight and out of mind. Life would be easier that way.

He knew which album to choose, the pages falling open displaying his true love.

There she was in all her glory. S615 JEN. He could feel the throb of her V-Twin Yamaha engine between his legs, chrome exhaust pipes gleaming with the hours of his devoted attention, the irresistible growl on the flick of her throttle.

He wished to turn back time. Instead, and as he had done a hundred times before, he turned his back to the bookcase. Out of sight but not out of his mind.

The Search

Lucy Brighton

I traipse through the mud wishing I'd worn different shoes, wellies perhaps. But I'd no idea the alarm would be raised so quickly. Sometimes my father could go days without a visitor. The social worker visits Tuesdays and Thursdays and today is Saturday.

Luckily, the woman from the adjacent bungalow had called to question him about why EXACTLY his bin had remained uncollected from the end of the path for an entire day. Rosie? Rosemary? I try to bring her name to mind, but all I can picture is her barely concealed snout protruding from her starched white net curtains. Rosaline, maybe.

"Your father is missing," the disembodied voice had told me over the phone.

Missing? My initial feeling was panic, swiftly followed by relief. My cheeks flush with shame.

Brambles scratch at the exposed skin between the bottom of my shorts and the top of my socks; I push aside the worst of the undergrowth with a stick. I'm surprised so many people have turned out for the search. Covering my eyes with my hand, I count twelve bowed heads, all scrambling in the scrub for any sign of my missing father.

The woodland backs onto the assisted living complex and, shortly after Rosaline had alerted the warden, the search had begun. A picture of him had been quickly photocopied and handed out to the swarm of volunteers. I overheard one of them say, "We must find this poor old man."

I can't quite reconcile with the fact my dad is old. At six foot three and seventeen stone, he'd towered above me all my life. I'd never grown big enough to fill his shadow and he's never let me cast my own.

Now he's 81 and his tongue is as sharp as ever. If anything, the belittling remarks had become more frequent in the past few years. More than the, "You a man or a mouse, Lad?" or "You ever going to grow into those ears?" which had been the soundtrack to my formative years. Now, his comments were crueller, digs about my life's unyieldingly flat stomach. "No lead in your pencil, Lad?"

I shake the thoughts away and focus my attention on the task at hand. We've all been given a designated search area and mine is complete. I skulk furtively further into the woods, no doubt encroaching on somebody else's 'quadrant'.

The day is bright, but the deeper I venture, the less the sun can penetrate. A chill gathers around my shins and I pull my thin jacket closer. It's gloomier here, so I move slower, probing the undergrowth, my knuckles white around the stick.

I think I see something. I rub my eyes and wait for the shadows to reveal themselves. I look again. A leg, pale and donning a tartan slipper. Dad's slipper.

"Over here," I shout.

Movement and voices are closing in. I look before they arrive. My dad is splayed, dead, his accusatory eyes still staring. Right where I left him.

Hollow Home

Gary Preece

He watched her silhouette disappear before retreating inside the house. The dining table, normally so cluttered with vibrant coloured fabrics and her old sewing machine, lay bare. The cupboard doors, usually impossible to close with all her creations, shut tight. The sofa, a place where they had laughed, cried and planned their future together, empty – a monument to times past.

He picked up the two sides of the broken photo frame from the floor and held them together. Through the shards of glass, he could just about make out a happier them, laughing together on the beach.

He looked up and stared at the door. He yearned for it to fling open, with her bursting through, slipping her arms around him. He desperately wanted to hear her voice softly saying it would be ok.

Sinking against the window frame, he watched beads of water trickle down the glass. Then sighing, he opened the window, and tossed the photo into the rain.

What's Left of Love

Alison Wassell

Every night at ten o'clock Bill would start rumbling like a train, and every night at five past ten Edna would shout "Bill, you're snoring." I imagined her jabbing him in the ribs with her elbow. He'd grunt and turning over, make the mattress creak, and five minutes later he'd start snoring again, with a different sound. Sometimes he whistled, sometimes you'd have sworn he was sawing logs. They carried on like that all night, the pattern only broken by one of them getting up for a wee. I heard it all through my bedroom wall and swore I was never getting married. Just the thought of their wrinkled saggy bodies lying side by side grossed me out, but Mum said that was what was left of love, when all the hearts and flowers had gone.

I followed them round Morrisons once, for a laugh. Bill put things in the trolley and Edna took them out. She denied him a pack of bacon because he needed to watch his cholesterol, a tin of sardines that would stink the place out, and Uncle Joe's Mint Balls, because he might fall asleep sucking one and choke. When Edna turned her back Bill would sneak the things in again. I wondered what would happen when they got to the checkout. Maybe Edna would think she was losing her marbles. Maybe that was Bill's plan.

One morning, Edna banged on our front door, and I realised there'd been no snoring for hours. Mum phoned an ambulance, but it was too late.

I'd see her sometimes doing her shopping. She always had the same three things in her basket – a pack of bacon, a tin of sardines, Uncle Joe's mint balls.

"My husband's favourites," I'd hear her telling the cashier.

The goats

Camila Posada

Anywhere South will do. Loose shirt, bulky backpack, pocket-able multi-tool.

You take your stove this time, long for something to gather around—can one 'gather' in solitude?—during cold nights.

An imperceptible mood separates this morning from routine. You step once more onto the same saddle, ride once more down the same quivering road. Today you will ride until sundown. Ride south until the world appears big, unnervingly boundless.

One could say you are escaping life. The room you leave behind is full of dirty laundry.

But escaping suggests something inevitable, daunting. Seeing you leave is a dance that offers no resistance. Only beauty, restlessness.

Your body moves like a samba, half joy and half *saudade*. Through coastal roads, old villages, mountain air that smells of nothing.

The leathery roughness of your hands stiffens around the handlebars. You build furniture, roads, houses. You think only of the movement, never see the product through.

The only thing worth building are these thin orange lines. Bellac to Saint Aiguilin. Basel to Bern. Elbistan to Baskil. They remain alive for a couple of days, then drown in some better news.

In the afternoons you sit with men drinking espressos, Turkish tea, Georgian wine. The old dark furniture intoxicates you, intoxicates them. The world shrinks, re-scales, closes in.

You become decreasingly stronger. The lines around your eyes deepen. But your eyes remain distant, piercing. They still look straight through lovers. No building.

You have lost and gained body weight, lost and gained body weight. The goats have given milk and died, have given milk and died.

Yet the days of a life that treads simply, productively, undeceivingly, have accumulated. You have built assets and stocks.

Escaping begets a void. But it takes too much to build a void.

And I—will I have built anything, while I wait, in my admiring disdain for the life you have chosen? These pages may be the closest resemblance, I gather. Yes, in solitude, I gather.

Requiem

Johanna Nauraine

This morning I woke up crying. My dream hung in the air like fog, so thick I couldn't see.

You sat in a wheelchair, your children on either side, faces slack with boredom. Restless dogs circled the room.

Upon seeing me, you tried to speak. I could see what it cost you, your chest rising and falling with each breath. I knew what you wanted to say. Between us, it has always been love.

Eighty-seven years marks a long life, and yet for me, it is only a blink in time. I think of all the places we have been over our shared decade — India, Croatia, Greece, Prague, Budapest, Australia, Hawaii. Yet, there is more to see — the pyramids of Egypt, the sands of Morocco, the frontier land of Montana. You are always my desired companion

It has been clear to us both that I will live decades beyond you. But our closeness, though sweet and unexpected, remains a shimmering star — beautiful and everlasting.

The Great Ghosts

Dorin Schumacher

Les Grands Transparents

As I entered the house I hadn't occupied for four years, I looked back at the six-foot tall oval mirror with those words in black longhand and the tiny artist signature, *Man Ray,* at the bottom.

The room was still, everything in its place, as though the occupant suddenly departed without looking back.

The woman I felt still here knocked me silent. She was present in the soaring cathedral ceiling and the wall of glass that brought stands of tall north Georgia trees into the room. Glimpses of the sunlight she loved reflected off the surface of the private fishing lake.

She was a living presence in her creation, but I was no longer her. I no longer had the energy, esthetic taste and drive that gave birth to this beautiful sunlit space where every object was infused with her memories.

The French reproduction Louis XVIe bergère chair with the carved fruitwood frame made in China that my first mother-in-law gave me that I covered in soft, off-white leather. The three-seat 1960s couch, now covered with the same soft leather, that I had surreptitiously moved out of my dead mother's condo to keep from my grasping stepfather and his new paramour. The teak Danish Midcentury Modern desk I bought in Pittsburgh while in graduate school and the matching teak wall unit, sideboard, and tea tables I found in Atlanta. The artwork, framed museum exhibition posters by Juan Miró and Matisse from the Fondation Maeght in Saint-Paul de Vence. Whimsical wall clocks from MoMA by Charles and Ray Eames. And purchased online, an oval white Corian dining table with intertwining chrome legs. The image of my brilliant, witty husband appeared, sitting there, staring into space and signaling his years-long decline that would end five months before I re-entered this room. The graceful white Panton chairs and the soft light the elegant lamps gave. A Bang & Olufsen stereo and speakers I chose for their ultra-modern design. The delicate handcrafted coffee table I searched for so long and finally found at a Spoleto USA craft show in Charleston, South Carolina. My collection of books on the wall unit and pottery and ceramic bowls on table surfaces.

I tried to keep my stroke-victim husband alive through the brutally inefficient emergency room visits and hospital stays, in artless claustrophobic rooms in overpriced assisted living facilities with underpaid nurses who never had the privilege of seeing a Monet, and finally, our ten-month separation while they "sheltered him in place" which enabled his dementia to wreak its full devastation. At last I could bring him to me so I could help him sink into a morphine sleep.

And now here I am. Years later. A sadder, depleted woman who gave her all to the only man she loved completely.

I don't know if I can pick up where that talented woman had to stop creating the beauty that lies before me.

Or has too much of her been lost?

Timing

Fabiana Elisa Martínez

The cold air of your city is the only one that does not make me retreat inside immediately. I always wonder why. My practical conclusion is this frigid wind is something that belongs to you completely, a part of you that still envelopes me with ardor. People inside the museum café are looking at me over their coffees and early, sweet wines. There is a young man who has been following me along the galleries. He is sitting now in a corner close to the counter observing me. I cannot turn and confirm his actions but I feel his questioning gaze on my shoulders, almost as heavy as the wind. I wish I could look through this glass wall, move this metal chair slightly, and peep inside the café. All my spectators, astonished at the woman sitting outside in the cold, would have to lower their eyes at once, scurrying pupils taking refuge in books, timetables, and plates sprinkled with scone crumbs.

Instead, I look into the garden or, more properly, into the future image I can compose of what this wasted frozen land will look like next spring. I see the possible roses and tulips through the real tears the wind shapes on my lashes like the glass blowers of Marinha Grande shape their transparent paperweights. My only source of warmth is the cup I nest in my hands. I am not sure whether the dark chocolate is warming my fingers or my gloves are keeping it hot. And as I look down into the dark abyss of the cup, the recurrent question and its recurrent void of an answer pop up inside my chest. If that man had not jumped in front of the train at Marquês de Pombal on August 1st eighteen years ago, exactly at 7:52 am, would we have met?

This stubborn question materializes when I am afraid. Afraid of not seeing you ever again, afraid of your silence, afraid of knowing that you might die but nobody will tell me soon enough.

Some people fidget when they are impatient. I could not move much in the backseat of that old taxi taking me to you for the first time. But my sense of smell grew more perceptive and as I looked at my cheap watch with desperation, I could sense the reek of tobacco in the driver's words: "No idea how long we're going to be here. Nobody's moving. People are coming out of the metro station like flies. Getting in buses and taxis like it's the end of the world. I didn't hear about any strikes today." He flicked on the radio and, after plucking the stations brutally with the worn-out dial, he stopped at the lugubrious voice describing the suicide, how the young man with thick, black-rimmed glasses had just let himself fall onto the rails slowly, obliquely, in front of the speeding train like a dead tree, like the sails of a boat untied by a merciless wind. I immediately thought with a guilty fury that he had chosen the worst time to die and that I would be extremely late on my first day of work at the international bank where the new manager from Boston needed my assistance.

I paid the taxi driver his full fare, immense for me at that time, and walked the five blocks rabid with pedestrians, as fast as my rickety heels would allow me, to the ornate golden doors of your building. It was difficult to imagine your disappointment at my lateness because I did not know your face, the exact hue of your blond hair, the way you express frustration that I came to love so much. Nor did I know you would be wearing a wedding ring, a detail that was not crucial at that time. I could not even pronounce your name properly.

I greeted the guard at your floor and still gasping for air, I explained that I was there to meet the new expat who needed help with all the immigration paperwork in Portuguese. He frowned. "I thought you were already here," he said, reading the signatures on his log. I mumbled: "There was an incident on the metro and traffic has been jammed." He brought me to your office, and to the grateful realization that you were also late. I sat in that cubicle relieved and curious, wondering why someone who should have a magnificent corner office was confined to this fragile, partitioned box.

Years later, as we galloped in the procession of time through a mountain range of tension, distance, passion, and pain, we came to the conclusion that another new assistant came to meet Mr. Parker while instead, I was sent to your office because we were both late that summer day. Nobody corrected the guard's mistake. We decided he should not be corrected thirty minutes after you said "bom dia" in the worst Portuguese I have ever heard.

Six months from now roses and tulips and perhaps timid violets will flourish in this garden again with their scent and colors. By then I will have given my lecture on the second floor of this museum, I will have returned to Lisbon and sat many times on our bench in Rua do Vigario and this cup of hot chocolate will have been forgotten, consumed by the void of actions and mistakes. All obliterated like the young man with black-rimmed glasses, who chose the wrong time to disappear so you and I could meet.

Fifty Happy Years

Chris Hall

To celebrate their 50th anniversary, Alf suggested circumnavigating their way around Australia in a Winnebago.

As reluctant as she initially felt, it turned out to be like a second honeymoon for Edith. Being outdoors made her feel fifty years younger. That was, until Edith forgot how old she really was and, during a spot of foolhardy trekking, fell heavily onto her left hip.

Several harrowing hours later the emergency department confirmed a fractured hip and hooked her up to traction.

Exhausted, Edith fell into a deep stupor. Alf was disconsolate. The nurse suggested he go home and get some sleep.

"Can't I stay with her?" pleaded Alf. "We haven't spent a night apart in fifty years."

The nurse reassured Alf, "She needs her rest, we'll take good care of her."

Despondent, Alf caught a taxi back to the caravan park. He blamed himself. Edith was right, they were far too old to be gallivanting around like a couple of teenagers. What was he thinking?

He didn't sleep. When he arrived back at the hospital, Edith was conscious. Alf felt a tear trickle down his cheek as he took Edith's hand. Her languorous features managed a wry smile. "I'll be fine, the doctors know best."

Reassured by her apparent recovery, Alf felt more content leaving her once she drifted back to sleep.

That night in the Winnebago, Alf lay on the bed, overwhelmed by sentimental reminiscence. If anything were to happen to Edith, life would not be worth living.

The following day when he arrived at the hospital, a doctor explained, "During the night Mrs. Johnson's breathing became laboured. She has early signs of pneumonia, so we administered medication to clear her lungs."

Alf nodded, "I understand, but why is she so sedated?"

"We need to keep her comfortable." Noticing Alf's obvious annoyance at his attempted justification, the doctor's expression switched to indignation. "We know what we are doing Mr. Johnson, we will call you when we have some news."

The next day Edith had gone. He asked the nurse of her whereabouts and was told Edith had been transferred to Intensive Care. Her breathing had deteriorated and she needed artificial assistance.

"You mean she is on a ventilator!" exclaimed Alf.

"That is correct. Her pneumonia exacerbated and she was unable to breathe on her own."

"What caused the deterioration?" asked Alf.

"Bed rest. Being motionless. It's very common."

"Is she conscious?"

"No, everyone on a ventilator is heavily sedated."

"Can I see her?" asked Alf.

"Not while she is in Intensive Care."

"Not at all?"

"No."

"What medication is she on?"

"The hospital protocol."

Alf stared directly at the nurse. "I asked, what medication is she on?'

The nurse gave him the name of an antiviral medication, then added, "Please don't raise your voice, Mr. Johnson."

"Please don't treat me like an imbecile," Alf responded.

The nurse turned and swiftly left the room. Then four burly security guards arrived. "You need to leave!"

Alf was dumbfounded and refused. Finding himself strapped into a wheelchair, he was conveyed from the hospital and banned from re-entering.

Alf's loss was profound. Edith was slipping away and he was powerless to intervene.

Alf researched the drug. The W.H.O. issued a conditional recommendation against the use of this drug in hospitalised patients, regardless of disease severity. The National Library of Medicine stated, kidney injuries have been observed in animal studies.

At two-thirty a.m. the phone roused Alf from his troubled sleep.

"Am I speaking with Mr. Alfred Johnson?"

"Eh … Yes!"

"I am the duty doctor at the Gehenna Hospital. You are the husband of Edith Johnson?"

"Yes."

"I regret to inform you Mrs. Johnson died earlier this evening."

Silence!

"Are you there, Mr. Johnson?"

"Yes."

"It was sudden and unexpected. She did not suffer. I am sorry, Mr. Johnson."

"What did she die from?"

"Preliminary reports indicate acute kidney failure."

"Due to the drugs you gave her."

"No, Mr. Johnson, we did not veer from the recommended protocol. It is a frequent complication in patients your wife's age."

"Because of your protocols!"

"Mr. Johnson, I understand you must be very upset. Would you like to come to the hospital to view the body?"

"The dead body?"

"Yes."

"Will you let me in?"

"Just go to the security gate, I will leave a message to expect you."

"How thoughtful of you."

"Thank you, Mr. Johnson, I will see you when you get here."

Rubbing the thick coat of oil on his brow reminded him he had not showered for several days. Nor changed his clothes.

Distraught and distracted, Alf climbed into the Winnebago and soon found himself at the gates of the hospital car park.

A security guard approached.

"I've been called in to see my wife."

The security guard shook his head. "Sorry, no visitors after hours. Come back in the morning."

Alf stared blankly at the man.

"You need to reverse your vehicle back and keep this entrance clear."

"But my wife just died!" Alf exclaimed.

The security guard shrugged, "Then you can wait until morning."

Alf flicked the gear stick back and forth before engaging first and planting his foot on the accelerator pedal. The wooden barrier splintered into an array of shards.

In his rage, Alf picked up speed across the car park and slammed the Winnebago through the main doors.

The ear-splitting cacophony resounded throughout the building's foyer until the vehicle came to rest against an immense pillar, lifeless and paralysed.

Alf was found slumped over the steering wheel, battered and bloodied. Amongst the chaos and confusion, he was extracted from the vehicle, despondent when he realised he was still alive.

"What were you thinking?" a voice asked.

A disconcerted Alf replied, "If you won't let me see her in this world, I'm sure as hell going to find a way to see her in the next one."

Before and After

Alison Morretta

Our verdant acre of land is well kept and free of trash so it's safe for her to explore after years of urban living. She sniffs out nature's refuse, though. Treasure troves of deer droppings hide in the grass like spilled Raisinets, and she smiles wide and mischievous when she discovers them. The brown patches around the stone path at the bottom of the back-deck staircase mar the pristine lawn, but they don't bother us one bit. It's her chosen spot to pee, so it belongs to her and not to us.

We relax in our his-and-hers Adirondack chairs near the tree line, watching her play. Dense forest rings our property, the trees like sentinels protecting us from onlookers. It is private and secluded, like it's all parkland exclusively for her. The peaceful suburban quiet is broken by the jangling of her collar tags and the thump of her stumpy legs as she barrels across the ground. She's in hot pursuit of a lime-green tennis ball but the perfect stick distracts her. She plops next to it and chews, breaking off the smaller branches one by one before gnawing on the thickest part.

The sky is blazing pink and violet as the sun prepares to set, but even nearing 9 pm, it's still delightfully warm. We sip our wine as she rests under her favorite tree: a two-trunked white birch with enough shade to keep her from overheating. When she's had enough, she ambles up and trots off, leaving a pile of broken wood covered in slobber at the birch's base.

She barks at a squirrel scrambling up a tree. She chases a bird into the forsythia bush where it nests. She runs off a family of deer who had the audacity to graze on her grass. She stops at the tree line, sits, and stares into the woods. She's daring the distant pack of coyotes to show themselves, but they know better than to trespass when she's on patrol.

The humidity hits me as soon as I step out the back door. I'm swimming through the air, nearly choking on it, as I walk down the steps. The deck needs a power washing. The second step is giving a bit too much under my weight, but I can't be bothered to fix it. The brown spots around the stone path are starting to fade away now. As far as our grass is concerned, life goes on, but though nature may be healing, I am not.

I stop and stare at the second stone on the path—the place where she vomited a bile-yellow puddle the morning we didn't know would be her last—before continuing onto the overgrown grass. It itches my ankles and I nearly spill my wine as I swerve to avoid a landmine of deer shit. I slump in my Adirondack chair. His is empty. He can't stand to be out here anymore, so I take my sunset drink in solitude.

All I feel is the vacancy she left, though there is life all around me. The family of deer feasts on her lawn. The squirrels and the birds dart around undisturbed. These beasts are far too brazen, cocky even, and I glare at them as they go about their evening unbothered. The incessant twittering shrieks out of the forsythia. The vermin rustle through the leaves on the forest floor. But all I hear is the absence of a lively, piercing bark announcing her presence to the other creatures, telling them whose land this is.

The thunderstorm that blew through a few days ago left the lawn littered with sticks, but they lie intact where they fell. The birch tree remains unsniffed. The tennis ball sits lonely at the wood's edge. I can't bring myself to throw it away.

The sky is a fresh bruise as the sun gives up for the day, and I can hear the coyotes yipping and howling in the distance. The pack is far too close for comfort since she left us, and now all manner of dangerous things lurk just past the tree line. I can feel them watching me, unseen eyes in the creeping darkness, impatient to stake their claim on the land that once was hers.

Dementia Vignettes

Joan Seliger Sidney

1.

I picture Stu lying on his back on the cold concrete basement floor, calling, "help, help," in a voice from far away. How did his plea travel across the house to my ears alone? Is that how love works, waves vibrating through walls until they touch my ears and heart?

2.

Was it Covid that melted his legs at the bottom of the steep stairs, miraculously not at the top? His memory blank as our turned-off TV.

3.

"There's no evidence of a fall, heart attack, stroke, pneumonia, or UTI," the ER doctor reports, but since Stu is Covid-positive, they keep him isolated in a private room for 1 ½ days, until we transfer him to Mansfield Center for Nursing & Rehabilitation. Two weeks of private pay instead of by our insurance, because the ER PT said, "He's perfect."

4.

What does "perfect" mean when the patient is incontinent and slides to the concrete floor with his wet boxers in hand?

5.

Every day I visit Stu at Rehab. His slacks sag, his belt looks
almost doubled up, emphasizing his frailty from Covid and
before, with continued episodes of incontinence. I bring a pack
of Depends for men. He insists on wearing boxers on top,
maybe for security.

6.

Stu almost trips himself getting out of the chair where he's been
slumping, not sitting upright, as he takes baby steps to the toilet.
He coughs deeply but I have to tell him to go spit out the Covid
crap instead of swallowing it.

7.

Already Jen worries about her dad's safety when he comes
home. She insists we alarm the front door in case Stu wakes and
wanders into the neighborhood night and steps into the
headlights of an oncoming car. "But Dad sleeps with his Apple
watch," I say, "we can track him." "That's not soon enough,"
she says, worry lining her 50-year-old face. "It would be
different if he slept in bed with you. But he doesn't, so you
wouldn't know when he's out the door and in the street."

8.

Since his heart, hip, & knee surgeries, Stu can't scoot into bed
with me, so he's sleeping on the living room couch. But after his
basement landing, he didn't use his Apple watch to call for help.

9.

Minutes pass as I chew my yogurt with granola, a late breakfast
from a sleepless night, wondering if Jen's right. Should we

prepare to move from our cozy 5-bedroom house to an assisted living, where, as his disease progresses, we'd both be safe?

10.

Am I self-centered because I refuse to leave the PT practice which keeps my secondary progressive multiple sclerosis stable? Spoiled by my floor to ceiling book-lined study, with its three windows overlooking perennials, oaks and hemlocks? So connected to my university colleagues that I'm denying the inevitable? Or is it inevitable? If Stu has "markers for Alzheimer's", must he become a full-blown case? Why aren't there meds to stop the brain from shriveling? Only Aricept, that did nothing to slow Mom's dementia back in the nineties.

11.

Stu opens the mail. "It's a holiday card from Rebecca." I think of the five years she worked as my personal care assistant, driving us to Jen's 75 minutes away, and taking me to out-of-town medical appointments. "I think she'd enjoy visiting with you," I suggest. "Is she still driving?" Stu asks. "Isn't she older than us?" "No, she's 12 years younger than you, and yes, I'm sure she's still a good driver."

12.

Stu surprises me by his short-term memory bouncing back from time to time. "Today is Wednesday. I did your Copaxone shot yesterday and I'll do it tomorrow." "The new checks you ordered are coming January 5th."

13.

But then he regresses: "When your next helper comes, she'll be amazed at how your study has been reconfigured." "Who do you think helped her uncle move my files, books, and desk?" "I forgot she was here, helping," he says, continuing to mark down his upcoming PT appointments in his 2024 planner.

14.

Change is good, change is bad. We sit catty corner at the dining room table. I glance out the bay window and watch the leaves stumble down in the wind. It's almost time for December snow. The Farmer's Almanac predicts a hard winter. I fear more than snow will challenge both of us.

15.

I like Stu's gerontologist's OT, whom we met for the second time online yesterday. I was able to vent about his general confusion as I struggle to be patient. It's not Stu's fault that he has poor short-term memory. It will happen to all of us if we live long enough. Isn't that what life's about: Holding our loved ones close so they don't feel endangered?

16.

Here I am with my to-do list growing locker room long, keeping me up these nights. What is life if not one project after another never finished, always a light on the horizon? Siri, you're a pain, scrambling my words (which I corrected late morning), but at 3:15 a.m. it is very helpful to dictate my thoughts. Maybe now I can go to sleep.

17.

There are some things Stu loves to do: load and unload the dishwasher. I watch his method of stacking the bowls, one against the other, so tightly that you can barely separate them. Then he puts them in their place in the dish rack in the cabinet. Very thorough, no wonder it takes him at least a half hour to accomplish. This may be tiresome but at least it works for him and finally I begin to understand. It's a chore he revels in. So what if it takes longer than it used to take me, back in the days when instead of being wheelchair-bound, I stood and reached the cabinet? For what are our lives if not living with loss?

The Turquoise Mask

Kresha Richman Warnock

When the pandemic hit, I made masks. I used up ribbon and elastic from old craft projects, ordered more elastic online. My fabric tote emptied. I sewed for cousins and nieces and nephews and siblings, my husband and my grown kids.

I wanted to make something especially beautiful for Kayla, my son's beloved. I used a swatch of deep turquoise, covered with purple flowers, green leaves, little streaks of gold running through it.

I love that Kayla insisted on being the one to propose marriage to my son. They had planned a romantic trip to Ireland from their Seattle home in late March. She would pop the question there. But no one was doing any pleasure travelling in the spring of 2020.

Undaunted, she asked me to set up a secret Zoom call on a Tuesday night. *Kayla and David have something to tell you*, the invite read. She decorated the Seattle apartment with Irish props. Unsurprisingly, David said "yes." We all jumped online to hear the joyful announcement. Cheers! Champagne!

Kayla's face on the screen, porcelain skin, fine features, sky-blue eyes framed by shoulder-length ginger curls, like a renaissance Madonna, light rays radiating from her face. The one advantage of communicating on Zoom was that you could see her smile. Unmasked.

That night, I met Kayla's mother, Robin, for the first and last time. She looked out from that computer screen, one face in a crowd of twenty other small, squared people, a continent away. I think she was happy. I know she'd met my son and thought he was a good match for her daughter. But when she offered her congratulations, we all struggled to hear her quavering voice; the Parkinson's was stealing everything.

Our son called a few weeks later to ask us to take care of their new puppy. Robin had died in the night. Kayla was flying home to New York to sit shiva, to be with her father. In the tumultuous early days of the protests of the summer of 2020, David, a police officer, couldn't get even three days off to fly east with her.

That day, my husband and I drove to their home in silence. We took the elevator up to their fifth-floor apartment, despondent calm. Even the active little puppy sat still. Our daughter, Anne, wearing a green and black checkered cloth mask I'd also made, stood in the entry with Kayla. Each of them is a tallish young woman, but Anne, with her dark hair and athletic frame seemed to tower over Kayla, so fine-boned, so determined to do this thing, even as her lithe body curled into a fragile standing fetal position. Over the turquoise flowered mask, Kayla's eyes had lost their sparkle.

Anne dropped her at the near empty Seattle airport. I guess that mask kept Kayla safe from Covid. It must have covered half her face on the flight that took her to JFK. Did it absorb her tears? When the cab pulled up at her dad's Manhattan apartment, did they break the rules and hug?

I imagine Kayla keeping up a strong façade for her father, while inwardly collapsing in the pain of grief. In a few days, she flew back out west, took up her lawyerly work responsibilities at her home desk. She and my son planned their wedding.

I helped shop for the wedding dress, but I couldn't make up for the loss of Kayla's own mother. I can only love her like a daughter. I know I cannot protect her or my other children from the terrible pains of life and death. I only wish I could have done more to help during that dark trip than sew her a pretty mask and watch the dog.

In My Father's Shed

Suzette Thompson

The door of the tin shed is jammed, the open padlock dangling uselessly from the front bolt. I wrestle the sliding door open and there is a grinding noise as the bottom scrapes along the concrete slab. This is the shed he was so proud of and my mother disliked. Inside he kept all his gardening tools, the stakes for the tomatoes he loved to grow, the rose fertiliser.

The star item was the Weber. He delighted in setting it up on the lawn to barbecue a chicken for visitors and at Christmas a large lamb roast. The barbecues, or braais, were accompanied by continual reminders, threats and questions about time from my mother standing at the front of the kitchen door. How he loved those social occasions, spending the whole morning around the Weber in his favourite faded blue shorts, beer in hand and a too small cloth hat on head. He was always shirtless, basking in the sun and the thought of all of us coming around to talk and eat and drink.

The plastic table and chairs he arranged on the lawn are gone. I threw out the last warped, misshapen remnant the other day. The round table so central to our family occasions had been languishing with one dicky leg and a few splits across its surface for the eight years since he died. My mother refused to throw it out. The lawn is sparse and dried up. He is no longer here to scatter the fertiliser and sand on its surface and pull up the weeds, to ensure the grass is cool and inviting for grandchildren to roll on and for grown-ups to sink their feet into its damp softness. For a brief moment I see us pull our chairs together under the shady peppermint and settle in for a night of food and drink, stories and songs.

No one sits here anymore, not on the grass, not under the verandah and not in the house. My mother who was once a busy, lively hostess to my dad's laid-back entertainer, then the gatekeeper as he became ill and, finally, the jailer, is now none of these things. She stands solitary guard at the entrance to the house, stooped over her walker, blocking entry.

I feel my father's presence as I stand bowed in his shed sweeping the spider webs from my face and squinting into the dark. There is the red Weber taking pride of place and I don't have the heart to add it to the growing pile of junk. I look at the old hoses, a garden snipper and the fly mower that no longer works. He used to mow the lawn regularly: no hat, no shirt and after a few hours in the sun return to the nagging of my mother, with a red face and shoulders – "Just a touch of sun my love, be nicely brown tomorrow."

A Ruined Christmas

Tim Law

The phone's ring broke the silence as we all sat around my brother's kitchen table. The spread was incredible, as it was every Christmas: turkey, ham, vegetables roasted to perfection and a pudding burning bright blue, all the trimmings of a celebratory feed. Beyond this delicious meal we could all see the perfect tree, tinsel, baubles, twinkling lights, and the pile of gifts that lay beneath, waiting to be unwrapped. Everything that we could have needed for a wonderful Christmas Day was there. Well, almost everything.

"Hello," said my dad into the phone. "Yes? Thanks for letting us know."

Normally any calls on Christmas Day would have been family, Dutch relatives, sending well wishes as they too celebrated the silly season. We knew though that this call, at this moment, was one from a place closer to home. It was not going to be good news. It was a call about Mum.

My mum has always been a child at heart, my best friend and fellow dreamer. Just like her father, she was the life of every party, making up silly stories and fun games to keep me, my brothers, and our cousins entertained. Birthdays, New Year's Eve parties, and always at Christmas time. Every gathering was a special one with Mum around. With her imagination we never knew what adventure we were about to experience, only that time with Mum meant laughter, joy, and hours of fun.

That Christmas, the Christmas of 2009, Mum's absence was draining our desire to smile. We tried, for our own kids, to keep the spirit of Christmas alive, but Mum's grandkids were so young, they did not have the same memories of their Oma, as we did. Over the years Early Onset Alzheimer's had chipped away at Mum's spirit and mind, until she reverted back to a child herself, a shadow of the woman who inspired me to dream so big. The person they had grown up knowing was a smiling, giggling mess who spoke in garbled, stuttered sentences, someone we all felt sadness and pity for.

I remember Mum was the first to wear a Christmas crown, the one who laughed at the terrible jokes, the loudest voice as we sang all of the carols we knew, the funniest dancer who made all of us giggle. These memories are the most precious gift of all.

Memories can also bring tears to our eyes. So clearly can I still see my mum in the aged care home, far too young, and yet far too gone. I regret not wanting to visit her then, and I regret even more not spending extra time with her when I did choose to go. It was difficult though, because who she was, who I remembered so fondly, that person had already left us well before the dreaded phone call came, and it hurt seeing the person that Mum had become. Bit by bit we had been watching our beautiful mother transform into a blank shell; the woman we loved had become nothing but anger, frustration, confusion, regression. Nothing was good, nothing was joy; everything just ended up in that pit of shit which was 2009.

And so we were on autopilot with Christmas hats on but not at all in a celebratory mood. Our kids still laughed, young enough to know that the day was special, so young that we decided to shield them from our melancholy. The adults watched in stunned silence as the lady of the house presented the pork. It was dry, like our Christmas spirit, but nobody had the heart to say. Those crappy jokes hidden away in the crackers, something that would normally coax at the very least a grin, that year, this time, none of us found even remotely funny.

"She's gone," Dad told us as he hung up from that call.

His voice was flat, emotionless. We had all been mourning the loss of someone special. This call came almost as a relief. The wait was over, Mum was finally at peace. So why didn't we feel the weight was lifted? In that moment, hearing those words, all I could think about was Mum dying alone, in that hospital, on that bed, no family beside her.

And then my youngest brother piped up with, "Well that's ruined Christmas now, hasn't it …"

He could not have been righter.

You Would Have Known

Judith Shapiro

It's been sweltering here all week. You would have loved it. It reminds me of that summer when you traveled in the Sinai desert wrapped in a sheet. I wasn't with you but you modeled your outfit and regaled me with your escapades when we met up later in Athens. Then again, some days everything reminds me of you. If someone says salt, I think, you loved salt. You fed me grits with salt and pepper, a childhood staple of yours. You salted your greasy cheeseburgers before tasting. Salt and pepper, no ketchup.

From Athens we flew to Crete, early in the morning when only shopkeepers were up, sweeping sidewalks, readying for the day. We stayed at a tiny hotel recommended by the cab driver who picked us up at the airport. He spoke no English. We spoke no Greek.

We took turns sitting on the tiny balcony, only room for one, so close to the building next door that I thought if I reached out, I could touch it. We ate yogurt, almonds and figs; drank sweet, syrupy, Greek red wine.

Then to Rome for me to run the Rome marathon. Italians wore fancy track suits in the scorching summer heat, stopped to talk to friends and strangers on the sidelines.

We drank cappuccinos at stand-up coffee bars, often the only women there. I held the tiny spoon perched on the edge of the thick white saucer like a treasure. Every afternoon I bought cannoli from a street vendor in the park near our hotel. He had dirt under his nails, which for some reason, gave me comfort. Added to his authenticity.

We took the train to Florence. Every seat taken in six-seat coaches; windows open in the summer heat, blasting with hot air. The man next to me lit a cigarette. I spoke little Italian, actually no Italian, but I got by with my college Spanish. I pointed to the no-smoking sign prominently posted on the wall above his head. He shrugged. Continued to smoke. At home I would have demanded he put it out, found the conductor if he refused. But this wasn't my home, it was his, and I thought that must be what they do here. We became fast friends, miming, gesticulating, laughing with barely any shared words. We traded addresses, believing, pretending we'd see each other again, knowing full well that we wouldn't.

We rubbed the nose of the Bronze Boar at the Mercato Nouvo. Ate dinner at a restaurant filled with American tourists. Clearly, we all consulted the same travel guides. A man occasionally stared from across the room. We didn't notice him following us when we left. He came up alongside me and in a delightful British accent politely inquired if I'd be interested in seeing an extremely large phallus. I declined and he peeled off, presumably to go find a more willing observer. Had he been wearing a hat, he most assuredly would have tipped it as he left.

Where did we go from there? So many travels over the years in planes, trains and automobiles.

Sleeping in an oppressively hot car in the Florida Keys with the windows rolled up, rest area swarming with moths and skunks. So many memories. That's all I have, all that's left of you, of us, is memories. Was it Key Largo or Marathon? You would have known.

It was Key Largo, you'd say. You'd remind me that it wasn't skunks but raccoons. The skunks, you'd say, were years earlier in a campground on a dried up river bed in Kansas. That's where the skunks were. But the Keys, it was definitely raccoons.

The Loss of My Father

Yonnie Murphy

I am not sure when I lost my father.

Maybe I lost my father when he was a child and took a fall and hit his head. That was when his family said he started falling asleep at all the wrong times. They were told he had a form of epilepsy called narcolepsy. Much later, in his fifties, he was diagnosed with sleep apnea. For much of his life, the lack of quality nighttime sleep would cause him to fall asleep at odd times and during any activity of the day. His family knew something was wrong with him, and the strangeness of it, the shame and stigma of it, kept his weakness close within the family.

Maybe I lost my dad when he was a teenager. Although he was the oldest son in a farming family, it was well understood that he was not the favorite. Later, he went to great lengths not to talk about his years growing up. He was most certainly scorned, maybe he was abused. Decades later, we would look at a rare photograph of him, standing with the two steers he was raising for Future Farmers of America. He would earnestly and softly-shyly, leak out, "I would have licked my Daddy's boots."

Maybe I lost my father when he married my mother. His undiagnosed sleep apnea had landed him in the ditch on the way home from one of their dates. My parents married right out of high school with the secret still undisclosed. This belated revelation became part of the distrust and grievances between the in-laws. Having struggles of her own, my mother took charge; telling my dad what to do and when to do it.

There wasn't a doubt in my mind that I had lost my father the day my mother announced she was leaving him. She declared she was taking us three children with her. We moved that very day, in the storm of her rage and our bewilderment. He cried and begged her to stay, but I knew he was already gone.

I so hoped to see a glimpse of him on my wedding day. I asked him if he would wear his cowboy boots and walk me down the aisle. He grimaced with his whole body, looked embarrassed, shifted, smiled slowly, and said "Well, sure."

I don't remember that anyone from my dad's family came to my wedding—not uncles, aunts, or grandparents, although I received wedding gifts from several. For years I told myself that perhaps my paternal grandparents were ill the day of my wedding. They lived only a block from the church.

Over time, I continued to look for my father. I tried once more when my children were older. I arranged for my dad to fly to our home, hoping my children could have some small connection with their grandfather; for him to at least learn their names, see their faces. He stepped off the plane wearing his slippers. He was carrying his socks in his hand looking awkward and uncomfortable. He said he hadn't had time to put on his socks.

I had prepared questions, gentle "getting to know you" questions. Thinking it might be the last time I had such uninterrupted time with him, I asked if I could record him. He did not mind. He seemed not to notice. He talked incessantly, without pause, even for meals. I could leave the room and he would continue talking and not notice.

When I asked questions, he just continued talking. He did not tell stories; he did not speak to the children. He did not mention my mother, his parents, or siblings, my sister, or my brother. There were no words of substance, no opinions or hopes in anything he said. He was agreeable in every way, even self-abasing, not wanting to cause any trouble, eating what was put before him. He did not take note of any of his surroundings. He seemed impervious to anything and everything. He was lost to me.

My father died several years ago now; the sleep apnea had taken a toll on his heart. I think of his passing as I walk to the hall closet. I must move several picture albums before I find my wedding album. It is a bit worn from years of standing there so stolidly. I have to grasp it firmly to keep the insides from falling out. All the photos are loose—it is the old kind of album where you slide the pictures in between two sheets of plastic. Some of the pictures are jumbled and overlap with each other. I work to straighten them and peer at each closely. Of course, we all look so young. "There he is," I say to myself. In the pictures he is the only representative of my paternal family tree. There is my dad in his blue suit and his cowboy boots. "Yes, there he is," I reassure myself.

The Hottest Day of the Year

Henry Bladon

The radio promised 'the hottest day of the year so far.'

Toby was in the bathroom and pumped the air with his fist. It was not often he got to sunbathe all day on his day off.

Ian shrugged at the news. He was due back at his flat today after his recent stay at the clinic.

Jenny cursed as she pulled on her thick black tights. The wards were always oppressive in the hot weather.

Gavin, who had already cleared the dinner plates and other leftover items from last night, was ironing his work trousers.

And the radio was true to its word. In fact, the day was even hotter than the authorities had predicted. Buses ran with all their windows open, and trains carried wilting passengers from one station to the next until eventually the cooler evening air soothed the city.

Now, in number 26, Jerome is massaging after-sun into his partner's torso because Toby fell asleep in the sun without his top on. Toby's chest is red, and he is already fussing about the white marks where his neck chain has been resting. Jerome knows now to expect several more days of complaining but he will counter this by cooking his special lasagne this evening.

When he is finished work, Ian the accountant in flat 29 who is always smartly dressed but looks like he might write crime fiction on the train, is thinking of playing chess by himself as he does most evenings. He has recently been away but is now clearing out his kitchen cupboard having been cured of his obsession to hoard cleaning products but never use them.

Jenny the nurse from number 5 is in a hurry to arrive home from work. She doesn't want to get caught in a conversation with Mr Ackerman from 22, but she slips and rips her tights, grazing her knee in the process. She will miss the musical tonight as her knee will swell up and start throbbing. Her Tinder friend Nigel will think she is making another excuse.

Gavin is ironing his work trousers; the flat still smells of last night's curry. He shares flat 7 with a man who thinks all female footballers are lesbians. Gavin likes women's football and dislikes ignorant misogyny, so he is working on a plan to force his flatmate to leave that involves cooking curry every night and ironing his work trousers twelve times a day.

All of which is overshadowed when, as dusk arrives, Ian jumps off the roof of the apartment block leaving a note saying that he just can't go on.

What To Do With This Weight of Ashes?

Karen Arnold

She lifts up the white box, strokes it gently. Choosing the box was the last thing they did together, in a cold room smelling of lavender furniture polish and the heavy scent of white lilies.

She remembers him standing beside her, mute with sorrow, as she wiped the sticky jelly from her stomach, both dodging the words that whined like bullets from a sniper's rifle, words that explained the space and the shadow on that grainy, twenty-four-week image.

On the walk home, she had forged ahead of him, trying to build up enough speed to outrun what was coming towards them, invisible in the May sunshine, sharpening its claws. Three weeks later he disappeared into a lemon-yellow dawn, with the soft click of a lifted latch, and a note explaining everything but saying nothing. She had rolled across the bed in the silent aftermath, into the warmth of the hollow left behind, breathed in the last of him.

She feeds the cat. Wipes pristine kitchen counters. Ignores the voice message from her mother. Deletes the text from her oldest friend. Pours away another cold cup of tea.

She holds the box in the crook of her arm as she scrolls through gentle, euphemistic websites. A firework, a necklace, a paperweight. She wonders how big a firework would this weight of ashes make?

She presses balled fists against hot, dry eyes. Watches purple rockets, soft golden rain.

The Crossing

Lesley Middleton

Slumping down on the shingle, exhausted and sniffing back her tears, Beth looked back at the mainland. It was only half a mile away, but it looked much further. It was ten years since she'd last sat here, a few weeks before she and Matt had been due to get married. They'd been full of plans for their future as they'd ambled over the tidal track linking the islet with the mainland. Now there were notices warning people of the dangers of crossing on foot. But Beth had walked across the causeway, retracing the last steps she and Matt had taken together.

Biting her lip, Beth savoured the briny tang of the sea as she watched dark clouds obscure the rising sun. Her denim jacket wouldn't provide much protection against heavy rain. She tucked her wild auburn curls under a baseball cap and tied a knot in the scarf loosely draped over her shoulders. She would need both hands free to clamber up the rocky outcrop to the small plateau that had been their special place.

Not a day passed without Beth thinking about the events that had taken Matt from her. Her fury was still raw and her anger still rolled in waves, as strong as all those years ago. At this early hour she had the steep crags to herself. Each time the loose stones beneath her feet crumbled, her fingers gripped the next handhold more tightly.

Reaching the flat rock where Matt had proposed to her, she sank down, gasping for breath. The sombre clouds had thickened and the wind had changed direction, a sure sign that the tide was turning. She should start walking back across the causeway but there was something she needed to do first. She shrugged the small rucksack off her back and emptied out the contents. Several dozen small stones rattled onto the bare patch of granite as her tears splashed over them.

Each time she and Matt had visited the island Beth had taken a pebble away with her. After she lost Matt, the stones had been a source of comfort. Their smoothness in her hands had given her solace and she'd marvelled at their multiple colours and shapes.

A swooping gull sounded its long call. Much as she wanted to linger, she daren't delay any longer.

The water had risen and the wind was whipping up frothy peaks on the waves. She hesitated briefly before stepping onto the crossing where she would retrace Matt's last steps.

Exactly ten years ago Matt and his best friend, Ed, both lifeboat crew, were called out to rescue two injured men from the islet. Other emergency services in the area were already out rescuing passengers from a ferry that had caught fire so they launched a small inflatable dinghy to reach the island. There was only enough space for the two casualties and one crew member so Matt chose to walk back over the crossing. The tide was rising fast and the wind was whipping up the waves but he'd rather get wet feet than hang about waiting for Ed to come back for him.

After helping the two injured men into an ambulance and stowing the dinghy in the boathouse, Ed looked out over the causeway and waved to Matt who was about halfway across. As Matt waved back he stumbled and fell. Seconds later, a wave washed over the place where he lay and Ed realised his friend must be hurt too badly to stand. He re-launched the inflatable and sped back to where Matt was floating face down in the water beside the submerged causeway.

A gust of wind blew Beth's hat off her head and a wave crashed over the causeway, spray soaking her. She was about half way across; exactly the place where Matt had fallen.

The water was splashing over her feet and she waited for each wave to drain off the track so she could see the crevasses. She shuddered at the prospect of falling into a deep water-filled hole and not being able to scramble out.

Beth covered her head with her arms as another wave drenched her. The causeway was under water. Her feet slipped on the wet cobbles. She wiped the water from her eyes, not sure whether it was sea spray or tears. Perhaps she should stop and let the tide take her as it had taken Matt.

The wind dropped and in the distance she saw the sun shining on the village church. Calm enveloped her.

"Beth!"

Someone was calling her name. *Matt?*

"What were you doing out there?" Ed asked as he held out his hand and helped Beth onto the quay.

"Saying goodbye." Beth wasn't sure Ed would understand why a heap of stones had been such a comfort after losing Matt and how important it had been to her to take them back where they belonged.

"You and Matt were together a long time," Ed said. "But he wouldn't want you to still be grieving. He'd want you to share your life with someone else."

"I know." Beth smiled. "Liam's a good man and he wants to marry me but I'm sure Matt still watches over me."

"You might be right," Ed said. "The tide would have taken you if I hadn't looked out across the causeway when I did."

Looking back across the sea, Beth shivered, realising how close she'd been to being swept away. Setting the stones free had been her final goodbye.

Now she could give Liam the answer he was hoping for.

Foul Play

Carol Adams

The year is 1955. I am sixteen years old and I'm wearing my first pair of stilettos – three-inch stilettos to be precise – black patent leather with a buckle. I'm a bit wobbly, but it's ok.

The dance band on a wooden stage thrums out a beat – old Mrs Farmer at the piano, Mr Harding playing accordion and Thomas Duck rat-a-tat-tatting on a single drum and symbol.

Mothers trundle up steps and into a back room to cut sandwiches and make large quantities of tea for the dancers. Nice people drink tea.

Girls sit hopefully around the walls of the old town hall. Boys slouch at the front door, disappearing and reappearing and increasingly loud and unsteady as the night wears on. My mother says they're 'fast'. She says if Wayne Bridges asks me to dance, I'm to decline and head for the toilet.

But I've got my eye out for Brian Patterson. I spot his mother across the room – an elegant woman: gathered skirt and net under-skirt frothing out over two seats, legs crossed and ending with real silver shoes. She is not working on tea and sandwiches with the other mothers. She has red fingernails. Beside her and half buried in a fluff of petticoats is that bitch from school, Desiree.

My mother says Brian is potentially a good catch but I am what is known as a 'nice' girl and so far, haven't had much luck with boys, including tonight.

I cross my ankles, smooth my floral skirt and look around – hopefully.

And there he is, standing with the other boys, looking a bit bleary but steady on his legs. I send out vibes across the dance floor. Oh Brian, Brian, pick me.

It's 'ladies' choice' at last. I catch Brian's eye and our gaze locks. A small smile leaps the distance and burns up the air. I stand and take a step. I figure it's about fifteen dainty steps to where he is, or maybe ten if I stride it out a bit. Brian, I'm coming.

If I teeter on my new heels it won't matter. Brian will slip his arm around my waist and hold me up. The band blasts out a new song. Three more steps and I can ask.

But what's this? Desiree had pulled up alongside and I detect Brian's expression light up. A glassy smile hovers on his vacant face. Desiree sticks out one tiny, shiny foot – sideways. I topple and smack onto the dance floor, face down. A gasp rises from the crowd. Ladies rush to my side with embroidered handkerchiefs to mop up the blood spurting from my nose. Their closeness is stifling. I push them aside and roll to my knees. One shoe has disappeared.

I lever myself up. Dancers give wide berth to the splattered pool of blood congealing on the boards. They wouldn't want to slip in that mess. Blood is all over my white blouse, has added flowers to my skirt and painted a grotesque, clownish mouth across my face.

On the dance floor Desiree sparkles, spins, twirls with Brian.

F★ you, Desiree!

Sunrise in Cappadocia

Diane Lee

Sunrise, and I'm awake before the alarm.

I turn onto my side and I see you, and marvel again at how you came to be in my bed. We have nothing in common, aside from being on the same tour – the tour I took to celebrate my birthday. A milestone birthday. I have passed the halfway mark if I live to the Biblical age of three score and ten years. I won't. My doctor told me that this birthday could be my last. So here I am, travelling, ticking off my list.

I notice you at the meet and greet dinner on the first night, with your bright, white Foo Fighters tee-shirt tucked casually into your jeans, slung low on your hips. Your sandy hair brushes your collar bone and I wonder why you aren't on a Contiki tour. You approach me after dinner and introduce yourself. I'm Lukas, you say. Hello, I say. I'm Alison. I keep the question to myself but I'm curious about you in other ways. We talk small, just minor details. I am grateful you don't mention my head scarf.

On the road, I'm intrigued and watch you. Sometimes you catch me out. We lock eyes a few times over lunch at Turkish truck stops. We brush against each other at the Grand Bazaar in Istanbul, and again at the Blue Mosque. You sit next to me on the cruise of the Bosphorus and tell me the river is like dancing sapphires. At each hotel, after a long day of driving, I'd freshen up, change my scarf and go for cocktails before dinner. You'd be there with your old-fashioned, and the irony was not lost on me. You didn't say much, but you'd flash me a smile every now and then. Of course, I was flattered. Who wouldn't be?

Last night, you ask me to watch the sun set over Cappadocia. I say yes. We make our way to the roof-top bar, cocktails in hand. We sit close, thighs touching. And as the ancient, moon-like landscape swallows up the sun, and the sky turns lavender, your arm slips around my waist. I remove my scarf, and my bald head is warmed by the setting sun. You tell me how lovely I am.

Now, you reach for me, and I laugh and kiss you lightly on the nose.

"Come on, Lukas. Get up. We can't be late." I force myself out of bed, and padding naked to the window, draw back the heavy curtains. The inky darkness is fading to a pinky-orange. I can just make out the hot air balloons in the distance, the blue flame of the gas inflating the colourful fabric.

"They look like giant Christmas ornaments," I say. "You don't know how long I've been wanting to do this."

"Longer than I've been on this planet?"

I laugh and blow him a kiss. It's another day and I'm still here.

Sunrise, and I'm awake before the alarm.

Parting

B. E. Nugent

Her mother should be here.

I glance across at Julia, her hands lightly clasped over her swollen abdomen, pulling the seat belt and shifting, trying to get comfortable.

It's like falling backwards, through the years. Tumbling and spinning. Almost twenty-five years to the day. The same, but different.

"You ok?" I ask.

"Yeah, I'm fine. Just getting used to having my own gravitational pull."

"Not for much longer. Happy birthday, by the way. Next week."

"Thanks, Dad," she answers.

"Have you got everything? Check your bag. Passport, wallet, boarding pass …"

She places her hand on mine, resting on the gear stick.

"Don't be worrying about me. I've done this before, you know."

"And Chris. He'll meet you at the airport, won't be late or …"

"Dad! I'll be fine. Stop worrying."

We lapse into silence. Focus on the road. Think of what to say. I wish her mother was here.

"Mammy should be here," she says at last. I swallow hard. Elizabeth was so much better at this, saying the things we couldn't. Always checking and assuring. Then rechecking. Reassuring.

"She never liked these runs to the airport," I answer, finally. What a stupid thing to say.

"I know. But at least she was waiting for you. When you arrived home. Will you not go to Janet's for Christmas? I don't like to think of you ..."

"I'll think about it. No, really. I will."

"And Jack's taken up fishing as well. He's dying for you to take him out."

"Nations have invaded their neighbours with less fuss than Jack wading into a river." We both laugh. "Yes. I'll think about that, too." I don't look but I know she's smiling.

I carry her bags from the carpark to the departures lounge, checked in and ready to go, back to Adelaide and her Australian husband. It's time to go. She reaches for my hand, places it against her bump, her other arm around my neck and she whispers.

"We're going to call her Beth."

I pull her closer.

"She'd have liked that," I say. I hope I've said it out loud.

Who might she take after? Might she have my nose? My ears? Let's hope not. Who will know? Who around her might recognise the familiar? Who might recognise that one look of her grandmother's that would wither an oak tree?

They'll just have to take Julia's word on it.

I stay behind a little while after she's disappeared through the gates. There's no need to hurry. There's a finality that I'm glad to delay. There will always be a place for her back here, a piece of home that will forever belong to her. I'll be there too, hanging on FaceTimes and phone calls. They will sustain me, after a fashion. My heart won't be in it, though.

No. What's left of my heart is boarding a plane for the other side of the world.

A Premeditated Farewell

Joy Nevin Axelson

April 1992
(My journal entry about losing my grandmother when I was 19)

I can't believe I haven't written anything about Grandma's passing in here. I clearly remember the last time I saw her alive – but let's go back to the last time I talked with her. I might have described this before, but the true reality and impact of the situation only begins to sweep through in retrospect. I was hosting a visitor from France. I was weary of having someone with me all the time, trying to meet her needs and make her visit good. I wanted to be alone.

We drove up to the small rural nursing home. Grandma had been informed of my visit. She was having her hair washed when I walked in. Happily, she recognized me. A sigh of relief swept through me. We accompanied her to her room where she cautiously sat, gently belted into a cracked vinyl chair on miniscule wheels – strapped in by a blue apron she wore with yellow strings.

I remembered her frail-bodied strength, back on the farm, in the old familiar apron, feeding the outdoor cats, making cornbread, playing Karam, and hugging us on the lawn by the cornfield. There she sat. The poor thing ... she was feebly attempting, with deformed bony knuckles, to unravel her restraints. She didn't realize they were fastened in the back and kept trying to undo a nonexistent knot in front. Her eyes betrayed her weariness of life. Frustrated, weak, and old – like a geriatric whippet with its legs tightly bound – after an hour of yelping, softly whimpers in frustrated exasperation.

I knew … I knew … I knew this was the last time I'd see her alive, functional, speaking. She was more coherent than I had expected notwithstanding the occasional mental slips. When I informed her I was going to college, she asked me if Carol, my fifty-one-year-old mother, was going too. I told her that "Carol" had graduated and was doing well. Her foggy eyes gazed softly into the distance as she murmured proudly, "Carol's such a nice girl!"

It was finally time to go. In a way, I was relieved because I had long before run out of things to say. I usually love to "visit" as they say in rural settings, but, under these sad circumstances, conversation would either be pointless or a stab to the heart, twisting slowly. The nurse wheeled her to the door on high-pitched, squeaky wheels because it was lunchtime. She invited us to stay, but I told her I had to eat lunch with my cousin. I didn't know if I could even bring food to my mouth or swallow it – my throat was so constricted with teary lumps. Ultimately, it didn't matter. I had no desire to prolong my agony. I knew the lump in my throat would soon erase my words and I'd cry like a baby. I choked out the words, "I love you, Grandma" – the first time and the last time I ever remember saying it. She responded, "I love you," in her fragile little voice that so aptly matched her frame. I kissed her wrinkled, almost translucent cheek, and she kissed mine. Pond's cold cream. She always smelled like Pond's cold cream, laundry drying in the sun, and a farmhouse kitchen.

I think the last thing I said to her was, "Have a nice lunch," or something corny and awkward.

I didn't want her to know how swiftly I was falling apart inside. I didn't want her to realize I had seen death prowling in the shadows of her room. I yearned to create a loving goodbye that I would remember when I was older – that would make me smile faintly each time I pictured it. Everything had gone just as I had planned. It was the first time I had the chance to say goodbye to someone for eternity. So that was goodbye ... how strange.

I walked two paces ahead of my French friend, wiping away my tears. I felt foolish crying. I wish so much that my French friend wasn't there – that I was at home in my boyfriend's embrace, who would gently rock me in his arms and let me cry tears of sweet remembrance. But no ... I needed to be, in this instance, a responsible adult alone in the world. I could not afford to linger or give full rein to my longing to temporarily break down. I had to quickly pick up my emotional pieces and move on. I had to drive us to my cousin's. Yes – I had to drive. I couldn't cry. And that's what I did. That was my premeditated farewell.

Requiem

Gail Sosinsky

Madeline smiled at the couple ahead of her in the line at Burger King. Not that they noticed her, wrapped up as they were in each other. She knew society expected her to frown at their public pawing, but the boy acted so like Jack had – eager for touch and skin and together.

She remembered that time in the hay mow when everyone else was in town. Or so they'd thought. Her parents stopped arguing against her engagement that night, though Daddy never did forgive her for making her own choice. But Jack had been a good son-in-law, pitching in with farm work without complaint even though he came from a long line of CPAs and continued the tradition for his own career.

The young couple approached the counter, and Madeline stepped forward and tilted her head up to scan the familiar menu. The onion rings were what had brought them here, in the days before Jack's blood pressure had nixed the salt. It was a Catch-22 – go to Burger King and remember going with Jack or go to McDonald's, Arby's, anyplace else and remember this wasn't their regular haunt. At times the idea would flit through her mind that it would be easier if she could just forget everything, but she would grab her mental broom and chase that evil thought from her skull as quickly as she could.

Remembering was her job. Remembering was really all she could give Jack any more.

She chose her reliable grilled chicken salad and a cherry ICEE. The drink was so big, she and Jack used to share one. They'd shared pretty much everything. She shook off the maudlin and pushed the door open to the parking lot.

The young couple had parked right by the door, not in a handicapped spot, but still. The girl slid into the driver's seat. Well, there was a mark against *him*. Jack had always opened Madeline's door for her, even when she drove. It made her crazy during the height of the women's movement, but when she'd complain, Jack would say, "I love you," and move on. She would give just about anything to hear those words one more time.

Madeline juggled her food, pulled the car door open and settled the ICEE. Her new SUV was much easier to get in and out of than her Camry had been, but she was long past the graceful sit and pivot of the young girl. Damn, but she'd had good legs once, too!

It hit her then, as it did at times, the utter grief that batted her perpetual nostalgia out of its way like a withering balloon. She grasped the wheel at ten and two, closing her eyes. Deep breaths. Deep breaths. Little by little the crushing pressure in her chest resolved into a sob, and Madeline leaned her head against the wheel and let her shoulders shake until the storm had passed, eroding her spirit, washing away all but the hard rock foundation of a farm girl who played the cards she was dealt without complaint.

Madeline dug tissues from her purse and dried her face. She sipped a bit from the cherry ICEE, wrinkling her nose at the cloying sweetness. With a fresh tissue, she mopped the cold condensation from the cup and pressed it against her swollen eyelids. She pulled down the visor mirror, wiped a mascara smudge and reapplied her lipstick. Pretty as her wedding day, as Jack would say, and she caught and released a melancholy smile.

When she arrived at the parking lot of the assisted living complex, Madeline pulled into her usual spot, a farther walk, but with afternoon shade.

"Let me get the door," said George, one of the residents and a terrible flirt, pushing the handicapped door button.

"Thank you," she said, walking through.

An administrator behind the desk turned like a sunflower to the shine of Madeline's money, a sheaf of bills blossoming in her hand.

"After lunch," Madeline said firmly, turning her back on the woman and punching in the lock code to the Memory Unit.

The door hissed shut behind her. She could hear music from the common room, but this wing was quiet today. That was good. Jack wasn't wailing. Step by trepidatious step she approached the room. Through the open door, she could see Jack's roommate. The man would die soon. She hoped. He hadn't woken for three days.

Madeline straightened her shoulders, put on the soft smile from her wedding picture and walked around the drawn curtain.

"Hello, Handsome," she said to the stooped figure in the wheelchair.

Jack slumped to the left as he slept. Madeline set the salad and her purse on the bedside table and carried the ICEE to Jack. Lightly, she touched his hand.

"Hi, Jack. How is everything today?"

He blinked and looked toward her voice, eyes blank until he saw the ICEE. His eyes lit, and he reached.

"Let me help," she said. "It's a big cup." He latched his lips on the straw and sucked greedily.

"Not so fast. You'll get a headache." She pulled the drink from his mouth and his awareness. The light in his eyes faded.

"You'll never guess what I saw today at Burger King," Madeline said. With a napkin, she dabbed a bit of ICEE escaping from the corner of Jack's lips. She could hear the roommate's labored breathing. She took a deep breath of her own. "There was this young couple in line." She uncovered her salad and stabbed a piece of chicken with her fork, telling the story, remembering theirs.

Lost and Found

Suzanne Purvis

Dad passed on a snowy Wednesday morning in January. The world crouched in the midst of Covid, I traveled to Canada through a snowstorm, arriving the Monday before he died.

Stress was the monster that greeted me at the door of my parents' home. My brother and his wife oozed tension and anxiety. Mom, married to Dad for sixty-two years, wore a thick and heavy cloak of denial. She couldn't accept Dad would no longer be there, lying in his hospital bed in the den where they watched an immeasurable number of hockey games. Though he was ninety-two with Parkinson's, and the palliative care doctor had shared the news his time was short, Mom stubbornly fought the inevitable with her every word.

I stayed with Dad through the next forty hours, administering low-dose pain meds through his IV, carrying on one-sided conversations, holding the phone for him to hear messages from family, keeping him comfortable. And I was the sole witness to Dad's passing that Wednesday morning. He died with a short inhalation, no exhalation, and I believed he could now rest, in peace.

As for the rest of the family, peace remained a stranger.

Again, with the dark shadow of Covid, the funeral service would be rushed, in two days, and no preparations had been made. Mom, still holding hands with denial, ducked all discussion of planning a funeral. My brother dealt with his grief by wanting to do, do, do, demanding decisions. Me, ever the meditator, fixed firmly in the middle of this funeral maelstrom, donned my assigned role like an old coat. I was to coax Mom to take action. All nerves were frayed and sparking.

I knew I needed to do something to ease the tension. I thought what would Dad do in this stressful family situation? "Why don't we open a bottle of champagne," I suggested. (My parents' house is well stocked with wine and champagne.) "We can toast Dad, and reminisce about some fun times."

"Yes, I'll get out the flutes." Mom opened the china cabinet.

"To Dad." We wiped tears, raised our glasses, clinked, and sipped.

Soon, laughter and bubbly alcohol lifted some of Mom's burdens. After a few bottles shared with visiting family and friends, I persuaded her to meet with the funeral home the next day. Whew, step one.

We talked and something we all agreed on — a closed casket with a suitable, framed portrait of Dad nearby. And we also agreed on the photo to use.

"That black and white headshot of Dad on your dresser," my brother said.

"How old was Dad then?" I asked Mom.

"Probably about thirty-two. It was taken to use in industry magazines when he started his big-time corporate job," Mom said.

Another step toward saying goodbye.

Not wanting to rock Mom's frail, rickety boat of acceptance, I snuck away from the conversation to search for the photo. I didn't realize my mission would be grueling and baffling.

No Dad photo on her dresser. No Dad photo in any of her dresser drawers. No Dad photo in her closet drawers.

My parents are children of the Depression and while very well-off, they don't throw much away. Years and years of paperwork, memorabilia, knickknacks, coins, cards, candles, and everything and anything that might be saved, was saved and stored in their 3500 square foot home.

Afternoon wore into evening, I scoured every drawer, closet, cupboard and couldn't locate the elusive photo.

No way the photo had been tossed, but where, oh where was Dad? And again, I rummaged on the sly, in between conversation and meals. I'd had my share of champagne, but determination fueled my search for the one request Mom had made that day.

I continued the hunt. Everywhere.

Ten o'clock, eleven, time ticked, no photo. I rifled again through each nightstand, each closet drawer, and as a last resort their bathroom. Coming out of the adjoining bath, I plopped down in one of the two chairs across from their bed.

I'd failed. My chest squeezed and crushed my aching heart. My eyes threatened to spill for at least the tenth time that day.

Discouraged, dejected, disheartened, I slumped back into the chair and thought, *Please. I need to find this photo.* Then, I noticed a table between the two chairs where I sat. The table looked the same style as their nightstands, but turned, with the usual front side facing the wall.

I got down on my knees, shifted the chairs, heaved the table around. Yes, just like their nightstands with a drawer and an open shelf. I fished inside the shallow drawer — no photo. The open shelf of the nightstand was crammed with a two-foot-high stack of old papers, magazines, files, likely the reason to be facing the wall.

I contemplated the pile, knowing it was more outdated, no-use clutter. Out of ideas, out of energy, and out of desperation, I thought, *Dad, help me. Please. I need to find this photo. For Mom.*

I considered the stack again, and with no enthusiasm and little hope, I randomly lifted the top two inches. There, sandwiched between who-knows-what junky paperwork (much smaller than I remembered) was the portrait of Dad.

With great care, I dusted the silver frame with my shirt, and hugged the photo to my heart. My eyes brimmed with grateful tears, and I said a silent *Thank you, Dad.*

I have no doubt Dad guided me and my hand to his portrait.

Two days later, an enlarged copy in a much bigger frame rested in the funeral home beside Dad's casket. Almost every one of the small number of attendees commented on the surprising, yet endearing portrait of Dad.

As time passed, I've wondered if I wasn't just searching for the photo, but for the Dad I lost on that traumatic day. But all I had to do was ask, and he was found.

The Substitute

Carl Chapman

Jim Starling stared at the screen before him, trying to decide just who or what situation he should get off with today. He liked watching the fem videos and recalled watching one that took place in the woods and while in the woods, two female hikers talked a male hiker, whom they just met, into letting them tie him to a tree, and once they'd done that, they immediately began cutting away his clothes until fully nude, jerking him off, and then just leaving him there. Now that got him hot. They completely dominated the guy and took control and sexually forced him to do whatever they wanted him to do. In some of the videos they even had sex with the guy while he was tied up and unable to do anything, not even able to touch them with his hands, it was like pleasure and pain, desire and denial, all at once. Even in the gang bang videos, he often fantasized himself as being the object of desire for another person's gratification, with each orifice being used for pleasure, which made him wonder if he was a switch hitter, as they called them, because the thought of pleasuring men also had its appeal. Whenever the men had double penetration sex with the women, he couldn't help but question if the men got turned on by feeling another man's penis next to theirs as they had sex.

Other than the sexual acts, he honestly didn't really know what was going on in most of these videos because he never turned on the sound and just pieced it together with the visuals. He couldn't stand the fakery of what was said or the horrible sounds they made when they had sex, it just spoiled everything for him and took him out of the moment, which in turn, made it more difficult for him to get off. He remembered hearing on one of the many late-night talk shows how the host had mentioned that viewers of porn could now get captions on the videos and wondered why would anyone care what was said in them?

His thoughts then went to his wife and their lack of sex, which wasn't really her doing but more his own. The more he watched porn, the less he craved the real thing. Now why was that? Yes, he wanted real sex with a real woman, but for some reason watching porn was more stimulating and easier. He could screw a different woman in his mind every day without any repercussions. No one to say he wasn't good enough, no one to say not tonight, no one to instruct him or deny him in any way. All he had to do here was play the voyeur and watch, which with some of the point-of-view videos was even more stimulating because the man held a camera, and all you could see was the man's point-of-view as he screwed the woman who was more than willing to pleasure him.

Yes, he had found that as he got older this sexual fantasy life was allowing him to experience all sorts of situations and all types of women. It was true that he felt a bit depressed afterwards, but the brief rush was worth it. This was harmless compared to drinking or doing drugs to get through the day. This was much easier and cheaper because all he had to do was hit a few keystrokes and he was with a new woman, fantasizing of being pleasured by her. He couldn't help but wonder if once porn video technology became virtual reality with the ability to add sensory touch to the game, would men or even women ever want a real mate again? All one would have to do is turn on the computer or television and tune in to the partner of their choice and the sexual situation of their liking and go from there. No need for foreplay, no need for coaxing, no need for small talk or cuddling, no need for commitment. It could be the perfect substitute for the real thing. Then he thought about the real thing and how when having actual sex with his wife the faces and bodies of all those women he viewed online would creep into his mind while performing actual sex. Instead of viewing his wife's face and body, the bodies of these strangers would appear and interrupt what should have been exciting and pleasurable. He had lost his desire for the real thing. He surmised that every vice had its downside, and he'd just have to learn to cope with it.

Hearing the engine of his wife's car as she pulled into the garage, he quickly shut off the computer and collected himself. Had she seen him undressed this way she would have quite a few questions for him and might even want to have sex, and he really wasn't up for it today.

Dad Lost and Found

Ellen Notbohm

My dad worked his brand of offbeat magic on my mother at their first meeting, a blind date wherein he greeted her with "Shall I impress Superwoman by playing the buffoon, the sophisticate or the intelligentsia?" She was hooked. He had done all three at once, in the space of a single sentence. And when, a few months later, in the depths of a Chicago winter, she showed up at his birthday party with her face scabbed over from a recent Florida sunburn, he knew for certain that a girl with that kind of aplomb was the one for him.

The magic lasted almost half a century until, twenty-four years ago, we observed what would be Dad's last birthday, he in the hospital cancer ward and me in denial that we were only days from losing him. Acceptance came hard. For the first few years, his February birthday was agonizing, the grief and disbelief paralyzing, the sense of my children having been robbed too soon of their beloved grandfather, the regret over things I wish I'd asked. But now I experience his birthday as sort of a reverse holiday—a time of discovery rather than loss, to reflect on the many inimitable gifts he gave me.

He left a trove of indelible madcap memories, wacky stuff only my dad would do. Who else, when screamed at on the streets of downtown by religious or political fanatics, would calmly listen to what they had to say before politely inquiring, "Does your mother know what you're doing?"

Who else would meet me for lunch one day, chuckling over this: While walking the half-mile from his downtown office to mine, a seemingly deranged young man had followed him for blocks, muttering "Stop following me, man! You're following me!" Dad had finally whirled around and thundered, "Cease your harassment of me while I am attempting to proceed *unimpeded* to my destination!" The pursuer stopped dead with "OK! Sorry, man! Sorry!" and ran. Dad was a big believer in the power of well-chosen words.

His most enduring stunt, born of his love of music, might have sent even Tchaikovsky reeling. He kept a cassette tape in his car cued up and waiting. When a teen in a souped-up car pulled up next to him at a red light, radio blaring, chassis heaving, Dad would gleefully hit the Play button and blast the kid out of the intersection with the *1812 Overture*, complete with real cannons, adding his off-key tenor to each BOOM!!

Though in time I found comfort in these stories, losing Dad was harder than I could ever have imagined. And on top of my own grief, I had to explain it to my very literal-thinking autistic six-year-old, who calmly but firmly rejected the idea that Grandpa was "with the stars" or other spiritual explanations. He wanted the truth—so that's what I gave him. That the body ceases to function but the spirit is inextinguishable. That the part we see and touch and hear goes away but the part we can't see can never be taken away from us.

So Grandpa will be a skeleton?

(Swallowing hard) *Yes.*

Cool!

In the aftermath of explaining this to my child, a wondrous thing happened: my own sense of loss turned to found. In the years since, I've been able to see and hear and touch parts of Dad that I never did while he was alive. In many ways, we're closer now.

We received a flood of letters and emails after Dad's death, extraordinary remembrances stretching back through his career, military service, college years, and childhood. But one stood out. It came from a coworker of mine, who had lost her own father to cancer.

> "It's hard to let go of the ones who brought us into this world, but the time comes when their pain and suffering must cease and we have to forge on without them. You will never be alone. You will have your memories of your time with your dad and somehow magically your boys will have an expression or look that will remind you of him."

She was so right, and I have paid her words of consolation forward many times since.

I try not to dwell on all the things Dad has missed. He was a master's swimmer, and my oldest son followed his example. Dad would have reveled to the melting point over my writing career, which he unwittingly inspired with his own writings and research I discovered only after his death. All his grandchildren have racked up achievements and experiences small and large, and most have nurtured quirks reminiscent of him that seem to me to be the true definition of immortality. So it doesn't feel crackpot to believe that he hasn't missed it all, that in fact he's had a sky box seat. Just as my friend promised, I've never been without him. All these years on, I spend more time thinking about having him than losing him.

The gift of memory is the unbreachable conduit that unites life with life. I can feel celebratory on his birthdays now, unlike that final living birthday when, hooked up to a morphine drip, he worried that this was the way his grandchildren would remember him. My 11-year-old son led us all out of that morass, spewing outrage that his grandfather could think such a thing after a lifetime of never missing a birthday party or a ball game, a ride in a wheelbarrow full of grass clippings or endless hunts through neighborhood baseball card shops. "Grandpa," he said, "was all about *being there*."

And so he is, twenty-four years later, still here, not lost. We know it in so many ways that can never die, but never more so than when we happen across the classical music station and get knocked sideways by the *1812 Overture* and those deafening cannons, our own throaty sing-along BOOMs echoing the buffoon, the sophisticate and the intelligentsia, all in one.

Burma

Claudette Currie

People who didn't know him before think he is quiet, unnaturally quiet. He always sits in the corner, drinks one beer, nurses it all night. He never has a conversation. Well, not with anyone he doesn't know well.

I can still remember exactly what I was doing when he returned. I heard a knock at the door. My hands were sticky with dough as I stuffed the New Year dumpling into the old pillowcase, and the weans were capering round the kitchen squealing and shouting.

I wiped my hands on my apron and opened the door.

A tall thin man stood on the landing. Dark patches discoloured his bone weary, pale face.

His clothes drowned him. His shoes were battered but clean and polished.

"Can I help you?" I asked him.

His eyes filled with tears. That's when I really looked at him.

That pronounced widow's peak, those almost black eyes.

My stomach dropped to my feet, my heart hammering in my chest like a trapped bird.

My youngest Alec broke the spell, running headlong into my legs, flinging his small arms round them.

"Mammie, I'm hungry," he said. He looked at the man, and shuffled behind my legs, never taking his eyes off the stranger.

"Who's that man?" he whispered.

My voice sounded odd, high pitched, cracking.

"This is my brother, your uncle, Peter".

"Why are you crying, Mammie?"

My brother sagged in the doorway. I reached out to catch him, his jacket rough and itchy against my hands.

I pulled his arm around my shoulders, put my other arm round his thin waist and we limped along the hall into the bedroom.

I eased him gently onto the bed and pulled off his shoes.

I tucked the quilt right up to his chin, the way he liked it. He turned on his side, closed his eyes and began to sob.

The weans were full of questions and noise so I took them across the landing to Sadie's. She would keep them entertained.

He was asleep when I returned, muttering under his breath, his face and neck bathed in sweat.

I used a damp face cloth to gently wipe his face and neck, scrutinising the familiar profile. Stroking his close-cropped head, remembering the luscious dark curls that were the envy of all his sisters.

He never spoke of it. The screaming nightmares, the bouts of illness where he sweated and soaked the sheets. He never went back to Mass;

I asked him about it once.

"I've already seen Hell," was all he said.

Departures

Abha Iyengar

My daughter is married. She is working. She lives in a different city. I cannot afford the travel to go see her. You see, the city is across continents. I am in India and she is in America. Also, I am old now. I will be unable to undertake the solo travel. Why, you may ask, after all, people in their fifties travel nowadays. They are fit for flying. But that is not true for me. My eyesight is weak. Not that I have lost it, yet, but I see things hazily. I can survive on my own with the helpers who come and go, cooking and cleaning and taking care of the house in which I live all alone. It's a big house but there is only me living in it now. My daughter wanted me to sell the house and go live with her but who wants to live in a cold country with no language or people to call your own. Here, at least, I have Sulekha, my full-time maid. She is young, a few years younger than Vandana, my daughter, and talks my language.

Sulekha also reads to me from the books that line my library.

Yes, Vandana had taught her to read long ago, and it has stood her and me in good stead now. One should not think of how a good deed done once returns to you, because this one did return in this life itself. I can hear well and it's good to listen to the stories. I loved reading once but the words now swim before my eyes, so I don't even try. Sulekha is like a daughter to me.

She takes good care of me. She is not married yet so I worry for her but at the same time a part of me is happy because if she was married, I would lose her too, isn't it?

Who would have thought that Vandana would marry and leave me and go so far away? Sometimes I think she just wanted out of all this caretaking, but I think she has not got herself a good deal. Her husband is rather demanding and old-fashioned. I don't know what she saw in this older man. Maybe she was looking for a father. Harish, my husband, left for his final abode when Vandana was just ten years old. She has some memories of him, but she says they are not enough. It's good, for she does not know that our relationship had already begun to flounder. Maybe if he had not died tragically in that accident, he would have left me with the young child and gone away to another city. How would Vandana have lived with that, I wonder? She has some great memories of her father and I let her live with them. I know that after Harish's death, I had been sad for a while, but then realised that this was a loss the world and I could live with. I did not have to explain to anyone (if it had happened) why our relationship had not worked, why we were not thinking of the small child, why a family should stay together etc. The world cannot forgive departures from one city to another. It does forgive departures from one world to another.

I am doing the same. I cannot forgive Vandana's departure to another city. She is alive but not for me.

It is something I have to bear. A tear trickles down my sadly lined cheek.

Sulekha looks up from the book she is reading. "Why are you crying, Auntie? I just read a funny story to you. You did not enjoy it?"

I nod. "It's good, Sulekha. I think my eyes are watering again. Do fetch me the eyedrops. Then, after putting them in my eyes, please draw the curtains. I want to sleep."

I actually want to think about Vandana. How we were together for so many years. I thought she would never leave me. Then she left me and went away.

I look at Sulekha as she walks quietly towards me. She looks so much like Vandana. I reach out my hand to her and say, "Don't get married. Stay with me. This house is yours. Tomorrow I will dictate the words to you. You write it and then I will sign it. But promise you will not go away."

I wait for her answer.

Life Sentences

Chris Leonard

He soon found that women on websites like E-Kiss-met and Grin-je did not want losers. The past must remain just that; opaque, unmentioned and loss free. He should be: "sincere and trustworthy"; "well sorted"; capable of returning a Hollywood smile through impossibly white teeth and to "make me laugh". He must "love me, love my dog" and "after a walk in the woods or on the beach enjoy a Sunday roast dinner with a good glass of red". The thought of "helping me achieve my travel cruise bucket list" made him feel queasy. He knew he was unlikely to meet any of these requirements.

There was something else though that made any thoughts of a new life difficult. Lately, he had noticed that, without warning, he could be moved to uncontrollable tears anywhere and at any time. Sometimes, during normal conversation, his eyes would fill with tears which slid across his cheeks and dripped from his chin. When this became impossible to ignore, he would claim some form of allergy.

It was not unusual for him to be the solitary figure remaining in a cinema seat long after the film had ended. The first time this had happened, he had been watching a film which celebrated an entirely female gaze. Two lovers were unable to sustain their relationship because of convention and circumstance. As the music accompanying the final scene welled up so too did his tears and he needed more than the duration of the closing credits to compose himself.

An adequate supply of paper handkerchiefs became part of his ritual checklist before leaving home. Once, whilst watching a live performance of "Macbeth", he became horribly aware that the whole audience seemed to be looking at his tear-bathed face shining in the limelight spilling from the stage.

This tendency to be lachrymose was not the only new thing in his life. He had always been proud of his memory, especially his ability to recall the minutiae of things others had forgotten. Now it was different. The past, which had once seemed granular, became a solid indecipherable mass. When he did manage to recall specific events, these would occupy his entire consciousness as he replayed them repeatedly until something jogged him back to the present and then the memory would disappear, perhaps forever.

His closest friends had always complained that he attached too much weight to reflection on the outcome of past events and relationships. He adopted various tactics to address their concerns. All he had to do was avoid any thoughts of time spent in hospitals with a two-year-old child, elderly people or even watching any form of medical content on television. Certain films, pieces of music and geographical locations had to be deleted. Then there were friendships which had been formed in the company of a former partner. When the partnership broke up choices had to be made as the reality of these friendships was re-defined and re-constructed. He questioned the value of certain acquaintances and tested the degree of mutual loyalty apparent. As each part of his life came up for final review, scrutiny and despatch to oblivion, so too did certain accompanying friendships.

"Well at least I've saved us all the inconvenience and upset of attending one another's funerals," he joked darkly with himself as more and more people were consigned to the incinerator of his past life.

Practically, jettisoning these friendships and the clutter of attendant memories was no great loss and, as most of them were very painful, he began to feel a certain lightness. He no longer discussed with himself the insoluble problems of the past and new things were able to fill the vacuum.

The rate at which he was processing these memories and their associated losses quickened and he felt more able to consider the challenge of meeting new people by subscription to dating websites. After all, if the past was no longer there then, surely, he could now concentrate his attention on what remained of his future? He threw himself and his opposable digits at the screen of his telephone. Each dating site claimed to be able to avoid any random selection of potential partners by using artificial intelligence and clever algorithms, but he also developed new skills of socialisation through this new medium.

Deborah wanted to "avoid being my friends' third wheel" and was "looking for someone who wished to develop a relationship which allows each of us to remain independent but together".

They met for the first time in the relatively safe confines of a bookshop. She briefly explained her past and he was impressed by her resilience. She listened to him without making judgement. To his amazement she seemed willing to take him as he was today and not how he might have been in the past.

Early conversation turned positively into lunch and then, to his surprise, and against the rubric of all dating guidelines, to bed where they clung to each other as life-wrecked survivors in a sea of mutual loss.

As their relationship grew, his tears would still appear, unprovoked and unannounced. He would apologise to her, but she would reassure him.

"Your life has been so full of loss it is no wonder you cry. Your tears are long overdue, and you deserve to be able to shed them," she said.

She would hold his head close to her. She seemed to accept that he had experienced more than his fair share of loss in his life and said to him,

"The thing with loss is that you don't always know that you are losing. It's a process, a series of sentences unravelling, sometimes chaotically or uncontrollably, and then comes the full stop. The full stops are the losses, the rest is the living."

Empathy

Josh Sherman

He'd been making the trip to the long-term-care facility twice a week for four years. There was never any question about it. None of the mounting resentment you so often see. He'd always been so close with his mom.

Close, despite how different they were.

Different, like how he was different from everyone else in his family.

None of his relatives shared his interest in language. Or anything intellectual. They were practical people. When, in the mid '90s — and after several of his avant-garde short stories were published in prominent literary journals — he began teaching creative writing at some prestigious program (Bennington? The Iowa Writers' Workshop? Does it matter?), he'd never felt more removed from his family. At the time, his mom was a hairstylist. His grandmother, a homemaker. His grandfather, an insurance salesman. He had an uncle who was a plumber. An aunt in some nebulous admin role.

His dad — he hadn't been around.

He'd learned that his dad wound up an office drone at a telecom company. Apparently, even in his absence, the man disappointed. He'd long hoped his dad had done something creative, something to help him understand himself, to provide context.

After his mom's dementia diagnosis, he began obsessing over his family tree. But it was like consulting a map without a cartographic scale. The distance between things unknowable. He no longer felt alienated or bitter. He just wanted an explanation: who, or what, was responsible for how he'd turned out?

Then he remembered the word searches.

When he was a kid, his mom had often worked through the puzzles as she sat in front of the TV, recovering from a long day on her feet at the salon.

Sometimes, he'd do them with her.

He loved it when she let him circle the words by himself. He realized then how some words could be special. How you could set them apart from others. The significance of arranging letters and words on a page.

These thoughts gave him an idea.

During his mom's first year at Whispering Pines: a HomeCare Inc. Home, he started bringing her word searches. She hadn't done them in years, but outwardly, at least, she welcomed another distraction.

Anyone could see why.

It would be more appropriate for facilities like Whispering Pines to have numbers for names. They're industrial. People are processed. Patients are treated with all the tenderness of an assembly line. His mom's, he knew, was no different from other long-term-care homes. Years ago, with an ex-girlfriend, he'd visited a different one. Sunny Meadows. His ex's mom had suffered from dementia, too. The conditions were identical.

No use dwelling on it.

Just do what you can.

Keep showing up, celebrate whatever the calendar prescribes.

Naturally, early enthusiasm fades. Yet for a time, even as his mom's condition worsened, the losses mounting, there were random flashes of her old self. Sometimes, he was convinced the word searches were the trigger. She'd notice the puzzles and start talking as if they were in front of the TV, back in his childhood home. The doctors had told him this sort of thing could happen. However, to his disappointment, his mom had recently been sleeping more and more.

The situation had to be weighing on him when, two weeks ago — on the eve of another scheduled visit — he saw it on the shelf at the corner store: *The Biggest Word Search Book in the Universe: 1,328 Puzzles (Volume 1)*. Lately, he'd been bringing cheap spiral-bound booklets, which had failed to arouse his mom's interest. Could this hulking neon tome revive her?

He paid the twenty-dollar price advertised on the cover.

Around the same time on the other side of the city, a personal-support worker was wheeling his mom out for dinner in the Whispering Pines cafeteria. The Monday menu: Southwest Fried Chicken with Syrup, Creamy Coleslaw, Waffle, and Fruit Cocktail.

It's unclear which she choked to death on.

Later — perhaps the day after the funeral? — he picks up *The Biggest Word Search Book in the Universe: 1,328 Puzzles (Volume 1)* again.

How could he throw it out?

He decides to finish the puzzles.

This evening, that's exactly what he's doing. He's seated across from me on the subway, concentrating on another word problem.

Our train rushes along Line 2. He's about halfway through the book. He flips a page, bites his pen. I assume the pen is embossed with the long-term-care facility's logo.

Two evergreen trees bookending Whispering Pines, perhaps in a light serif font.

I'm not sure, though.

To be honest, I can't verify any details about this guy's life. Not beyond this moment, around 7 p.m. on February 16, 2019, somewhere between Castle Frank and Sherbourne Stations.

We are complete strangers.

But the thing is: I'm trying to be less of a jerk these days. To better understand my fellow man. Before Isabella left me, she'd said my outlook was too negative. I was too pessimistic. She needed a partner with a *kinder disposition*. Well, a man can change, Izzy! This guy with his word search, though, he's testing me: how can any fully grown adult become so engrossed in something as fucking inane as a *word search*? They don't even have educational value for children! (I googled this as our train hurtled over the Prince Edward Viaduct.)

He could be solving a chess problem. There's sudoku, the *New York Times* crossword, best-sellers, cult classics. Podcasts, streaming music, books on tape. Last week, I observed another man looking at what appeared to be printouts of grisly crime scene photos. That, too, is a healthy alternative. Even zoning out and retreating into your own mind before the brain calcifies seems like a better use of time ...

But that's the old me speaking up. The new me wants to comprehend, to accept. So I've come up with a reasonable justification for this man's behaviour — a backstory. I'm putting myself in his shoes, giving him the benefit of the doubt.

It's called empathy.

All the Dead He Carried

Thomas Reed Willemain

Having wandered long through that gray day and coming upon a quiet glade with a soft patch of moss, the old man rested. Closing his eyes, he listened not to his thoughts but to the sounds of the glade: passing birds, rustling leaves, the quick sounds of a squirrel, and the weary slow notes of the last crickets of summer.

The crickets reminded him of the passing of summer. The passing of summer reminded him of those now gone whom he had known and loved. Embracing the grief, he gathered paper and pencil from his pack and began to list all the dead who had touched him in life.

He began his list with the keen-eyed girl Annie who had sung him songs and seized his heart and given him children. He added the names of the children they had lost before even having names. Secretly, he'd named the first Danny. The second he could not bear to name, so she became Girl. It surprised him that, so very many years later, he felt the urge to cry at their memory. To break the spell, he lifted his eyes to see wind gifting him bright leaves, reds for Annie and Danny, yellow for Girl.

He blinked away grief and resumed work on the list. Names of other dead kids appeared at random. James, the first kid he knew who had died. Charlie and his younger brothers who died in that fire. Bill called Beefy who was big and kind and slow and did not like being called Beefy. Beefy's adopted brother Bob who saved that Marine at Cu Chi instead of dying himself in the 'Nam. Jamie, who tried but could not recite her graduation speech because her mother was dying of cancer.

Because there was a bit more light and a bit more paper and there were many more names, he continued the list. He turned from the young to the old. The grandmother he never met who died so young. The grandmother who was his second mother who it seemed would never die. The grandfather who set his face like flint against his sons. The grandfather who always had a boring chore for him to do. The father who showed him how to sustain love and dignity through disease. The mother who stayed through it all.

Eventually his mind caught up with his emotions and suggested organization for his list. Soon there were subheads for cousins, high school friends, college friends, work friends, former students, neighbors, colleagues from his writing work-shops. Professional antagonists who did not live to see that he was correct and they were not. One barber.

In a while, he had no more paper and no more heart to list all the dead who crowded his heart. He could only look from the trees to the bed of moss, from the moss to the past, from the past to the approaching dark. He whispered, "Requiescat in pace," folded the list into a pocket, tried to rise to his feet, surrendered to a great weariness, reclined, and closed his eyes.

As the small group dispersed from the grave site, his granddaughter Jeannie kissed the list the rescue squad had given her, then laid it on the grave that also bore Grandma Annie's name.

On her drive back to the airport, she thought of names for her own list. She wondered how many dead her heart could carry.

Last Contact

June Rogers

Sasha hunkers down on the cold, steel table. The room reeks of
disinfectant and feces. Barks echo down the hall from the
kennel. Harsh neon lights bounce off the white walls.

Her grey-and-white striped fur is matted, her eyes, glassy.
The vet pads into the room and clicks the door closed. He greets
me, places his hand on Sasha and rubs her ears. She drops her
head.

Grabbing the loose skin behind her ears, the vet injects a
tranquilizer in her neck. "I'll give you two a moment to say
goodbye and then I'll return to finish up." He leaves as quietly
as he came in.

Sasha tucks her paws under her bony chest and closes her
eyes. I pet the rough fur down her back, telling her how much I
love her and will miss her. "So sorry for all the times I yelled at
you when you peed outside your litter box. And, please forgive
me for picking you up gruffly when you barfed on the carpet
the other day."

She stretches her left front leg out and touches my hand.

Ticket to Elsewhere

Christine Johnson

After dinner, Alex heads upstairs to sort Greg's washing. She sighs. His bag still lolls full in the bottom of his wardrobe. That last trip, he was away for a week.

'Business,' he said.

She sorts casual against business shirts, light colours away from dark trousers. Checks pockets for tissues, paper clips, odds and ends. This is when she finds it.

The ticket.

Her fingers unfold its creases. Used, but quite clear. Fiji Nadi. She checks the date. Such a cliché, but it's true; the confirmation makes her chest constrict.

Over time, Alex's pretence of belief has worn thin. She is watchful, alert to any hint of who another unknown woman might be. Greg's long meetings, weekends away, lump sums disappearing from their bank balance. Yet still she stays, inertia a powerful force.

Greg hides all traces. The pattern started early in their relationship. Unable to stay faithful, she knows he doesn't want to abandon his married state. The dream lifestyle, the intelligent wife whose successful career is a supportive reflection of his own. It suits him.

Alex straightens, takes a deep breath, and returns to the lounge.

'Did you enjoy your island getaway?'

His blustering begins. 'What do you mean?' And continues. 'I was at that conference in Melbourne!'

How can he continue to lie? What does he hope to achieve?

Quiet voice. 'I found it. Fiji Nadi.' Silence. 'The ticket!'

She displays it. He stares. In an instant, the inappropriate little piece of paper overwhelms them both. It points to the potential end of their marriage; confirms a betrayal that leaves their relationship unmapped. They both know it.

'I need to clear my head,' he says. 'I'll pack some things, leave for a bit.' But he clings on. 'I don't want a divorce.'

On automatic pilot, she ignores him; returns upstairs to fetch the washing for the machine, dumps her load in the laundry, then stays in the kitchen. Sticks to routine. Her thoughts lock in one direction.

'Got to carry on,' she murmurs.

Until, his control lost, she hears Greg stumble out the front door. *Click.* One sound closes the relationship forever.

Although Alex knows this is coming, she freezes. How will she cope? That night, she sleeps but keeps waking, expecting Greg to be there.

But the ticket waits. Its proof is absolute.

The next morning, tearful with self-pity and fury, she opens his wardrobe doors. She gathers his suits, shirts, ties, and shoes, carrying them to the dining room table. Rough piles complete, she then clears out all his drawers and shelves, tossing the contents beside the rest.

That done, she gets ready for work. The suit and her makeup are a prop, a reminder of what's normal. On her motorway drive to the office, she pushes her car to the limit, releasing pulsing exhilaration.

At her desk, she freezes her emotions and focuses on the tasks at hand. When the day is over, she can't remember what she did or how she did it.

Back at home, cold and determined, she moves his blue relaxer chair into the dining room alongside his clothes. She stacks his books beside them. Settles the boxed bottle of port she gave him for their last anniversary into its place. Scans the scene. Frowns. From the kitchen, she brings out the huge black pepper grinder that was a souvenir buy from their last holiday. With a symbolic flourish, she places it on top of the pile.

Greg rings. Just as she's expected.

'I want to come over.' His voice bends, softens. 'Talk about things.'

'Of course,' she says.

They stand in the kitchen, both aware that everything has changed. One look at him and Alex knows he's no longer there. She shows him the pile of clothes and the chair. Shocked, he chokes.

'I can't fit all that in the car!'

'Yes, you can.'

She helps him pack his vehicle, together lifting, shuffling, and squeezing in the favourite blue relaxer. Civil, he side-tracks; asks whether he should take the port or the pepper grinder.

'Which?'

Adamant, she insists. 'You take both.'

An awkward goodbye and he drives away. She returns to the house.

The ticket lies on the kitchen bench.

Alex smiles, face shining. A ticket signalling the loss of one life. And, for her, a positive detour into the next.

Eye for Eye

Howard Brown

Wendell Harp's father—Mister Buck—was a hard-core shit kicker. And even that, at best, was a charitable appellation. Most people, including his son, thought of him as a senile, drunken old peckerwood, who surrounded himself with suffering and misery the way stink clings to a day-old turd.

So, Wendell found himself more irritated than surprised when he read the note his wife had left him on their kitchen table: "Your daddy's dog, Rip, done killed another one of Settlemeyer's hens this morning. You better get on out there before all hell breaks loose."

Although they were neighbors, there'd been bad blood between Mister Buck and Settlemeyer for as long as anyone could remember. And the last thing Wendell wanted to do was drive all the way out to Hurricane and get involved in another dust-up between the two old bastards. Except he knew how things might play out if he didn't.

The Constable had warned Mister Buck about letting Rip run loose. But when Wendell pulled up in front of his father's house that afternoon, the log chain to which the dog was supposed to be tethered was empty, stretching across the yard like a coiling, rust-colored snake. "Rip ain't the only one needs to be chained," Wendell mumbled to himself, as he sat listening to the ticking of the truck's engine as it cooled.

Settlemeyer was standing on his front porch and Wendell waved as he got out of his truck. But the old man ignored him, turned and stepped back inside his house. Have to go over and try to *set things right once I deal with Daddy*, Wendell thought. *Offer to pay him for the loss of his hen.*

"Oh, Daddy," Wendell yelled, banging on his father's front door. There was no answer, so he pushed, and the door came open with a screech. "Daddy," he yelled again, stepping into the front room.

"Get your sorry ass off my property, Settlemeyer," Mister Buck croaked from somewhere in the back of the house, his voice barely audible over Rip's barking.

"It ain't Settlemeyer," Wendell shouted. But the words were scarcely out of his mouth when the door which separated the front room from the rest of the house erupted in a shit-storm of splinters.

By the time the shotgun boomed again, Wendell was back outside, crouching behind the open door of his truck. He surveyed his injuries, then crawled into the cab, reaching for the ignition. But the keys weren't there, they were in his pocket.

He was still dancing about in the driveway fumbling for the keys when his father came out onto the front porch, a shotgun laid across the top of his walker. "No, Daddy," Wendell yelled, as Mister Buck shouldered the gun. And when the truck's windshield exploded, showering glass all over the inside of the cab, Wendell was off and running again—this time across the road toward Settlemeyer's.

He could hear Rip somewhere behind him and, from the sound of his frenzied barking, fast closing the gap between them. Wendell made it safely across the road but stumbled when he tried to jump the drainage ditch on the far side and was lying in a shallow stream of fetid water when the next shot came. Only this one had a sharper sound to it, more like a rifle. And as he looked up, Rip went limp in mid-air and dropped beside him like a sack of flour.

Wendell lifted his head just enough to see out of the ditch, and there stood Settlemeyer on his porch, cradling a deer gun. He ducked as the old man aimed and the rifle cracked one final time, kicking up dirt at the edge of the ditch. Then there was silence.

At length a door slammed, and Wendell peeked over the lip of the ditch again. It was almost dark now and Settlemeyer had disappeared once more. But when he looked back across the road, his father lay sprawled in the front yard beside his overturned walker, his chest covered in blood

"Goddamn, Daddy," Wendell whispered. "This thing has done got completely out of hand. What the hell am I supposed to do now?"

He hesitated, struggling with the inevitable consequences of the decision which confronted him as he crawled up out of the ditch. Then, shaking his head, he turned and headed back across the road to his truck. And as he reached for the .45 automatic which he kept in the glove compartment, he knew precisely what his father's answer to his question would have been. *Shit-fire, boy, you know what the good book says—eye for eye, tooth for tooth—now get on with it, by god!*

Different, Yet the Same

Michael Webb

The TV screen flickers, but I'm not watching it. It's some kind of a reality program, where the contestants try to go from one end to another while huge foam clubs and walls and hurdles attempt to knock them from their path. And when they inevitably take a wrong step, they slip and fall and tumble into the water, emerging seconds later, dripping and embarrassed. It is loud, and there are lots of colors and motion, yelling and fake enthusiasm, like what might happen if you asked a kindergarten class to design a television show. I don't like it, but I leave it on because it makes me feel less alone.

Their shift ends at 8, and it's now approaching 11, but I know better than to expect them home on time. They have explained it, but every job I've ever had has ended when it ended – your shift ends, they stop paying, you stop working. Their job isn't like that, and no matter how many times they tell me how it is, there is a tiny part of me that gets jealous that so much of their energy goes to people who aren't me. I know that's how it is. But I still hate it.

The door opens and they are there. They set down their backpack, and kick off their shoes. We have a routine, since the contagion has come – I pretend I don't see them until they are able to go straight into the bathroom, shower, and change. That gives them a chance to decompress some, and in a more practical sense helps make sure, to the extent we can, that any microbial grossness they have gathered is washed away.

I can see their face from here, and their face looks tight. They don't say anything, and they take off their Mariners cap and whip off their blue, blocky scrub top, letting it fall at their feet. They come across the room and half stumble, half fall into my arms. I set my book down, unnerved by the deviation from routine, and open my arms as they come to me. Their face finds my shoulder, and then presses hard, almost uncomfortably, against my pectoral muscle, and they emit a low, shuddering sob.

The tears come now, wetting my shirt, and with them great, gulping, animalistic crying. I have only experienced tears like this from them a couple of times, and I have learned that I need to let them have space, so I sit with them, holding them, running my hands over their gray tank and down their back, waiting for the words to emerge, smelling the sweat off their hair, whispering against their skin.

After an eternity, they began.

"There was this girl. Not the virus, an MVA. She was crossing against a light, stupid, I know, but someone was speeding, and the witnesses said she just flew. She was a mess. Crushed ribs, broken back, blood everywhere, and we were scrambling, trying to do what we could, but it wasn't enough. I was holding her hand at the end. This amazing thing happened. She became a thing, right in front of me. She was a person, and then, just, suddenly, she wasn't. I've never experienced anything like that. Just person to object, in a half a second."

I held them as closely as I could. If I could have unzipped my skin, they would have climbed inside. They were speaking against my chest, their words vibrating my ribs, their hot breath on my dampened shirt.

They continued, "and then the chief resident went out and told the family. It was awful. They made a sound … it was pain, of course, and fear, and this kind of rage, and this animal, guttural sound. I've never had to notify, but I have heard them react – there was a time before, and then there is now, and nothing is ever going to be okay ever again. It's a terrifying sound, and I never get used to it. "

They stood up, stripping off their pants, then walking back towards the door to gather their shirt. Heading towards the shower, they stopped and looked at me, their face still streaked with tears, so beautiful it made my heart ache.

"You know what the funny thing is about the sound they make, though? The sound the relatives make?"

"What?" I say.

"They are all completely different, and they are all exactly the same."

Gone

Nod Ghosh

I should have held onto him this time, but I didn't know how.

When Ronan came back to me, I'd been waiting for him for almost a decade. I always knew he'd return. But he's left me again.

I haven't been able to face work in the two weeks since he went. I rang in sick. Later, I said I'd fallen while running in the park. Eventually my lies disintegrated, and they fired me.

I didn't care.

This morning, I changed out of yesterday's clothes, cleaned my teeth and showered for the first time in days. I sprayed myself with the lily-of-the-valley scent he'd bought me when we'd found each other again. Then I took the stack of empty bottles out and went for a run in the afternoon sun. I needed the heat, wanted to feel something.

The house smells like a sewer. I must find another job. But first I have to clean up.

I bump into my ex-husband at the carwash café. As I'm out of work, I probably should clean the car myself. But since I bought the Honda, I've had her valeted regularly, as if by looking after the car, I'm also caring for myself.

Abe is friendly enough, even buys me coffee. I ask about our son. Kyle's partner is active on social media, so I know we've had a second grandchild. Abe tells me the baby is babbling and reaching out for toys. He updates me as if I'm an outsider, like an old neighbour, or perhaps someone who once taught Kyle at school, not his fucking mother.

We talk about Abe's work, his in-laws in France. There's an easy confidence between us, as if once being married has stripped away our shyness. Things can go the other way with an ex, but we parted without hating each other. It happened a long time ago, before Ronan. Perhaps we'd married too young.

"Are you still living in the same place, Madeleine?" He drains his coffee.

"I don't ever want to leave." I remember the two of us painting every room when we moved in years ago. Abe likely has no idea how close I've come to losing that house. He knows I was forced to leave teaching after my *indiscretion* was discovered. I've flitted from one low-wage job to another, often working two together. I'm determined to keep my home, despite the crippling mortgage and having an arsehole of a neighbour. It's where I raised our son. And it's where Ronan and I have been at our happiest. We'd have stayed there until one of us died if he hadn't left me again.

Abe is a good man. He doesn't judge me as everyone else does. It's as if the turmoil of being rejected by our son, kissing my career goodbye, and being pointed at in the street is someone else's fault. I suspect Abe was pleased when I started a relationship with someone, even though that someone was with a child. It let him off the hook.

When most people were demonising me, Abe and his wife Sondrine were supportive. As a stepmother, Sondrine offered to talk to Kyle, to encourage him to speak to me. Kyle hasn't followed her advice.

The distance between my son and me is an ocean. He doesn't need me. He has his father. He shares good times and bad times with Abe and Sondrine. Kyle has never forgiven me for falling in love with his best friend.

Abe talks about Sondrine's sister's new partner, and asks whether I have anyone special in my life.

"Not just now," I reply. I can't face telling him there was someone until very recently. I make an unnecessary trip to the bathroom, so Abe won't see my tears.

When we reunited, Ronan asked to take things slowly. He wanted to keep our relationship *private* until the right time.

The time never came. When I pushed for a decision, he was cruel.

"I don't know what I ever saw in you, Madeleine," he said.

"But you love me," I'd pleaded. "You know you do."

"I never should have come back."

"We were so happy. Remember?"

"I was never sure about you." He'd turned his back on me. "I wish I hadn't wasted my youth on you."

Youth. That had stung.

I'd understand the pull of a wife and children. But Ronan isn't going back to wretched Gretchen and their children. He's left me for an office girl he'd been seeing behind Gretchen's back. She's just turned eighteen; not much older than Ronan was himself when I first took him to my bed.

After I return from the bathroom, Abe asks if I want another coffee. Our cars are ready, he says, but he doesn't have much else to do. He can stay for a bit. Do I have the time, he asks. We haven't seen each other for a while, he says, adding that it's good to chat.

"I have all the time in the world." I order the drinks.

"Does Burt Hartley still live next door?" Abe asks when I come back.

"Unfortunately."

"I thought he'd be dead by now."

"Trust me," I say. "He would be if I had anything to do with it."

Abe laughs and we talk about how Burt might die, complicit in our murderous thoughts. I imagine a giant boulder rolling down the hill, crashing into Burt's house, missing mine by centimeters. Abe suggests wild mushroom poisoning. Burt is a forager. We laugh, and I love how easy it is between us. I wish Kyle could share this. I wonder what it would be like if we'd stayed together. But the idea is unappealing.

There's only one person I want, and that person has left me. Again.

Perhaps Ronan will come back. He's returned so many times before.

But this time, there's something different in the way he's severed our ties.

This time, I think he may have gone for good.

The Wake

AR Neal

John Junior stood at the back of the sanctuary, tightly gripping his mother's hand. 'Now John Junior,' she said gently, 'he can't hurt you. It's like he's asleep.'

The boy shook his head vigorously and planted his feet. Victoria squatted and looked into her son's eyes. 'John Junior, you understand what's happening, right?'

The six-year-old looked at his mother and nodded.

She smiled. 'You are such a big boy. Remember how you sat with Auntie Lucille when Sister Browning died?' Another nod. 'This is very much the same except it's your granddad.' She stood back up, her knees creaking loudly in the empty church. At first, Victoria had planned to preach the eulogy for her father, but the deacons and deaconesses thought it wouldn't be appropriate. Even though she preached often, they felt a woman's place at such times was on the mourner's bench. Her husband John would oversee the services for the Right-Reverend Doctor Josephus Claymore, while she sat on the front row, draped in black lace.

Since she wouldn't be in the pulpit, Victoria said she and John Junior would sit with Reverend Claymore's body. Since it was early, she thought it would be the most appropriate time for John Junior to say goodbye to his grandfather. Like her, he was being raised in the church, so he'd already been to several funeral services. But for some reason, he was reticent to walk down the aisle to the casket.

'Mother,' the boy said quietly, 'I'm sad.'

'Me too,' she answered.

He stared into her eyes, his face solemn, reminding her so much of her father. With a deep breath, John Junior tightened his grip on Victoria's hand. They marched down to the casket. He was too short to see, so Victoria hoisted him onto her hip. He looked down at Pastor Claymore, resting peacefully in his favorite pastoral robe.

Reverend Claymore had been bedridden for the last four years. She and John had argued with him about moving his room to the first floor of the house. He felt it was undignified to lay in the sitting room, but he couldn't go up or down the steps and it had become difficult for Victoria to care for him while also looking after John Junior. He'd finally relented after Victoria's husband John built a sliding door for the sitting room and after everyone made over him like a king.

Victoria had been at the church when he died. As she walked up the lane toward the house after bible study ended, she saw all the lights turned on in the house. Lucille stood on the stoop … and Victoria knew.

She looked down at his wrinkled face and watched as her tears splashed dark spots on the silk strips running the length of her father's robe. John Junior wriggled in her arms until he was in front of her. He wiped her tears with his hands and said, 'Don't cry, Mother. You said when people die and go to heaven, they never get sick, and they are happy. Isn't that what you said?'

The door opened and the deaconesses walked in. It was difficult to tell the difference between them since they all wore black lace veils. Victoria leaned over to let John Junior stand on his own and walked to the front bench, where they sat. As she pulled her veil over her face, she said to him, 'You are such a smart boy, John Junior. Granddad would be so proud.' They held hands and waited for the service to begin.

The Almost Mother

Delphine Gauthier-Georgakopoulos

CW: miscarriage.

The Beginning.

The first few weeks, I was cautious, didn't tell anyone except my husband, because it wasn't safe yet. We all knew what could happen in the first three months when an ethereal life tried to grow inside. Women rarely talked of it, but it was there, a cloud hanging low, threatening with rainy days.

A lot of friends and family members had been through it. I had seen the tears, the haunted faces, the shaky hands rubbing desperately empty bellies. They whispered the news. It was an invisible loss; it happened. As if life had just been passing through, almost unnoticed. 'Hello—goodbye—my mistake. I changed my mind. Sorry, I have other plans. I won't stay.'

So, the first twelve weeks, I kept quiet, just grinned a lot.

When the twelve weeks mark passed, I exhaled with relief and we announced to the world the wonderful news. Oh, the pride in one's body! I finally gave it the respect it deserved for doing such a brilliant job at not only keeping me alive, but also bringing another life forth.

'Yay body, you're amazing!'

Although I had some nausea, it wasn't bad. Nothing much had changed, yet I grew teary-eyed out of the blue, my temper flared faster, I showed my teeth on occasion, getting ready to protect the life inside. I was almost a mother.

The Middle.
I shrieked when the little shrimp kicked for the first time. This time, it wasn't gas.

This time, it was *my* little shrimp.

Placing a trembling hand to my large belly, overwhelmed with love, I started a unilateral conversation.

'Hi there, Little Shrimp, I'm your mum.'

My eyes filled with joyous tears, the exultation over-whelmed my hormonal self and I sobbed—loud. Ridiculously loud—with happiness. The little being wasn't an invisible thing anymore. I could sense, feel, talk to the little shrimp and she kicked back. Communication. Pure love.

I reached five months. Halfway through. I wasn't blooming—the books lie—but beamed with anticipation and my happiness hid the lack of blooming.

We started listing all the things she would need. I read books and magazines to understand where the little shrimp was at, and what to expect. We discussed names and chose one that seemed to meet the little shrimp's approval if her kicks were anything to go by.

I was getting huge, but I didn't care. There was a magical life growing inside, and I was madly in love with it.

The end.
It was a Friday, on a cold February night. I was lying in bed, under a fluffy duvet, pillows on the side, ready to place between

my knees to avoid back pain, waiting for the little shrimp to calm down.

'You're having a party in there, Little Shrimp?'

After half an hour, the movements stopped. I settled for the night.

I woke up on Saturday feeling odd. Something was off.

I got scared. I knew.

The cat came and massaged my still belly as if to give chest compressions to the little shrimp.

'It's too late.' I swallowed hard as I whispered the words.

He knew too.

We had plans that weekend, a big event to attend. I was so tense and desperately grief-stricken that I pulled a muscle in my shoulder. I welcomed the physical pain.

All evening, women, young and old, ran excitedly to rub my belly. I plastered a weird smile on my face for a few hours while wondering if I was bringing them bad luck.

On Sunday, I called the doctor.

'Something is wrong.'

The scan on Monday confirmed it, the little shrimp was no more. My little shrimp had suffered an aneurysm.

'It's rare, but it happens, and it's nobody's fault,' the doctor said.

It's not my fault.

It became a tuneless chorus on repeat.

It's not my fault.

I needed to accept that fact, or I would have lost my mind.

The nightmare was not over because I, the almost mother, had an almost baby to give birth to. To give death to.

As I pushed, a fountain of desperation poured out of my eyes. The physical hurt of the "delivery" matched the agony in my heart. It helped a little. The pain was my friend at that point. It made the loss real.

They gave me pills to stop my body from assuming that there was a live baby. I took some to avoid lactation, but it came anyway because my body insisted that I was now a mother. It was still doing its job.

I didn't respect that anymore.

I looked at the milk flowing, useless, and it broke my heart further.

I, the almost mother, had a ghost baby to mourn, a life dream to let go of. It had been there, and then it wasn't. It was an intangible death, almost an unknown quantity, a ghost loss, a ghost baby.

Also from Pure Slush Books

pureslush.com/store

- Achievement Lifespan Vol. 8
ISBN: 978-1-922427-34-2 (paperback) / 978-1-922427-35-9 (ePub)
- Home Lifespan Vol. 7
ISBN: 978-1-922427-32-8 (paperback) / 978-1-922427-33-5 (ePub)
- Marriage Lifespan Vol. 6
ISBN: 978-1-922427-30-4 (paperback) / 978-1-922427-31-1 (ePub)
- Work Lifespan Vol. 5
ISBN: 978-1-922427-28-1 (paperback) / 978-1-922427-29-8 (ePub)
- Love Lifespan Vol. 4
ISBN: 978-1-922427-26-7 (paperback) / 978-1-922427-27-4 (ePub)
- Friendship Lifespan Vol. 3
ISBN: 978-1-922427-24-3 (paperback) / 978-1-922427-25-0 (ePub)

Also from Pure Slush Books

pureslush.com/store

Also from Pure Slush Books

pureslush.com/store

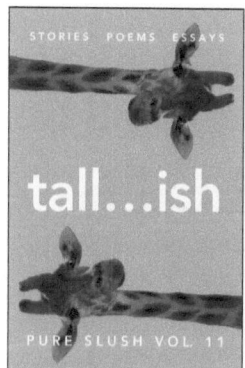

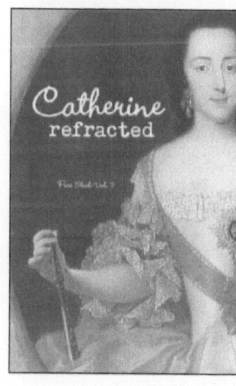
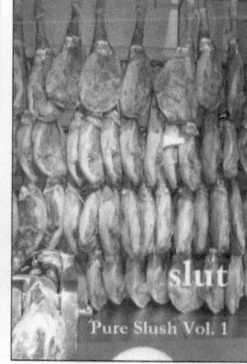
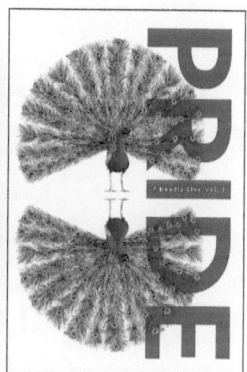

- tall…ish Pure Slush Vol. 11
ISBN: 978-1-925101-80-5 (paperback) / 978-1-925101-98-0 (eBook)
- Feast! Pure Slush Vol. 9
ISBN: 978-1-925101-63-8 (paperback) / 978-1-925101-66-9 (eBook)
- Barcode Pure Slush Vol. 8
ISBN: 978-1-925101-00-3 (paperback) / 978-1-925101-01-0 (eBook)
- Catherine refracted Pure Slush Vol. 7
ISBN: 978-1-925101-78-2 (paperback) / 978-1-925101-79-9 (eBook)
- Slut Pure Slush Vol. 1
ISBN: 978-1-4716-0674-8 (paperback) / 978-1-925101-99-7 (eBook)
- Pride 7 Deadly Sins Vol. 7
ISBN: 978-1-925536-72-0 (paperback) / 978-1-925536-73-7 (eBook)

Also from Pure Slush Books

pureslush.com/store

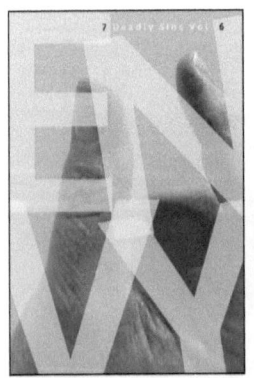  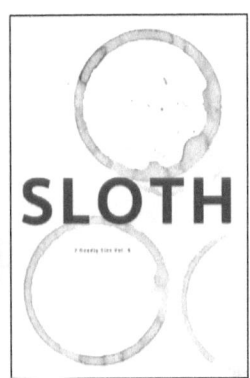

- Envy 7 Deadly Sins Vol. 6
ISBN: 978-1-925536-70-6 (paperback) / 978-1-925536-71-3 (eBook)
- Wrath 7 Deadly Sins Vol. 5
ISBN: 978-1-925536-68-3 (paperback) / 978-1-925536-69-0 (eBook)
- Sloth 7 Deadly Sins Vol. 4
ISBN: 978-1-925536-66-9 (paperback) / 978-1-925536-67-6 (eBook)
- Greed 7 Deadly Sins Vol. 3
ISBN: 978-1-925536-64-5 (paperback) / 978-1-925536-65-2 (eBook)
- Gluttony 7 Deadly Sins Vol. 2
ISBN: 978-1-925536-54-6 (paperback) / 978-1-925536-55-3 (eBook)
- Lust 7 Deadly Sins Vol. 1
ISBN: 978-1-925536-47-8 (paperback) / 978-1-925536-48-5 (eBook)